# Jack D. Breckenridge

SURGEON FISHIN'
first published in United States by J & J Breckenridge

Cover design and cartoons by Jack D. Breckenridge

First U.S. edition, 1998, published by
J & J Breckenridge 1918 Harrison Ave., #7
Centralia, WA 98531-9388

Library of Congress Cataloging-in-Publication Data
Breckenridge,Jack D. 1920-

Library of Congress Catalog Card Number: 98-092814

Surgeon Fishin/Jack D. Breckenridge p. cm.
 ISBN 0-9656993-1-5

Also by Jack D. Breckenridge: PUMPKINS ARE ORANGE


Printed by Gorham Printing
Rochester, WA
1-800-837-0970

# Dedicated to...

THE MEMORY OF GEORGE BROWN, my fishing and hunting companion for many enjoyable years.

# Thanks

To MARGO and VADEN, my daughter and son-in-law for many memorable Sturgeon fishing trips, furnishing many ideas throughout this novel.

To JOHNNY JOHNSON, my friend. An excellent, dedicated, fisherman and sportsman, for his help and encouragement from Chapter One to the finish.

# CONTENTS

AGE IN YEARS

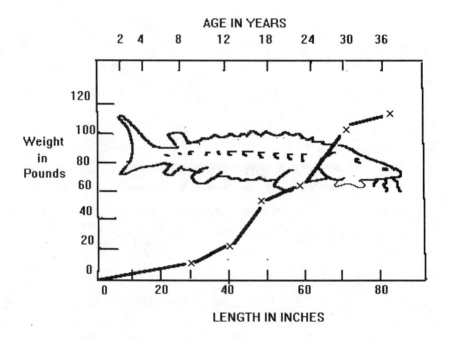

Weight in Pounds

LENGTH IN INCHES

# The Surgin' Sturgeon

I saw him jump and I made my wish
   I wouldn't rest until I had that fish
He's lived in our rivers for a long long time
   That big sturgeon just has to be mine
The tide came in and then started out
   I thought my efforts would go without
Then the line peeled off at a frightening pace
   I had hooked the old devil, I was in for a chase
The rod bent double, I adjusted the drag
   Keep him off the bottom away from a snag
This fish is smart , he ain't no dope
   He headed straight towards the anchor rope
With a flick of my knife I cut the boat free
   We were driftin now, just the fish and me
After a three hour struggle he came up to float
   So I guided him carefully to the side of the boat
We were both exausted, completely out of stamina
   That's when I shot him, with my wide lens camera
He had a sad look of defeat in his eye
   As I removed my hook and said goodbye
With a flick of his tail my monster was gone
   That's when I noticed...I'd left the lens cap on.

*Poetry done specifically for— SURGEON FISHIN'*
*© By Tony Hickman*
*Adelaide Australia.*

# 1

# Now What?

Snooks and I are having our morning coffee and I get up nerve enough to ask her why she shut the door in my face when I asked for a little help separating all the stringy pulp from the pumpkin seeds of my Giant Pumpkin? She tells me that her memory is still very vivid over many disastrous experiences she's had in my other "help-me" projects, and she could see nothing but disaster involved with any part of that stinking seed-sorting mess. She says also, that she has learned much about any involvement in my projects, and a straight out "no" answer will always keep her dignity and well-being safe from harm.

I admit things don't always go exactly according to plan, but Snooks all at once seems to be very cautious about becoming in-volved in any projects with me. A few little setbacks, of no conse-quence, shouldn't sour a person for life. If a person takes that atti-tude all the time, he can never accomplish anything. I wonder how far Thomas Edison and Henry Ford would have gone with an attitude like that. We would still be without lights and automobiles! I hope this attitude is just a passing phase.

We finish our coffee and I ask Snooks if she would like to take a ride and head out toward the coast to see if the salmon are starting to move into the rivers yet. After all, we might want to do a little salmon fishing this fall. Snooks says "Well, I'll go, but you know the salmon won't move until the fall rains start. You do know that, don't you?"

"Sure, but we can see if the jack salmon are starting to move yet. It'll do us good to get out of the house for a while." After we get started in the car, Snooks asks why they call them 'jack' salmon? And is that another form of male chauvinism?

I tell her "No, all of these small immature salmon are always males. There's no such thing as a female jack salmon." Then Snooks says even the salmon have turned chauvinistic, and she's sure they learned it from the American males.

It's hard to explain things to the one-sided mentality like Snooks has. It certainly couldn't be considered an open-minded approach.

I tell her that the State Fisheries Department sets a catch limit of six jack salmon per day per person, but they really should let you catch all you can. The jack salmon don't reproduce, yet they eat the eggs of the spawning mature salmon, thus creating a nuisance factor. The more jacks removed, the greater the benefit to the mature spawning salmon and also the more pleasure to the sport fisherman. But the Fisheries Department Directors are appointed by the Governor and many of them don't know any more about fish than that they taste good batter dipped and deep fried! So to impress everyone, the Directors discriminate against the sport fisherman. It makes them look like they're really doing something and of course the sport fisherman is the only one without some clout to change things, and the only one not motivated by greed.

"I'm sorry Snooks" I say as we drive along, "I didn't mean to get carried away, but you might just as well know the facts. It's a cruel, unfair world out there and the sport fisherman is always on the short end of the stick."

We head for tide water and one of the larger coastal rivers. When we get near the boat launch, there must be forty fishermen all lined up fishing from shore. Either the salmon are in or there's a phenomenon going on that I don't know anything about. They're just fishing, they don't seem to be doing any catching, which happens more often than not anyway. However, something is definitely holding their interest.

Two or three fishermen and I wouldn't think anything of it, but forty some is certainly odd! To say the least. They aren't all here to get away from nagging wives.

It's really a waste of time to talk to fishermen, but the answers are sometimes amusing, and even if they tell you nothing, you may be fortunate to stumble onto the bragger who spills everything he knows to enhance his ego, then you do learn something.

Also, I may not find out anything about today's fishing but almost all of them talk freely about off-season fishing; they can brag and tell you all, you're bound to forget it eight months down the line anyway. This information is usually factual and valuable. Filed away, you can forget the lies about today and if you can remember the truths about tomorrow, it's not been time wasted.

These are lessons I've learned over the years and there's no point in telling Snooks because she trusts nearly everyone and wouldn't understand my vast knowledge of fishermen in general.

Fishermen are so strange: the guy you fish with today is your companion and confidant, but if he's with someone else tomorrow and meets you, chances are the truth isn't in him. These are facts you must realize, accept and ignore, if you're to remain friends with other fishermen. It's all part of the game.

This is one place you really gotta be s-w-a-v-e [sic]. If you ask a bunch of silly questions you'll get nothing, the safest way to act is like you know all about it and just couldn't fish today yourself, but came down to see if the bite's on.

It doesn't look good today, so I say to one lone fisherman, as I walk up close to check everything out first hand, "Seems to be sort of slow today. I did pretty well last week, but then the tide was different too." I really haven't said anything specific, but sound like I know the ropes.

He replies "Yup." I wait for more, but this guy just is not a conversationalist. Just my luck to pick the silent type.

I climb back in the pickup and drive way down past the parked boat trailers and all the fishermen. Four or five fellows are leaning up against the side of a pickup, and every once in while someone looks in the truck bed and then continues on with conversation and laugh-

3

ter. This looks to me like the prime place to try to get a little information.

I holler out my window at the fellows by the pickup, and ask what they caught. I figure this is not a dumb question, and doesn't lead to giving away any pertinent information, and I'll probably get an answer.

They each glance at one another real quick, because they know that whoever answers will get hell for owning up to anything. Finally, a short, pot-bellied guy with his baseball hat on backwards, hollers "SURGEON!" Now he's in trouble but doesn't know it yet. He won't know it until after I leave and the rest of them chew him out for even acknowledging my presence.

My sweet wife Snooks says "Well, now that you have the door open, go talk to them." Snooks' real name is Rose, but she hates that name and I never call her that to her face unless she has really upset me. This is one of those times. Why did she have to be so quick to tell me that which is so obvious? She must think that I can't think.

Now this is a time to be really swave. Just me alone against five strangers. I start out by saying "Not as good as last week, is it?"

One guy says "Oh, I don't know, Carl here got one yesterday.....a 52 incher."

Carl pipes up and says "Lost two besides."

To which I reply "Yeah, I had two days like that last week up river a ways." Now, so far I'm doing pretty good. I want to look in the pickup bed real bad, and see just what one of these surgeons looks like, but I know if I run right over there I'll have tipped my hand and will get no further information.

Then a fellow wearing a Tony's Bar and Grill sweatshirt pipes up and says, "The bait's not so good this week."

And Carl says "Yep. The sand shrimp are real soft for some reason."

Then Bar and Grill says "Willie here larned the hard way that you cain't fish these hyar babies with no steelhead gear. He's gone to straight 40-pound test monofiliment."

Willie says "Yep, ah fought that thar feller mor'n a ahr on 15-poun test then just busted him off. Jes as quick as ah git my Walfar check ahm goin' raht quick down to the Tackle Shack an get me sum of that that 40-poun stuff."

Then the fellow who's got the baseball cap on backwards and hollered "surgeon" says "Game Warden come by yestidy and picked up Pete for not havin' a license. We kept tellin' him it would happen and sure as shootin' he got caught. A hunert-an-fifty bucks it cost him! He didn't show up this mornin'. I hope it didn't break his spirit; then again, maybe he's jes waitin' for the incoming tide."

A short little guy in a red shirt says "Yeah, incoming tide's always best, all right."

I move slowly over by the pickup and look nonchalantly into the bed and HOLY SMUT! There, without a doubt, is one of the homeliest, meanest looking critters I've ever seen; little tiny beady eyes, mouth that opens like a funnel under the chin, a long snout with whiskers like a catfish, big sharp bumps all down the back and both sides, a white belly and a battle-ship gray back. It has NO SCALES! and in many areas, like the top of it's head, is a very rough-looking surface. There are some strange markings in an odd pattern on its head, too. Just a quick glance, but to me it appears as if it might be a cousin to a shark.

This one is about 45 inches long, yet from what they say I don't think this is a braggin' fish!

Then the guy in the red shirt says "Had a chunk of that one I got last week. Flo fried it like chicken and it was out of this world."

The guy with the baseball cap says "Pete told me how to pickle some. Now that's a rare treat."

Then the one called Willie says "Ha! Don't think you can beat em' batter dipped and deep fried; they go mighty good in a fish chowder too. In fact, ah ain't never seed a way they warn't dern good."

The fella with the Bar and Grill sweatshirt adds, "You know, it don't even smell like fish when you're cookin' it. Best fish I ever run across, and to think they been around forever."

5

Then the guy in the red shirt says "You can talk about how good they are to eat, but if you want to taste something bad just cut into that there notocord. That's the one thing you can't do is mess with that cord. Pull that cord before you start to butcher or it ain't never gonna be fit to eat. That's one thing we all agree on."

I say "Yep, that's for sure." I tell them I gotta go, but I'll probably see them on the river again, in the meantime not to let all the big ones get away.

As I walk away I'm mighty proud of myself. I out-swaved myself on this one. I got more good information that I even dreamed possible! Yeah, a real bonanza.

As I open the pickup door Snooks says, "Well, you've been gone long enough to be a world authority by now, or did you waste your time talking to a bunch of true fishermen?"

"Snooks, you won't believe how much I found out! I wrung them out like wet sponges, and they didn't even suspect a thing. If you have a spare hour or two I'll fill you in with all the details. Those guys sang like canaries; I think that was the swavest I've ever been.

"You know Snooks, you can learn a lot more by listening than you can by talking. You should remember that little bit of wisdom, Snooks."

Snooks says "Well, Great-Wealth-of-Knowledge, clue me in on all your recent learning."

"Snooks, their name is 'surgeon' and you know what? These fish were here with the dinosaurs! They don't even spawn till they're 20 to 25 years old. They live as long as man or longer. They get REAL big! A four footer is just barely legal; you need heavy tackle, 40-pound test line at least. They use a bait called sand shrimp; best fishing is incoming tide; they are the best eating fish that was ever invented and you can cook 'em any way you want. They're the meanest, homeliest looking thing I ever saw. No scales, whiskers like a catfish, little beady eyes; their mouth comes out in a round extendable tube under the chin, and they really don't have a chin or mandible. They're sort of a cross between an alligator and a shark. Got a cord down through the middle of them called a notocord, if you cut into that while cleaning your fish, it ruins the meat, and you better just throw it away; and you need a license. Now Snooks, how's that for a lot of information from some close-mouthed fishermen?"

"I'll have to admit, you did learn a lot. I also have a feeling by the look in your eye that you'll know a lot more real soon. It's funny you never stumbled onto these fish a long time ago."

"Well, I was always happy with lake and river fishing for trout, Snooks. I didn't think the tide water had anything to offer, and besides it was a little too far to travel."

"I hate to bring this up, but I don't think you got the name right. A 'surgeon' fish is one I read about in the encyclopedia, and it's found in warm tropical waters, and this sure isn't tropical waters."

"Snooks, I heard what I heard, that guy said 'surgeon' twice and I don't give a damn what the experts say! I know what I heard. Those guys catch them, they ought to know what they are."

"Well, you know you do have a hearing loss and wear a hearing aid, and with their tarheel accent, it's just possible that you misunderstood what they said. But then, you know what you heard."

"Rose, I don't know why you bring up these little things to make me look bad, but it really annoys me. I know I'm right and let's just drop the matter here and now, O.K.?"

After a mile or two of silence Snooks finally speaks again. "Now what? I do hope you don't become as involved with this as you did with the Giant Pumpkins." I don't feel this needs an answer.

"Snooks, how would you like to go down and try out a little fishing for these surgeon?" Snooks says that after I find out a little more she might try it, so I tell her I'll look into it.

"The first thing you better do" Snooks says "is check on the license and where to get the shrimp things for bait." I can tell right now that Snooks is interested. This may be easier than I had figured.

"You know Snooks, you're absolutely right. Those are the first things to do and I'll check on those licenses first thing in the morning down at Peak's Plunkin Shack. I can get the licenses and maybe a little dope on sand shrimp. When it comes to tackle, if Pete don't have it in that Plunkin Shack, it just isn't made."

# 2

# License and Information

Snooks says "Well, you act like you can't even wait for your coffee to cool this morning. What's the hurry?"

"Snooks, I'm not in a hurry, but it's a fact if you drink cool coffee you have a chance for heartburn and bad gas. Mickey Muldoon drank cool coffee for years. Nobody would ever ride in a car with him and people were real careful never to have a conversation with Mickey on the downwind side. People learned it from dogs who have much more sensitive noses than we do. You never saw a dog on the downwind side of Mickey."

"Did Mickey have heartburn too?" Snooks asks.

"Well, if he did nobody ever noticed. Anyway, after numerous questions and tests, the doctors found it was due to Mickey's craving for cool coffee. Once they got him programmed to drink hot coffee he became an acceptable member of the human race."

Snooks then wonders why people who drink iced coffee in the summer don't have any problem? I can see with this question that she is a mite skeptical of my story about Mickey. "As a matter of fact, Snooks, they do; but the reason it's not so evident is because summer is a time of year to be outside and some things are not near as evident as in the confines of an enclosure, such as a room or a house. But Snooks, I think this is poor conversation over breakfast coffee, and I'd appreciate it if you would just change the subject to something more pleasant.

"I think I'll just mosey on down to the Plunkin Shack and pick up a copy of the fishing regulations; find out where those little shrimp hang out and maybe stop and see Billy Booze in the hospital. Billy and Hank Edwards had a real close call you know. Hank was patched up and released in an hour, he only had 43 stitches in his right leg. He was driving and was wearing his seat belt, but poor old Billy wasn't wearing his, and he took the brunt of the damage when they hit that big maple out on Curly's Curve on Highway 6. If they had hit the tree square, it would have killed 'em both outright, but they just tore the bark off one side. It was the double rollover down the hill on Smith's Ranch that did 'em in. Poor old Billy was banging around in that car like a marble in a tin can."

"It probably served them right drinking and driving and all," observed Snooks.

"I think that's a terrible thing to say before you know all the facts, Snooks. Matter of fact, drinking had nothing to do with it. It would never have happened if they hadn't had frog trouble."

"What in the world do you mean, 'frog trouble'?" Snooks asks.

"Well, it was one of those real warm summer evenings and Hank and Billy decided to go bullfrog spearing down to Swanson's Pond. They figured with the warm night, those frogs would all be out a-bellerin' and a-courtin' all over the pond. I guess they were right because they said they had about 50 big old bullfrogs when they headed home. They just speared them and dumped them in a sack, tied a string around the sack opening and dumped it on the floor in the back seat.

"I guess they would have stayed longer but the batteries went dead in their light and they couldn't butcher the frogs without light. Billy said he could do it by feel in the dark, but Hank wouldn't let him. Billy had almost cut his arm off cutting the heads from some chickens they stole one night. So they figured they'd cut the legs off when they got home to a good light in Billy's kitchen.

"Now, as anybody knows, you can't hardly ever kill a frog. You even have to put a lid on a skillet full of them frying on the stove! There's still enough life left in 'em to jump out of the pan and away from that heat. The only way you know when they're cooked is when they quit trying to jump out of the skillet. The only other thing

I know of that tenacious about hanging onto life under adverse conditions, is a Mississippi River catfish.

"But back to Hank and Billy, they're driving along home at a pretty good clip because it's after midnight; they still have 50 frogs to remove the legs from, and that takes considerable time itself. Frogs are so tough that they don't even flinch when you run them through with a triple-prong spear. These frogs in the sack are feeling pretty frisky, they've never traveled in a car before. They want to see what's going on and get out of those cramped quarters and stretch their legs a bit. They wiggle around until the not-too-secure string gives way and they're free, out in the big wide world.

"All at once in the pitch black confines of their vehicle, Hank and Billy are inundated with cold wet projectiles careening off every angle. Snooks, can't you just imagine how unnerving a thing like this could be?

"Hank, not having the calmest nerves in the world anyway, loses complete control, and the car caroms off the side of that tree and goes end-over-teakettle down the hill.

"When the patrolmen arrive they find frogs jumping everywhere in and out of the car. Hank is sitting on a stump holding his leg and hollering 'Poor Billy.' Poor Billy is right! He's got to be hauled out on a stretcher, and very carefully to boot.

"It ends up with Billy having a broken left arm, three broken ribs and a mild concussion. The concussion was bad enough that Billy thought he was a frog and kept hollering 'I got skinny legs, skinny legs! You don't want my legs!' Now Snooks, after you heard the facts, aren't you sorry you blamed it on drinking?"

"Well, I still say Billy never got a last name like Booze without there being some problem somewhere."

"The officer didn't find any evidence of drinking, however he gave Hank a ticket for reckless driving and each of them tickets because Billy wasn't wearing his seat belt. The Game Warden gave them tickets for thirty frogs over the daily catch limit (estimated because loose hopping frogs make it hard to get an accurate accounting) and another ticket for not having a hunting license. Hank and Billy both thought they only needed a fishing license for frogs, but the law does not recognize ignorance as a valid reason to be wrong. Total cost for almost dying and going to heaven was $653 bucks, a pretty price for an evening's entertainment.

"Well, I'm off now, and like I said Snooks, I'm going to find out about a license for surgeon; find out where those shrimp come from and see Billy. I should be back before lunch."

Peak's Plunkin Shack is not only a place to buy fishing tackle but there's always two or three fishermen sitting around the big chrome and black pot-bellied stove, either telling about the big one that got away or the injustice and lack of gray matter of the Fisheries Department.

Snarly Krautkramer is sitting by the stove and really blowing off steam about Hank and Billy getting tickets when they're half dead and they never deserved any tickets at all. Snarly doesn't understand how the gillnetters can take tons of incidental caught steelhead and other fish with no penalty, and we can't fish for even a peamouth chub without a license. Snarly asks "What the hell's a 'peamouth chub' anyway?"

Elmer Erkel says "Snarly, it's sort of a cousin to a squawfish; both worthless."

"You know" says Snarly, "the Fisheries Department is real thoughtful and giving though. You can catch albacore tuna, carp, crawfish and smelt without a license. Now ain't that generous of them? We really have an abundance of albacore here! Nobody cares about carp! They don't even rate being a part of the food chain, they won't even make good fertilizer! Those guys have got guts even listing them at all."

"You know" Elmer answers, "one of these days they'll put a license on smelt! There's a lot of people dip smelt, and some day one of those air heads will figure out how much revenue they're missing out on. Anybody having that much enjoyment sooner or later is going to have to have a license for it. You know you can't even have legal sex without a license, matter of fact I think the marriage license was probably the first ever license."

Pete Peak pipes up with "According to that 120 page book of fishing do's and don'ts that takes an attorney to figure out, it says you need 16 separate licenses to make everybody legal."

Some people call Pete "Pikes" because his prices are sky high, but most fellows are willing to pay because he's got what you need on hand and you don't have to wait a week or ten days to get it, which is what happens when you use the catalogue order system.

Fishermen are funny, if somebody finds a hot lure then everybody wants it right now, to hell with expense, time is the denominator. This is where Pete and the Plunkin Shack make hay, because he usually has the article in question in stock. I have never seen so much variety in fishing gear and paraphernalia in such a small square-foot area anywhere else. You name it, Pete's got it in a 25x40 foot area.

The only space not occupied by fishing gear is around that pot-bellied stove or the coffee pot. You might think this is wasted space. Not so. This is where the conversation leads to the success of new equipment and the rush to buy quick and try it out before the fish get wise. Next to the cash register, I'd say the stove area is his most lucrative area in the whole building.

You may never have noticed, but some fish won't touch last year's hottest item, they're off on something totally new and this is what keeps Pete's cash register ringing.

A lot of terminal tackle was never made to catch fish, it's made for only one purpose and that's to look fishy to fishermen and they're the ones that get hooked. Every tackle box has a fair amount of fishy-looking fish catchers that were never intended to catch anything but the guy paying the bill. Every one of us falls prey at one time or another. Fishermen seldom talk about it because none are totally immune.

Harvey Carbone is probably the one fisherman with the most non-fish-catching fishing lures in his tackle box of anybody I've ever seen. Pete says Harvey just can't resist those fishy looking new things that are always popping up on the tackle store shelves. If it's bright and wiggly looking, sure as shootin' Harvey's got to buy it. Willie Wicks is a sucker for any lure with big eyes. His whole tackle box is full of big-eyed, non-catching fishing lures. But then I guess we all weaken once in a while.

I ask Pete how much a couple surgeon licenses are going to set me back and he tells me $18.00; $8.00 each license and $1.00 each to fill them out, that also includes a punch card each, and a book of regulations so we stay within the law. Pete says he'll throw in a tide book free.

Pete starts doing all the paperwork. I say my wife's first name is Rose, maiden name was Thorn; she figured her dad wanted a boy and in disappointment named her Rose for the thorn on a rose bush. She hates the name Rose. I only call her that when I'm mad or upset with her. Pete fills out both licenses and punch-cards; puts them with a tide book into a sack. I hand him $18.00.

Then I ask him where those sand shrimp live and Elmer pipes up and says "Down in the salt water by the beach. Better take a clam tube, it's better than a clam shovel. Also a bucket to put them in. Smelt are supposed to be just as good. Let me know how you do, I've been thinking about trying some of that myself."

As I start out the door Snarly asks "Did you read the regulation about 'in transit'?"

I say I have not, and Snarly says, "You read that the way I read it, and about the only way fish are not in transit is if you have the fish with you while in your home or motorhome, in your bathroom, door locked, sitting on the john. Read page 8, and see what you think."

Snarly and Elmer are not happy unless they're after the Fisheries Department. If the Department gave them free licenses, they'd still find something wrong.

I head over to the hospital to see Billy before I go home. Billy really enjoys attention and company. In a way, this hospital stay has been great for lots of attention. I get his room number and walk in on Billy.

14

"Hey, am I glad to see you," says Billy. "I've only had three visitors so far today and I was getting lonesome."

"Billy, it's only 10:30 a.m. you know," I say. "Hey, how did you get such a fancy room, private potty and excellent view of the mountain?" Billy says he isn't sure, but he does remember a nurse's comment that might have made a difference.

I interrupt and ask Billy just what had happened to cause his accident. I had heard all the rumors, but I wanted the facts. You know rumors and second-hand information are most of the time wrong and often damaging to your otherwise normal thinking and outlook on life.

Billy says he and Hank had headed home after their flashlight burned out and they did have a few too many frogs. It was such a nice warm evening and the frogs were real cooperative, which was probably the reason for the accident. They had too many frogs for the size sack they brought. There wasn't enough sack left to make a good tie with the string around the top of the sack. They didn't have far to go so they weren't too fussy about a good, solid, secure tie on the sack.

The frogs wiggled out as I had heard, and Billy continues, "I would have been all right but Hank just ain't very stable under even the slightest bit of adversity, and with it being pitch black and us being bombarded with a large number of unknown cold, wet flying objects it was a mite unnerving even to me, but poor old Hank went half-way to the loony bin in a split second, and from then on it was topsy-turvey bedlam with Hank a-hollering 'Lord, where are ya?' I knew then Hank was out of his mind, because even under the worst conditions I had never ever heard Hank ask the lord for anything."

"I hear you boys got arrested besides. When did they give you your tickets?"

"They stuffed them in our shirt pockets while we was waitin' for the ambulance, I guess they was afraid we might die before they could serve them."

Billy continues, "When they got us here, the first thing I knew

15

there was a gal with a clip-board asking if we had insurance and the guy pushing my cart telling her he didn't know. She asked if he could remove the oxygen mask and find out? It was critical; she really needed to know. He told her they weren't sure I would make it if he interruped the oxygen, but he did it anyway and I mumbled out 'Medicare and good supplement' and back came the mask. As I was passing out from temporary lack of oxygen, I heard her say, 'Oh, after surgery put him in the room with the view of the mountain.' Hank ended up in a ward, but then he only stayed overnight and he didn't have insurance."

Billy stops and says he'd give anything if he could just take one deep breath without feeling like he was going to split apart in the middle.

I figure I better leave. I've only been here an hour, but Billy's voice is beginning to quaver and he looks pale. I just can't understand these people who stay forever when somebody is as sick as Billy; besides I looked out the window and saw Slim Rogerson coming in, another friend of Billy's.

Before I leave I ask Billy when he thinks he might get out and he says, "The rib doctor said come Monday. The brain guy wasn't too sure, said I might need some sort of therapy for a while. I guess I thought I was a frog and he wants to make sure I know I'm human."

Here comes Slim through the door and I tell Billy I'll see him and leave.

When I get home I tell Snooks I got us each a surgeon license and also found out where to get the sand shrimp. "Elmer Erkel told me they're in the salt water down by the beach, and a clam tube is better than a clam shovel. So Snooks, I think we should go down and just scout things out so when we get real serious and all rigged out, we'll know how to catch the bait. After all it's better to be prepared ahead of time and we have time now. What do you think?"

Snooks wants to know how much the license was and I tell her $18.00 for the two of us. She asks for her license because each person is supposed to have his own in his possession. I reach in the sack and dig out the regulations, licenses and tide book.

I give Snooks her license and punch card and start to check for low tides in the tide book to go get sand shrimp, because anybody knows that low tide is the time to prey on any shellfish or crustaceans. I find a good low tide next Thursday and start to tell her, when right out of the blue she bellers out at me..... "I KNEW IT! I KNEW I WAS RIGHT!"

"Snooks," I say, "what in the world bit you this time, pray tell?"

"They are STURGEON!" she crows. "Not surgeon! I tried to tell you, but no, you knew, you heard what you heard. Well Buster, just read what it says on both your license and punch card. Two places like that prove to me that it is definitely Sturgeon, with a 'T'. What have you got to say now about surgeon?"

"Snooks, I just don't see all the fuss. There are eight letters in Sturgeon, I missed one letter out of eight. Now in my book that makes me 7/8ths right and you 1/8th right. So tell me who was the most right? Mine was only a slight hearing misunderstanding anyway, could have even been a low voltage hearing-aid battery. You seem to want to take advantage of any opportunity to prove an error on my part. If I were you Snooks, I'd just drop the whole thing before you make a complete fool of yourself.

"As far as I'm concerned, we have far more important things to discuss, like low tide on Thursday and the pursuit of sand shrimp. Tide's low at 11a.m. We wouldn't have to get up early, and could have a nice breakfast on the road and be there in plenty of time to investigate their capture. I'll have those two old clam tubes ready, get a bucket and my hip boots." Snooks reminds me that she doesn't have any hip boots and I tell her I'll throw in her low, little farmer boots. After all, I'll be the one down on all fours and she won't need any more than that for foot gear. Snooks agrees, and I proceed to gather up everything and tell her we should be ready to leave the house by 7:30 a.m., Thursday.

I don't know about Snooks, but I'm really looking forward to this new experience and new knowledge. I tell Snooks there's no way we can get in trouble because sand shrimp have fewer restrictions than almost anything else. No license required, take them anytime, anywhere and ten pounds per person. "I don't know about you Snooks, but I'm really going to enjoy this. It will make a nice change for us. Some sea breeze and fresh salt air."

# 3

# Trickery and Goo

"Rise and shine Snooker! It's a beautiful day. The sun's peeking over the hill and we are ready for a whole new wonderful adventure, plus breakfast out."

Snooks stumbles out and starts to dress. I tell her to just wear the old grubbies that she's going to wear on the shrimp expedition and she informs me that no way will she be caught dead looking like that at the restaurant, let alone anywhere else in public.

I don't even try to argue with that little bit of feminine mentality. Besides I don't want to start a beautiful day out on a sour note.

We have a nice breakfast and arrive at the beach just at low tide. We head out toward the ocean with our clam tubes and bucket. Snooks asks "Now just where do we find these shrimp and what do they look like anyway?"

"Snooks, I think you just dig down anywhere, but not where there's a dimple in the sand; I know dimples mean razor clams, and I never saw anything but razor clams where there's a razor clam dimple. Razor clams like to be by themselves, they're real antisocial except at razor clam mating season and even then they're only sociable with another razor clam.

"These shrimp look just like any other shrimp only they live in the sand instead of in the water." Snooks wants to know if I ever saw one and I have to admit, that no, not alive and kicking.

Snooks' answer to that is "No, and I'll bet not still and dead either! I'm beginning to think you brought me on a snipe hunt. Your knowledge of our quest is sub zero. I'm not digging another hole in this sand until I have more facts and concrete information."

How's Diggin?

"Snooks, it's a beautiful day. Try to enjoy the day and not be so pessimistic."

About this time we find we're not alone on the beach, which up until now I hadn't given a thought. This fellow wanders over with clam shovel, hip boots and an old beat-up windbreaker and asks "How's diggin'?"

"Real slow. How are you doing?"

He replies "Real slow until just now, but business has picked up remarkably in the last 30 seconds. I'm with the State Fisheries Department," he says as he flashes a bright silver badge from the inside of his worn windbreaker. Innocence has suddenly turned into wickedness and trickery. Snooks looks across at me like I have led her into the lion's den to be eaten alive, when actually I have no idea what this is all about.

The officer says "I'm sure glad I put a brand new unused ticket book in my jacket pocket this morning because, as I see it, I can almost fill a book with just you two alone."

I say "Well SIR, (you always address anybody with a badge with 'Sir' and respect) I just don't see where we have viol—"

He rudely interrupts me at this point and says "For starters, you are digging in a 1/4 mile permanently-closed sanctuary; number two, the season's closed and you don't have a license visible on your clothing, you don't each have a separate container, and your clam gun is under the four-inch minimum opening. That's five separate counts for starters, and I'm not even down to the fine print yet. This is one of the most flagrant out-in-the-open, broad-daylight miscarriages of law breaking that I have ever seen in all my thirty years with the Department. You deserve to have the book thrown at you!" This tirade leaves me totally speechless, and I watch in stunned amazement as he asks for all the pertinent information to fill out numerous separate violations and tickets. "I'm going to let you off with just the five basic tickets."

People with badges always say that to make you think they're being nice to you and are giving you a decent break, when actually they are mercilessly throwing the book at you.

"This comes to a total of $375.00————each. I put down the minimum on each count. You will be due at the County Courthouse next Tuesday at 3:00 p.m. Pacific time. Be prompt, the judge hates tardiness."

"Officer" I say, "I hate like hell to break your lucrative bubble, but we were not digging clams but sand shrimp. If you'd get out from behind that little tin star you would find out that we were perfectly legal, and all this bombastic, superior, idiotic attitude is a total waste of the taxpayers' time and money."

At this point the Game Warden hesitates, then replies "Fella, I've been handed a lot of excuses, but in all my born days I've never heard a weaker one than that. Anybody in his right mind would know that you don't find sand shrimp on the ocean sand beaches. They're over in that mud flat cove by the Coast Guard Station.

21

"I'll see you in court, and I hope you can come up with a better story than that one or you're both dead pigeons, and I will surely remember your insolence and disrespect."

The Warden walks away and Snooks lights into me with both feet. "Now Buster, look what you got us into just because you didn't find out more about what you were doing! I knew better than to get involved in this hair-brained scheme. $750 because you couldn't take time to find out the facts instead of wandering off half-cocked into the wild blue yonder, oblivious to reality!"

I don't feel I'm entitled to any of this abuse from either one of them and I really resent it.

I tell Rose to quit her bellyaching and just drop the whole thing. "We came to get sand shrimp and by the powers that be, that's exactly what we're going to do! So, Snooks, just stop sniveling and let's go get 'em." I tell her "We'll just find the Coast Guard Station and go down in the mud flats and use our sucker tubes and get some shrimp one way or another. I have my dauber up and by golly, we're not going home without that for which we came, despite any adversity that can be thrown at us!"

We return to our vehicle, our pockets stuffed with tickets, but our spirits still intact (at least one of us.) We find the spot the Warden spoke of and we only had to ask three other people. We grab our gear, bucket and high spirits (at least one of us) and head out to the mud flats.

Snooks right away starts to complain. "No self-respecting critter would live in this stinking, slippery, slimy stuff. What in God's name is that mess over there? It looks like a ghost threw up! Ugh, how awful." I tell her not to get upset, it's just a helpless jellyfish that got trapped and left when the tide went out. Then she wants to know who left all those long, brown bull whips all over the landscape? I tell her that's just another form of seaweed she apparently isn't familiar with.

By now the tide is coming in and we don't have too much time left. I stick my clam tube down as far as it will go and pull it out fast.

**My gracious, Snooks**
**you've got to be more careful**

Lo and behold! There are four pinkish-orange, wiggly things about two to three inches long with pincers, one much larger than the other. "SNOOKS, LOOK! Here they are!" I cry jubilantly. We pick them up and put them in the bucket. Snooks says they look like they might pinch, and looking at them I have to agree. So I tell her to just watch how she picks them up. Well, Snooks gets several and now she's really caught up in the whole operation.

The tide is coming in fast now and we have probably 20 or so shrimp. Snooks decides to take them down to the salt water about 20 feet away and wash them off.

I keep getting a shrimp or two each try with the clam tube, when I hear a muffled little cry of fright and turn towards the sound. Snooks' every step is sinking deeper into the mud; soon she's out of her boots. As she attempts to return to solid footing she tangles her bare foot in a bullwhip seaweed, slips and falls full length on her backside. She cannot get up without rolling over, and ends up with her face in the muck before she finally struggles to her feet. From head to foot, her entire body is covered with stinking, slimy, brownish-black goo. A real pathetic sight, to say the least.

23

"My gracious Snooks, you've got to be more careful. Gather up those spilled shrimp and your boots and we'll head out of here."

Snooks replies "I DON'T GIVE A DAMN ABOUT THOSE @#%&*#+ SHRIMP! I'M GOING TO THE CAR AND HOME!"

I tell her just to calm down, raising her voice and blood pressure will not help. We need to keep our cool and rationalize the best way out of this predicament. I suggest she walk up to the car and I'll retrieve the bucket, boots and sand shrimp.

If I were not wearing hip boots I'd be in the same fix as Snooks. The mud tries to suck my boots off at every step, and at each step I struggle and sink a little deeper. I do just make it back in one piece, and realize I am totally out of breath and in far worse physical shape than I had ever imagined.

I arrive at the car to find Snooks wondering why I had locked the car? "Snooks," I tell her "in your present condition I do not feel it advisable for you to enter the car.

"See that sign up the other side of the Coast Guard Station about a block and a half away? It says Car Wash in neon letters. Put your boots back on and head up that way. I'll be right alongside of you in the car, and when we get there, they'll have a pressure hose and we'll get you cleaned up in no time.

"My, you do smell bad Snooks. Reminds me of the time baby cousin Rickey fell through the hole in the outhouse and we had to fish him out and clean him up; what a stinking mess that was. You're lucky we have a modern car wash with a warm-water pressure hose. All we had for little Rickey was an ice-cold, horse-watering trough."

Snooks finally agrees and heads up the street, and as I promised, I'm right alongside of her. We don't go half a block before I see trouble coming. I holler to Snooks to cross the street, but in her present state of mind I exist only as some pesky vermin and she chooses to ignore me.

Staggering down the street toward Snooks, wearing four or five layers of filthy, cast-off clothing, comes tattered trouble, wine bottle

in hand. As he meets Snooks head on he remarks "Well honey, yer jest my type of gal. Why don't we wander down to my shack under the railroad trestle and I'll heat up a nice cup of octopus nectar for you? As soon as you get warm we can commence to get better acquainted. Say honey, what's that thing wigglin' in yer hair?"

With that Snooks completely loses it, and goes hoppity screaming off down the street toward the Car Wash, pulling at her hair and shaking her head till I think she might dislocate her neck bones. I arrive at the Car Wash when she does but I have to shift into high gear and full throttle to make it at the same time.

I get Snooks in the stall where you wash cars and put in my $2.50 and start the wash. Just as I get things going well, Snooks' new boyfriend ambles up to watch the transformation. I spray her with soap, and when Snooks looks like a sheep ready to be sheared, I figure she's ready for the rinse.

The boyfriend pipes up with "Hey fella, be sure and give them headlights an extra special hand wash; and you missed a big gob of goo on that tail gate."

I figure this is about enough out of him, so I turn and say "Fella, just bug off with your remarks and get out of here before I get the cops."

He flips me the finger and ambles off with a remark that "she ain't half as interesting as when we first met anyway."

In my excitement and confusion I inadvertently also finish Snooks off with a wax job. The wax is very uncomfortable and she complains bitterly. I tell her as long as I paid for it I want to use it and she can wash it off very easily when she gets home in her own shower.

Even pressure washed, Snooks still doesn't smell like a bed of roses. I suggest to her that while there is no one in sight, she should peal off those wet clothes. We'll wrap the blanket around her that we keep in the back seat so the dog hairs stay off the cushions. That way she can stay fairly dry, and I'll turn the heater up to keep the chill away on the way home.

Snooks doesn't answer but begins to comply. She's down to her pants and bra when out of the stillness comes a lone wolf whistle; the boyfriend is still watching from a distance. At the sound of the whistle, Snooks jumps the four feet through the already open car door in one instantaneous vault. Hollering bloody murder at me to get her the blanket and throw her smelly, wet clothes in the trunk! Her last words are: "LET'S GET THE HELL OUT OF HERE!"

As we head home with about 25 sand shrimp, I decide to try to break the silence. I can tell by the set of her jaw that Snooks is about like Mount St. Helens on the 17th of May, 1980; almost ready to explode and cover half the free world with her wrath.

I say "Snooks, I'll bet this is a learning experience we'll probably never forget. Are you warm enough?

"You must be hungry, I'd be glad to stop and pick up hamburgers and hot coffee."

Through clenched teeth Snooks says "I-just-want-to-get-home-so-

I-can-shower-and-dress! Then see a lawyer and find out which is cheaper, a divorce or a hit man."

"Snooks, I'm utterly amazed at your attitude. After all, it wasn't me that told you to go give the shrimp a bath. They didn't feel dirty, that's home to them. They were born and raised in that stinking, slimy mess. Did you ever see an unhappy dirty pig? Probably the last thing they wanted was to be all fresh and clean in pure salt water. Also, I didn't trip you and roll you around in that black, slimy, stinking mess. These are all your own doings. And Snooks, before you plan my demise; stop and think about this: is it worth going to prison forever over a mistake you yourself made and are now trying to blame on me?"

Snooks is silent and I can tell still thinking about what I just said. But I'm not safe yet, her jaw still has that firm, determined set. I feel it will be a long time before sex is ever mentioned in our house again.

I continue to tell Snooks that she'll be back to her old self as soon as she has a nice warm shower and clean clothes. Also, we have to maintain a compatible relationship at least until after our trial. I explain to her that we'll have no problem with the Warden's terrible miscarriage of justice, because Elmer will go to court and testify that I was not completely informed as to the exact whereabouts or habitat of sand shrimp; after all, Elmer hates any mention of the Fisheries Department. "So you see Snooks, things are not as bad as they look."

Snooks finally talks, and asks in a quietly controlled, guarded manner, "Do you remember your exact words this morning shortly after the bubbly Rise-and-Shine scenario? They were: 'We are ready for a whole new wonderful adventure.' If that's what you call this day, I hope and pray that I never live to experience a day with a BAD adventure, because neither of us is strong enough to come out of it alive. In my wildest imagination I could never have come up with the likes of today. I've seen spine-chilling horror movies that were mild compared with my experiences today. I hope you're proud to

27

be the sponsor of my worst day on the face of this earth, and if you haven't got the idea by now, you're beyond hope, which is a definite possibilty; and Buster, don't even mention sex for at least a year!"

"I know Snooks. I already figured that out, that's always the first thing you women take away."

I suffer with verbal abuse all the way home, I'm glad to be able to escape the confinement of the car. Snooks goes in and proceeds to shower.....twice.

The clean clothes and make-up seem to dull her wrath some- what. I make her a cup of coffee, which she accepts. This is the first step on the comeback trail.

Then Snooks tells me in a very calm mild manner, that she doesn't think she wants to accompany me down by the boat launch and sit on a little stool by a fire with all those men, and fish Sturgeon. Besides there's no bathroom down there and her plumbing is not as simple to get at as mine. "Why don't you get your friend Johnny Johanson to go with you? He just lives for fishing and I bet he would enjoy learning about Sturgeon fishing with you."

I think this is a good time to agree and besides this is a very good idea. I think Johnny and I would enjoy it. Next time I see him I'll just ask him.

I tell Snooks we got home with 23 shrimp. Snooks' reply is "Big deal. If the Warden makes his accusations stick, then they cost us $32.60 each, not counting gas. I think that's a record for the most ex- pensive fish bait in the history of mankind."

I assure Snooks that there's no way the Warden can win on all counts. "And besides, I don't know why you take such a pessimistic attitude to any project that interests me, Snooks. I just hate constant negativity."

I tell Snooks I think I'll drop by the Plunkin Shack and see if Elmer's there. Tuesday is court day and we have a lot to do if we're going to beat the Warden. He's a professional at this and we're just amateurs.

I head down to the Plunkin Shack and there's three or four sitting by the pot-bellied stove. Elmer is telling a story about three guys who were talking about how far back they could remember. The first one said he could remember when he was six and in the first grade; remember his teacher's name and all the kids. The second one said he could remember when he was four and all the rooms in the house where he lived and all his toys. The third one hadn't said anything and one of the others asked, "Well Sam, how far back can you remember?" Sam replied, "I can remember going to the dance with my father and coming home with my mother."

Everybody laughs at that, and when things quiet down I ask Elmer if I can talk to him outside for a minute. I then proceed to tell him just what had happened and all the charges against us, and the fine for us both is up to $750.

Elmer says not to worry; he remembers not being very exact about the location of sand shrimp, but he warns me we've tangled with Norman Nugent. This Warden, whose name is on the tickets, is one of the worst in the State to deal with. He brags about never losing a case in an honest court. He's got the nickname, 'Nail 'Em Nugent.'

Elmer thinks I should go right in the Plunkin Shack and tell everybody, and we'll muster up all the help we can get. He says with this guy's reputation he thinks we're gonna need it.

I ask Elmer if he's just trying to scare me or is he serious? Elmer says "You walk in that court without some backing and you'll know I'm serious. You need all the help you can get, now let's go back in and drum up some support."

We go back in the Plunkin Shack and Elmer tells Pete "The fishing fraternity has got a buddy and his wife in a mess with the law, and we have got to help them."

Pete listens to my story and says he'll get on the horn and get Snarly and a half dozen other good old boys; then have me tell them the facts first-hand and whoever can get away will go with us to court and give us the protection and support we need.

I return home and tell Snooks that we have no worry. Pete and

Elmer are going to line us up some help. I'm to meet with them in the morning and give them some details. After dinner I get a call from Pete and he says to be down to the Plunkin Shack at 10:30 or so. Several of the fellas want to hear the facts and give their help. I assure Pete I'll be there. Pete says this is the way it should always be. We should all stick together. Lord knows nobody else looks out for the sportsman.

10:30 a.m. pronto I walk in the Plunkin Shack, and Snarly Krautkramer is wondering how we could have got into such a mess? I tell Snarly it was due largely to lack of proper information as to the residential area of sand shrimp. "Nobody in his right mind," I tell him "would be down there digging clams in broad daylight with the season closed and in a restricted area besides. Then we tangled with the worst ticket-crazed Game Warden on the west side."

Snarly says "I believe you've hit on the answer. We'll go in there and prove to the judge that you two are mentally incompetent." I tell Snarly it might work but I couldn't add this to Snooks' embarrassment over being arrested. Tom Snavly says he could act plum loony for $750.

Before I know what's going on, they have all decided that this is the only possible way they are going to get us out of this. Already it sounds like a totally out-of-hand funfest, with all the giggling and laughter. I hate to hear a grown man giggling like a lovesick teenager.

Pete asks for a show of hands, and it's five-to-two in favor. Pete says "You go on home now and don't worry. We'll stay here a spell and get all the details worked out. I wouldn't be surprised we might get you off with maybe a $50 fine and very little jail time; could be you two might have to spend some time with a shrink though." Then the giggles and laughter start in again. Somehow I just don't feel too comfortable. I think I would have been way ahead to have never breathed a word about this.

But it's too late now. The cat's out. I haven't the faintest idea how I'm going to tell Snooks about this scheme they've cooked up.

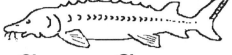

# Court Capers

As soon as I arrive home, Snooks wants to know exactly who was at the meeting and what were their ideas to get us out of this horrendous mess? I tell Snooks when I finished telling them the true story, they said it was kind of dumb to be trying to get sand shrimp on a clam beach, but to go on home and not worry, they would work up a fool-proof plan.

Her female intuition leads her to believe that all is not right and I know more than I am telling her. I can tell she senses a fly in the ointment. Her concern and questions are becoming more direct and frantic. I just don't understand how women can hit the nail on the head with very little, if any, information to point them in that direction.

Snooks looks me right in the eye and asks "Just what did they mean, 'it was a dumb thing to do'?"

By this time I'm beginning to get a little nervous. Most folks would never notice it, but Snooks knows me far too well. She notices the slight tremor in my voice, but lucky for me she can't see the little rivers of sweat trickling down my back clear to the cleavage of my posterior. A similar feeling to a Gestapo interrogation.

A mind can only take so much, and even with my strong, unrelenting will-power, I finally crack under the relentless intimidating questioning. I tell her "Snooks, I believe they're going to use a mental approach." Snooks asks exactly what I'm getting at, and I say "I believe it's like proving you're not mentally capable of knowing you were wro—"

"YOU DON'T MEAN AN INSANITY PLEA!?!"

"Well, yes, Snooks. Something like that."

Right at this moment I don't think insanity would be too hard to prove. Within half an hour though, I can begin to understand some of her babbling and gibberish. I say "Snooks, Tom Snavly said he could act plum loony for $750."

"Well, I'm not Tom Snavly! Tom wouldn't even have to act, that's normal for him."

I tell Snooks that Snarly Krautkramer was taking up a collection when I left. They were going to try to get us some legal counsel. Again the questions. "How much did they collect?" I tell her they were still collecting when I left. "Well, how much did they have when you left?" I inform Snooks they had $23.48, counting the 20 I put in, because after all they were doing it for us.

The phone rings and gets me away from the quizzing, at least momentarily. It's Snarly and he tells me they raised $27.50 and they were real lucky to get Slinky Shinkle out of retirement to represent us in court. He would even be there a half hour early to talk to us in order to get the facts, and build a strong case.

As soon as I hang up Snooks is back at it. "Who was that and what did they say? Was it about court? Was it good or bad?"

"Snooks, Snooks. Not so fast. It was Snarly and they raised $27.50, and we're lucky enough to get Slinky Shinkle to represent us. We're to be there a half hour early to let him talk to us and build a case."

Snooks explodes with "HOLY TOLEDO! Could you sort out the good from the bad for me? Because right now, all I can see is bad. If you gave them $20.00 and they took up a collection to stick together and help the poor sportsman in trouble and only added $7.50, it doesn't look like our friends are very friendly! Then you say they were lucky enough to get Slinky out of retirement. Slinky was so bad that he was retired for ten years before he retired! and he's been retired for at least twenty years! The last case on record that he won was back in 1958.

"I think we'd be ahead to mail in our $750 and call it quits before Slinky proves us mentally incompetent in front of the whole town. I don't know about you Buster, but I've half a mind not to go to court and just forfeit my half of the fine."

"Snooks, we can't do that. After all, that would just show that we were guilty and we know we're innocent! No, we've got to get to court and exonerate ourselves of this terrible miscarriage of justice.

"Let's get a good night's sleep and go down there a half hour early, meet with Slinky and hope he can convince the judge that we're innocent. Court is at 3 p.m. We'll get there at 2:30."

On awakening the morning of our trial, Snooks tells me that my idea about a good night's sleep might have worked for me, but not for her. She had horrible dreams about being pronounced mentally sub-normal and needing psychiatric counseling. I tell Snooks not to worry, it was only a dream, besides I think that before she could be committed and need a phizeekeeatrist, I would have to sign some papers. Snooks answer to that is "OH MY! Now I am really worried. It seems that any time you enter my personal life I end up much, much worse off than before."

I tell Snooks I think it would be good idea to dress down and look real poor and unkempt, then the judge might think we don't have any money and if he does find us wrong, he'll not fine us as much as rich people.

Snooks doesn't like the idea because women always want to look their best at all times (and I might add, at all cost.) I tell her it wouldn't look good if one of us looks real good and the other real scroungy. She agrees to that and decides to go along with my idea. She really goes all out and looks about as poor as I could imagine; much worse than I do, and I think I look really bad.

We arrive at the Courthouse half an hour early and meet our attorney. I hadn't seen Slinky in six or seven years. He looked old then, but now he's just a shaky shell of his former frail self. Snooks whispers in my ear "We ain't got a chance." She needn't have whispered, I doubt if he could hear a box of dynamite explode if he were sitting on it.

Slinky takes us to a little room, we all sit down and I say "Mr.

Shinkle (you have to respect this much age,) what do you think our chances are?" Slinky cups his hand to his ear and says "This here new hearing aid helps some when it's on high blower, but you still better speak up and stop that mumbling."

Snooks says "Lordy, lordy, what has God wrought?"

Slinky listens to our story and he feels that we might use an entrapment plea, before we stoop to an insanity plea as a last resort.

Snooks says "My yes. Let's try that." He then explains that we'd tangled with the most ruthless, ticket-happy Warden on the west side of the mountains and it will be almost impossible to get off Scot free.

It's time to go on into the court room and wait our turn. There is one case ahead of ours, but we don't mind. We need to get the feel of things anyway. We march in and take seats well back from the action.

Pretty soon they bring in two guys in orange jump suits, handcuffs, and leg irons. I figure these guys have to have done something real bad to deserve this kind of treatment. They take their places up front and just as they get seated, somebody in a sheriff's uniform and a badge hollers "Judge Hollingsworth. All rise." As I stand I hear a sound like air escaping from a ruptured rubber duck. I turn toward the sound and Snooks is as pale as a ghost and whispers to me "Do you know who that is? I was going with him when you came along. I dumped him for you."

As we sit down I say "Snooks, it's been a long time, maybe he's forgotten."

"No, not a chance" Snooks replies, "he said at the time that if he lived forever he'd never be able to forget me."

I try to whisper to Slinky but that's like trying to get sign language across to a blind man, so I write him a note and try in brief to explain the sudden and unexpected complications and wonder if it's too late to get a change of venue. He gives me a thumbs down which means —too late.

By now the proceedings are starting on the case ahead of ours. It seems that the two guys in orange jumpsuits took the victim out in the woods and tied him to a tree, then rubbed him down with bacon grease and put two pounds of bacon in his pockets and down the front of his pants, and left him there; hoping that during the night the bears would smell the bacon and come and eat him!

The problem was, he untied himself and turned the two men in the orange play-suits over to the police and now it is time for the judge to pass sentence. The men are charged with assault with a deadly weapon. I would never, ever, have considered bacon a deadly weapon. Live and learn.

The judge sentences them to 20 years apiece for attempted murder, five years for possession of a deadly weapon and six months for malicious mischief; with possibility of parole in eight years if they promise never to come in contact with bacon again. The judge raps his gavel and the orange suiters are led out by the guy with the badge.

I think that might have been a good case for an insanity plea. Now our case is next.

The judge retires to his chambers and we are seated at the front. Across from us sits Warden Nugent; jaw set, shoes and badge each with a new high-gloss shine. He has the look of complete confidence.

The judge returns and again we all rise. Our case is called and then we are sworn in and the judge asks Warden Nugent what the charges are. He begins by telling the Court that the defendants (us) were digging clams in a closed, protected area, during a closed season, without proper licenses, and with illegal equipment. He adds "I have never seen anybody in his right mind flaunt such total disregard for our laws in broad daylight, as these two. Then the man lied to me, used profanity, also disrespect, and told me they were digging sand shrimp! Your Honor, that really topped it off. Anybody would know sand shrimp don't live on the sandy, ocean beaches."

The judge turns to our attorney and asks if he has any questions for the Wildlife Agent? Slinky replies that he most certainly does.

35

First he asks how long Mr. Nugent has been a Warden, and immediately Nugent fires back he is not a Warden, he is a Wildlife Agent. Slinky apologizes, and I feel if this continues in this vein, our goose is cooked.

Then he asks Nugent if we had any clams and Nugent admits, "No, they did not." Slinky then asks how long he had observed us on the beach and Nugent says we had just got there.

Slinky then implies that Nugent was living up to his reputation as being ticket happy, and was so intent on writing tickets that he had not taken sufficient time to really observe what we were doing, therefore he could not honestly say we were digging clams.

Next Slinky inquires as to how Nugent was dressed; was he in uniform or beach wear? Nugent admits we could not have known he was an Officer as he was not in uniform. Slinky then accuses him of trickery to gain an admission of guilt. Nugent is beginning to get a little red in the face and I begin to feel we might have a chance. Again, Slinky asks Nugent if he had asked us what we were after, and he answers that he had. Slinky asks what exactly he had said to us and Nugent replies he'd asked "How's diggin'?"

Slinky then tells him, "That question asks about the quality of digging and has no reference as to what the defendants were after. You made an assumption and a wrong one at that. Then you proceeded to bully them with threats of numerous infractions and multiple and montrous penalties!

"I have no further questions of this witness, your Honor."

Nugent steps down and resumes his seat, very red in the face.

"I have one more witness to call to the stand, Your Honor. Will Elmer Erkel please come forward?"

Elmer is sworn in and Slinky asks him if he was present the day I came down to the Plunkin Shack to get the Sturgeon licenses. Elmer replies that he was. Slinky wants to know if we had any conversaton and Elmer confirms that we did. Then Slinky asks Elmer to elaborate on our conversation. Elmer clears his throat and proceeds to tell Slinky and the court that I had specifically asked where sand shrimp live, and he had told me down at the beach in the salt water. Elmer adds "After he left, we all had a good laugh at the Plunkin Shack because Pete sold sand shrimp right there by the dozen, but the defendant had asked where they live, not where you could get them."

Slinky says "Thank you, Elmer. You may step down. Your Honor, I rest my case."

The Warden is visibly shaken. All that look of triumph has left his face. He knows he has lost a big one due to his overly ambitious attitude at the beach.

The judge says "I believe these two to be innocent of any crime; and rather than a fine, should receive an apology from Officer Nugent for their inconvenience." He raps his gavel and says "Case dismissed."

I notice a look of disappointment on several of the Plunkin Shack bunch who have come to see us end up with the insanity plea.

Slinky Shinkle could not be happier, wants to take us over to the Blue Danube for a cocktail to celebrate. In his happiness we cannot refuse. You know, he even looks younger. Actually, we feel he did a fantastic job, and we make sure we convey that feeling to him. He says it was one of the two most enjoyable cases in his lifetime. I have a feeling the other was the case in 1958, he also won that one.

As we walk down the Courthouse steps Judge Hollingsworth passes us, and in a very low tone says "I hope all is going well for you, Rose."

# 5

## At Last

After a couple of celebration drinks with Slinky we head home feeling no pain. As soon as we enter the house Snooks remembers her down-grading appearance, which in all the excitement of trial and all, she had totally forgotten. "OH MY GOD!" I hear from out of the bathroom. Snooks has seen herself in the mirror and realizes what the judge has seen. "No wonder he made the statement he did as he walked down the Courthouse steps. I look like maybe my richest relative is a recipient of food stamps!"

The court appearance was interesting, and with a rewarding outcome. Plus, poor old Slinky Shinkle has regained his self respect and rightful place in society. All for $27.50.

As we turn in for the night, and have our last, just before sleep conversation, I ask Snooks, "Exactly what did you do when dating Hollingsworth to have him make a statement like you said he made?"

Snooks answers, "I don't recall what you're referring to. I'm really tired. Do you mind turning out the light now?"

I say, "Snooks, in the courtroom today, in your surprise and anxiety at seeing him in court, you mentioned going with him before me and that he had made the statement to you that if he lived forever he'd never be able to forget you. What female magic did you use to make him make a statement like that?"

"I just told you I'm tired. I have a migraine coming on. Will you please turn out the light and discuss such trivial things some other time? Now good night."

"Good night Snooks; an aspirin might ease your migraine.....and conscience both."

During morning coffee I ask Snooks how her migraine is and she tells me it seems to be gone. I tell her that as fast as that came on I feel it was stress related. She wants to know what stress I'm referring to? Just as I'm ready to continue the lights-out conversation, there's a knock at the door.

It's my old friend Johnny Johanson. I pour Johnny a cup of coffee and the three of us sit around the kitchen table; soon the conversation gets to the trial and Sturgeon.

Johnny remarks how pleased he is at the outcome of our court appearance. Snooks tells him that she is really glad he stopped by. She wants to know if he's ever had any inclination to do any Sturgeon fishing. She tells Johnny her introduction to this sport ended in two cases of embarrassing situations in the first two hours of exposure to this new and exciting hobby.

I feel this is as good a time as any to ask Johnny if he'd care to join me. "Johnny, Snooks doesn't care to go any further with this Sturgeon business and I wonder if you'd care to join me in this exciting sport?"

Johnny remarks that he doesn't feel my great exuberance or excitement, but it's sort of off-season for everything else and he would accompany me on a trip or two.

Snooks says "Johnny, do you have any idea what you're letting yourself in for? This husband of mine can turn the most innocent circumstance into a total disaster easier and quicker than you can blink an eye. If he walked across the street to get an ice cream cone I'd not bet against the possibility of him ending up in jail."

Johnny laughs and says "Well Snooks, I've known him a long time and I'm not afraid. I think I can hold my own. But thanks for the warning, I'll be very careful."

He says for me to look up the next good tide and he'll pick up a license and then get the sand shrimp the night before at the Plunkin Shack. That sounds good to me. Now maybe at last I'm going to get a chance at some real honest-to-goodness Sturgeon fishin'.

As we pour a refill on the coffee, I tell Johnny the story about the fellow who stumbles up to the only other patron in a bar and asks if he could buy him a drink? The patron agrees, and the man sits down. As they drink, the first man asks where the other man came from, and is told he's from Ireland. The first man is surprised and says he too, comes from Ireland so they should celebrate with another drink to toast Ireland. When asked where in Ireland he's from, the second man says "Dublin" to which the first says he cannot believe it, for he, too, is from Dublin! So they have another drink to Dublin. They keep talking and the first one asks where the second went to school? When he's told the second man went to Saint Mary's and graduated in '62, the first man is absolutely astounded and says he did too! So he suggests they have another round, this time to celebrate Saint Mary's and the Class of '62. About that time in comes one of the regulars who sits down at the bar. He asks the barkeep what's been going on, and the bartender says "Oh, nothin' much. Just the O'Malley twins, getting drunk again."

Johnny has a good laugh over that one and about three minutes later Snooks laughs. I tell Snooks "He who laughs last, thinks slowest." Snooks wants to know where I get all these fortune-cookie expressions. I tell her I just think them up and she tells me I'm either part Chinese or missed my calling, but for her sake she wishes I'd keep them to myself.

Johnny decides he better leave. I tell him I'll call after I check the tides. Snooks asks me to walk out with Johnny and get the mail. As I walk back thumbing through the mail, it dawns on me that we seem to be getting a lot more contest-type mail and it's all in Snooks' name.

I hand Snooks her mail and she starts going through it eagerly. I ask her if she has become addicted to the contest gimmick? Snooks resentfully tells me it's no gimmick as I call it, and that our little Japanese neighbor Yoko enters lots more than she does, and Yoko has won six bars of soap, a dinner trip for two on a steam train through the Redwoods in California, and last, but not least, Yoko won a $100 check to be used on the purchase of any car model later than 1990 at Slicker Williams's Used Car Emporium!   When our Japanese neighbors the Myamoto's, Eiichi and Yoko, come over for their morning cup of tea and conversation, I right away ask "Well Yoko, when are you leaving for your big steam train trip through the Redwoods and dinner?"

Itchy pops up and says, "We not go, no money to get there, cost too much."

"See" I say to Snooks, "it's all a gimmick. After you spend five or six hundred to get there, then it's free. They give these things to make them look good but they know most people can't take time or don't have the money to travel to the free part."

Yoko pipes in defense of it all and says "But I only had to buy foah boxes of Ding Dong Dog Biscuits, then I win big pwize; good too, Atsumi wike them." As I see it, the only winner was their Shar-Pei and if that dog didn't just happen to like them, it would have been a total loss.

It only takes a few minutes to find out that these two gals are hooked on the lure of the contest. I might just as well shut up and let them enjoy their fun.

Snooks and Yoko spend the rest of tea time discussing the good and bad merits of one new contest they have been picked out of 2.3 million to enter. Snooks says "I think the Red Rodent Trap contest is the best chance I've seen yet. I don't know how we were both lucky enough to be among the twelve finalists for the eight million top prize money. With only ten prizes for 12 finalists the odds are great that we're bound to win something. I sent my entry blank and money for two Red Rodent Rat Traps this morning."

As Yoko gets ready to leave she remarks "Good ting and only thwee days weft, I send entwy and twap money today."

After they leave I tell Snooks I'll see if I can get a couple of rats to turn loose so the expense of the rat traps will not be a waste. As I see it, we need two rat traps about as much as an Hawaiian surfer needs ice skates. Snooks turns and walks away without an answer but I know she heard me. I can tell by the stiffness of her walk.

I can't seem to find my tide book so I drop down to the Plunkin Shack to pick up another one. As usual there are two or three fellows around the pot-bellied stove, coffee cups in hand, telling fish stories or any others they can think of. Snarly and Elmer are both there, and Snarly says "It was a pleasure to see Slinky beat old Nugent out of your tickets yesterday; the Warden felt pretty sure of himself, but Slinky fixed that in short order."

I think all Snarly really wants is a little praise for the donation and getting Slinky to represent us. I tell them how it would never have been possible without their help and we really are thankful. Pete pipes up and reminds me that he has live sand shrimp for sale every day and in the future it would probably be cheaper to just stop in and pick up what we need, then he laughs as he hands me the tide book.

After checking the book, I find the next good low tide will be 7:32 a.m. next Thursday. I call Johnny and make a date to pick him up at 5:30 that morning. To some people time just doesn't mean a thing, but Johnny is always on time. I know one character who figures if you're ready to leave at the time you're supposed to arrive, then you're on time! this I just can't tolerate. You can't beat time, so you just better learn to go along with it.

Talking about time, one of the fussiest things is a soft-boiled egg. If you don't pay strict attention to time it's hard to tell what you'll get, but it won't be soft boiled. Me, I like mine cooked 3 minutes and 45 seconds at 375 feet above sea level.

Thursday finally arrives and Johnny and I head down to the river mouth and the boat launch. The bank fishermen, or plunkers, fish alongside the boat launch on a cleared- off parking recreation area. They sit in lawn chairs by the river, bait up and cast out, put their rods in rod holders and wait for some action. If it's bad weather they do the same but sit in their cars and wait for action.

Speaking of action: this is not fast and furious fishing; it's sort of a social club of welfare or social security checks, waiting for action.

Johnny and I are early enough to find a decent spot and set up our chairs, rig our outfits and get ready.

We watch in amazement as others arrive. It's definitely more of a social club, almost a ritual. One fellow hollers over to another close by and asks "Where's Ned?" The other one answers that Ned's sister is here from Spokane and he had to stay home and entertain her. The first one replies, "Too bad. Ned had the record, 88 days without a miss. Last time Ned missed was when he had his heart attack, even then he only missed two-and-a-half days."

Johnny and I look at each other and wonder if this bunch will ever accept a couple of newcomers. After about an hour we have not been spoken to or even noticed as being present. Johnny says, "Well, I'm going to wander around and see if I can at least get a rise out of someone." Johnny isn't gone more than five minutes and he's back. I ask how come he's back so soon? And he says "I barely got my mouth open and that guy over there in the blue shirt told me it's illegal to leave my rod unattended, I'd better get back and stay close or Warden Nugent could be watching and give me a ticket. On the one hand he's telling me to mind my own business and on the other, acts like he's giving a newcomer some helpful advice and he really doesn't care which way I take it."

Finally one of the regulars saunters over and strikes up an inquisitive, guarded conversation. I have a feeling he was hand picked to find out as much as possible without telling anything at all. Probably a retired lawyer.

Without a handshake or an introduction he asks "Where you fellows from?"

I answer "Up the road a piece." This guy is going to find that two can play the same game. Then he inquires how long have we been fishin'? Johnny asks if he means fishing in general or just Sturgeon? This throws the fellow's cadence off, because he was to do the asking and now he is in a position to have to do the answering. I don't think he's a lawyer, they wouldn't let themselves get in this position so quick.

All at once he looks towards his rod by the water and says "I better go check my rod, I think I might have a nibble. See you fellows later."

A fellow about eight guys downriver from us all at once hollers "FISH ON!" and everybody near reels in and runs over to watch the fun. This fellow is using a rod that looks as though it started life as a pool cue and ended up retired with a handle and guides. The way this fish is fighting, it looks like the rod had a much easier life as a pool cue. Forty-five minutes later we're still undecided as to who has who. The fisherman is sweating profusely and dropping one arm now and then, and it's becoming more now than then. He wiggles his fingers on the dropped hand and shakes his hand to improve the circulation.

It's obvious that the fish is too big to keep, but the fellow is in a situation where it will reflect on his macho image if he cuts the line. On the other hand, a few of the other fishermen would like to end this and get back to fishing. The fellow fighting the fish is between hell and high water. It looks like the fish is winning, and this fellow looks like he would like any excuse to end this battle if he could do it and save his manhood. It's been close to an hour-and-twenty minutes and everybody is starting to grumble a little. One man asks "What's the matter Sam, he got the best of you?"

Sam answers in a shaky voice "Not on your life! This dude is starting to weaken, it won't be long now. I just saw some bubbles; that's a good sign."

"You know it's too big to keep, Sam. Why don't you cut your line and let us get back to fishing?"

Sam's answer is "Well, I just want to get a look at it."

About now the fish comes toward shore much too fast for Sam to keep up with it, and about 20 feet out, right in front of us, it jumps clear out of the water. It's an awesome sight to say the least; it must be all of nine feet in length! As it goes back in the water it drops across the line and breaks it. The fish is gone, but the memory will probably be with me forever. Johnny says "I had no idea there were fish anywhere near that size in this part of the country! We're going to keep after these guys till we learn all about it. This is really something special!"

Everybody settles back, baits up and goes back to fishin', except Sam. He's over in the shade wiping the sweat off and getting a sandwich and a cold beer. I think he's too tired to bait up.

The tide's almost high now and fishing is about over for the day. The boat fishermen are beginning to show up. As they do everybody is curious as to their luck and to see how they did. It's surprising, but out of seven boats there is a total of six fish and one boat has two! The bank fishermen are three times as many but only one bite maybe and one lost fish. The boats give a definite advantage. I can see that right quick.

As Johnny and I pack up and head for home we are both ready to try again; this holds a real interest for both of us. I tell Johnny that before we go again I'm going to have to buy a complete new outfit because there is no way I'm equipped to do battle with something like we've seen today.

Johnny says "Me too. Let's go down to the Plunkin Shack and re-equip."

When I get home I tell Snooks all about the battle the fellow had with the big Sturgeon and how exciting it was to see it jump clear out of the water right in front of us. Then I tell her that Johnny's coming over in the morning and we're going down to the Plunkin Shack and get us new outfits to fish those babies with, because what we have would be about as effective as using a slingshot for an elephant.

Snooks says "I see that gleam in your eye, and I'm afraid we're off and running again. Just don't expect me to go down there and sit on a stool with all those men. You and Johnny can have that fun. And please don't spend more than our income."

"Snooks," I say "there's no way to run into any large expense; it's almost over as soon as we get our new rods, reels and line. After that it can't be more than a few sinkers and sand shrimp."

45

Snooks raises her eyebrows and says "I've heard that line of bull before. Look what two free packages of Giant Pumpkin seeds cost you last year, over $2,500! All I say is, please don't get carried away. I know you, the on-purpose expenses are almost as much as the accidental expenses."

I ask Snooks what she means by accidental expenses and she reminds me of the power saw I borrowed once to cut a tree, and when the tree accidentally fell on the power saw I had to replace the saw with a new one. Snooks says that's what she means by accidental expense. Rose can be cruel at times.

Johnny shows up ready to go the next morning, and over coffee tells Snooks all about the big fish. She says "Johnny, I believe you two have been bitten by the big fish bug." He has to agree.

Johnny rushes through his coffee and says, "Well, we better get down there before they raise the prices." I ask Johnny if he knows exactly what he's after and he tells me he has a pretty good idea because he looked over a lot of outfits yesterday.

As soon as we enter the Plunkin Shack and our intentions are known, we start getting help and advice from all sides. I pick up a nice looking heavy-duty reel and while turning the handle and looking at the $38.34 price tag, Pete Peak comes over and says, "Brand new, just out, a beauty, 185 yard, 45 pound line capacity. 3.3:1 gear ratio. I can give you boys a special price on two."

"Like what?" Snarly asks.

Then Elmer pipes up and remarks that the gear ratio is nowhere near fast enough, no wonder they're so cheap.

At which point Pete gets a little upset and wants to know if either Snarly or Elmer is buying the reel, and if not to just tend to whatever they were doing before we came in; or were they just leaving?

Cross-eyed Krause turns around in his chair by the stove and says, "Buy an American-made reel, then you get a warranty you can read. I'd suggest one of those old standbys that have been dependable for years." Cross-eye knows Pete doesn't handle those and now Pete's upset. Cross-eye can see this and he decides he better get home with that quart of ice cream he left in the car.

After Cross-eye leaves Pete says, "I've been told never to sit at a counter in a restaurant next to Cross-eye, because he'll look in his plate and eat out of yours."

Pete then gets a long tong grabber rig and reaches way up on the top shelf above his head and brings down a green box, blows off the dust, and says "This is the reel you boys want for that heavy-duty fishing you're planning. I can't keep these in stock; one of the most popular heavy-duty reels made. Models are so good they haven't changed a thing since '79." Pete is really at his best right now, he figures we can't pass with this sales pitch.

Pete continues, "Made in Sweden. Nobody has craftsmanship like the Swede's do." I interrupt this spiel to ask the gear ratio and Pete ignores me and continues with: "Three ball bearings each side for friction-free spool rotation. Swedish stainless steel no less, and three grease cup fittings for easy lubrication. A genuine Lars Hjelm original, a masterpiece in fishing excellence, only $87.25 or two for $157.33, almost a $10 savings apiece. I'll set these on the counter while you're picking out a suitable rod."

All this time Johnny is off by himself looking over several other reels, not listening to or being swayed by Pete's sales pitch. Finally he asks Pete "What about this Japanese reel made by Shingitchy? It's got 200 yard 40 lb line capacity with sealed stainless ball bearing spool, zirconia level wind pawl, 6.3:1 gear ratio for lightning fast retrieve, Helical brass main and pinion gears, die cast aluminum frame, thumb button release, centrifugal brake system to prevent backlash, total weight 9.6 oz. and a lifetime warranty. Only $81.20 with $20 off when you mail in your owner's certificate."

Johnny tells Pete he doesn't know how anybody can beat that, and besides he saw four of them in use on the river yesterday; they must be good. He tells Pete that's his choice. I chime in and ask "How much for two?"

Pete's whole attitude changes in the flicker of an eyelash. He snaps back, "Can't give you no break on that Jap stuff. You guys are making a mistake passing a genuine Swedish Hjelm reel, a real mistake."

We pay Pete for our purchases and as we leave he's trying to reach up and put the two Swedish reels back. It was so close and yet so far away. Oh well, sooner or later he'll catch somebody; probably poor old Harvey Carbone, he's a sucker for fishing tackle.

As we walk out I tell Johnny that I think his reel choice is impossible to beat and we should go back again tomorrow and pick out a rod, and maybe even some line, but for now I suggest a visit to the Blue Danube, for a little libation would sure be in order. Johnny says it's sure in order as far as he's concerned.

As we enter the dimly lit watering hole, we see Rotgut O'Riley at one end of the bar, and off in a corner Harvey Carbone, of all people. Harvey pipes up and invites us over, and as we sit down he wants to know "What in the world have you been up to, and what brings you in here this time of day?"

We order our gin and tonic and then tell Harvey that we just came from the Plunkin Shack and Pete Peak tried to pawn a couple of out-of-date Swedish reels on us.

Harvey asks if those were the Lars Hjelm Swedish masterpieces? We say "Yes, but we ended up with a Shingitchy model X-40." Harvey laughs and says Pete has been trying to pawn those Swedish lemons off for at least five years. He says Pete forgot and even tried to sell him one twice. I had wondered why Snarly and Cross-eye were both sitting back there snickering like two school kids, now I knew. We all laugh about that and how Pete has lost out again. Harvey says "I think selling those lemons has become a lifetime challenge for poor old Pete."

We decide to have another round on poor old Pete Peak's pet project, and we're soon confronted with another step toward relaxation and camaraderie.

Rotgut O'Riley, a glass of muscatel held in a shaky hand, is up to the bar already deep into a husky-musky stupor. Rotgut is trying to tell the bartender a story but he can't keep his thoughts straight long

48

enough to finish it. I ask Harvey if he has any idea what story he's trying to tell and Harvey says, "I think it's the one about the blind guy who was swinging his seeing-eye dog around and around over his head and a passerby wanted to know what he was doing? And the blind fellow replied, 'Oh, just looking around'."

Then Johnny wants to know if we've heard the one about the fellow who stuttered real bad who had gone to the doctor and found he had prostate trouble and needed an operation. He was horrified and asked the doctor "wha—wh-wah— i—i—i—if a—ah—ah— d—dd-do—don—don't ha—h—haaa—have i-i-i-it d-dd—du—dun—done?" The doctor said "Well then, you'll be pee'in just like you talk."

I tell Johnny that I'll have just one more round, because I told Snooks I wouldn't be too long and she'll be waiting for me. She promised Grandma Two Dogs she'd be over today and balance her check book. The poor old soul is pleasant enough, but just has a lot of trouble with even fourth-grade math. In fact, she never did learn her multiplication tables.

Harvey says "Well, she doesn't need multiplication tables to balance a check book. All she needs is addition and subtraction." I tell them that she never learned them either. Harvey adds, "Yep, she needs help all right. There are three kinds of people, those who can count and those who can't."

Johnny and I both nod and answer "Yeah, you're sure right on that Harvey."

Then Johnny pipes up and says, "Ya know Harv, yer always cumin up with them smart sayins, I don't know why I kin never think of them things."

"Guys, I haven't bought no roun yet and I'm gunna buy this here next one, then like I tol ya, I gotta git on home. TONY, BRING US ONE MORE ROUN!"

As we're all three leavin' I tell Johnny to com'on over for coffee 'bout nine and we'll go and pick out a rod an' some line. Johnny says he can't make it in the morning 'cause he's gotta dental 'pointment. "What's the problem?" I ask. "Gettin' a root canal?"

"Nope, I lost a fillin' and I'm gonna get it put back."

"Hey Johnny, thas very unushal these days," I tell him. "With 'shurance an' all, mos everthin is root canals, crowns or both. Your dennis mus be ole-fashion. Do you have in-surance?" He says he don't. I tell him that maybe thas the dif'rence.

Harvey says "Yep, any time I see a physician or dentis' thas the firs thin he'll ask, even before my name. You can't tell me that 'shurance don't determine the type of treatment you get. If you got 'shurance you get x-rays and all the good stuff. If you ain't, you gotta wait weeks to get a 'pointment, mos of the time you're well by the time you get it an' then you don't need it. Have you guys tried to get a tooth pulled lately? That went out 20 years ago. Now it's save all teeth at any cost, 'ticularly if you got any 'shurance."

"Harv, some of thas true and some is booze talkin'."

Harvey says "Are you tellin' me I had too much to drink?"

I say with a smile "Yep Harvey, somthin like that."

Harvey grins and walks off down the street to his shoe repair shop. Johnny tells me he will be over right after his dental 'pointment and then we can go back to the Plunkin Shack for the rest of our 'quipment.

When I arrive home Snookums says "Well Sport, it looks like you boys have been out solving all the world's problems. What's in that sack you have there?"

"Snooker," I say "thas the bes gol-dang fishin' reel in the whole state."

Snooks replies, "My gracious, why don't you sit a spell and have a cup or two of black coffee, then go take a nap? Maybe when you wake up your eyes will focus better."

I don't for the life of me know how she figgered out I'd had a couple at the Blue Danube, but you can't fool ole Rosie no way, no sirree. The nap idea sounds great....then maybe everything'll quit movin' round all over the landscape.

Next morning I wander out in the kitchen and get a big glass of cold water, and then another and Snooks remarks that I seem to be extemely thirsty this morning. "You look like you might have a bad case of the Blue Danube flu. I told you to get a flu shot, now don't you wish you had?" She's smiling, but Rose can be cruel at times. Then she tells me that the aspirin bottle is on the counter by the sink. I ask Rose why she thinks I need aspirin? Her reply is, "No magical powers, just careful observation."

Johnny shows up about 1:30 and he doesn't look so good either. Right away Snooks starts in on poor Johnny. "John, you don't look too good. Have a rough trip to the dentist, or is there a little Blue Danube flu involved, too?" Johnny switches the subject real quick and wants to know if I'm ready to go look for a Sturgeon rod and some line. As we're leaving Snooks says, "I don't expect you to dilly dally around after your shopping, but if you boys promise to be back by 3:30 I'll make fresh coffee and a batch of cinnamon rolls." Johnny and I both promise, and we're on our way.

Pete is not quite as sociable today after the big let down yesterday. He remarks that he imagines we're both after heavy duty rods, to just look around and when we find what we want, bring it up to the cash register and he'll take care of us. Right now he's in the middle of fall inventory and doesn't have time to help us make our choice.

I know I want a rod 7 1/2 to 8 foot long, with medium action, double cork grips with locking reel seat, 35 to 40 pound line weight, two piece, 8 fugi hardloy guides and made of fiberglass.

Johhny wants about the same thing in graphite. He asks me why I don't want graphite?

"My experience with graphite has been that once it receives a sharp blow, even falling against the boat edge will weaken it, and down the line under stress and cold it'll break, leaving you in an awkward situation. I like the advantage of a more rugged, less temperamental rod. Besides glass is cheaper and my preference."

Pete pipes up that the cheap part is probably the big factor with me. He is even more bitter than I thought. My answer to that one is

51

that I can always order out of the catalogue; he doesn't have a monopoly on me.

I tell Johnny I'll be waiting in the car when he's through, "Remember, Snooks is making cinnamon rolls for us."

Johnny comes out and says, "Pete says you're really thin-skinned and let little things bother you too much."

I tell Johnny I'll order the rod and line out of the catalogue, to hell with Pete and his Shack. Besides the catalogue offers a much better selection and exactly what I want for less money.

Johnny tells me the tide will be excellent next Tuesday, and wonders if I can get everything here by Monday. "Hey John, that gives me four days" I say. "When we get home I'll phone in an order on my credit card and have it sent two-day air. Sure, I'll be ready for Tuesday fishin'."

We get home and Snooks wants to know if we got everything else we needed. I tell her that Johnny did but I just couldn't find what I wanted. "You told me when you left that Pete would have just what you need, what happened?"

As we sit over hot coffee and eat fresh-baked cinnamon rolls, Johnny clears his throat and tells Snooks that Pete and I had a little argument and I wouldn't buy anything more from him.

Snooks then reminds me, "Honey, it was Pete who took up a collection to get Slinky as our lawyer for our recent trial. You should remember some of these things. After all, you two have been friends for many years and it's a shame to let some little thing come between you. Don't you agree Johnny?"

Johnny's answer is that his filling is high and he better get down to Doc's office before five and get it fixed. Just when I need some backing, my good friend bails out on me. I just don't know what things are coming to.

I remember I have to call in an order to Gables for that rod and line to get here by Monday. I find the catalogue and look up just what I want and dial. I get a busy signal for 25 minutes; then at last, this sweet southern voice drawls "Gaabells. Ah lines ah awll buusy aet the moment, plaese hol." She's gone and then the funeral music starts and about every 30 seconds a voice comes on and reminds me I am not forgotten and then back to more music.

About the time I call to Snooks to bring me another cinnamon roll and warm my coffee, I get another voice with even more of a drawl. I ask "Where are you from?"

"Suh," she answers "we'all ah lowkated raht hea in Mowdock, Joja. Wha?"

"Well, I knew you were down south some place with that accent."

She comes right back with "Suh, ah dew nawt hayve an aycsent, yew do!

"Ef yew waunt a caytalouge, push won. Ef yew waunt tew ohdah, push tew. Ef yew hayve a cumplaynt, push threa." She's gone, I push two and the funeral music is back.

Then another voice comes on and says "Suh, will y'all be placin an ohdah today?" I reply yes and she wants to know which catalogue I will be using: trapping, sailing, waterfowl hunting, boats, salt water fishing, fresh water fishing, or outfitting? I tell her I'm not sure because I'm fishing close to the mouth of a river that flows into the ocean and the water flows both ways with the tide, and it will depend which way the tide's going whether it would be more fresh or salt water. Therefore, I don't know if I want the fresh water or salt water catalogue. After a moment she says, "May-o-mah, eksquese me, suh." She's gone and the funeral music comes back again.

After about five minutes or so, a man without an accent comes on and says the young lady said she didn't know what "tide" was. "Now sir, what would you like to order? Will it be on a credit card? How do you want it sent? Please give me your name, address, credit card number and expiration date." I give him my order and all the rest of the stuff and after thanking me for my order, he assures me that it will arrive by Monday noon.

By the time I finish I've spent at least 35 minutes that seem like an hour but it's done. Snooks wants to know how much cheaper they were? I say "Rose, Pete gave me a dig about being cheap and now that's the first thing you mention. I don't like that thought from either one of you, because I'm not cheap."

Rose says "You're a little thin-skinned about this cheap business; it must touch a nerve someplace."

"That's exactly what Pete said, have you been talking to Pete? Those are Pete's exact words to Johnny; that I was thin-skinned. How would you both come up with exactly the same words, exactly the same thoughts and phrases?"

Rose tells me "It's a common phrase and it would not be rare to hear it many times in one's lifetime. It's not something to get into a total all out snit about.....unless of course, it really does touch a nerve."

Monday rolls around and still no delivery on my important order by 4:30. I tell Snooks I'm going to call and find out what's happened. Snooks tells me "The day isn't over, and you have to give them all day. After all, they did promise you it would get here, or did you have them send it third class to save money?"

Old Rosie don't know it but she's just a hair away from living as a lonely old divorcee; I'm not going to let her know that her statement even reached my brain, let alone gone deep into the Etched-on-your-memory-forever File.

Just about the time I can't keep away from the phone any longer the delivery man comes to the door with a skinny little package. Yea! This is it. But before I can unwrap it Rose calls me to dinner. Right after dinner I rip the wrappings to shreds and am shocked to see a little short flimsy whip of a thing, that looks more like an antenna on a radio-activated toy car than a fish rod! Certainly a far cry from my order; they did get the line correct Maximum, 200 yds, 40 pound mono. Rose wants to know if I would like some help putting the line on the reel. I ask her, "Why would I want to put line on a reel when all I have for a rod is a baby buggy whip?" Rose remarks that I certainly am touchy these last few days, either I'm coming down with something or it could be a touch of male P.M.S. This little sweetheart is really pushing her luck.

I get hold of Johnny and tell him, "I can't go fishing in the morning. They screwed up my rod order real bad." Johnny thinks maybe we could get Pete to open up and I could get the one from him I liked.

I tell Johnny that I won't go back in there. Johnny says, "Well, I know what you want. Let me see what I can do. I'll call you back in a little bit."

In about an hour, there's a rap on the door and it's John with a new rod in his hand and a big grin on his face. He hands me the rod and pulls an envelope from his jacket pocket. I open the envelope and it's a nice note from Pete explaining that he was just joking and had no idea I'd take offense and he is really sorry. He's giving me 20% off on the rod with the hope his joking has not destroyed a 20-year friendship and that we can put it all behind us and go on from here.

Snooks pours Johnny some coffee and says, "What's in the letter?"

"It's an apology from Pete."

"Are you going to accept it?" she asks, and before I can answer she tells me that if one person is big enough to apologize then the other should be big enough to accept it and a friend is a thing to be cherished.

Johnny, who has tried to stay totally neutral, pops in and says, "Snooks is right. And here's the bill on the rod, you owe me $48.75."

I think for just a second and while Snooks pours my coffee; then pick up the phone and call Pete and thank him for opening up to get the rod and for the 20% off, and tell him I'm sorry I got upset and yes, we'd be better off to forget the whole thing.

Snooks says, "Now, don't you feel a lot better? I hope that changes your whole disposition."

Johnny says "Let's put some line on that reel and get ready to go fishing in the morning."

"Yes Honey, you go fishing, and while you're gone I'll call and get that catalogue outfit straightened out on your order."

We put the line on the reel and with Johnny's good night he says he'll pick me up at 6:30, and we'll breakfast down at the restaurant, then go get 'em.

I'll have to admit I sleep a lot better than I did the night before. I'm all ready when Johnny stops by, and we head out after breakfast with high hopes for a successful day.

We again arrive early and pick our spot. With all the latest and best equipment we rig up our tackle and prepare to do battle. As the others arrive I notice an awful lot of the same faces as last time and several of them speak to us. I guess they figure if we're going to be around fairly regular they might as well be civil; they still don't tell us much of value, but as the day progresses they do accept us much better than last time.

The guy next to me called Shorty, says "Fella, you got one workin' on you there, right now."

I say "It must be a bullhead, because it's so easy."

Shorty is more insistent now and replies "Damnit, you can't tell the size by the bite, set the damn hook, NOW!"

I can't imagine a bite this light being anything to get too excited about but I do what Shorty tells me and pick up the rod and really rare back on it. It's hung up; there's no fish there. I tell Shorty "I'm hung up, there's no fish there."

Shorty says, "You must be green as grass. Just don't relax, because I'd bet a dollar to a pinch of goose crap that you got a fish on there." Just about that time a real authoritative force takes out about 20 feet of my line and stops. Shorty, with a big grin says, "Now damnit, do you believe what I'm trying to tell you?"

AT LAST! After weeks of thinking about just this very thing it's finally a reality and not just a myth. I'm really on to one! Everybody for 30 feet on each side of me reels in and then they all begin giving advice; some helpful, some just idle talk. Johnny really sticks right with me and helps in a quiet, calming way. After about 20 minutes of up-and-down the bank maneuvers, someone says "It won't be long now, I just saw some bubbles."

I was just about ready to ask Johnny if he would like to take it on for a spell and see what a Sturgeon feels like, but if it's about played out, Johnny can just wait and hook his own. Besides it's my first ever Sturgeon and I'm eager to catch it. It's a good thing there's a limit of one Sturgeon a day; that law must have been put in effect to save the lives of fishermen, not the depletion of the Sturgeon population.

At last it surfaces and shows definite signs of ending the battle. Now the guesses are as to whether it's going to be legal. As we ease it flopping up on dry land, one of the fellows takes out a tape measure and another holds the other end; one end at the head, the other at the tail. This one is legal, but they always measure them anyway. This one's just a 1/4 inch over five feet, just a nice average fish. Everybody is shaking hands and making a big fuss over this fish. I have a feeling we'll be "one of the boys" from here on. Tony's Bar and Grill sweatshirt hollers and says "Hey guy, don't forget to punch your card!" Yeah, we're now one of the boys.

Johnny and I lift the Sturgeon into the pickup bed. As we get ready to leave, Willie comes over and says "That's a beauty; best fish caught from the bank all week. That's not as big as the one I lost a couple weeks ago, but keep tryin' fellows, you're on the way to bigger and better things."

Later, as we head down the road I say "Johnny, you know Snooks is gonna be real proud of us."

I know one thing for sure, I'll probably be too stiff and sore to get out of bed in the morning. But I doubt if I'll ever have a bigger thrill than this.

Johnny says "When that thing first came to the surface I thought you had an alligator! They're the homeliest, meanest-looking piece of marine life I've ever seen. I sure hope they taste better than they look."

I ask Johnny if he has any idea how to butcher this thing after we get it home? He says Joe Ramus, an old Frenchman who used to catch and smoke a lot of them, really knows an easy way to prepare them; he'll call him and ask, before we make a bunch of mistakes.

When we arrive home with the horn honking, Snooks runs out and looks at that fish and says "Oh my gracious! Now there is one beautiful fish! Look at those pretty patterns running around the top of it's head." Johnny and I look at each other both wondering if Snooks might have just escaped from the loony bin.

Johnny calls Joe, comes back and says "There's nothing to it, simpler than salmon."

I say "Okay, but what about the notocord?"

"No sweat," Johnny replies, "we never get anywhere near it, in fact we fillet the Sturgeon without even gutting it." Johnny adds that Joe told him these fish don't have any bones either. Both facts sound good to me.

Forty minutes later we have two beautiful big fillets of the prettiest white meat you ever saw. The job is done, the day is ended, and I'm tired but extremely happy.

# 6

# Butane Bungle

Johnny comes over for coffee the next morning and remarks that he's afraid he's been bit bad by the Sturgeon bug and Snooks says he's not alone. "This idiot was talking about that fish in his sleep. He slept well, but I sure didn't."

Then Snooks asks him to come for dinner this evening and we'll see how fresh Sturgeon tastes broiled, and by then his half will be frozen and he can take it home.

Johnny likes that idea then says that I should check the tide book and see what time the tide is tomorrow, because he's ready to go again. I look and it's not bad, low tide is about 11 a.m. and outgoing till about 5 p.m. Johnny says he'll pick me up about 9 a.m., have breakfast out, and we'll give it another whirl. "I'll be ready but I hope I'm not this sore and stiff by then" I tell him.

After John leaves Snooks predicts "I can see it coming, the only way you two are going to be happy is when you're on the river after those big fish." Snooks adds that Johnny looked real tired to her. I tell her she always worries about Johnny, but he's O.K. and just excited about this fishing.

Johnny arrives early and we have a little liquid refreshment before dinner. He tells me that he went over to Pete's Plunkin Shack and bought a sinker mold for 4 and 6 oz. pyramid sinkers, and next week on the off-tide time we can melt up that twenty pounds of scrap lead and make us up some Sturgeon sinkers. Snooks says "Johnny, I believe you're bit worse by the bug than your fishin' partner."

Dinner's great, the Sturgeon is even better tasting than any of us had imagined. Snooks says "That's the first fish I ever cooked that didn't smell up the kitchen like an Alaskan fish cannery during the heat of the summer. This hasn't any odor at all."

We all like it's texture and mild flavor. It almost has the firm texture of lobster. I mention I'd heard it's excellent smoked and even pickled. Johnny says that since he's a Swede, he'd probably like to try some pickled. Snooks wrinkles her nose and says "Yuk, count me out on that one!"

Johnny picks me up the next morning and we head to breakfast. I order bacon and eggs and Johnny orders a buttermilk hotcake, and little pigs. We get our meal and I see Johnny is having some trouble with his hotcake. He has cut off about five bites but when he tries to pick up one, the others all tag along. With all that butter and syrup it's sort of messy and it takes a little longer to figure things out. "Johnny, what's your problem?" I ask. Johnny informs me that this hotcake is so fond of itself that when he attempts to eat one bite, three or four more try to follow.

Finally Johnny pushes his plate away in disgust and says "It's a hair! A great big long hair in my hotcake, right in the batter, cooked right in."

I tell him to call the waitress and order something else but he refuses, saying he's totally lost his appetite, and furthermore doesn't know if he can ever look another hotcake in it's flat face again.

I think it's time for me to tell Johnny about the gal who used to come in when Snooks and I owned our restaurant, and eat most of her meal and then drop in a hair and show us and refuse to pay. We knew what was going on but just couldn't figure how to stop it. But a hair cooked right in a hotcake is something that has to start in the kitchen; it can't be self-manufactured.

Johnny drinks his coffee while I finish my breakfast. "Don't hairs in food bother you?" he asks. "How can you sit there and eat?"

I inform him that first, it wasn't in my food and second, I guess I must have a stronger constitution than he does. "John, you better get a donut or something; you'll starve."

He replies "No. I have a nice roast beef sandwich in my lunch and by that time I'll be all right."

As we head out, I tell Johnny that I want him to pull into the nearest gas station and I'll fill his tank. If he's going to take his car the least I can do is buy the gas. I grab the nozzle and start the pump. Johnny inquires as to why I'm standing there hopping from one foot to the other and looking as though I'm dancing the watusi? "It's just one of those unexplainable things, but whenever I pump gas I have the strongest urge to pee!" Johnny laughs and says he never heard of anything so ridiculous. "Well," I tell him, "some people can't pump gas, and some freak out when they see a hair in their food. It's a *comme ci, comme ca* sort of thing."

We get to the fishing area again in plenty of time. Get everything set up before most of the others show up. Finally Carl comes over and wants to know if we have eaten any of the fish yet and then tells us how he likes it cooked. One by one the others come around and do their best to let us know that we're now accepted.

But during all this, two of them call me "Toad." Then the one called Herman asks "Ya gonna get another big one today, Toad?"

"Herman, who told you my name's 'Toad'?"

Herman replies "Nobody, but when you had that big one on the other day you were hoppin' and jumpin' around; and after you left we said you reminded us of a toad with all the hoppin'. So whether you like it or not, when you're with us guys, you're gonna have to answer to 'Toad'."

I hadn't intended to go that far to be one of the bunch, but I'd rather be Toad than Toad-aly ignored.

The man called Irish comes over and tells us that in the future it's customary when you know you have a fish hooked, to holler 'FISH ON,' then everyone will do his best to see that you catch it and not accidentally foul you up.

The fellow who wore the baseball cap on backwards and hollered 'Surgeon' to me the day Snooks and I stumbled onto this fishing, turns out to be Alex. He walks over and tells us that we'll need really strong bait to catch the big Sturgeon.

He tells Johnny and me to go down to the chicken slaughter house and get a bucket of chicken guts and leave them out in the sun with the lid on for three days. Then take off the lid for three more, then three on again, and after ten days of this we'll have prime big-fish bait. Boy, these fellows really have taken us into their confidence to tell us their innermost secret baits!

All at once there's a FISH ON! and everyone flies into action like a bunch of firemen. It's Toughy's, and he says it's not very big, not to get too excited. In about ten minutes it surfaces, and in five minutes more he beaches a 44 incher. A keeper, but nothing to brag about.

Alex tells Toughy that he better hurry and get that notocord out of it. Johnny goes to Toughy and tells him how to clean it without ever entering the body cavity or getting near the notocord. I think for us to tell these self-proclaimed experts something useful they don't know, will help our standing a great deal. The tide's about high and some of the guys are getting ready to quit. Those with left-over sand shrimp are giving theirs to the fellows who will be back fishing tomorrow.

After we put everything in the car we walk over to watch the returning boats. Each boat has at least one legal fish and some have two. There's no doubt the boat boys do the best. I notice every one of them, except one, is using sand shrimp. That one has smelt, he also has one fish. I also notice that nobody, absolutely nobody is using smelly, rotten chicken guts! This gets me to thinking and before we leave I walk by Alex' layout and he's using sand shrimp; no chicken guts in his bait bucket either.

As we crawl into the car to leave, Alex hollers over and tells us there's an extra good tide next Tuesday. "Johnny, you and Toad better be here!"

We head home with no fish but more knowledge. I comment to Johnny that we have to watch Alex. If his rotten chicken guts bait is so good why wasn't he using it?

Johnny agrees and thinks we should work on some idea to get

back at him just so he'll know we're wise to him. At least we woke up to him and his tricks before we started fixing a bucket of guts. John says he thinks if he'd started that, Snooks would have put the kibosh on it in a hurry. I also doubt if Johnny would have let us carry it in his car and I say so. Johnny says "Yeah, you got that right."

Then out of the blue Johnny asks me "Toad, do you think we can make it back next Tuesday?"

"Where do you get that 'Toad' stuff? If you go home and tell that to Snooks you're going to be in more trouble than you can imagine. If you thought that hair in your hotcake was bad, you tell Snooks about Toad, and your next hotcake will look like it's wearing a toupee!"

Johnny just grins because he knows now he has something to hold over my head. His answer is, "I wonder if they had seen you jumping around pumping gas, what they would have nick-named you? The closest thing I can think of is a chicken that's just lost his head, but that's hard to use as a name. I guess they did pretty well with Toad. Now that I look back, you did resemble a toad. Yeah, those guys are pretty observant."

"All I'm saying is, Snooks better not find out. Keep that in mind."

"O.K., Toad."

"To answer your question John, I think we better make it a point to go fishin' Tuesday; tide's 9 a.m. In the meantime, maybe we can find time to make up some sinkers with that new mold."

When we get home Snooks comes running out to see how we did. I guess she thinks we have good luck every time. I tell Snooks that the last time was exceptional and we can't expect that every time. Johnny tells her that although we didn't catch any fish, at least we're now accepted members of the Sturgeon plunkers of the northwest. I can see he's just dying to tell Snooks the Toad business, but one look from me stops that.

Johnny says he'll be over about ten and we'll work on the sinkers. I have the butane portable camp stove that we'll need to melt the lead.

Snooks wants to know where we're going to make sinkers, and I tell her we're going to set up in the kitchen because it's supposed to rain tomorrow, and besides making sinkers is good clean work; and I might add, fun, without any chance of trouble. Snooks looks skeptical, but says "Well O.K., but I'm telling you right now I don't want any part of it."

As we turn out the light for the night I ask Snooks if she knows where the flame goes when you blow out a candle? Snooks wants to know why I always come up with these idiotic things just as we're turning out the lights for the night? I tell her it's just to give her something to think about if she can't sleep. Snooks tells me I've got it all wrong: it's to give her something to think about all night, so she won't sleep!

Next morning Snooks makes some batter for buttermilk hotcakes and decides to call Johnny to join us. After she talks to him she remarks, "He must be mad at us because when I mentioned buttermilk hotcakes he never hesitated a second, but straight out refused. I thought buttermilk hotcakes were his favorite breakfast. He always liked my hotcakes before; something is wrong. I told you he doesn't look well, I mentioned that the other day."

"Yes, it sure is strange" is all I say.

Johnny shows up about 10:15. There is no mention of breakfast, which I'm sure just adds to the strange behavior of our friend Johnny Johanson in Snooks' mind.

After a cup of coffee we get right to work setting things up for the big pour. John has a piece of cedar board to set things on, and I put an old towel down under the camp stove.

Snooks wants to know why all the protective action for such a clean, safe, fun thing? I inform her that she didn't want any part of this and that includes questions. "Snooks, why don't you go play with your laundry and stop being so concerned?"

Johnny says we're ready to melt the lead and if I'll light the butane camp stove, we'll go ahead and get started. I ask Snooks if she would be so kind as to run out to the car and bring me those heavy gloves on the front seat? Snooks says "You're not getting me involved now, are you?" I assure her that this little chore will not lead to any involvement whatsoever. Then she asks "Well then, why don't you go get the gloves?"

I tell her "I'm busy. I have to light the stove and get things going, and when I'm lighting the stove I can't be after gloves too; I really have to tend to business."

Snooks goes after the gloves and I light the match as I turn up the butane; the pressure from the gas jet blows out the match. I reach in my pocket for another match and find that was the only one I had. I walk out to the matchbox by the fireplace, grab two and return to the stove. I light one of them, and quicker than a cat turns over when dropped from six inches, there's a blinding flash of heat, light, and thunder mixed! For some reason this mixture robs you of all of your senses except sight, which is cut to 20-800 for a spell; also direction, time and reality are suddenly missing.

The first thing I'm aware of through this haze of half life, is Snooks asking if we're hurt? Why would a person ask a question like that of two people who she has just watched go through the shock of an A-bomb explosion? I'll bet if a fellow fell down eight floors in an elevator shaft she'd want to know if he's hurt! I won't say anything because it's just possible that she's also goofy from the aftershock, and doesn't know it.

Johnny starts to wobble to his feet and remarks, "I'm sorry my friends, but I must refuse the great honor of another term as President of these United States. I have to spend more time with my family. Life is so short." I do believe Johnny and Snooks are escapees from the same nut house.

Snooks asks "What's that puddle on the floor?"

"Snooks, don't ask any more damn-fool questions! Just get the mop."

As reality sneaks back into these shell-shocked brains, we find two cracked window panes and one completely gone. Then Snooks notices three of her prize antique Waterford crystal goblets with the stems broken.

Snooks is visibly angry and she looks me right in my foggy eyes and says, "Well, how close to being through with this fiasco are you?"

"Snooks, actually we never even really got started" I say. "But once we gather everything up it shouldn't take too long. It's really quite a simple procedure."

Her reply is, "You are through ever making sinkers in this house for the rest of your natural and unnatural lives! Get this mess cleaned up and out of here! Go find a place in the middle of a forty-acre stump ranch!"

Johnny is still raving around about refusing a second term.....I hope he snaps out of it before I have to have the President committed.

About this time we hear a siren bearing down on our very position. I meet a fellow in fireman's garb, ax in hand, ready to destroy what real estate we have left and another fellow rigging up a high-pressure hose preparing to finish off what the ax man doesn't accomplish.

We tell them we did not call them. It was just a slight explosion, absolutely nothing to get excited about. They look disappointed, then tell us that if they make a run they must make a report and if they make a report it automatically ends up in the daily paper. Which publicity we could do without. They finally realize there is no problem, but still write a report before they leave.

Snooks remarks that she will call our insurance company and turn in the house damage, also the Waterford crystal.

Within an hour an adjuster shows up, big smile and hand extended. I tell him I won't shake his hand because he's only here to beat us out of what we have already been promised. He goes about his business without a word, remarks that we should get three bids, take the lowest one, have the windows repaired, send in the bills and the insurance company will pay them. As for the Waterford crystal, unless it was on a separate rider, we cannot collect.

We bring out the rider and he flushes slightly and takes out his magnifying glass, looks through the fine print and finally says with a smile, "Right here it states that any damage caused by a man-made force between daylight and dark is not covered unless on Sunday while you're at church. I'm sorry folks, but your glassware is not covered.

"We will however, have to raise your general rates substantially, because you are living under very hazardous conditions. I'm so, so very sorry about your loss. Please tell others how quickly we came and took care of your claim. Good day."

I say "Snooks, I told you he'd beat us out of what we have coming."

Snooks replies "He was right about one thing.....I'm living under very hazardous conditions."

Johnny wobbles toward the door and I ask him where he's headed and he informs me that he's going down to the Plunkin Shack and buy some sinkers. It might cost a little more, but it'll sure be safer. Snooks tells me that if this was my idea of fun, she sure doesn't ever want to be around when it isn't!

I tell Johnny that he should look in the mirror before he leaves, because he sure looks odd without his eyebrows and mustache.

Snooks says "You both better go take a look, you look like the gold dust twins."

Then as Johnny walks out he says, "Well, if nothing else, it's the end of a most memorable day, to say the least."

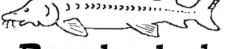

# Rapykacked

Johnny shows up right on time Tuesday morning ready for breakfast and heading down to the fishing area. We look forward to this because the other fishermen seem to think it will be an extra good fishing tide.

At breakfast Johnny stays away from his favorite hotcake breakfast again, and orders oatmeal; says he's watching his cholesterol. Ha!

Willie Wicks and Harvey Carbone are in the restaurant and they both come over and sit with us. Each wearing a big mischievous grin. Harvey says "Boy, you guys sure look different this morning. Don't know what it is."

Willie says, "Yeah, they sure do. You don't suppose it's because they both shaved off their mustaches, do you?" Harvey agrees that's part of it all right, but the eyelashes and eyebrows are also missing! Willie wonders if there's any connection between the new look and the fire truck and aid car stopping at our house?

I say "O.K., O.K. We were going to make some sinkers and the butane stove blew up while we were lighting it."

"Yeah, we know. Have you fellows read this morning's paper? You both made the front page." We haven't read it so we don't know a thing.

On our way to fish, I tell Johnny that Snooks really will be upset about us making the front page. Johnny answers that when we come home this evening he's not going to come in, but will just drop me off. I tell him that's a coward's way out and he better come in and face Snooks with me.

68

His answer is, "Well Toad, I don't think so."

This Toad business has got to stop.

I tell Johnny that anytime we catch a fish we should thank Alex for tipping us off to the chicken-gut trick. Then tell him that we have a little variation in his method; that we use just a little bit of the residual juice from the rotten chicken guts, which we then inject into the sand shrimp with an insulin syringe. Then we'll just sit back and watch the whole thing backfire on Alex. Johnny laughs and agrees that it's worth a try.

Again we arrive a little early, but this time there are several ahead of us; Alex, Carl, Shorty and Irish. Irish is the first one I met the day Snooks and I discovered this setup; the one who wouldn't talk, but that's just around strangers, he's almost as talkative as Alex when you get acquainted.

We set up right next to Irish and he saunters over and remarks that it's a beautiful warm, sunny fall day. The tide's the best in six weeks and we really ought to catch some fish today.

Alex agrees and says, "Maybe this would be a good day to make some bets on first and biggest. The two winners split the pot; each of us put in two bucks." Johnny and I agree and the other three think it's an excellent idea. Shorty pops up and says he'll go to the car and get a little half-pound lard bucket to hold the bet money. Shorty sets the bucket on our chopping block in plain sight so everybody can put in their money. All six of us ante up when Toughy and Herman show up. We mention the bet to them and Toughy says he can't, he's short on cash till he gets his disability check. Herman says he's real short on cash too, and unless we want to take food stamps, he'll have to pass; he's sorry, but he spent his last two dollars on sand shrimp, and in fact he won't be able to fish any more until Thursday the third, when he gets his welfare check.

We turn down the food stamps so those two have to pass, but then along comes Willie and he just can't wait to get his money in the can. That makes seven of us, so now the two winners will split $14, unless somebody else shows up.

We all settle down to fishin'. Jim, in the red shirt, shows up late and spots the lard bucket with the money and wants to know what's the bet and is it too late for him to get in on it? Alex hollers down and says "Toad, tell him the bet. He's not too late, because nobody has had a bite yet." I tell Jim what's what and he sticks in his two bucks so now there's eight of us and $16 bucks to split on the two wagers. First fish and biggest fish.

Johnny mentions, "It used to be first, biggest and most. Now, with a one-a-day limit, that knocks out 'most'."

About that time an outfit backs down a ramp with an 18-foot narrow, old wooden boat, with a 30-horse motor. They spend considerable time loading a wheelchair into the boat and getting a crippled-up fellow from the car into the boat, and then onto the wheelchair. It's quite a slow, involved procedure. These fellows know they're late and the tide has already turned but the more they hurry, the more fouled up they get. They are going to have four people in that boat, counting the wheelchaired man.

Looks to me like that puts them at least two over the safety factor in that leaky monstrosity, even if they were regular healthy people, which they ain't.

Johnny pipes up and says "Isn't it amazing the things you see around a boat launch? You know Toad, someday we should just go and watch the boats at a boat launch. Like say, opening day of trout season on a busy lake." I tell Johnny that would be fun because I don't ever fish opening day anyway, it's always too crowded. He tells me "We'll just make that a date next opening day."

At last, after at least thirty minutes of antics equal to the best of The Three Stooges, they realize they don't have a life jacket on the guy in the wheelchair. One runs back to the car and gets one. Now this guy in the wheelchair is about a 46 extra large and they're trying for ten frantic minutes to squeeze him into a 32 small. They finally succeed, but now his arms stick straight out like a scarecrow. I tell Johnny that I hope he don't have to pee because there's no way he can get his arms down to unzip his pants.

Johnny frowns and says "Looking at that boat, it has very little free-board, and with him sitting way up high in that wheelchair and his arms straight out, he really does look like a scarecrow."

It seems like everything happens at once. Willie, about four down from me, hollers "FAYSH AHWN!" sets the hook and starts to play his fish, when the four in the boat take off, full bore. Thirty feet out they make a sharp right-hand turn to head up river, and as they do, they catapult the scarecrow about 40 feet through the air, hollering like a mashed cat until he disappears under water. Johnny, who was trying to reel in his line to get out of the way hollers, "FISH ON!"

Now we have two fish on at the same time, and a handicapped fellow overboard. Needless to say it's pandemonium. The fellow running the boat turns back and one of them throws the spluttering scarecrow a round-ring life saver, which hits him on the head. He's not hurt, but this just infuriates him more. They try to haul him back into the boat but it's impossible, so they make him hang onto the side of the boat and take him slowly back to the boat launch. The language that man uses would make an Aberdeen logger blush. However, for the time being, they're half safe and out of the picture.

Johnny says he feels he has a pretty good fish. Willie is saying "Ef'n we-uns both git them faysh landed, theyn that thar wan to git his landed first gits that thar ayet bucks." Willie is really trying to land his first, and it looks like he will because his fish doesn't seem to be too big. Johnny is without a doubt into a real nice fish. In fact up to now, he hasn't made much headway. Finally after about twenty minutes Willie says "Thar he is! I seed him, it hain't gonna be vury long now. I'm a'gonna beat ya, Johnny."

Willie finally lands his fish and we hear him hollering. "Oh shucks, that durn fool is jest a mahght too short! Dad gummit!"

The word from Willie that his fish is too small definitely puts Johnny in the lead for first fish unless his is too big. Thirty minutes later Johnny beaches his and it's 53 inches. A good, legal fish and a cinch for first fish.

Johnny has his one fish and is through fishin'. He punches his card and folds up his tackle. Everybody else baits up and gets back to fishin'. The wheelchair group have packed up and gone, nobody noticed when during all the fish action.

Alex says at least the field is wide open for the biggest fish and that's true. They were right, it is an exceptionally good day. About ten minutes later I have one working on mine. Johnny asks, "Aren't you going to set the hook?"

I tell him that at this moment I have a distinct advantage. "I know he's down there but he don't know I'm up here. That will all change when I set the hook." Johnny tells me that's fine if I don't let him eat all the sand shrimp first. I set the hook and I guess he's right, because there's nothing on the other end.

Johnny grins and says "Well, you still have the advantage, because he still doesn't know you're up here. Put another shrimp on and maybe he'll take that one, too. You still might have a chance."

John wanders off while I'm baiting up and goes down to talk to Alex. In about ten minutes he's back with a big smile. He has thanked Alex for the chicken gut secret, but told him that we have a little variation with the injection of rotten chicken juice right into the shrimp. Alex falls for it hook line and sinker, wants to know where we get our needles and how we inject the shrimp?

Irish, who is right next to me, hollers "FISH ON!"

Johnny turns to me and says, "I'll bet that's your fish that you didn't want to know you were here." After twenty minutes Irish beaches his fish, but it's not as big as Johnny's and at the moment John could win first and biggest. The tide's about full and Irish decides to stay though he has his one fish; he wants to see if Johnny wins both bets.

About this time Warden Nugent drives up, saunters over and asks how fishing has been? We tell him it's been better than average. He says that he really came down to check the boat fishermen when they come in; but just to kill a little time, he'll check us over, if we don't mind. He checks the two fish, Johnny's and Irish's, and both punchcards for the two fish. Then he checks two random outfits for

# Who's going to win the money?

© Jack O Breckenridge

barless hooks. Everyone is legal and as he turns and walks toward the boat ramp he spots the lard bucket on the chopping block and asks "Who's going to win the money?"

We tell him it looks like Johnny is going to win the 16 bucks for both first and biggest.

Alex says "Yeah, it's a shame when one guy wins both, you'd have thought out of eight of us it would sure have got split up."

Warden Nugent turns back with a great big grin as he reaches in his shirt for a pen and his hip pocket for his ticket book. He says "Fellas, I want to read you a little something out of the regulation pamphlet, it says here on page 10 Fishing Contest ——

'Any event where six or more people fish competitively for game fish and determine winners, regardless of the prize value, is defined as a fishing contest and requires an application be made in advance to conduct a fishing contest. There is a $24 fee for the permit.' Now, do you fellas have that permit handy?"

Someone tells Nugent, "No, we don't have any damn fool permit handy and we don't think you can show us any stupid regulation like that!"

Nugent shows it to Herman, and Herman reads, then nods and says "Yep, that's what she says."

Now, Nail 'Em Nugent is right in his glory, eight guys all at once, what a bonanza! This is sure gonna look good on his arrest report at the end of the month. He opens that ticket book with a flourish, licks the tip of his ball point and says, "Who's first? Just all eight of you heavy betters line up. Don't crowd, I'll get to you just as quick as I can. Have your license in hand and ready."

Willie whispers "Gawl dang disgustin' ain't he." Nail 'Em hears it and looks up but decides not to push his luck any further.

After writing several tickets it's my turn; he looks up and remarks, "You look familiar, where have I seen you before?"

I reply "Oh, last month my wife and I were looking for sand shrimp and you ticketed us for digging clams. In case you don't remember, you lost that case in court."

Nugent continues to write my ticket, saying nothing, but I know by the slight flush in his complexion that he heard and remembers.

About now Alex looks at his ticket and remarks, "If the permit is $24, why is our fine $50 apiece? It ain't right, we been Rapykacked!" Nugent ignores this remark and continues writing the rest of the tickets, then tells us he'll see us all in court on Thursday, 2 p.m. at the County Court House.

On his way by the lard bucket, Nugent grabs the $16 and says "Evidence, you know," and saunters off down to the boat launch to check the incoming boats.

We all gather round and Irish says "Alex is right. We really been Rapykacked this time. What in the world are we gonna do? That old reprobate is really gonna hang it on us!"

"I'll get hold of Slinky Shinkle" I say, "and I'm sure he'll represent us in court. He beat Nugent last month and I believe he can do it again."

Irish says "O.K. Toad, we'll leave it up to you and Johnny."

We load up the gear and Johnny's fish and head for home. On the way Johnny is really upset that Nugent took his 16 bucks winnings. I tell him not to be concerned, that I'm sure Slinky can clear us and get his winnings back.

As we go through a small town I notice an ice cream place across the street and ask John if he'd like an ice cream cone? It sounds good. We both settle on strawberry, so I run across the street to get the cones. When I get to the other side there's a cop with a ticket book in hand and he writes me a $25 ticket for jaywalking! I buy the ice cream and walk a half block to cross in a crosswalk, and as I do, I look back down the street and see the cop and two others jaywalking!

By the time I get to the car I'm ready to tear this one-horse town apart! As I hand John his cone, he wants to know why the cop gave me a ticket and I tell him for jaywalking.

"But" he says, "I just saw the cop and two other guys walk across in the middle of the block!"

"Well, as soon as I finish my cone, I'm going to go ask that cop what kind of a deal they're running here."

Johnny says "Well Toad, you can ask him right now, because here he comes."

Sure enough, the cop has walked up to the front of the car and looked at the license plate. Then he comes and leans on the window ledge. I ask him why those two who just jaywalked across the street with him didn't get tickets? He says "You must be mistaken. Nobody else has crossed the street since you did. I came over in the line of duty, to suggest that you two should probably be leaving town before I have to give you another ticket, this time for loitering."

I start to say something and Johnny pipes up with "Yes sir, we're on our way. In fact, we're already late for dinner."

As we drive slowly and cautiously out of town, Johnny remarks that a situation like that is the worst thing you can run into. Most small town cops never had another job and now the badge and all that authority makes them drunk with unchallengeable power. No matter what you do, all you do is get yourself in deeper.

We arrive home and Snooks comes out to see if we had any luck. She notices that even with one nice fish we're still not overjoyed.

We tell her that eight of us got arrested by Nugent because we bet on our fish and it's illegal for more than six to bet, and we have to go back to court on Thursday.

Then Johnny tells her that I got arrested for jaywalking besides. Snooks shakes her head and says "If you can't stay out of trouble any better than that, you better go back to work to make enough money to pay for all these arrests and fines."

She doesn't seem to be mad about the newspaper article, and mentions that Harley David called up to tell her the article reminded him of a story: A sky diver jumped out of a plane and his chute didn't open and he notices a fellow coming up toward him. He hollers over and asks "Do you know anything about parachutes?" And the other fellow hollers back and says "No, do you know anything about butane camp stoves?" I tell her that I'd heard that one before, and it fits.

I tell Johnny to start cleaning the fish and I'll see if we can line up Slinky Shinkle to defend us.

Slinky says he'll be glad to help us and only wants to be paid if we win, and then only $10 apiece; cheap at twice the price if we can beat that ticket-happy maniac. Slinky wants us to drop off a copy of the fishing regulations for starters.

After Johnny leaves Snooks again mentions that he really looks tired. She says "You know, I've told you for two weeks now that he doesn't look well, and today he just looks terrible! I'm really worried, I don't know how you can help but notice it. As soon as he has time to get home I'm going to call and invite him over for breakfast, and then just point blank ask him why he looks so bad."

Johnny accepts Snooks' breakfast invitation and now he's in for a real quizzing. Frankly, he may look a little tired, but nothing to get all worried about.

Snooks mentions that she gave Itchy, our Japanese neighbor, a piece of our Sturgeon and he sort of hinted that he'd like to go with us sometime.

I tell her if I had a boat I could take him, but we just got in with this boat-launch bunch and they sort of have an unwritten law that you don't bring any newcomers, and I don't want to break that trust. Snooks remarks, "Fishermen are strange."

As I turn out the bedstand light for the night, I ask Snooks "If the moon has the power to move billions of gallons of water twice a day on earth, then isn't it possible to affect the large amounts of fluids in our bodies the same way? Have you ever considered the possibility that people acting strangely during the full moon may truly be related to this phenomenon?"

Snooks retorts "I knew it! Another big nighttime problem to think about and lose sleep over. If your father was anything like you then I can understand why your mother had a separate bedroom."

Next morning as we three finish breakfast and relax over coffee, Snooks begins her relentless quizzing regarding Johnny's present health. She says "Johnny, you've been looking a little more tired and haggard every day now for the last two weeks. Is there anything bothering you? Do you feel well? Have you been sleeping well? Are you having headaches? Can we help?"

John takes a sip of coffee, puts down the cup and stares into it for several seconds and then says "Yes, matter of fact I have been having some problems, but I can't tell anybody about it. I just can't talk about it." Snooks asks if he has picked up a bad social disease? Johnny says, "No, it's nothing like that, it's something strange in my head."

Snooks asks "Like what?"

Johnny replies "I'd just rather not talk about it because it's really weird."

Finally, with the tenacity of a bulldog, Snooks weasels it out of him. It seems that every night when Johnny goes to bed he hears music and people talking; almost like a radio station, but in his head. He cannot make out the words but he sure can keep time to the music. I tell him, "John, old friend, it sounds to me like you need to see a phyzeekeatrist, a shrink."

"See," Johnny says "that's exactly why I didn't want to say anything. You think I'm crazy, you just said it. I knew that's what you'd think. I should never have mentioned it. Someday I'll learn to keep my mouth shut. For heaven sakes, don't let this go any further than this room. I don't want to end up in a nut house wearing a straight jacket waiting my turn for a lobotomy."

Snooks says, "Johnny, I think I know what you should do. I know you're not crazy, even if your feather-brained friend here doesn't. There was an article in last month's Collywobble Health Journal, Odd and Unusual section, about a situation very similar to yours.

"You just had the dentist put in a new filling last month, didn't you?"

Johnny nods yes.

Snooks says for Johnny to go back and see his dentist; she's sure it's connected with that filling and if he will just replace the filling, John's troubles will be over!

In the article that she read, the new filling acted like a crystal radio set, and the man's head was the sounding board; the ears registered the sound, the saliva acted as a conductor and the bed springs were the antenna. Thus, music in his head when he went to bed.

Johnny jumps up with a big smile, gives Snooks a big hug and says "God bless you Snooks! May I use your phone?" He then makes an appointment to see his dentist to hopefully get the problem solved. As he gets off the phone he says, "Next Tuesday at 10."

Slinky calls and wants to know what we were fishing for? I tell him Sturgeon, he says "Thanks" and hangs up. I tell Johnny that Slinky is working on our case already.

Thursday rolls around before I know it. Johnny picks me up and we head down to the restaurant for a late breakfast. John orders oatmeal; I just don't know if he will ever get back to his favorite hotcake breakfast.

I ask if they have a real waffle and they tell me, yes, Belgian waffles. I tell the waitress that's not a real waffle. I don't know how the American Waffle Union allowed those Belgians to come over here and totally monopolize and ruin the regular, good old-fashioned, American waffle business! It's so bad that it's almost impossible to get a good American waffle anyplace anymore. I decide to have oatmeal, too.

Johnny says "Boy, you're really wound up on that waffle business. I didn't know you cared that much. I hope the rest of the day doesn't affect you the same way."

After breakfast we swing by and pick up Slinky. On the way to court we ask him what our chances are and all he will say is "Slim, mighty slim." Yet he has a smile, and an air of confidence in his voice and manner. I think the old boy has things pretty well under control and justs wants to keep us in suspense as long as possible.

I ask Slinky if he knows who the County Judge is and he replies that he's pretty sure it will be Judge Lynch, the hangin' judge. Despite his name and reputation, Slinky has always felt Judge Lynch is very fair, so he's not afraid to speak his feelings.

We arrive in plenty of time and right off the bat run into Nugent. Now I'm sure that he feels this one's in the bag, but when he sees Slinky with us, he just sort of looks like a whipped puppy.

The rest of the fellows show up one by one and we enter the courtroom on schedule. It is Judge Lynch, and after all the formalities His Honor asks Nugent what this group is charged with and is told, "Your Honor, they were making illegal bets."

The judge asks for clarification. Nugent explains the law and the judge asks how we plead? Slinky replies for us, "Guilty, Your Honor."

Well, this response really upsets every one of those accused of betting, and they look at Johnny and me like we sold them short.

Then Slinky explains to the judge that it's just eight fellows who made an innocent, fun bet, not enough certainly to be misconstrued as a contest; hardly different than a bunch of grade school kids playing marbles for keeps.

The judge agrees that it's an absolutely stupid regulation, probably put together by a bunch of fisheries biologists on their lunch hour to continue the legal harassment of the badly, and constantly-abused, sport fishermen. However, the law is the law, and as stupid as the law might be at times, it's his duty as an Officer of the Court to uphold it. He tells Slinky that unless there are extenuating circumstances, and in view of the fact we have all pled guilty, he will have to pass sentence. Slinky breaks in and says "Your Honor, before you do that, may I please call Officer Nugent to the stand for a few questions?" The judge agrees and Nugent is sworn in.

Slinky asks if Officer Nugent actually saw the betting taking place? Nugent replies "The defendants admitted betting to me, and I confiscated $16 out of a lard bucket that they admitted was bet money; $2 each from eight of the defendants. That made it a fishing contest and then they also admitted that they didn't have a $24 permit, therefore I arrested them."

Slinky then asks Nugent if he knows what we were fishing for? Nugent answers "I think Sturgeon." Asked if there was any doubt in Officer Nugent's mind what we were fishing for with the type of tackle and type of bait we were using, Nugent answers that it would have to be Sturgeon. Slinky then asks Nugent which classification according to the law does Sturgeon fall into? Nugent replies that Sturgeon are classified as food fish. When asked what kind of fish require a permit to bet on, Nugent answers he thinks all fish. Slinky informs him that rather than run around arresting people at will, perhaps Officer Nugent should spend a little more time reading the fishing laws than writing tickets without sufficient and proper knowledge.

"Your Honor, the regulation clearly states 'Game Fish;' therefore the defendants were not wrong in betting, but Officer Nugent was wrong in arresting them; and I feel he should return to Mr. Johanson, the winner of the bet, the confiscated 16 dollars and in writing, by mail, apologize to each and every one of the defendants."

Slinky turns again to Nugent and says "Had the defendants been fishing for suckers, squawfish or peamouth chubs, then the arrest would have been correct, because those are game fish, Officer Nugent. But not Sturgeon; Sturgeon don't rate the distinction of being classified as game fish."

Judge Lynch remarks that he is not going to elaborate on attorney Shinkle's statement, he feels it could not have been stated better. He makes Officer Nugent hand over the 16 bucks to Johnny and then tells us if we do not get an apology written on departmental stationary within one week, to contact the Court and the matter will be handled swiftly.

Case dismissed.

It's obvious that Nugent is livid. He not only lost the case, but Slinky humiliated him again in front of the enire court. Slinky Shinkle has again come through in great shape. We each walk up and pay him the ten bucks he asked for, and every one of us gives him an additional pat on the back, which he surely deserves. We head home much relieved, and very happy over the outcome of a second encounter, at least for me, with old Nail 'Em Nugent.

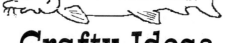

# Crafty Ideas

As we're getting in the car, Nugent walks by and remarks, "You, one and all, should constantly be looking over your shoulder because after this humiliation I will not rest until I can nail each and every one of you on a legitimate charge." Then he looks at me and adds, "Particularly you and Shinkle."

I ask Slinky, "Could that be construed as harassment?"

He replies, "Possibly, but I think he's had enough for one day."

As we drive down the road, Slinky wants to stop in the next little town and have a couple beers to celebrate our victory. I tell him there is no way in the world I'll stop in the next town but there is a little roadside tavern about a mile further and we'll stop there.

Over a beer I ask Slinky if he's any relation to Homer and Otto Shinkle? He tells me they're his cousins. I tell him that I've heard a lot of stories about those two. Slinky says, "Yeah, and most of them are true."

Three beers later we head on down the road. Slinky reminds us to watch our steps with Nugent and be sure we're always within the law, because from here on out any confrontation with Nugent will be tough; he'll be out for blood.

We drop Slinky off with a sincere word of thanks and appreciation. Johnny reminds me that he has a dental appointment on Tuesday, but the tide looks real good for Wednesday and he thinks we should go fishing. I agree with that. Tide's at 10 a.m.; down to breakfast at 7:30 and we should be in good shape. It's a date.

Snooks is overjoyed at the outcome of our trial and, of course, having personally tangled with Nugent, this means more to her than normal.

I tell her "In view of our victory in court I'm going to take you out to dinner. I understand the Purple Oyster has a pan-fry special right now. Because pan-fried oysters are one of your favorites, Snooks, that's where we'll go."

We order a Purple Oyster Margarita which isn't like any margarita you ever tried. It's equal amounts of Tequila, fresh lime juice and simple syrup in a tall glass with a lot of ice and topped off with beer. In Mexico City they call it a Bull or an El Toro, but the Purple Oyster has adopted it as their margarita. After three of these, we're feeling pretty good and about then in walks Nail 'Em Nugent and his wife.

I doubt if I'd do it under normal circumstances, but I order a couple Purple Oyster Margaritas for Nugent and his wife. Snooks says, "What do you think you're doing, twisting the enraged bull's tail?"

I tell her "No, I just sort of feel sorry for him. Twice he thought he had an air-tight case and both times it blew up in his face."

Snooks says she doesn't believe that at all, she thinks I just want to watch the reaction when he finds out where the drinks came from. She says it's a sadistic attitude I have. I wouldn't call it that, although the thought did go through my mind that maybe I could kill him with kindness. I think it's a shame to let anybody get to know you as well as Snooks seems to know me.

Nugent's drinks are presented, and he takes a big long pull on the straw and then asks something of the waiter and looks in our direction. He squints through the hazey dim light and finally makes out who it is across the room.

He gets up and without a smile walks to our table and wants to know if this is in the form of a bribe? I tell him that had it been pre-trial he might have taken it that way, but after the judgment he lost, it's more of a "Let's let bygones be bygones."

He thanks us for the drinks but then adds a warning about making sure I stay on the straight and narrow or he might have the long-overdue pleasure of writing me a ticket that I can't wiggle out of with a shyster attorney. Then to emphasize his point, he adds "Even my mother would get a ticket if she violated our fish-and-game laws." It's evident real quick that this guy is just a plain, poor loser.

I say "Nugent, just remember that all's fair in love and war and this sure isn't love! So keep in mind you have to catch me first; but thanks for the warning, at least now we both know where we stand."

He smiles and answers "Third time's the charm."

Just when the banter gets downright nasty, what do you think Snooks does? She gets up and goes over to Nugent's wife and invites her over to our table. I'm absolutely beside myself! I doubt if old Rosie has any idea what she has just done.

I have only seen a similar situation once in my entire life. An Army First Lieutenant and a Major were walking along together and were approached by a Colonel. Well, the Lieutenant knows he must salute the Colonel and does so. Then the Colonel returns the Lieutenant's salute but also at the same time is forced to salute the Major; therefore forcing the Major to return the Colonel's salute. In all innocence, the Lieutenant has just perpetrated one of the most horrendous mistakes of his young military career. He has forced a Bird Colonel to salute a Major, a breed barely recognized by a full Colonel; and on top of that a lowly Major returns a full bird Colonel's salute! A terrible military blunder.

Now this wouldn't bother normal people, but there's nothing normal about the Army. There's much too much time and effort put into such trivials as saluting, anyway. But officers and gentlemen love to play these silly little games.

Well Rose, in real life, has just created a very similar type situation. I am now forced to sit, fraternize, drink with and try to be sociable to——someone who has threatened, bragged about and admitted being out to get my hide!

A terrible social blunder if I've ever seen one. I will definitely have to discuss this with Rose in private later.

Mrs. Nugent brings her drink and joins us. After the introductions, she and Rose take off on a get-acquainted conversation the likes of which I've never seen. They seem to have more things in common than a mother hen and chicks. She seems like a really nice, pleasant lady; how she ever got tangled up with the likes of Nugent I'll never know. Also, how she could stay so seemingly pleasant living with him is the second mystery, and if she and Rose would shut up for a second I'd ask her.

Nugent tries to strike up a conversation, but I have to make my answers so guarded that between us we're having as much trouble trying to get a conversation started as two oysters at high tide—— twenty feet apart in their shells.

He wants to know if I spend much time fishing? Now why would he want to know about that? Besides, it's none of his business. I tell him "Enough to keep me happy." You have to watch every word with a guy like this; you can't let down for a second.

I'm hoping they'll drink up and go back to their table before we order. I should never have ordered them a drink, and Lord knows Rose should never have invited her over to our table. Now Rose pops up with "Are we all ready to order?" That's the second big blunder for Rose in less than thirty minutes!

Nugent is visibly as uncomfortable as I am and just as he has his mouth open to speak, his wife Nancy answers, "Yes, I'm going to have the pan-fried oyster special."

Rose says, "So am I, that's why we're here tonight."

By now I'm beside myself and say, "That's only part of why we're here. The main reason is to celebrate my victory on a dumb, bum rap in court this afternoon; which I'm sure is not the reason you're here, Nugent."

At this Nugent turns purple, stands up and tells his wife that he came here to enjoy an oyster fry, not to be humiliated by riff raff. As he takes her hand and heads back to their table, Nancy Nugent says "Snooks, I'll meet you at 11 and we'll go antiquing and lunch as planned."

The waiter takes our order. I'm so upset I don't know if I'll be able to even choke down an oyster! Rose however, seems oblivious to any problem, and is just overjoyed with her new-found friend. She remarks that she hasn't run across anyone so interesting in a long time. "We share so many similar thoughts and ideas! Nancy seems like a wonderful person."

Our oyster fry arrives and I manage two bites but feel nauseated and quit. Rose however, enjoys every bite and even orders dessert.

What a terrible turn of events! In my wildest imagination I would never conceive that the wife of my absolute worst enemy and my dumb Rose could become bosom buddies in one short disastrous hour.

As we leave, Nugent and I do not even look in the same direction but the two women are waving and hollering clear across the dining room like a couple of idiots; totally disgusting.

I feel this is not only the turning point in our marriage but may be the end to decent fishing for me forever. I can't wait to get Rose home and tell her just what I think of this horrible mess she's created.

As we enter the car Rose again remarks what a wonderful evening it was, and what a nice person Nancy seems to be, and how much the two of them have in common and can enjoy together. She is really looking forward to tomorrow. Rose is wound up like an eight-day clock.

I say "Rose."

She immediately retaliates with "Don't call me Rose! You know I dislike that."

"ROSE," I say. "I really don't care what you like right now. You put me in a terribly awkward situation tonight. I resent it very much and you don't seem to care."

Rose answers, "You were the one who ordered the Nugents a drink, and that was just a nasty thing to do under the circumstances. Besides, he was gentleman enough to come over and thank us, and I wasn't going to be so rude as to leave that nice lady sitting by herself. If anyone is to blame it's you, not Nugent, not me, and certainly not Nancy!"

It's funny how women can take any situation, no matter how much in the wrong they may be, and turn the whole thing around to place the blame squarely on your shoulders, and she's done it again. I might just as well not carry this any further, I can't win. But that doesn't stop me from being about as upset as I've ever been. I'll probably be mad until I forget what I'm mad about, and this time I think that's not in the foreseeable future!

The rest of the drive home and the remainder of the evening is spent in total silence. The next morning starts out the same way, a double dose of silence all the way around. Rose even resorts to pointing at the coffee pot, a reversal to sign language which is the first step toward improvement. It's still the silent treatment but now it's a show of wanting to communicate.

About in the middle of this unhappy standoff, in comes Johnny all excited. He has been to the dentist and had his filling changed, and the dentist is sure this will stop him trying to sleep while keeping time to Ripped His Corsettoff's Third Movement.

Nobody offers Johnny a cup of coffee so he gets his own, sits down and soon senses a wee mite of cool tension. He has already stuck his foot too far in the door to gracefully back out, yet knows he's in the wrong place at the wrong time.

All at once he says "Oh, darn it, I almost forgot. I'm supposed to pick up my brother's mother-in-law at the depot and the train's due in right now. I gotta go." Then he turns and asks me if I'd like to go and help him because she always has a lot of heavy baggage. That's one thing I'll give Johnny credit for, he's always been able to think his way out of tight spots real quick like. I remember when a bunch of us kids were caught stealing chickens out of old Eli Carvonon's hen house. Johnny was the one who told Eli we were just running off a weasel we saw in his hen house. John thought so fast and was so convincing that old Eli bought it, and Johnny saved our hides that time for sure.

I say "Sure, John, I'd be glad to help you." As we get in the car

Johnny asks me what in the world is going on between Snooks and me? He felt it was so cool he might need an ice pick to chip his way out.

"John, it's a long story, but I'll try to collaborate it for you."

Johnny smiles and says "Why don't you just condense it for me, I'd like that better."

"Well John, I took Snooks out to dinner last night and Nugent and his wife were there, so just to add salt to his wound I bought them a drink. Sort of rubbin' it in for us winning and him losing. Now don't you tell Snooks that or I'll just deny it! Well anyway, Nugent came over to thank us and damned if Snooks didn't invite his wife over to our table. Now she and Nancy Nugent are the best of friends and Nugent and I are still at it tooth and toenail.

"I'm mad at Snooks for getting friendly with his wife Nancy. I don't want a bloody thing to do with either one of them! Do you know he had the guts to call us riff raff? He's on a destruction course to get me. I hate his guts and I don't want any family fraternization at all, no-how, ever! I'm really upset with Snooks this time."

Johnny says he doesn't think I should be so upset with this turn of events; after all, I might just turn this terrible catastrophe around and into a definite benefit. I ask him just how he figures that? "Well," Johnny says, "I figure with Snooks and Nancy friends you can probably get Snooks to find out from Nancy where Nail 'Em is going to be and then we'll just fish some place where he isn't and it would sure take the pressure off us."

I tell him that isn't a bad idea and we'll refine it a little bit on our way to fishing in the morning. You know, sometimes that John comes up with a good idea and this seems like one of his better ones. Another good idea was to get me out of the house. There wasn't any brother's mother-in-law at all, he just thought fast like, to get me out for awhile. I have to admit it's nice to have a good friend who can think fast like Johnny.

"You know when you get home, you might just as well speak and smooth things out or you might be putting up your own lunch in the morning." Yep, that John is thinking all the time.

When I get home I start a conversation like nothing ever happened and Snooks joins in and before long we're a little bit of the way back to normal living.

Next morning Johnny picks me up and the first thing he wants to tell me is that he slept like a baby. There was no music playing in his head. Thanks to Snooks' suggestion and the dentist changing the filling. Then we start to work up a plan to keep track of Nugent through Snooks' affiliation with Nancy Nugent. We decide that Snooks must never know that she is the go-between to keep us informed as to Nugent's movements and whereabouts.

Johnny thinks it would be easier if Snooks knew and could help us, and I agree with that, except he doesn't know Snooks' temperament like I do. "Johnny, Nancy is now a 'true-blue friend' and Snooks would never collaborate against a friend, even if the friend were married to your most dastardly enemy, which she is, and out to make life miserable for Snooks' loving husband, which I am... most of the time."

We decide we will have to try to get our information through Snooks without either of them being the wiser. It may not always be available, but at least what we'll get will be accurate. You gotta be swave to come up with this sort of ingenious scheme. I'm proud of both of us. Now we have a pipeline right to the lion's den.

Johnny is almost as swave as I am to come up with these kinds of wise ideas. I think we've got a good, workable, fool-proof plan.

When we arrive at the boat launch Willie and Irish are already there ahead of us. I ask Irish how the fishin's been and he says not too good all week. Then Willie pipes up and says "Them thar guys in them fancie hai-clays boats, they been limitin' aver day up yonder. We'uns ony got sex fesh all week atween us. Gaul dang pour, ah'd say. But then ya know that thar old sayin, 'Them that has, gits'."

Eight of us fish the entire tide and there is only one fish hooked and it turns out to be too small, then one other nibble missed. Johnny and I decide to stick around until the boat people come in off the river and just see if Willie is right.

Yep, Willie is right. Out of seven boats and twelve fishermen there are eight legal fish and they all talk as though they could just be pretty selective.

Johnny and I head for home empty-handed, and as we travel out of the parking lot we look at each other and I ask him if he's thinking what I'm thinking? He answers "I'm thinking what Willie said 'Them that has gits' and that means boat; and after what I saw come in with the boat people, that has to be given a lot of thought."

"I think we should put fishing aside for a spell and take some time to get an idea of what kind of craft would best suit our purpose. The big boat show of the year is on next week in the Dome. We better go up there and give it a serious look. Probably no better place to find out the fundamentals of what we think we need to know." Johnny agrees and we decide to run up next Tuesday and check things out.

I tell Johnny that it shouldn't take too long. After all, a boat's a boat, and it just can't be a very complicated decision to make.

# 9

# Crafty Decisions

Tuesday morning rolls around and Johnny and I take off for the boat show with open minds; ready to soak up a sponge full of knowledge about boats. Johnny tells me he doesn't think there can be too big a problem because when he got home after fishing, he started eliminating all the boats that he knew would not interest us, and there were only about two left that would fill the bill. "John," I ask "what did you start with?" His answer was submarines and air-craft carriers, with the Queen Mary in ninth. "Gracious Johnny, you really did make an extensive and complete search into our needs, and what, pray tell, did you finally come up with?"

"There are only two that should really interest us," Johnny says. "Number one: a jet sled 16-to-18 feet with either an inboard or out-board engine having enough power and speed to move us rapidly on a distance run, like maybe a mile or more. Number two would be a small cabin cruiser with lots of open fishing area in the back."

"Now that we're thinking of becoming nautical it would probably be a good idea to get in the habit of nautical terms rather than land-lubber language," I tell him, "so for starters use 'stern' instead of 'back of the craft'."

I guess he doesn't like my suggestion because he continues on by saying, "Like I said, it should have lots of fishing room in the ass end." I probably won't mention nautical terms again.

Right off the bat I like this Dome show, we each get a free captain's hat as a door prize for being in the first hundred to attend the show. We spend four hours wandering around the boat show getting all kinds of information on all kinds of fishing boats, inboards, outboards, gas consumption, propeller size, gear ratios, depth and fish finders, automatic anchor winches, boat hulls, fiberglass, welded aluminum, riveted aluminum, with canvas tops, solid tops, without tops, trailers, trailer winches, wheel sizes, wheel bearings, grease for wheel bearings, jet pumps, batteries, battery cases, dual batteries against single batteries, trolling motors, signal horns, lifejackets, running lights, CB radios, and marine radio telephones.

By the time we leave, we've signed up to receive everything advertised that is free and informative. We carry home with us at least an apple box of brochures and helpful information. You could call it helpful, or confusing, however you want to look at it.

Each person we talked to had a reason his product would fit our needs better than anyone else's. I guess that's what you call salesmanship. I'd call it an underhanded way to confuse people on a subject they know very little about.

Well, as we head home wearing our captain's hats, I tell John "Maybe we better go make a bid on the Queen Mary, because it probably has all that equipment already on it, plus a crew who know how to run it!"

I thought this would be a simple thing, instead I have never felt more confused! Plus the fact that I don't think Snooks will hold still for one minute for me to spend the kind of money those guys were talking about for a boat to catch a few fish, which, according to Snooks, smell up the house when you cook them. I tell Johnny maybe we better just go back to bank fishin' and give up this confusing, hair-brained idea.

Johnny offers another idea that may still save us; he thinks now that we have some information to formulate our wants, we should look for a good, used boat that comes the closest to fitting our needs and pocketbooks.

Just when I'm ready to abandon ship, Johnny throws us a life preserver. This sounds like another good idea. John adds that he has seen a great many nice boats for sale for a third-to-half the new price or better, and many are only a year or two old and just like new.

We talk about everything we looked at today, and it seems the one we both feel would serve our Sturgeon fishin' needs best would be about a 16 foot jet sled with a collapsible canvas top, and an outboard motor, 85 to 90 horse-power.

"I don't understand about horse-power, John. Is water horse-power different than land horse-power? If you had eighty horses swimming and pulling a boat would it make it go any faster? I think horse-power is a term that should have been left with the horse and buggy. I wouldn't be a bit surprised if it wasn't something Henry Ford cooked up to fit the needs of the time and then out of respect people just kept using the term till long after it meant anything. It's sort of like candle-power, that's another one that's outdated. I bet old Tom Edison cooked that one up. It sounds like something he would do."

Johnny says "You know, Snooks told me that you come up with some of these off-beat questions with her. Are you trying to do the same thing with me? If you are, I don't care a thing about trying to change or explain the units of power or light. As long as everybody else is happy with them, then I'll just go along. And I think you better, too. I don't see any reason to complicate our lives with that sort of thing. If Henry Ford and Tom Edison figured all that out and it worked then and it still works for everybody else, than more power to 'em."

Boy, is he touchy today! All I was trying to do was carry on a little normal conversation about an out-dated way of figuring things.

When we get home we go in to tell Snooks what we've come up with after spending the day at the boat show, and there sits Snooks and Peggy Parkinfarker both looking like somebody ran over their pet poodle.

I say "Hey gals, why the long faces?" Peggy starts to cry, and Snooks starts to tell us what's wrong.

It seems that Pete and Peggy had been out for an afternoon of golf and on the way home Peggy said to Pete "You know Pete, we're getting along in years and one of us could die. If I died Pete, would you remarry?" and Pete said he supposed so, if the right gal came along.

93

Then Peggy asked him if he would continue to live in the same house? Pete said that yes he would, it was his home and he could see no reason to move. Then Peggy asked him "How about the bed; would you sleep in the same bed?" Pete replied he couldn't see any reason to break in a new mattress. Peggy then asked "How about my golf clubs, would you let her use my golf clubs?"

Then Pete replied "Naw, she's left-handed."

Well, that last statement gave Peggy a bad case of the collywobbles, so she came right over to see Snooks, hoping that Snooks and she together could pick up the pieces of this terrible tragic bit of If, When, and Maybe.

I put my arm around Peggy and say "Peg, there's absolutely no problem here at all. You just have to concentrate harder on livin' and not so much on dyin'. Just outlive that wayward old rascal."

Now I don't know what's wrong with that statement. It seems to me like a very logical, sensible solution; but Snooks is pounding on my leg under the table like she's playing soccer at the state championship finals. It must have hit 'em both the same way, because Peggy starts crying and carrying on all over again. I'm sure after the under-the-table thrashing I got, that I'm bound to hear more about this later.

Well good ol' Johnny comes right to my rescue and says, "Peggy, I wouldn't be a bit concerned. The only left-handed female golfer I know of died about six months ago and that was Hacker Hackett's wife Holly. Holly was as good a left-hand golfer as there was. She made three holes-in-one in one year and that's how she got the nickname 'Holy Holly'."

Peggy dries her eyes and smiles with one of those I-remember-Holly looks, and says "Oh yes, I know it could not have been Holly. Pete didn't like Holly at all. Mostly I think it was because she always beat him."

I say, "Well, that's one down. Now all you have to do Peg, is keep your eye peeled for any other female golfer with a left-hand swing. Personally, I don't think you have anything to worry about; but then, only time will tell. Probably a good idea to golf with him whenever he golfs."

I wish Snooks would quit practicing soccer on my leg all the time! After all, a leg can only stand so much without coming up with a noticeable limp sooner or later. I'm not sure whether it'll be a limp or broken until I stand up and test it. I have no idea what I did or said this time for Snooks to whale away at my leg like that.

Something has started Peggy crying all over again. Johnny clears his throat and asks, "Why don't we go down to the Plunkin Shack and see if there are any used boat ads on the bulletin board?" I tell him that's a good idea as soon as we finish our coffee, and he says he thinks it would be a better idea before we finish our coffee. I don't know what's the all-fired hurry, but I'll humor him along as much as I hate to leave an almost full cup of good coffee.

We get down to the Plunkin Shack and check the bulletin board but there is only one boat that even sounds remotely interesting. We write down the address and stop to gab with Snarly Krautkramer and Harvey Carbone.

You can figure if those two aren't fishing they're going to be where they can talk about fishing. They figure if it don't involve fishin' it just ain't worth talking about. Snarly wants to know where we've been lately, as we haven't been around since we tangled with Nugent on the sand shrimp deal. We tell him that we've tangled with Nugent once more since then, and beat him both times in court with Slinky Shinkle's help. Pete Peaks pipes up and says "You better be careful; you may drive Nugent into an early retirement; or else be lookin' over your shoulders, because he don't take defeat lightly!"

Snarly says he thinks we probably forced Nugent to give up any thoughts of early retirement. "Until he nails you two red-handed Nugent won't quit unless forced to!"

Harvey says "Hey, I hear Snooks and Nugent's wife are buddy-buddy. Is that right?"

I say "Yes sorta, but that don't change things one iota between me and Nugent. There's no love lost between us. He already warned us that he won't rest till he nails us." Snarly says it was nice of him to warn us. "Yeah, and you can bet we'll test him right to the limit. But can't we talk about something more pleasant than Nugent? If any of you guys hear of a good buy on a used sled about 16-to-18 feet, let us know."

With that we leave and head out to check the one ad that might be worth looking at. When we finally find the place we both go up to the door and as we're ringing the bell a snapping, snarling, mongrel dog comes out from under the porch we're standing on! This dog is smart, you can tell that right off the bat. He didn't expose himself or his intentions till he had us the greatest distance as possible from the safety and protection of our car, and then he greets us with an offer we have to refuse as rapidly as possible. As one, we head off that porch.

I can see I'll never make it to the car, so I stop, squint up my eyes and prepare to meet my fate, which seems at the moment to be a full-course dinner for Fido. It's funny, when we bolted from the porch I was his choice to consume first, but strangely, when I stop, the dog immediately switches his interest from me to Johnny, who at the moment is trying to set a new broken-field twenty-yard dash, world record.

Well, I can see right away that now is my chance to make one more desperate flashy bid for intact survival. And by now, Johnny realizes that four legs make twice as fast a runner as two legs, and stops dead eight feet from the car and prepares for hopefully, a sudden, merciful demise. Again the mad mongrel turns his attention to me but fortunately he is only able to rip the heel off my shoe as I jump through the open car window. As I sit up and look around Johnny also gets a new lease on life, and makes that last eight feet in a blur-of-lightning speed into the safe confines of the car.

We have both made an impossible bid for life that thirty seconds ago seemed to be an absolute impossibility, and with only the loss of one shoe heel, while moments before it looked like we would both lose our souls.

"Johnny, I don't care if he'd pay us to haul that boat away! I wouldn't venture back there for anything on earth! Besides we're not even sure he has a boat. Let's just chalk this one up to life after death."

We head on back to see how Snooks did with Peggy and as we enter the house we see that Peggy has gone. Snooks asks how I developed such a bad limp? I tell her "Snooks, that's from you kicking me under the table. I don't know what I did to deserve that one-legged-under-the-table-beating I got."

Snooks answers "You know, I spent an hour trying to calm that poor girl, and you tore down every bit of it in a matter of seconds! You're lucky you just have a limp. I thought about murder twice in ten minutes. But I am sorry you're hurt."

At which point dear ol' John pipes up and says "Snooks, you didn't give him that limp. A mad, vicious dog tore the heel off his shoe in an escape attempt." Sometimes I wish Johnny was more like me and would think before he blurts out some of these idiotic statements that would be better left unsaid.

One thing it did though, was to get us off Peg's problems, because now Snooks has to hear about everything that went on at the boat show and the mad-dog show, too. This takes up the better part of an hour to get everything aired out. Snooks thinks we're smart to look for a good used boat. At least there is some agreement on what I thought might be a ticklish situation.

Johnny and I decide to check the paper first thing every day and keep at it till we come up with what we want; which could be very difficult because we're not sure ourselves what we want.

Snooks wants to know if we think our research at the boat show did us any good? We tell her that at least we got a look at everything available and now have some idea of what we don't want. I see that look in Snook's eye and instantly realize that what I said didn't come out the way I intended it to. In fact, I hope she doesn't ask me to explain it, because now that I reflect on it, it would be a lot harder to explain than to have said it. With Snooks you have to weigh every word twice before you expose it to the air-waves.

Snooks says "You know, I've heard some dumb answers before, but that one takes the cake." Johnny is just sittin' there with a big grin on his face looking into his coffee cup, which indicates to me, 'Fella, you got into this on your own, now let's see you dig your way out.'

Snooks doesn't waste a second to jump on that one and makes a remark like "That's the strangest answer I could imagine. Anyone else, under the same circumstance, would say they found a few things to help them figure out what they want; not what they don't want. With a backward mentality like yours, it will be a marvel if you don't buy a birchbark canoe with a 100 horse outboard without a propeller, and no paddle!"

Johnny can see that I'm no match for this, seeing as how I laid my mentality on the line. I have to admit I feel a little like the skinny dipper who looks up to see someone of the opposite sex standing by his clothes on the bank with a big smile, waving and saying "HI!"

Johnny breaks in and asks Snooks if he can use the phone, and thankfully this changes the drift of the current a bit. He calls the local marina to see if there are any new boat ads on the bulletin board. They talk for a moment, then there's about a three minute pause and they talk for about a minute, and I can see by the change in John's voice that he is just a mite upset. After he hangs up I ask him, "Johnny, what's the matter?"

Well, I had no idea, but this is just like stirring a stick around in a hornet's nest; it's one of Johnny's pet peeves. John says, "You know, it used to be when you used the phone, you got service. If you called long distance, you talked to a real live person with a desire to help. If you couldn't connect with your party, the operator would kindly ask 'Would you like us to continue for the next ten hours to contact your party?' Now if you ask for a little help, you talk to a machine with a strictly business attitude. You seldom get a suitable answer, but either way your conversation with a brainless mechanical voice ends up on your monthly statement."

Johnny takes a deep breath and I can see we're in for a lecture so I grab the coffee pot and give each of us a refill, then I ask him "What about that conversation with the marina, what upset you so?"

"With all these modern telephone nuisance conveniences," Johnny says, "they have two that are changing everybody's lives and egos. One is Call Waiting and the other is having more than one phone line. The problems are very similar. That one with the marina happened to be an extra phone line.

"You talk with a friend and all at once he says 'Oh, just a minute. I have a call on the other line.' You wait till they diddly-damn well take a notion to get back to you and then they always say something like 'I'm sorry, but that was the President of Princeton and he wondered when I can break away to present a paper to the senior class on advanced triggernometricks.' I have never once had anyone say it was the garbage man and he wanted to let them know that he is sick of picking up unsacked garbage that the dogs strewed around. Hell no! It's always somebody important that they interrupt our conversation for or maybe a Very Important Call from Arabia, Nepal, Japan or at least Montana! But rest assured, it's always from a Very Important Person or a long ways away. It's definitely a grand opportunity for an ego trip. Both systems work exactly the same so either one is as bad as the other."

Johnny continues, "And another thing! I don't know why we have to try to remember so many numbers to make a simple, little, cross-town call. Used to be just two numbers, simple and quick, through an operator with personal service every time. Now they are rude, mechanical-voiced dummies."

I say "John I agree, but those rude mechanical dummies are wonderfully intelligent compared to the Fisheries Department. Those people are a few clowns short of a circus."

Soon after this, Johnny leaves but calls bright and early the next morning and when I answer the phone says, "Meet me down at the restaurant. I got a real slick idea about how to get a boat without watching ads all the time. Be there in twenty minutes."

As I hurry around, Snooks wants to know what hair-brained idea has me all fired up so early in the morning? I tell her Johnny called and he has an idea about an easier way to find the right boat than compete over newspaper ads with everybody else. Snooks says that as long as it was Johnny's idea, she won't worry. I never understand why she doesn't have any faith in me and ask her why she doesn't trust my ideas and judgment? Snooks replies that after the rototiller I bought from Slicker Williams she's afraid to let me loose alone to make any business transactions more complicated than a book of stamps at the post office. Rose can be cruel at times.

I meet Johnny and we have coffee and order breakfast. I notice one of the waitresses has lost about twenty pounds so I tell John I'll bet him breakfast that I can write on a piece of paper why she has lost the weight and then we'll ask her, and if I'm right he'll buy, and if I'm not, I'll buy. Johnny agrees and when she brings us our order I say, "Janice, I notice you've lost some weight, you look real trim." She beams all over and is so glad that it shows.

She says she just had to lose some weight before August 10th. "You know, I gotta look my best for our 25-year class reunion."

As she walks away, I flip Johnny the piece of paper; he opens it and says "Well I lose, but how in the world did you know that?"

I tell him, "First, you just have to be s-w-a-v-e and second, you have to understand human nature and timing. First off, she can't lose 45 pounds in a short time. Second, there is more weight lost getting ready for any class reunion of twenty years or more, because it takes about twenty to get to the point that if you ain't been watchin' it you're going to have to try to bring it all back, so the old boy friend you didn't marry will wish you had. It's one of the world's greatest ego trips and if you can pull it off, you can gloat for another five years.

"John, there's more weight lost over class reunions than any of these commercial weight-loss clinics ever provide. Just another fact, Johnny.

"The commercial weight-loss people will help you lose the

weight, but six months later 90% of it is back on and they're ready to take your money again. Now those people understand human nature. I know a gal who has spent $400 a pound with taking it off, putting it on and re-joining to take it all off again! She is now two pounds heavier than when she started twenty years ago and $6,000 poorer. Yep Johnny, those people understand human nature and have made millions off that very fact.

"But John, that's enough of that. Tell me about your plan to get ahead of everybody in finding us a good used boat." Johnny replies that we have been going at this all wrong. We have been answering the ads and we're never first to answer, and if there was a good one it would be gone by the time we answered the ad, soooo the best thing for us to do is run an ad ourselves, one day every week until we get what we want. This puts us in contact with people answering our ad! We'll not only be first, but be the only ones getting the message.

I tell Johnny it's an excellent idea and he's learning about swavery real fast. He laughs and says, "It doesn't take long when you have a master teacher."

After breakfast we settle down over a cup of coffee and come up with an idea for an ad that should find us exactly the kind of boat we want. Johnny pays our breakfast bill and we drop the ad off at the local newspaper office and head for home with high hopes.

As we enter the house, Nancy Nugent and Snooks are looking at some new dishes laid out on the kitchen table. I ask, "Which one of you found something you couldn't live without?"

Snooks says "Nancy and I went downtown antiquing and we saw this beautiful set of dishes and Nancy talked me into buying them. Aren't they just beautiful?"

"Snooks, you bought a set of dishes just two years ago, so why in the world would we need a new set so soon, already? Did the others get broken? Are they out of style? Do they leak?"

"No dear, the color doesn't quite go with our new kitchen paint job, and besides these dishes belonged to that old pioneer family, the Sturtevants. These dishes came across the prairie and survived two Indian attacks while crossing the plains! Only two pieces have tiny chips. They were a steal at the price and the dealer had just put them out this morning! We were lucky to be the first ones in the store after they put them on display."

Nancy suddenly remembers that she has to get home right away and fix her husband's lunch. Dear Johnny also finds a reason to abandon the premises with a promise to meet me again at the restaurant in the morning about 8:30.

As soon as they leave, I ask Snooks, point blank, how much she paid for this rare, out-of-the-distant past, absolutely necessary, unheard-of-beyond-belief bargain? Snooks says "You know, with a rare gem like this, price is not something to stand in the way of purchase or be something to quibble over. Why, I could probably sell them with their marvelous historical background for a great deal more than my original purchase price. After all, these are not just dishes, but rare priceless treasures of history."

"Snooks," I say, "one more time.....how in hell much did you pay for these gems of history?" Snooks replies that she has no intention of divulging information with a no-longer practical value; this was a done deal. And she's no longer going to be subjected to my Gestapo-like quizzing tactics.

"Snooks, I think it'll be to your advantage to never again mention my caper with Slicker Williams and the rototiller, because I have a strange feeling that was small potatoes compared to this little gem of monetary maneuvering."

She has suddenly become slippery as an eel, and I find it impossible to glean even a small hint on my quest for monetary fact. This requires further tactics, maybe even underhanded, but sooner or later the truth will come out. I must contact Weasel Woodard. Weasel can find out anything no matter how guarded a secret it might be. The man is a phenomenon when it comes to secrets no longer being secrets. Weasel should have been a private eye; he's a born natural gatherer of forbidden, hidden knowledge. I'll give him a week and I'm sure the truth will materialize.

I meet Johnny the next morning for breakfast and he has a big grin on his face and remarks, "I'll bet you the price of breakfast that you never did find out what Snooks paid for the dishes."

"No bet, John. You're right, I didn't find out a thing."

Johnny then says "Did you ever stop to think, that maybe Nail 'Em is trying to break you financially by getting Nancy to talk Snooks into overspending? This may just be the beginning of a master plan by Nugent to bring about your financial demise. You know he's a crafty, vindictive old coot and not above any underhanded form of trickery. He said he would get you one way or another. You better think about this, and if it happens again you may need to employ drastic measures."

I tell Johnny that he really doesn't need to bring up such horrendous ideas to complicate my life and unless he can think of pleasant conversation, just not to say anything! Johnny takes that to be a subtle hint to just shut up, and I tell him, "Yes John, unless it's pleasant, just skip it."

Johnny tells me that he does indeed have some more pleasant news. A telephone call he got in response to our ad; after breakfast we'll go take a look at a boat that the call made sound like just what we're looking for. It's out about ten miles west on Highway 12. Seems a fellow lost his job and has to sell in a short time to keep from losing everything he has in it. It's only 18 months old.

As we're starting breakfast in walks Weasel Woodard and he sits down at the counter and orders a butterhorn and coffee. I excuse myself from John, and head over to Weasel and give him all the information to help find out the cost of Snooks' dishes. Weasel says he'll get right on it and let me know by next weekend. He seems very confident, yet when I ask him how he's going to find out, he says it'll take time to form a battle plan.

I rejoin Johnny and finish a cold breakfast. Then we head out to check on the answer to our ad. We find this beautiful boat looking totally out of place in an old rundown, leaning, leaky tool shed, and the tool shed is the best looking building on the whole five-acre spread. Except for smoke coming out the chimney, the house looks like it's been unoccupied since struck by a tornado some years ago.

As we drive in, a short, well-rounded, unshaven, tobacco-chewing character saunters from the remains of the dilapidated shack and spits a stream of brown juice on a sleeping cat; then looks at us with a sinister grin and asks "What in the warld brings yew critters out this-a-way?"

I say "We're just out to take a look at the boat you told us is for sale."

"Oh yeah. My name's Rudy, fellers. It shore do pain me to hev to even thank a givin' 'er up, but atter ah done hurt ma back in that there loggin' assident, ah hain't got much choice. Ah jest cain't make all them ends meet nohow."

He hooks his thumbs in his wide, red, logger suspenders that hold up his stagged-off Levis; leans back against the side of the shed, spits juice toward the cat again and says, "Yew fallers look 'er over an then after a mite, maybe we kin do some dickerin'." He stands there as we check it out and just grins, but not another word.

I say "Look here Johnny, this has a beautiful power winch to lift the anchor."

Johnny says "They're O.K., but they run your battery down fast."

I say "Funny thing, I always heard how good they are. And John, look here; two beautiful outboards; a 7.5 for trolling and a 95 for speed. Boy, I'll bet there's a lot of money tied up in that big beauty! That's one of the highest recommended motors on the market, what a beauty!" Again Johnny tells me that Consumer Digest says this particular model has had a lot of ignition problems. I tell him if it does, I sure never heard it, all I've ever heard is good. It seems like no matter what wonderful thing I find on this craft, Johnny finds some fault. I finally just shut up. I'm tired of being made to look wrong on everything. As far as I can see it's even better than we expected to find, yet Johnny does nothing but find fault with every bit and piece of it. I'm just a mite upset with John, to say the least. This is exactly what we want but not the way John is acting. Sure as shootin' he's gonna make Rudy mad, and we're going to lose out on this beauty.

Johnny says "Well Rudy, let's cut out the bull. What do you figure you're going to have to have?"

Rudy says "Wha don't you fellers make me a offer?"

"No Rudy," says Johnny. "You know what you have to have. You set your price; we wouldn't want to insult you. There are several things that need fixing and some things aren't to my liking, so you tell us what's the least you'll take."

Rudy turns his baseball cap around forwards, spits another shot at a baby chick and says "Fellers, I'll lay it right on the line. I got eighteen-five in it, and I'd let it go for twelve but only because I really need the money, but ah cain't go nary a red cent less."

John says "Well Rudy, I saw three last week almost like this and the highest was six-two. We haven't got the money to go over seven, even. That, of course, would be cash."

Rudy throws his arms up in the air and says "That just ain't no use talkin' anymore because that ain't even a good insult, let alone an offer!"

Johnny says "Well, that's the best we can do. I'll leave you my card just in case you should want to contact us. It's a nice rig, but I don't think you'll come anywhere near twelve. Have a good day."

As we drive away I look in the rear view mirror and Rudy has thrown his hat on the ground and is kicking it across the yard; he's visibly upset.

I ask John why in the world he was so negative on a beautiful boat like that, I tell him I thought it was just what we wanted. Johnny asks me how many automobiles I've bought in my life and I tell him three new ones and seven used, but I can't see what that has to do with buying a boat.

Then Johnny unloads on me. He says "I doubt if you ever bargained on anything in your life. You not only lost your 'swaves' but also your common sense! There never was a used-car dealer who wouldn't try to get you for the best deal he could, it's always to their benefit, and yet the trick is to make you think they really got taken, where in reality they're laughing all the way to the bank. This is the same as buying a used car. I sold cars for twelve years and I learned a lot. You never let the seller know you're really interested; never agree to pay what they want.

"First, this guy is hurting and I'll bet you a twenty-dollar bill that within a week he calls us with a real good offer, and if we hang tight he'll finally meet our seven thousand. Remember he needs money; you could tell that by looking around. Second, he perked right up when I said 'cash,' and third, he took my card; he didn't refuse it. We'll hear from him. You want to take my bet?" I tell Johnny that I'll take that bet because nobody that mad will contact us; we insulted him bad. Johnny says "He's O.K. Rudy's bought a lot of used cars, he's been around the block a time or two."

Then Johnny tells me that just in case this deal does fall through there are other good boats around and on the next one, if it comes to that, just sit back, watch and learn a few things about the fine art of second-hand buying.

When we get home Snooks tells us "A Mrs. Tootie Zmelzem called, and said her husband bought a river boat just six months ago and only used it twice when he dropped dead of a massive coronary, and she would like someone to have it who would promise to give it tender, loving care and enjoy it the way her husband would have." Snooks gives us the phone number, we call and it sure sounds good. It's only a mile away and we head right over there.

We knock on the door with great anticipation; the boat sounds almost too good to be true. A nice looking, mild-mannered, gray-haired lady greets us. I'd guess her to be in her late fifties and normally I pride myself on guessing ages pretty darn close.

I just figure, O.K. John, old boy, now I'll do just what you said. I'll just sit back and say nothing and watch a smart, ex-used car salesman slicker this poor, defenseless, kindly, frail little lady out of her poor dead husband's last item of pride; his new jet boat.

106

She introduces herself as Mrs. Zmelzem, "My friends all call me Tootie." She invites us in the house and continues, "I presume you are the gentlemen who called regarding my poor dead darling's pride and joy. My, how Yugo did love that boat! It's just a shame he didn't live long enough to really enjoy it; but then you know when the Lord calls, we just have to drop everything and hightail it right up to heaven. I do hope they have fishing in heaven. Yugo would miss it so. I can just see him now with a big grin on his face and fishing up a storm."

I say "Yeah, and maybe with a cute little trick to bait his hook."

Talk about dirty, augered-in looks! Johnny gives me a look that would put Snooks' looks to shame. The first comforting little addition I make to Tootie's comment and John gives me that awful look. I have no idea what in the world has upset poor old John so bad, but like I said, I won't say another word. I'll just let John go ahead, he thinks he's so smart. I'll laugh if he self-destructs on this one, then maybe he won't be so critical of others. Particularly, others who are trying to help the best way they know how. Sometimes I think Johnny doesn't appreciate all my rare natural talent.

Tootie clears her throat and invites us to have a cup of tea. I could have figured her for a tea drinker. There's something about tea drinkers. I think it's the way they purse their lips on any word that starts with a "W." Also she's wearing a high neck blouse, you never see a real tea drinker show any hint of cleavage. I can spot 'em a mile away. Just another of my very swave characteristics.

We drink tea and talk about everything else in the world but what we came to talk about. After twenty minutes I just can't stand it any longer and say "Well Tootie, we came to see a boat. Where ya got 'er hid?" Johnny is pounding on my leg under the table to the point I think crutches will be a must to get out of here at all.

Tootie tells us it's out in the blue shed and she'll get the keys and show us. As she opens the big shed door, we see sitting there probably the most complete, nicest-looking craft I have ever seen. Johnny asks as to the length and Tootie replies it is 16 foot. I remark that it sure has got dusty and wonder if the batteries are still O.K.? Again a look from John. I can't say anything but what he gives me that look. Tootie says the batteries were brand new and may just need charging. Johnny asks Tootie how much she wants for it and she replies that she really doesn't care about the price, she's more concerned about someone having it who will enjoy and take good care of it and that's why she wanted to spend some time talking to us because she wanted to see if we would be the right ones, and she feels we are mature enough, and being retired, we will have time to enjoy it and "Oh, it's twenty-five hundred, plus bring the boat and trailer licenses up to date. I'd be pleased to have you take it." Also would we stop by sometime for a cup of tea and tell her about our fishing and maybe bring her a piece of fresh Sturgeon every once in awhile? "Oh yes, and will you please leave the coffee cup that's attached to the top of the big motor in place? You'll be surprised at the fun you'll have with that cup." I don't understand what Tootie means about the cup but I imagine we'll find out. "I'd also like you to leave the name YUGO'S DELIGHT on the stern." We agree to that and tell her we're delighted to grant her requests. "Do you have a place to keep it out of the weather and elements?" We assure her we do and she says then that settles it. She tells us if we'll come back in the house, she'll sign over all the papers and we can write her a check. She explains the money is not important and she would just as soon we don't tell anybody what we paid, because it's nobody else's business. "What's really important is that the right people get the boat and I'm very pleased for you to have it. I know you're not out for the monetary bargain but just the pride and fishing pleasure of a nice boat."

Johnny and I ask if we could leave the boat with her for a couple of days until we both get the proper trailer hitches on our cars? Tootie is agreeable.

Johnny writes a check, takes the paper work; we both thank Tootie and head for home, happy as can be, because we realize that through the kindness of a lady wanting to perpetuate the pleasure and pride her husband had with his new boat, we are the recipients of an early Christmas present ala Tootie's kindness. What a nice lady.

All at once I notice Johnny is not heading home but sure as shootin' it looks like he's headed to the Blue Danube. I ask "John, where do you think you're headed?" Johnny says he thinks we should have a little celebration drink and toast our new purchase. I was right, he's headed to the Blue Danube and for the life of me I cannot see any reason not to agree whole-heartedly.

Before we get out of the car Johnny says "I'm going to have to teach you the difference in dealing with a used-car salesman and a nice, kind lady in sorrow. You lost all your swaves on that one, too. I'm just not sure if there's any hope for you in the fine art of horse trading and making cool deals. But I'm still willing to try. Now let's go celebrate."

We walk in the Blue Danube and right off the bat Harvey Carbone and Snarly Krautkramer holler clear across the room and want us to come sit with them. They want to know what the occasion is that brings us into this palace of happiness? We tell them "We just bought Yugo Zmelsem's jet boat from his widow Tootie."

Snarly pipes up and says "Boy, I didn't know she wanted to sell that. Old Yugo had everything on that rig that you can imagine! It's probably the best-equipped little 16 footer in the county, and if I recollect right, it's probably only six months old. Man, that musta cost you guys a pretty penny."

We just grin and say "Yeah, we sure didn't get it for nothin'; but it's a beauty, that's for sure." Then Johnny calls the bartender over and says he'd like to order each of these boys a drink and he and I would also like double Martinis for starters. I got a feelin' we may be a while. So to partially save trouble I excuse myself and call Snooks, and tell her we bought a boat and we're having a celebration drink at the Blue Danube and I'll be home as soon as Johnny brings me. I haven't lost all my swaves, I'm not too dumb. I left it up to Johnny to get me home. Ha!

Our drinks arrive and Snarly wants to know if we heard the story about the gal in bed with her husband's best friend George? The bedside phone rings and Martha answers it on the second ring. After a brief conversation, she replaces the phone on it's cradle, snuggles closer to George and calmly says, "That was Harry, but don't worry. He won't be home for a while. He's playing poker with you." Good joke.

Johnny and I have been so busy for the last few weeks with this boat business that we've lost all track of fishing, and Snarly and Harvey proceed to catch us up on the local conditions. It seems that we haven't missed much. The new fishing regulations came out and of course, the sport regulations are even more strict than before, and the license fees are going up again and there are fewer fish allowed in the take-home purse. Snarly says something has to be done to protect the poor defenseless sportsman, but nobody does any more than just sit and raise their voices; they can't seem to come up with a workable plan. The only decent suggestion is to can all the brass and start over with personnel sympathetic to the sportsman.

Then Snarly has another joke for us. "It seems a little boy and girl were playing and the little boy pulled down his pants and pointed saying 'I've got one of these and you don't.' The little girl ran home crying. The next day the little boy does the same thing again, but this time the little girl is not upset and just continues to play. The little boy says 'Yesterday when I showed you, you were upset and ran home crying and today it doesn't bother you a bit. Why not?'

"And the little girl replied 'I told my mommie what you did and she told me,' pulling down her panties and pointing, 'when you have one of these you can get all of those you want.'"

Everybody figured Snarly's stories were pretty good ones. Then Snarly orders another round and we accept but tell them that we'll have to quit after that one. I'm glad, because this could continue into a real bang-up hangover which Johnny nor I neither one need anymore than a bad case of crotch crickets. We finish our drinks and decline another and head for home. I can't wait to tell Snooks all the details about the boat. I also need to write Johnny a check for my half of our new purchase. I'm so excited over our good fortune that I probably won't sleep a wink all night.

As we enter the house Snooks is eager to hear all about the boat, and I'm surprised but even Snooks can't find a thing wrong with our good luck and super buy.

As soon as we can get Bill to put on our trailer hitches, Johnny and I will start a new wonderful phase to our fishing lives. BOY, AIN'T LIFE GREAT!

# 10

# Makin' It Ours

Johnny and I take both cars and drop his off at Bill's garage, and since Bill says he's not too busy, he can have a hitch on in two hours. So we head on down to the restaurant for a bite of breakfast and maybe catch up on any gossip going around that may have gone by Snooks unnoticed, if that's possible. Normally either Peggy or Nancy get all the dirt that Snooks don't already know, and between the three of them they're never out of tune. But if once in a while, you can catch a morsel they haven't caught yet, it's like winning the Super Bowl or the World Series.

We order hot Polish sausage with eggs and just get started when Weasel walks in. He comes right over and says he's having trouble finding out about the cost of the dishes. The place where Snooks bought them seems to know he's fishing for information and instead of answering his questions they are asking him questions! Like: why would you want to know that when the dishes are already sold? Or, we can't tell you, we have to protect our customers. And, have you ever heard of the laws of privacy? Weasel says he's going to give up. When they ask more personal questions than he does, it makes him awful nervous for some reason.

Johnny asks me how I liked the hot Polish sausages and I tell him that I thought they were good. Then John starts in about all the good old American dishes that some foreign country has stolen for their own. The French are probabaly the worst with grabbin' off our stuff, like French toast; and the Belgians ruined the waffle with those crisp, oversized depressions. I tell Johnny that the waffle was patented and the only way the Belgians could beat the waffle game was to make the depressions bigger; then they could beat the patent and change the name to Belgian Waffle. (If Johnny buys that, I can sell him the Brooklyn Bridge!) Johnny says he didn't know that, but it sure makes sense. (Yep, I could sell him the Bridge.) I remind John of the Swedes and the Swedish pancake. Now if anything is American, it has to be the pancake. It all started with the Alaskan gold rush and those famous sour-dough hot cakes.

We pay our bill and it's time to head down to Bill's and pick up Johnny's car. We leave mine with Bill, and head over to Tootie's to pick up our pride and joy. Tootie is more than glad to see us, and again we have to come in and have a little cup of tea and just shoot the breeze for a few minutes. I'm beginning to think she is just plain lonesome since her husband's passing. I ask Tootie if she ever did any fishing with Yugo?

Tootie replies that on some occasions she did enjoy fishing with him, but that her favorite fishing didn't seem to interest Yugo. I ask her "What kind was that?"

Tootie replies "Sturgeon fishing. Yugo didn't think they were a sport fish and too, he thought they were so ugly.

"I felt they could outfight a salmon and you never knew how big they might be. Plus, if you ever looked close and paid attention, they had a beautiful design in the tissue on top of their heads. I think they are beautiful and a real fishing challenge. But much to my sorrow, Yugo seldom fished for them.

"Did you fellows know that when you cook Sturgeon it never smells up your kitchen like other fish? It's excellent eating any way you cook it."

Johnny and I look at each other but never say a word. We didn't picture this tea-drinking gal as any kind of fisherman, let alone Sturgeon fishin'.

We hitch up the boat and head for our big front yard to really look our beauty over and see what needs attention, because we figure it hasn't been run in the last few months. First off, it needs a good wash and wax job, that's one thing we're sure of.

113

As we pull in the yard, Snooks is frantically waving her arms and jumping up and down like she's just discovered the house is on fire and can't remember 911. As I get out of Johnny's car I ask what all the excitment is? Snooks says, "There's a fellow on the phone who wants to talk to you; this is the second time he's called in the last hour and he sounds like it's something real important!"

I go in and answer the phone and guess who's there? RUDY! And Rudy just wants to tell us that, as ridiculous as our offer sounded to him, he suddenly finds he owes a big income tax penalty on a logging operation and as bad as he hates to do it, he is forced to sell his boat quickly. He is willing to take us up on our outrageously ridiculous offer of seven thousand. I tell him "I'm really sorry, Rudy, but we found a much better buy even at the price we offered you and we just couldn't pass it up. We purchased another boat yesterday evening.

"You know Rudy, we would have gone along with our offer yesterday morning, but the moral of this story is: 'He who hesitates is lost.' We're sure sorry, but if we run across anybody else in the market we'll tell them about your boat. Can we quote the seven thousand price?"

With no more wind in his sails, Rudy answers in just above a whisper, "Yeah, I guess so."

I walk back out in the yard and hand Johnny a twenty-dollar bill. Johnny asks "What's this for?" I tell him that it's for understanding used-car salesmen and the human nature that goes along with them.

"That was Rudy, and it seems he's in a jam and needs to sell his boat quick so he felt he was forced to accept our ridiculous offer. It happened just like you said, only a little quicker than you figured."

Johnny replies "I think it was quicker because he told his wife what we offered and not having any knowledge of the boat's value, but a knowledge of their need for seven thousand dollars, she forced him into a hasty decision.

"She probably applied some good, old-fashioned female celibate power of persuasion, or FCPOP. It's absolutely amazing the strange power of FCPOP! Females all understand it's power and have used it since the beginning of time. It's not something learned but rather something in the genes; it's inherited."

I find it absolutely amazing that Johnny knows so much about so many things. He's got all the sandwiches in his picnic basket, that's for sure.

We decide we'll go over this boat from one end to the other, and read and understand all the directions for the 110 h.p. motor as well as the little 5 h.p. motor for trolling, the depth and fish finders, automatic self-starting bilge pump, ship-to-shore telephone, AM/FM radio and CD Rom player, the care of the jet pump, canvas top maintenance, refrigerated fish box, twin self-charging batteries, motorized anchor pick up and release, propane heater (with optional hot plate!) and last but not least, the audible, low-gas tank indicators.

This rig is really loaded and there may be more good stuff on it, but that's all the things we see at first glance. Johnny says he stayed up late last night and sent in all the paper work to transfer ownership and re-license both boat and trailer. We decide that each of us should take some manuals home to read, and then when through, we'll trade so when we finish with them, we'll both know all about everything.

I suggest the first thing to do is to wash the whole boat down and then start out and wax every flat surface we can find plus both motors. Johnny agrees and we run down to the marine supply to pick up what we need, plus we get my car from Bill, and everything is lining up fine, and we'll have our new beauty out for a trial run before you know it.

Everything is going along great and it's all washed. Even the clamped-in cup that is miracle-glued right tight to the top of the big motor is washed. I ask Johnny if he has any idea what Tootie meant when she said to leave that cup on there and we would have a lot of fun with it? Neither of us can make any sense out of that statement; I guess time will tell.

We have it all washed and cleaned and are about to apply the wax to bring out a high luster on the hull, when Snooks comes out and wants to know why a wash job wasn't enough, why are we going over every nook and cranny with spit and polish?

Johnny looks at me and I look at Johnny and we sort of wonder the same thing for a second and then I tell Snooks, "Well Snooks, we're just making it ours."

John turns to me with a big smile and adds "Yeah, Snooks, that's exactly right. Couldn't have been said better. When we're through, we'll feel it's all ours."

Snooks sniffs and says, "You men sure do have a funny way of looking at things. That's a stupid answer if I ever heard one. Wasn't it yours when you paid for it?"

"Well, Old Girl, you've really stuck your foot in it this time. You bought those dishes the other day, and paid God only knows what for them, and as soon as you got them home you took each and every one and washed it. You were making them yours, isn't that right?"

Snooks turns toward the house but I can clearly make out her mutterings. "You eat off dishes, you don't eat off a boat."

Johnny says, "For a minute there, I thought you had her."

"John, old pal," I reply, "you don't often get ahead of Snooks even when you're right. She's slippery as an eel. I did win that round though, because if I hadn't, she'd still be standing there. The only reason she left is because I beat her at her own game. She didn't think I'd remember the immediate washing of the dishes and the similarity."

We apply the wax and while it dries go in for coffee; then we can rub it down to a beautiful luster. We sit and drink our coffee and discuss the great luck in finding an almost new boat with the latest equipment available, and for a mere pittance, as far as money is concerned. I say "John, we owe it all to Tootie. We'll sure have to stop and see her and take her some fish once in a while; we owe her a lot."

Snooks says not to get carried away, that giving Tootie fish could lead to some dangerous things because she's a pretty attractive widow, as we have undoubtedly observed. I say "Now Snoo-oo—"

I'm looking out the window, and who drives up but Nugent! He stops, gets out a pencil and notebook and, while looking at our boat, seems to jot down a number of items. I ask Johnny what he thinks Nugent is doing? Why would he be writing things down? How could he possibly have found out so soon that we had purchased a boat; and what is wrong with our having a boat? I can see that this day was just going along far too nice. We should have figured the rat would smell the cheese.

I turn and ask "Rose, did you say anything to Nancy about Johnny and me buying a boat?" Rose replies that she can't remember, but she might have said something about us thinking about getting a boat, but she's not sure. "Rose, I don't like your association with that low-down rat's wife; and above and beyond everything else, don't ever tell her one thing we're doing here, not one thing! I'll bet she never tells you anything Nail 'Em is up to, does she?"

Snooks mumbles "Well yes, once in a while she does."

"Then Snooks, why in the world don't you let us know so we can stay out of his way? You know he's just dying to nail us with a big fat ticket."

Rose replies, "What do you think I am, a traitor to a friend?" Well, this is just about all I can stand. She tells Nancy things about John and me, but won't give us any information she gets from Nancy that could help keep us out of trouble with Nail 'Em. She says she doesn't remember for sure, but she knows she told Nancy about the boat, otherwise she would have come out with a flat 'no.'

Talk about being upset! This really takes the cake. Yeah, and talk about celibate. It's gonna be celibate around here for one long time, you can bet your booties on that! I'll bet I can even last a whole week!

Johnny and I go out and rub down the wax on the boat hull, which in my present mood gets an extra vigorous job, to say the least.

After we put in about eight hours of pretty hard work, we figure we're ready for a shake-down cruise in the morning.

We decide not to take any fishing tackle but just give it a run and familiarize ourselves with the boat, it's performance in the water at idle, and top speed. Also acquaint ourselves with all these nice new gadgets that will help us in it's performance.

One thing for sure that we really need to practice, is loading and unloading at the boat ramp. Launching a boat properly is of prime importance, yet one that few do quickly and efficiently. If there is anything more fishermen don't do well, it's either load or unload at the boat ramp.

Another universal thing is, that when he finally does get to the boat ramp, the fisherman is always in a hurry. He may have spent an hour over coffee at breakfast, or twenty minutes gabbing at the bait shop, but when he gets to the boat ramp, ready and waiting to launch, he is in a——HURRY! I think that this odd phenomenon stems from the fact that once he arrives and sees others launch, the thought suddenly enters his mind that he must hurry or someone else will beat him to his favorite spot. One reason I say this is, when you see a fellow with a small motor launch first and head out, the next one waiting to launch never seems to have the worried look on his face because he knows he has three times the horsepower as the one ahead of him. He knows that he'll be able to overtake the first one, if he has enough distance to go. Really, boat ramps are one of the world's best places to study frustration psychology. I'm fascinated with the goings on at boat ramps.

We decide to go to a lake where the ramp gets very little traffic, and then we can practice without bothering anybody or causing undo stress, because we won't hurry and we want to learn to do things right.

We have breakfast and gas up the boat and head out. We're near the city limits when some guy pulls up alongside, and frantically points back at the boat. We pull over, and he waves and drives on. Johnny and I get out and check everything, and can't for the life of us find what the fellow was so excited about. So we continue on our way.

We get into quite a discussion about how to combat this Nail 'Em situation, and we finally decide that we'll have to think up some tricks to pull on Nugent. Not worry about Snooks and Nancy, because that relationship seems to be so solid that we are on the outside looking in. I tell Johnny we can call in a few phony phone tips every once in a while to throw him completely off the track and maybe even force him into many extra h-o—u—r—— "What in hell is that guy who pulled up beside us waving and pointing at? He's just like the last guy.

"Johnny, I don't know what it is, but we've got a serious problem! Two of them now have acted the same way." Again as we slow up, this driver waves and drives on, too.

We again stop, check everything, but can find nothing to indicate all this frantic waving and pointing at the boat. We are at a total loss.

We get to the boat launch, and when we arrive we have it all to ourselves. We launch and load about three times and get better every time. Just when we start to feel pretty good about it (we think we're just about as fast and efficient as firemen answering the station alarm) up drive two guys guzzling booze and visibly bordering on bourbon collywobbles.

They get out and stand and watch. Pretty soon they're pointing, whispering, and slapping their legs, and making little comments. What had been a very efficient launching procedure all at once falls apart about as fast as a soaked sugar cube. We don't know what they find so amusing right off, or what all the whispering and laughter is about, but it takes it's toll and we can't drive the boat on the trailer, can't make the tie downs work. In fact, what had been so easy has now become a blundering, disoriented mess and getting worse by the minute.

Then they begin to call out snide remarks, like: "That guy in the blue shirt is in over the top of his boots!"

Then the other one says "Naw. He ain't got no boots on!" and they laugh as though it's real funny. Well, I'll clue you in, it's not funny to us!

We decide to try to load one more time, and give this up because now we're afraid to take off on the lake for fear they might damage our car or even steal our trailer. It's funny how little unforeseen happenings can change the best-laid plans.

We finally load, but we don't get the boat straight on the trailer even with the side guides. As we're pulling out, one of the slobs hollers to us, "You guys shouldn't be in such a hurry. You don't even know what you forgot!" and the laughter is still going on as we drive out of there.

Johnny asks "I wonder what they meant by that?"

"With them," I say, "I wouldn't worry too much. They're not too sure of anything right now. Myself, I'm just glad to be out of there and away from those two clowns."

We head towards home without further incident but only partly finished with our test cruise. We certainly didn't accomplish all of what we had planned to do.

As we drive along I tell Johnny that I have a plan to keep Nugent out of our hair. All we have to do is say something in Snooks' presence, but not to her, to the effect that we heard there's been a lot of deer poaching going on up Tillson Valley almost every week. Of course Snooks will pass that on to Nancy, and she will tell Nugent; and if we can keep him working nights he'll be out of our hair during the day.

Johnny thinks it's an excellent idea. I say "Yeah, John, you gotta be swave to turn adversity into an advantage."

We're going along the freeway at the legal speed and all at once five big eighteen wheelers go by us, one right after the other, like we're standing still. Johnny remarks about them and the danger they can cause as well as the legality. I say "Johnny, I can slow that whole bunch down, if you want me to." John says there is no way I can do that. "Well, John, I'd like to get that twenty back you won from me betting that Rudy would call us. I'll bet you that twenty, that in ten minutes I can have all those trucks a quarter mile behind us."

John says, "It's impossible; I'll take that bet."

I lean over and turn on the CB to channel 17 and say "County Mounty at the Maytown exit." Well, you never saw five trucks slow down to legal so fast in your life. The legal speed for them is ten miles slower than ours and in no time at all, they're all nice and legal and a good distance behind us. By the time we get to the Maytown exit they're a long way back. Johnny just shakes his head and hands me a twenty. Again I say, "Johnny, you gotta be s-w-a-v-e to turn adversity into an advantage and this time into money, too. I might also add, John, that when used right, the CB is a pretty slick rig." Johnny does not choose to answer.

It hasn't been a totally successful day but, on the other hand, it has been about a 75% day and I did pick up a quick twenty from Johnny. We go in for a cup of coffee before we put away the boat, and Snooks says she's had a phone call from someone wanting to tell Toad that the Sturgeon fishing is picking up at the boat launch. She informed the caller that nobody lived here by that name, but they insisted this was the number they had been given.

Snooks wants some sort of an explanation, but I just tell her they obviously got their wires crossed, because we don't know anybody by that name. Johnny is looking over the top of his coffee cup, with a big grin hiding behind it.

The next surprise is that Yoko, our Japanese neighbor, has been over and she told Snooks that her husband Itchy has seen our new boat and he would "shuah wike you husban and fwend to invite him fo fishing some day."

I say, "Snooks, you know we're going to have to learn a lot more about what we're doing with the boat than we know now, but maybe some day we'll think about it."

Snooks replies, "Whenever you say 'I'll think about it' that means no; and as good neighbors as they are, the least you can do is take him fishing in the new boat. After all, they share all their garden produce with us."

"Yeah," I say "that's right Snooks; mostly their precious zucchini at a time when everyone is right in the midst of the Big Zucchini Give Away. Anyone who raises anything in the garden, raises zucchini! You have to run, hide and be rude to keep from being given zucchini.

"Why, do you know Snooks, that's one of the main criteria for a salesman's job at Latimer's Used Car Lot? It's how successful a fellow is at giving away zucchini at the peak of the zucchini give-away season. Why, that's how our friend Phil got his job with Latimer. He gave some to a guy who raised them himself yet gave his own away because he was so allergic to the fool things. Now that's the height of salesmanship! That's why they started Phil out as manager of the sales force."

Johnny heads out to put the boat up and we decide to go right back to the same place in the morning and see if we can't complete this shake-down, get-used-to cruise. We want to go through all the procedures again before we actually get out where it's too far to get back if we have trouble, or find something we should know and don't, or lose a nice fish because we don't know our boat well enough.

Next morning after breakfast we go right back to the same boat launch; practice a couple more launches then head out to try maneuverability at slow and high speed. We find it handles beautifully at high speed, which with two of us tops out about 43 to 45, and it just wallows around at low speed unless we use the trolling motor. We check out the depth finder, radio equipment, anchoring and putting up the top. At the end of a long day we feel we have learned about everything there is for us to know about our new beauty.

As we load and head for home in late afternoon we look at each other with big grins. I say "Johnny my friend, we've learned most of her secrets and enough to be comfortable with her. We've made it ours, now let's go fishin'!"

# 11

# AGJS and Toad's Woes

When we arrive home I holler "Hey Snooks, we got 'er all ready! Now for some fishin'." I walk around the corner and see that Snooks is on the phone.

Snooks tells me the party on the other end just said, "Put Toad on, I just heard his voice."

Snooks says "Whichever one of you jokers is Toad; talk to this man.

"Since Johnny hasn't said a word, I presume he means you, Lover. Here, take the phone."

I guess Toad is finally out in the open. Even the best kept secrets sometimes fall to the fickle finger of fate. It's Alex, and he just wants to tell us that the fishing is hot as a pistol and we better get down there before somebody takes our places. I tell him "We haven't been down because we bought a boat and we're getting it ready; but we'll be down in a couple of days, and thanks for letting us know."

Instantly when I tell him we have a boat, his voice changes, and he's through talking. All he says is "That's nice, have fun," and hangs up.

"John, that was Alex down with the boat launch bunch, and he was all enthused about letting us know the fishing is hot until I told him we've bought a boat, then instantly he acted like he don't even know us. I wonder what got into him?"

Johnny says, "That's easy to figure out. It's called the Ain't Got Jealousy Syndrome. The AGJS is when somebody else doesn't have all that you do. Suddenly, they don't like you anymore; it's a basic form of jealousy. We're now better off than they are, and therefore, we're no longer one of the 'have-not-fraternity' but now belong to the 'have group.' So now we're outcasts, we've lost our former buddies over the AGJS.

"We'll just have to move along now with our former buddies ignoring us. It's too bad; we haven't changed our feelings toward them, it's they who have changed. They look down on our success. AGJS happens every time without fail."

Snooks pipes up and says "Well Sport, let's get this 'Toad' thing out in the open.

"The other day you lied when you said you never heard of Toad, and now today you are one. Please explain. I don't care who tells me, but one of you better start talking and quick."

I ask Johnny if he'd like a cup of coffee and Rose says, "No stalling around to find time to wiggle out of this 'Toad' deal. Just tell me about that and I'll get the coffee. My curiosity is just about to get the best of me." Rose is just like a pit bull; once she gets hold of something, she just won't let go.

Johnny finally tells her "When we were fishing with the boat-launch bunch, our mutual friend here got a big fish on, and in the process of landing it he was hopping around all over the place, and those guys said he looked 'just like a toad jumping around.' From that day on they called him 'Toad.' It's just a name those boat-launch guys thought up and hung on him."

Rose smiles and says "You know, come to think of it, at times he even reminds me of a toad. I think that's a good name for him, and I'll just continue with it from now on."

Rose can be cruel at times.

A person tries to protect himself, but it seems like some things get away from you no matter how hard you try. I sure can't blame Johnny. He never said a word about 'Toad' over these last months. And Rose could just drop it, but no; I have a feeling 'Toad' is here to stay.

I tell Snooks that Johnny and I will be heading out fishing in the morning and I'd like a nice lunch because we'll be gone most of the day. Snooks asks, "Are you going to take Itchy this time?"

"Snooks, no. We are not going to take Itchy until we know exactly what we're doing ourselves."

Snooks replies that she doesn't think Itchy would be any trouble, he would probably try to help as much as he could. "You know he's not the kind to have to be babied. Just look at his garden and that will give you a clue."

"Don't worry about it Snooks; when we get used to things ourselves, we'll take him, but not yet. There'll be plenty of time.

"The tide will be just perfect tomorrow and we need some actual fishing time to get really well acquainted with the boat under real, honest-to-goodness fishing conditions. Also, we need to see how much time all the procedures take, so we'll know how early to leave to be ready for the prime-time fishing. This is what you call swave boating and fishing knowledge; only the best fishermen take time for all this special procedure; another reason we don't need a greenhorn along on the learning trip.

"Besides, we don't know where the good fishing holes are. We have a lot to learn before we take anybody else with us. Do I make myself clear, Snooks?"

"Well yes, when you put it that way; but if you catch a fish," Snooks says "you can surely share some with Itchy and Yoko, can't you?"

"Sure Snooks. When we catch a fish we'll do that. For now just forget it. When the time comes, we'll take him with us." Like I said, Snooks is just like a pit bull, once she gets hold of something she just hates to let go.

Johnny comes by the next morning with the boat loaded and we head for the river with a whole new fishing method and experience ahead of us. We arrive at the boat launch and as we had anticipated, nobody even looks up. We know they know we're here, but they all totally ignore us. We're a new breed now, and don't fit in with them at all. A classic case of AGJS.

We launch flawlessly, and I'm sure thankful we practiced ahead of time, because I'd sure hate to have any trouble in front of our former friends. I hope some day they'll get over it. I hate to see bad feelings over nothing.

We head up river, which for some reason is what all the boats seem to do, as yet we don't know why. I tell Johnny we should watch where some of these boats fish and also spend some time with the new fancy depth and fish finders and see if we can locate any fish at all.

Johnny runs the boat real slow and I keep my eyes on the fish finder and all at once I spot about five on the bottom within a 50 foot area. Johnny takes a look and confirms my findings so we pull up ahead, drop the anchor, and drift back to where we can fish right in the middle of them. They almost have to be Sturgeon because they look big on our screen. They're in about 35 feet of water.

Already I can see a terrific advantage to boat fishing over bank fishing. We're all excited and it takes us twice as long to rig up. Particularly when we know we're sitting right on top of a whole mess of fish.

We each bait up with sand shrimp and cast out, rods in the rod holders, and sit back in our comfortable boat chairs and wait for the action. I tell Johnny I never realized how simple and positive this hi-tech boat fishing would turn out to be.

Forty minutes later we haven't had a sign of anything. This hi-tech boat fishing isn't all peaches and cream either. Johnny says that maybe the fish moved because we made too much noise getting the anchor out and everything ready. "After all," he adds "you know we didn't make any effort to be quiet. Next time, I think we should pull well up above, shut off the outboard and quietly drift back with the tide; then drop the anchor very slowly and quietly; because we know fish can hear.

"Have you ever seen dolphins respond to noise? I've seen three of them jump ten feet out of water in unison to a police whistle. You bet fish can hear under water."

After an hour-and-a-half with nothing to show but wasted time, we decide to look for a new spot, but after we pull the anchor and drift back over the same spot, the same fish are showing up on the screen. We think maybe we misread our fish finder and mistook sunken logs or something for fish. Johnny says "I think there may be more to learning to read these depth and fish finders than we thought."

As we head out looking for a new place we see two large fish break the surface ahead of us, and then a monster! almost too big to be believed, comes up about three feet out of the water and he's only just past the two fins right behind his head! I shout "JOHNNY, DID YOU SEE THAT?!"

John says, "YEAH! His head wouldn't fit in a five-gallon water bucket!"

Now we're really excited!

We decide this is the place to fish so we do what we'd planned. We continue forward and shut off the motor, then drift back slowly and quietly as we let out the anchor. So far, so good. This time we know there are fish here and we feel we have approached them properly. We don't even talk above a whisper to each other. I figure you gotta be really swave to outsmart these babies, and we're plenty swave and a little bit savvy besides. Now it's just a matter of time.

Two sandwiches, a bottle of beer apiece and two hours later; we still have not done more than drown seven sand shrimp. Not a thing except about every ten minutes to view in close proximity the surfacing of our quarry; large, inviting, seemingly close at hand but in reality very, very distant.

While we ponder our problem, our confidence is disappearing like smoke out of a chimney on a windy day. For the life of us, we cannot figure why we are right in the midst of fish and are not getting even a slight nibble of encouragement.

The stillness is broken ever so slightly by the slowly advancing put-put-put of a small outboard that stutters in a broken cadence like it may quit at any moment. We pay it no mind until we realize this boat seems to be approaching our immediate area.

It's an old wood, waterlogged scow about 10 foot, and by the sound of the constant bailing, has to be just one step from sinking. In fact, one man alone could not operate that craft, because it takes one just for full-time bailing. You can hear the men laughing as though they are perfectly safe; maybe the beer they're guzzling gives them a false sense of security. Talk about loud! You can hear every word at 200 yards above the hiccup of that ancient little outboard.

They know exactly where they're headed because the one bailing keeps hollering and waving his arms with precise directions. After careful maneauvering they feel they're exactly where they want to be, and the bailer calls out "W'ar raht on 'er. Let 'er go!" At which time a rusty bucket, filled with about 25 pounds of concrete, and held by a heavy inch-thick rope, is thrown over the side with a tremendous splash and a "YAHOO!" out of the anchor man as he pops the top on another beer. By the time they are settled in place, they're only 35 feet further out from the bank than we are, and right alongside us. A little close I'd say, but I don't want to start an argument; after all Johnny and I are here for fun, not a fight.

Yet it seems strange that with not another boat in sight and miles and miles of river, they would have to pick this spot right in our hip pocket.

After everything settles down, the beer drinker who had been running the motor, waves his cigar, leans over and asks, "Yew fellers bin havin' eny aykshun?"

I answer "Not much."

You never tell another fisherman any more than you have to unless he's in your boat, and of course, lying is all part of the game. Besides, Johnny whispers and says not to tell them anything. He's hopping mad because they crowded in so close to us, and says if they were any kind of fishermen, they shouldn't come in here making all that racket and heaving the anchor over like they did. It'd be a miracle if they catch anything. Besides that, with all their noise, they have undoubtedly ruined any chances we had.

John adds in a whisper that drinking and fishing never result in catching.

Yew fellers bin hayvin eny aykshun?

We can't believe it, because they have been here only ten minutes and already they each just opened another beer. Then the anchor man turns around and calls to us, "We'uns wun't a-crowded yew fellers, but ar uther bes feshin' hol was tooken up ba sumbuddy else, so we hada take secon' bes. Aw hup yew'all dun't mine, but all's far in luv 'n waar."

Then they both laugh and stomp their feet with glee; and the cigar man has the guts to add, "Asides, fellers, we'uns hain't gunna be very long. We'uns ony want tew ta smoke o'er the weeken."

Johnny and I are so disgusted with these drunks that we just ignore them altogether. After all, real fishermen we don't mind lying to, but these two aren't even worth a good lie.

We continue to fish, but our dispositions have turned to the displeased and upset side. Most of the fun is gone, thanks to these two beer-drinking clowns.

Right about in the middle of the first ten minutes of our full-fledged ignoring, the cigar smoker hollers "YAHOO! AH GOT 'IM!"

Well, as hard as we try, we can't ignore the goings on in the other boat. It's sort of like somebody pointing up to the sky and hollering "FLYING SAUCERS!" It's just impossible not to look, though you really wish you hadn't.

The cigar smoker tells the anchor man, "Throw the float; it's a big 'un!" At which time the anchor man throws out a big, orange-red balloon-looking rig tied to the anchor rope and they float up river with the tide. Now the cigar smoker is standing up leaning into a rod bent almost double. They disappear around the bend still fighting the "big 'un," as the cigar smoker would say.

I look over and see a slight twitch at the tip of Johnny's rod and say "Hey, John, I think you better watch your rod; it looks like maybe there could be something going on. I just saw a twitch there."

Johnny replies "Well, if it's a bite, it sure isn't very big," at which time he sets the hook and there is nothing. He reels in and finds his bait missing, so something has been after it for sure.

Again we hear the put-put-put of the little motor as the beer boat rounds the bend and returns. The anchor man picks up the big red float and throws it back in the boat and they settle down to continue fishing. "Let's git another, an' head fer home."

They purposely tie the fish on the far side of their boat so we can't see it, and I wouldn't ask to if it killed me. We really perk up our ears as the cigar smoker asks the anchor man to pass down the "gromafraw juice." We watch as a jar of greenish stuff is passed and the cigar smoker dips in his baited hook, then passes the jar back to the anchor man who does likewise.

They both cast out again, then settle back with another beer apiece and wait. Well, would you believe it? In less than five minutes the anchor man hollers "YAHOO! FISH ON!"

The cigar smoker starts to reel in to get out of the way, then yells "AH GONNIES, ME TOO!"

They each have a fish on at the same time; again throw out the float and head up river with the incoming tide. Their fishing time waiting for bites is not more than 15 minutes all told between them.

130

Our total fishing time is several hours and only one missed bite that could have been a bullhead or a crawdad; then these beer drinking, noisy Tar Heels come along in their leaky boat, and in less than an hour have three big Sturgeon on. It's a tough life.

Johnny and I look at each other in utter amazement. We felt that we were pretty good fishermen. We had our pick of the spot and they came in after we did.

We think they did everything wrong, even threw the anchor with no thought of being quiet, in fact, noise meant nothing to them! Granted our fancy boat and equipment doesn't catch fish, but it does make things easier and more comfortable. While we are looking at each other and trying to make some sense out of this, we hear the put-put-put of the little outboard as they return.

They lift the anchor, throw it in the boat, and as they drift past us the cigar smoker looks our way and waves, "We'uns won't be no more bothur. We dun ketched two buties ta smoke o'er the weeken. We tarnd unuther leegul un loose; figgerd you guys wud be a want'n to ketch yer own. Probly see yew fellers agin un a these days. Gu bah."

As the put-put-put sound of the little outboard lessens in the distance, we look at our watches, pull anchor and move over to the spot they just left; put on new bait and cast out.

We have three hours before high slack tide, and now that we know we're sitting in a hot spot, it's just a matter of no time at all and we also will be into fish.

I ask Johnny if he'd like a sandwich but he declines because he doubts we'll have time to eat before we'll have a strike.

After two hours Johnny says, "Toad, why don't you pass me one of those roast beef sandwiches, a piece of cheese and a cold beer? We've been right in the same spot that they were in, and we have no bites. I don't know what in hell we're doing wrong, but I'm afraid the secret is in that jar of whatever it was Cigar Man asked Anchor Man for."

"You mean the green stuff he called 'gromafraw juice'?"

Johnny nods and says "Yeah, Toad. That was it. Well, I just hope our future success doesn't depend on some idiotic thing like that. Something they have and we don't know anything about."

We finish out the tide with only one nibble and finally give up, pull the anchor and head for the boat launch and home; empty handed, but maybe wiser. At least we know we must look further into the gromafraw juice.

# 12

# Gromafraw Quest

We head home and suddenly realize that there are several things going on that must either be solved, obtained or controlled. As we drive along, one of those problems again surfaces.

A car pulls along-side and again points to the boat and goes on. This is happening so often we have learned to try to ignore it, but as hard as we try, we know a lot of people are bothered by something we cannot find. I say, "Johnny, what in the world do you suppose is so important that people feel compelled to point it out to us, but is of so little significance that we can't find it?"

Johnny replies, "I'll be darned if I know, but one of these days I'm sure we'll find out."

We continue on and our conversation turns quickly to the jar of green stuff the Tar Heels called gromafraw juice. Johnny remarks that it has to have something to do with attracting Sturgeon. Now that's an understatement if I ever heard one!

The fact is we were right next to them, and when they left we moved right where they had been. They seemingly couldn't keep the Sturgeon from biting, and we could not get a bite. This has to put the handwriting on the wall in big, bold letters. The message to us is: Get some gromafraw juice at any cost; beg, borrow, or steal!

Johnny says, "I don't think we can beg or borrow any. I think we'll have to steal it from them, and we'll have to figure how we can do that without it looking like we did."

"Johnny, let's work on that idea, I think between us we can surely outsmart those two. They may have the juice, but we got the brains and it's up to the brains to get the juice. We gotta be swave."

Our conversation then turns to Nugent and now that we're back to fishin', I'm sure he'll be trying to keep track of our activities. We must also use our smarts to keep him at a distance. "John, I'll go to work on that as soon as we get home. We'll put our deer poaching plan in operation. Plan Number One of several I have in mind for good old Nail 'Em."

I ask Johnny to pull in the next gas station as we better fill up. It looks to me like we've been running on fumes for the last ten miles. We've been talking and not paying attention to the finer points of driving. I have a feeling that the gromafraw juice could get us in trouble before we ever even get a close look at it.

Within five minutes the engine sputters, coughs and dies. Johnny says "%&#@+'!" and my answer is very similar, only not quite as colorful. We coast to a wide shoulder area at the side of the road and contemplate our next move. I tell Johnny to turn on the flashers so some idiot who is talking and not paying attention, doesn't hit us.

We then try to figure how to work our way out of this foolish dilemma. John says, "You know, in this day and age with a gas station around every corner, there is no reason to be so stupid as to run out of gas! I just hope nobody we know comes by and sees us in this mess."

We have two choices: try to siphon a little gas out of the stationary boat tank into the bait can and into the car, using an old piece of rubber tubing off a makeshift bungy cord as a siphon hose; or pour in what little gas there is out of the three-gallon emergency boat can.

Johnny says he has a real allergic reaction to drinking fresh gas out of a rubber tube; makes him break out in red blobs under his eyelids. I tell him I am against putting raw gas in my mouth because if the fumes ever ignited off a spark from a sharp tooth...well, KERWHAMBO! It would just be goodbye brains and anything else in close proximity to your mouth, like teeth and eyes and such.

We both decide that it's much safer and better for our general health to use what little there is in the almost empty three-gallon can. Just as we reach in the boat for the can, we hear the squeal of tires as two young loggers pull in behind us. They ask what our problem is and, as much as we hate to own up to our stupidity, we feel we have no other choice.

We tell them right straight out that our ignition system is out of whack and we have been just guzzling gas like you can't believe, but if we can just get enough gas to get to a station we'll fill up and then get that fool ignition system fixed in the morning.

They offer us a couple gallons they have in their pickup to fill their power saws, stating that should get us to the nearest gas station. It seems these loggers-of-mercy came along just in time to save our bacon.

We offer to pay them but they refuse and settle for a beer apiece. As they start to climb in their pickup, the one on the driver's side hollers up to us and says, "Hey fellas, you better take that cup off your motor, it won't stay there once you take off; you'll lose it for sure."

We thank them and wave as they leave. Johnny and I look at each other, just now realizing what all these people have been trying to tell us! All the poor, helpful people have been trying to tell us is to stop and salvage our cup before it blows off! "Johnny, how many of those people stopped to realize that there's no way in the world a cup would sit there on a car going 50 to 60 miles an hour? That's about as stupid as asking a guy who falls out a second-story window if he's hurt! I think we should leave the cup there and see just how many crazy people there really are, and how many really don't stop to think.

"Now that I think about it, Tootie told us to leave the cup there, that we would get a lot of fun out of it; now I know what she meant and she sure was right."

Johnny says he wishes we had caught a fish, he'd like to give some to Tootie. "After all, she just the same as gave us this beautiful boat." I tell John that the first fish we get, we'll make sure she gets some.....that is, if we ever catch one.

We find a gas station in about four miles and I ask Johnny if he

135

would mind filling the tank as I seem to have a lot of urinary problems, like a real sudden urge to go, if you know what I mean, but it only seems to happen when I'm filling a car with gas.

Johnny laughs and says, "Yeah, I guess you'd call that a 'pee-nomenon.' I hate to see you go through those hopping antics of yours, they also remind me of a toad with his feet in hot water. 'Toad' sure is a good nickname for you, and I'm afraid you're stuck with it now. Even Snooks sort of likes it, I think."

As we leave the station, one of the attendants hollers and points at the boat. It's amazing the reaction we get out of that fool cup! We just wave and tell him it's O.K., it's attached. "You know Johnny, most people act like they're a couple beers short of a six pack, but still just dyin' to be helpful."

When we get home I ask John to come in for coffee while we tell Snooks about our day. I'm explaining to Snooks about the little boat and the first fish hooked and tell how they threw out their float and drifted off upriver. Snooks interrupts with "Hold it right there, Toad. Will you please explain to me how anybody can drift 'up' river? I've heard of walking on water but you need a halo for that, which you don't have. But to float up river is just not possible."

I say "Snooks, I'll just bet you ten big American dollars that it's not only possible, but I can explain it so even you can understand it."

Snooks snaps right back with, "What do you mean by that crack, so even I can understand it? Do I seem so dense that it takes a special knack of explaining to get through to me? You act like I took an IQ test and came up negative! I resent your remark, it's a direct insult!"

I tell her not to get all upset and let her Rosy disposition surface over nothing. When you mention Rose, she immediately takes offense. It's like PMS; if you think the problem is PMS and it happens it is, it's just like throwing raw gas on a fire. All females flare up instantly. I can see this is going to be a tough show, because inadvertently I got off to a bad start and then just kept making it worse.

"Snooks," I say "either put up or shut up. Are you going to bet me so I can continue with this explanation?"

Snooks replies "You just bet your booties I'll take that bet, Buster."

I proceed to tell Snooks that when you're fishing a river so close to the ocean that the water is affected by the tide, then the river water will go upriver if the tide is coming in, and downriver if the tide is going out. The fellows in the little boat were anchored and the tide was coming in; therefore, the river was running upstream so they drifted upstream with the current as soon as they broke away from their anchor position.

Snooks says "That just doesn't make sense, because someplace where the river isn't affected by incoming tide, it is running down stream and the water running upriver from the incoming tide will meet the down stream water that isn't affected by tide, and there will be a big pile up of water running two ways at once and it wouldn't be safe to be there." She never heard of such a thing before; therefore, I have to be wrong, I'm just pulling her leg and I owe her ten dollars.

Then Snooks wants to know why the water can't make up it's mind where it's going, and how can the water rise five or six feet when we haven't had any rain to bring on the flood conditions? I tell Snooks that the tides are controlled by the moon, and at that point she accuses me of any kind of lie I can come up with to win ten dollars, and she is ashamed of me. I then tell her that only the dumb refuse to listen to reason.

We're going at it pretty good when Johnny speaks up and says "Toad, why don't you go visit Itchy and Yoko. Let me try to explain the tides and up-river drift of a boat to Snooks. I'm afraid this could end in a divorce court and over nothing of importance."

"All right Johnny," I say "but she's about as dumb as that state senator from the eastern part of the state who came over here and noticed the water level in the bay at breakfast, and when he went to lunch it was up four feet, and he remarked that he had no idea we had that much rain in such a short period of time. I'll bet I could even explain this to him easier than I can to old Rosie the Du—u—

137

m—." At which point Johnny shoves me out the door before Rose could find a dull knife to perform delicate surgery.

I go visit Itchy and Yoko and, of course, we have a spot of tea. Right away Itchy gets to throwing out little hints about wanting to go fishing, and Yoko is backing him 100 per cent. In conversational self defense, and a weak moment, I promise Itchy that on the next series of good tides we'll take him fishing with us. (Woe is me; what have I let us in for? May the Lord help us!)

After two cups of tea and the fishing promise, I head back to see how Johnny is progressing with his tidal explanation. If old Rosie can't understand it by now, she either won't let herself, or hasn't enough gray matter to absorb so much in such a short period of time. Rose can be really frustrating at times, and by now poor Johnny may have found that out.

As I walk in, Rose says to me "Well, there's nothing strange about this tide thing."

I answer "Then you do understand it, so you owe me ten dollars."

"OH NO I DON'T! You bet me ten dollars that you could explain it, and you didn't; Johnny did. So you can just go whistle for the money. I'd call it a stand-off, but I'm not paying. I just don't know why you can't explain things like Johnny does."

I thought my explanation was good but then Johnny was probably right. We had arrived at the 'I said, you said' stage of things and that is usually past the point of reasonable thinking. Johnny stepped in just in time to throw water on the fire.

I've come to the conclusion that women are all born natural lawyers; and they just don't apply for a formal degree. They're always looking for the little loopholes to wiggle their way out of things, and this is a prime example. I concede; anyway, I hope now we can start over from here, and behave like two human beings instead of a cat and dog.

Nancy Nugent walks in and would like Snooks to go with her tomorrow to an estate sale, and of course Snooks is rarin' to go.

Nancy casually asks how we like the new boat and we tell her fine; that we're still getting it organized the way we want it, and should have it ready to do some serious fishing within two weeks. Snooks pipes up and says "I thought that was serious fishing you two did today, or does it make it less serious because you didn't catch any fish?"

I can see that Rose is still upset over the tide business and this smart-mouth answer is just defiant retaliation. I'm just trying to get us a couple weeks without Nugent in our hair. Then she remarks that if it isn't ready, why did we mention trying to get in a day or two more this week? Now she's really getting dirty. Rose can be cruel at times.

Johnny decides to leave and I walk outside with him so we can talk in private. We make plans to go right back in the morning and try our luck again; maybe we just had an off day.

After everybody leaves, I think I'll have to have a heart-to-heart talk with Rose about this tendency to tip Nancy off to our every move. I say "Snooks, I don't think you should turn against Johnny and me and give Nancy any information to pass on to that miserable, no-good husband of hers."

Snooks' answer is "You lied. You knew you were ready to fish regularly and I knew exactly what you were trying to do. You know, I'm not as dumb as you think, and I won't stand here and let you out-and-out lie to such a sweet person as Nancy."

I can see that this is strictly a no-win situation, and I'm just going to drop it. Besides, it's difficult to talk with your teeth clenched and jaw muscles so tense they could almost cause a cramp.

Things are pretty quiet on the home front for the rest of the day. It's just a shame that Snooks can't understand that her loyalty should be with me and not Nancy. However, I think when we get down to serious fishing, there will be ways to handle this quirk of fate.

Johnny comes by bright and early and we pick up sand shrimp at the bait shop, then head for the river and, after an excellent launch, we head right back to the same spot.

We get it all to ourselves because the gromafraw boys are home smoking fish. That's one reason we decided to come right back to-day and maybe even tomorrow. There's nobody else around except one guy in a small boat way over on the opposite shoreline.

We get all settled, bait up, cast and begin our day full of anticipation. Nobody to disturb us. The guy in the small boat is trolling a small area, probably for trout, anyway surely no bother to us; we have the river almost to ourselves.

After about an hour and no luck, Johnny says that if we don't get something soon maybe we should move. I tell him I think I'll check my bait but when I pick up my rod, I find I'm hung up on the bottom real solid. "Darn it John, I must have hooked onto a sunken log or something, because I'm tight and can't move it. I know it's not a fish because I've watched my rod tip like a hawk, and it hasn't moved a tad except a slight quiver when a mosquito lit on the tip; plus, this is solid. I better just see if I can break it loose."

Johnny says that maybe I've tangled with one of the rare jelly-mouthed Sturgeon that can take your bait without you even knowing it, because it's so soft mouthed. I tell him that this is not jelly, but a solid log on the bottom. While we're discussing the different types of rare Sturgeon, John says "Say, it looks to me like your line has moved over about three feet to the right."

I'm looking at Johnny because it's not polite not to look at people when they're talking to you, and say "I don't think so; I didn't feel any movement and of course I was looking at you and not the line, but it don't look any different to me. It's no more active than a sunken log.....and they have a habit of total inactivity John, once they find themselves hooked. And this is no exception. I'm going to break it loose and get on with practical fishing, which we all know this isn't because when you have caught a log, nothing else will bite!"

I just start to apply a little pressure when I feel a violent tug and something takes out about six feet of line and again stops solid. Well, once I get my eyes back in their sockets I try to speak, but nothing comes out, just my mouth moving around but no words at all. However, I need not try to speak because Johnny also saw it move and

has already started to reel in to get out of the way. Then with a slow steady pace as though it can do anything it wants, the fish heads up-river with the current. I have the feeling that the fish has me, instead of me having the fish. On and on it goes. I tighten the drag and it still contiues on. Johnny says, "Well Toad, it looks like you finally have a real fish on there."

I tell Johnny to cut the bull and start pulling up that anchor FAST! because at this rate I'll run out of line before he gets the anchor up.

I must say I've caught a lot of normal fish: trout, salmon, bass, and even the Sturgeon caught at the boat launch; but I've never tangled with anything like this. Just as I'm sure I'm going to run out of line, John brings the anchor in and starts up the outboard. We slowly fol-low the fish until we gain back almost all the line and this monster is now right straight below us. We have weathered one crisis.

Already I have learned two things. But then I've always consid-ered myself a fast learner. The Tar Heels had the right system on that throw-overboard balloon, quick-get-away anchor; also, the way this fish feels, I don't know if even 40 pound line will hold him!

The battle continues on, and the mid-day sun begins to heat up and makes it's presence known. My arms begin to tire and ache, not to mention a new feeling similar to a ruptured disc in my lower back.

Johnny says, "You've been at that thirty minutes and you're beginning to look like a tired Toad; would you like me to spell you a bit?" I tell John that in my perfect physical condition I'm probabaly good for at least an hour or more, so far I'm not even beginning to feel any pressure and for him to give it no more thought. Johnny replies it's my physical condition he's concerned about, because he's never seen me get more exercise than picking up my morning coffee cup. Sometimes John's got a smart mouth just like Snooks; I wonder if it might be contagious?

Just about the time I feel I must tell Johnny of a sudden surge of weakness creeping through my entire body, I also get the feeling that I'm beginning to be able to control this back-and-forth tug of war.

All at once I see bubbles coming to the surface and I recall Sam, one of the boat-launch fishermen, telling us that when you see bubbles, it's a sign of a mighty tired Sturgeon and you have the battle almost won. Hopefully, Johnny will never know how close I came to throwing in the towel.

I also remember asking Sam where the bubbles come from and his answer was, "One end or the other, nobody's been down there to watch."

Another five minutes and we get our first look, and to tell you the truth if you've never seen one this big, it is an awesome sight. Sort of like a cross between a shark and an alligator, but without teeth. Johnny says "Boy! That thing looks like a gummy alligator."

I tell John to skip his comparisons and get out the tape measure. We have to see if it's too big to keep. His answer is not what I want to hear; "I forgot to put one in the tackle box; we don't have one."

My next remark does not bear repeating around children or in polite society. Then I say "Well John, a dollar bill is six inches long; now get busy and mark off ten dollar-bill lengths on the side of the boat.

You at least have a dollar bill, don't you?" Johnny confirms he has a dollar bill, but he thinks the fish is legal. "Johnny, there's no thinking! We have to know; 60 inches or 5 feet is the maximum legal length, and I'm going to be legal. I think the fine for one oversize runs into four figures and Nugent would love to catch us wrong; and you never know when he may pop up out of nowhere. We are the prime target of his very existence."

I keep dragging the played-out fish back and forth while Johnny keeps flipping that dollar bill over till he gets 5 feet on the side of the boat, then marks it with two Band Aids out of our emergency kit. We drag the fish by the marked-off area and it appears to be 58 inches, as best we can tell. Johnny confirms that it's for sure legal. He runs a rope through it's gills and out it's mouth. We tie it tight and leave it alive but hanging, tied over the side to the boat. It's just too big to put in the boat.

We regroup and head back to where we hooked this one. It really didn't go very far, just tried to stay on the bottom. Johnny says, "Toad, if you're going to be so legal, you better get your Sturgeon card out and punch in the date and location." I do that while he's putting out the anchor and he adds, "As soon as you finish with that punch card, we can get back to fishing."

"Johnny, you get back to fishing. I've caught mine, and I think Nugent would just love to catch me fishing for more. You fish; it's a sandwich and cold beer for me." I don't want to admit it to Johnny, but I'm too tired to even think of hooking another one that size today.

Johnny looks over the side and says, "That sure is a beauty. I hope we can take two home like that;" but the day ends without another nibble and as we begin to put things away, the small boat slowly trolls over to our side of the river and right up to our boat.

The little guy trolling turns out to be big bad Nugent incognito, and he has been over there all day, just biding his time, lying in wait to try to nail us. First he checks our licenses, which he had done already once or twice before, then he checks our punch cards, then checks to see if we're using barbless hooks. Last, but not least, he insists we meet him at the boat launch to stretch that fish out on a flat surface and make sure it might not be just a wee mite too big. This guy doesn't leave a stone unturned. He's determined to get us. It's so easy to hate a fellow like this. With Nail 'Em, a deep unfaltering hatred is actually fun. Yes it is, it really is.

After slow progress, due to his small motor, we arrive at last at the boat launch and even our former friends gather round and speak to us. After all, in a conflict of interest with Nugent, we boat owners become the lesser of two evils. We drag the still living fish up on level ground and Nugent proceeds to measure, and finds it to be 59-1/4 inches long, just 3/4 of an inch short of being illegal. Nugent comes back to the tail, pulls on the fish to make sure it's at it's full length, and takes another measure. He would give anything to find me wrong, but this is not to be the day. No matter what he does, the measurement remains the same, and in front of witnesses he must concede. As he heads back to his boat, several unkind remarks are made that could have double meanings, but Nugent knows what is meant, and knows for whom they're intended, and knows it best to act like he doesn't hear them.

All our boat launch buddies laugh and pat us on our backs; and now we're friends again and they realize we are not the enemy, only Nugent is. Shorty says, "Toad, if you split those fish gills and bleed it out, the meat will be a lot whiter, cleaner and better tasting when it's cooked." We do this and while we're waiting, talk to our old friends and find things should be better in the future. We leave them some left-over sand shrimp, which pleases them no end.

While we're at it, we ask about the two fellows in the small boat. Everyone is aware of whom we mean, and all declare the two spend very little time on the river, but always come back with a limit. Shorty says, "Those two out-fish everybody else on the river, always! I don't know what they know or what they have, but whatever it is, I'd shore give a bundle to know, too." The others all voice agreement to Shorty's statement.

144

Johnny and I load the boat on the trailer, pack up everything including a nice fish, and head for home. I notice on our way out that Nugent's car and boat trailer are not in the parking lot, yet I know of no other boat launch close. He must have a secret, private launch. I mention this to Johnny and he agrees. It sure would be nice to know where that launching place is.

The discussion on our way home involves two prime topics: Nugent of course, and the gromafraw, too. I say, "Johnny, this business of Nugent must be given a lot more serious consideration. We can work Snooks' attitude and feelings to a definite advantage as we've discussed before; plus the river is open to night fishing now, and between that and deer poachers, we may get him working enough nights that he can't stay awake forever, and that should help to give us free days."

"Toad, did you notice how he was shaking when he measured that fish? He was just sure he had us. He's a fanatic about nailing us."

"You're sure right there, John.

"You remember my friend Vic. Well, he has a plane; maybe I can get him to give me a ride and find where Nugent launches his boat. We have to spend most of our non-fishing time trying to outsmart Nugent, and Snooks and Nancy are going to be a great help without their even knowing it. Yes, indeed.

"Next Johnny, we must figure some way to get some of that gromafraw juice. We do know a little more about the Tar Heels than the other guys; at least we know where they like to fish and that they have a powerful, secret juice to help them. We must get it by hook or crook, and soon."

When we get home we take our fish out in the shed and clean it, getting two big, beautiful fillets about 30 pounds apiece with no bones of course, because Sturgeon have no bones, just cartilage.

Johnny trims one piece up special and says, "After I put the boat away, I'll just drop this off for Tootie. I'm sure she'd like that." I agree that's a nice thought.

We decide as long as the tides are right, we'll just go back again in the morning. The tides are just an hour later every day, so we won't have to leave so early. We also will not let our plans be known any more, until the morning we have plans for. I tell Johnny to call me this evening about 8 o'clock; not to say anything, just listen. I'll be sure and answer it because I have a plan; he'll make the phone ring and I'll do the rest. Just another little swave trick to outsmart Nugent. I think this project may become almost a full time job when we're not fishing. Anything one does well takes time and effort. I think Mark Anthony told that to Cleopatra, and you can believe Mark because they tell me he knew what he was doing for sure.

Johnny says he'll be by about nine in the morning; then he drops me back at the house. I remember hearing Snooks say she and Nancy were going to some fool thing early in the morning so they can get first pick. Maybe they'll be gone before Johnny picks me up. I don't think I'll even mention the little run-in with Nugent. With Nancy in the picture the best thing I can do is keep a low profile on that subject and it should make it easier to get around our problem. Swaveness is going to be the answer. We have been way too out in the open and it's working against us.

Snooks wants to know all about our trip, but I'm starting to wise up and although I tell her about catching the fish, I just give her minimal information and nothing of vital importance that could harm us if passed on. Johnny would be proud of the new way I'm handling things on the home front.

"Are you two going fishing again in the morning?" asks Snooks. I tell her that Johnny thinks he'll be busy but he won't know for sure till morning, so we probably won't. She says in that case she won't worry about fixing my lunch. Well, lunch or no lunch, she isn't going to make me talk. I've made a few sandwiches in my day; after all, I'm not helpless, you know.

Eight o'clock right on the button the phone rings and I answer and for a full two minutes say nothing except "Mmm, you don't say, how much? Uh huh, yeah; uh huh; mmmm, uh huh, yeah. Ah, mmmmm." Then I add, "Tillson Valley, mmmmm, mmm, does, too?

146

Mmmmm, don't that beat all." As soon as I hang up, Snooks starts with the questions. AH HA!

"Well, what was that semi-intelligent conversation about?" she asks.

I say "Oh not much. Weasel wanted to tell me that Joe Jacobsen is going to have to sell his new Jeep and wondered if I'm still thinking about one."

"Well, are you?"

I say "No, not since we got the boat."

"What was that about Tillson Valley?"

"Oh, nothing much; Weasel overheard two guys talking in the tavern that there sure has been some deer poaching going on up Tillson Valley way. They're taking does too. But that's no nevermind to me; probably just idle beer talk, sounds like to me."

I just drop it there. I figure the seed is well planted. I really had no idea how wickedly swave I could be when I have to. I even surprise myself sometimes.

I'm just pouring my 8 a.m. cup of coffee when Nancy swings by to pick up Snooks. She doesn't even come in the house; they're all fired up on a mission to secure cast-off junk at bargain prices before somebody else gets the idea their "mother had one like it" or "things like that just aren't made anymore."

It's a crazy hobby where some people are willing to pay fabulous prices for a possible hidden treasure which, more likely than not, turns out to be worthless junk.

Snooks and Nancy call it antiquing. I call it crazy. Funny thing though, it seems to be growing in popularity. I think some of these TV shows where they show all these fabulous finds keep people interested. All I ever got out of one of those shows was, if you have something old, leave it old, don't clean it or fix it, just don't mess with it.

John picks me up shortly after the gals leave, and he is laughing about my crazy telephone conversation. However, he admits it should help and every week or so we'll just put out a new rumor call

147

like that for Snooks to peddle to Nancy and then, of course, right back to Nail 'Em himself. We may be able to work him to death doing nothing.

We arrive at the boat launch, and our old friends come over and tell us how pleased they are Nugent didn't get us. In the conversation we find out that the Tar Heels are fishing, in fact they have been on the river much longer than usual. Shorty points out their pick-up and trailer. It looks just as bad as the rest of their stuff, boat and all, but you still can't deny, they do out-fish everybody else.

We launch and head up river. As we near the spot where the Tar Heels like to fish, we expect to see them, but no, they are way up river waving and carrying on something shameful. We shut off the motor and they're hollering for help! We figure anybody who hollers for help surely must need it, so we run up there wide open to see if we can be of any assistance.

The Tar Heels are very glad to see us because their little old outboard finally gave up; they're absolutely dead in the water. We can hardly believe our eyes; they don't even have a paddle or an oar, and I don't see any life jackets either. The Coast Guard would be glad to catch up with these two. They could probably write them enough tickets to support the Coast Guard base for a month.

I ask what their problem is and Cigar Smoker says, "Thet thar enjine dun jest up and quit, mayhow blow'd a payston. Shore dun make a bunch-a-rakit when she dahd."

Anchor Man agrees and says, "Yep, Jethro is rhaght, she shore dun make a parful lotta rackit wen she dun giv up."

Johnny says we'll be glad to tow them back to the boat ramp. I quickly add, "Yeah, under one condition."

Jethro asks, "An whut maht thet be?" I then tell him that we would have to have that jar of green stuff they been dipping their sand shrimp in before casting. Jethro is so shocked he even stops bailing and says "LAND O GOSHEN MAN! NOT THE GROMAFRAW JUOOS!!"

The Anchor Man says, "NO WAY ATTAL!"

I tell Johnny "Then let's get back to fishing. We'll send the Coast Guard unit down after high tide to tow you in. That is, if you don't sink first."

Johnny starts the engine, we wave as we pull out, and those two are jumping up and down like mashed cats, waving and calling us back. We swing back around and they reach down and hold up that prized jar of green juice. We pull up along side, they hand over the jar and we toss them a tie rope, then head slowly on back to the boat ramp.

The gods of opportunity have shined on us today. We have the GROMAFRAW!

# 13

# Tea, Tape and Tricks

After we turn the Tar Heels loose at the boat ramp, we fire up our trusty big motor and, at about forty miles an hour, immediately head back to our fishing spot. With an hour of good tide left we'll have a really good chance to check out this secret fish-catching find of the century.

We drop the anchor and drift into position, dip the baited sand shrimp into our new found treasure (namely gromafraw juice), cast and we're ready.....tensely awaiting a bit of action.

As expected, it's not long in coming. Johnny has one on in no time at all. I pull the anchor and we slowly follow the fish. In about ten minutes Johnny brings it in, and it's just a little over 43", a nice fish, just barely legal.

As we go back, we talk about the fact that we forgot to buy a float so we could save this anchor-pulling business every time we hook a fish. Also, we didn't mark 42" to 60" on the side of the boat to get some idea of legal size while the fish is still in the water. Nor did we buy a tape measure! Again have to measure with the dollar bill trick.

Johnny says he thinks we better quit fishing after today until the next series of tides; get ourselves better organized and catch up some of the loose ends. "I agree John, and one of the loose ends is to punch your punch card on that fish you caught." Johnny looks surprised that he did forget. "You know John, we don't dare slip up, not even once. We can't give Nugent any opportunity to nail us."

Within five minutes after re-anchoring I'm onto a fish, but I tell John that it doesn't feel big enough to pull the anchor for and it turns out I'm right; but we now know the gromafraw really does attract fish. A real stroke of luck for us.

"I agree with you Johnny. We've been hitting this fishing pretty hard and it's time we stop, take a look around and put a few things in order and perspective.

"Besides, Bud Breen called last night and invited us out to his lake on Saturday for a picnic and fishing contest. He's offering prizes for the biggest trout and bass caught, plus.....and get this John.....a million dollars for the first goldfish! Now can you imagine that?"

Johnny smiles and says, "Bud just threw that in as a joke to spice things up because it just isn't possible with all those bass in there, and besides how would a goldfish get in there anyway?"

We pull the anchor and head for the boat ramp and home. One real lucky day for us. On the way we decide we'll get a tape measure in the morning, also paint 42" and 60" on the boat where we can get an idea of legal size before we try to land the next fish. And buy a float and anchor set-up so we can move and quickly follow a big fish without losing our fishing spot.

I mention to Johnny that though we now have the gromafraw juice, it won't last forever, and we should give half of it right away to Wonder What? Chemical Analysis Company to find out what's in it and how much of what's in it. Otherwise, once it's gone, it's gone and we'll have gained very little but a few good fishing trips against a lifetime of good fishing trips. Johnny thinks that's real smart thinking and should be done right away as a Number One Priority. I figure you gotta be swave all the time to stay ahead, once you get ahead.

We arrive home and clean our fish. Again Johnny gives one piece extra special care and packaging. I ask, (even though I already know) "Johnny, how come you trimmed and wrapped that with so much special care?"

He tells me "Tootie was pleased with the last fish we gave her and she so loves Sturgeon, that I thought I'd just take her over a little more. Besides, it's right on my way home and no bother."

When Johnny arrives next morning, Snooks and Yoko are having tea and I'm having my coffee. John sits down, looks around and when Snooks offers him coffee Johnny replies, "Snooks, it looks to me like you and Yoko are having tea, and if you don't mind, I think I'd like the same."

"Johnny, I never thought I'd live to see the day a full-blooded Swede like you would be caught dead drinking that stuff. My father used to say 'All tea is good for, is to rust your boiler.' How come you all at once got a craving for tea? Your brain hasn't suddenly tilted you a little bit kattiwampus, has it?"

Johnny's answer is that he's had a little bit of upset stomach lately and thought the mildness of tea might help a bit. That answer might satisfy Snooks and Yoko, but by George, not me! I'm too swave to swallow that after watching him drink two bottles of beer yesterday. I'm not sure what the real answer is, but I'm thinking it will surface after a bit.

Yoko remarks that "Itchy shua would wike go fish too, some day." I tell her we have a lot of learning to do, but when we learn enough we'll for sure take Itchy fishing. A promise I'm looking forward to about as much as I would a root canal.

Johnny and I leave to do a little shopping and pick up the loose ends. First place we go is Herkimer's Hardware to get a tape measure to carry in our tackle box. We ask Herk to show us what he has in wind-up tape measures. Well, would you believe he brings out some big fancy ones from 50 to 100 feet?

Johnny tells him "No Herk, we don't want anything over 25 feet."

I tell them both "We don't want anything over 6 feet, because all we really need is 5 feet, but nobody ever heard of a 5-foot tape measure, and we don't see any reason to pay for any more tape than we're planning on using; 6 foot at the most, that's all we need is a 6 footer."

Herk says "We had some little cheap ones we sold at Christmas for stocking stuffers, and the way you two sound, 'cheap' should fit all the way around."

Johnny tells him "I think that remark was meant in a slanderous way and we'll just take our business down to one of those new chain-store outfits that carry everything."

I add "It won't be long until the corner hardware will be like the dodo bird. They'll force you little nickel-and-dime stores out of existence."

As we walk out, I tell Johnny I had no idea buying a tape measure could be so much trouble, but at least I guess we showed old Herk where the bear pottied in the buckwheat!

We drive down to the big, new Everything Homewise and check for tape measures. Well, they have 6 footers on sale, two for 99 cents, so we get two; one for the tackle box, and one to keep handy on the boat. I tell Johnny I'll meet him at the car. I'm going back to the pet department and get Snooks a bag of bird seed for her bird feeder.

Snooks doesn't like pet departments because she says some have snakes for sale and she won't go near one. So I have to go in to get the bird seed for her. Well, while I'm waiting at the counter to pay for the bird seed, there's a kid ahead of me paying for a couple of guppies; and do you know, they put the little rascals in double Ziplock bags full of water and some air! This immediately starts my mind on a frenzy of activity; this knowledge I'll store away for future use.

When I meet Johnny at the car he says, "You're grinning like the cat that just swallowed the canary. What's up?"

"John, I can't tell you now, but before the week's out, I'm sure you'll know." Johnny looks puzzled, but asks no more questions.

We then head on down to the marina and pick up one of those big orange-red floats and 100 feet of half-inch rope. This should match up with our anchor to give us quick-release anchoring.

From the marina, we drive to the Wonder What? Chemical Analysis Company with our precious jar of green, fish-getting joy juice. We walk in a big fancy office that looks like it was set up to impress people and intimidate them at the same time, so the company can take more of your money than they earn. I can just feel trouble. Somehow it reminds me of the Social Security office; even sort of smells like it.

Cora Cogger

We walk up to a reception desk. Name plate says "Cora Cogger." We are greeted rather coldly by Cora who seems to be in the middle of a full life-cycle of PMS. Glasses down on her nose, poker face and voice very similar to the whine of a mosquito right next to one's ear. This gal has never been bothered with, nor ever need worry about, sexual harassment; and who knows that may be the focus of her problem.....poor thing.

After a few questions she calls someone, then directs us to the second cubical-like office down the hall on the left, to talk to a Dr. Porter Prickelhaupter. As we approach the door we see the letters after his name are a bunch of degrees that take up half the alphabet! He is listed as a Chemical Composite Consultant, which must be important because it's in real genuine, gold-leaf lettering.

Seeing him seated behind his desk, John and I hesitate then walk in, seat ourselves and wait, without even being acknowledged as alive, in hopes that sometime soon he will finish whatever has him so preoccupied that he doesn't even know we're here. Or this also could be an act to impress us with his importance, which he doesn't have to do because the walls are covered with little framed certificates listing degree acknowledgments, and they have to be important because each of them has a folded ribbon stuck on with a fancy serrated-edge gold seal. This guy must be a chemist's chemist. Already I don't think we can afford him.

He seems totally engrossed in whatever he is reading and I think a mite upset, because he keeps drumming his pencil on his desk as he reads, sometimes almost stopping, then continuing like a woodpecker on an elm tree.

At last he sets his paper aside, clears his throat and asks "And what can I possibly do for you gentlemen?" I put our half-jar of gromafraw juice on his polished desk top. He reaches over, takes the jar, lifts it to eye level and shakes it gently, then removes the lid, and takes a deep whiff of it's contents. The frown and quizzical look suddenly change to one of wide-eyed horror.

He quickly replaces the lid and says to us, "What is it?"

I turn to Johnny and remark, "Well John, I guess we're in the wrong place because Port here, is asking us what we came here to have him tell us." I reach for the jar as Johnny rises to leave.

Dr. Porter Prickelhaupter suddenly springs to life and says, "Just a moment gentlemen, just a moment. Let's back up and regroup and start all over. I assume you gentlemen are here to have our company give you a qualitative and quantitative analysis of the contents of this container."

Johnny answers right back, "I don't know about that, but we want to know what in hell is in that jar!"

Dr. Full-of-degrees Prickelhaupter then replies, "Exactly, exactly. Now in order to do this for you, it will help us a great deal if we can have some chronological knowledge of the material's origin and it's intended utile function."

I'm beginning to run out of patience with this line of chatter and ask him if he means what the hell it's used for and where the hell did it come from? Prickelhaupter replies "Exactly, exactly. If you can just give me a little of it's history and what it's used for, we'll get right

155

on with our work."

We explain to him that it is called Gromafraw Juice and we obtained it from two Tar Heel fishermen. It's use is to entice and lure fish, namely Sturgeon, to swallow the bait presented to them. We also tell him that we must have total confidentiality on this matter, because if this information should leak to the general everyday fisherman, it could be as devastating to our fish population as the Fisheries Department policies already being enforced!

Dr. P. proceeds to tell us that in twenty-five years with the company, this will be the most unusual material they have ever analyzed and is, without a doubt, the strangest he has ever encountered, bar none.

We ask if we could possibly have some idea as to expense involved and a time frame for this project. Dr. Porter Prickelhaupter frowns and tells us that due to the unusual nature of this project it will be very difficult to put a defininte price tag on the eventual solution or outcome.

We tell him we understand, but before we can continue we must have at least a ballpark figure. He must think he's dealing with a couple of country bumpkins if he thinks we're going to turn him loose with a signed blank check. We're a lot more swave than that.

He frowns a while, and finally gets out his portable calculator, note pad and pencil, and begins to figure.

This is either a monumental task or he flunked fourth-grade math because it's twelve minutes by the clock before he comes up with an answer!

He tells us that there will be a base charge of $50, plus $10 for every ingredient found, and $10 more for the quantity of each ingredient, plus $75 for confidentiality. Not knowing much else about the "Juice" at this time, he cannot give us an exact figure, but to cover our question he will say the cost will be not more than $475, nor less than $275.

We decide we can't afford to do it. But we can't afford not to! And for the price we paid for the boat we're still going to come out ahead. The big problem is it may take up to a month to get complete results. Doc P. tells us that if we'd like, we can call him every week and check on progress.

As we're leaving he asks, "Could you please tell me what a 'Gromafraw' is?" John looks at me and we just grin and tell him we'd like to know that too, and maybe he'll find that in his chemical analysis.

We've had a pretty busy day and head back to the house and see what's been going on. Again Snooks and Yoko are happily drinking tea and again Johnny decides to have a bit of tea with the girls. They are both overjoyed because finally one of the contests they entered has sent them a check for $50! You'd think it was a million, as happy as they seem to be.

Snooks tells me that I should check the stuff on the hall table because all that information Johnny and I signed up for at the boat show is now beginning to show up in the mail. Now that we have our boat we're not interested, now it'll be just a nuisance.

Snooks inquires as to how our day went and we tell her we got a lot done but most important, we got our gromafraw sample over to the Wonder What? Chemical Company for analysis; and once old Doc Prickelhaupter figures it out, and we find out how to make it, we'll be set fish-wise for life!

Johnny says "Yeah, it may cost a bundle, but it will sure be worth it." Snooks asks how much we think the examination will cost? Johnny tells her, "We aren't sure, but we gave them a two-hundred-dollar deposit." (He should have been born speechless.....I wasn't going to tell Snooks how much it cost at all.)

Snooks raises her eyebrows and remarks that boys just put no limit on expenses when it comes to fishing or for that matter anything they consider pleasure. Now I just can't let that go by without mentioning all the money she spent on those dumb dishes she bought at the antique shop. Snooks replies, "Toad, you don't have any idea what I paid for those dishes, for all you know they may have been a door prize, and until you know what you're talking about, you better not make statements like that." As I've said before, there's no point in trying to argue with a woman because they are born half lawyer.

I hear a car and see Nancy at the wheel. She comes in and Snooks asks if she would like tea or coffee with us? I figure if a fella is real swave and careful, this would be a good chance to check on Nugent. In fact, if a fellow just listens real careful he may find out a whole bunch without even saying a word. Nancy asks Snooks if she got any word on the dishes and I can see instantly that this is something Snooks would rather we hadn't heard. Snooks ignores the question and asks Nancy what she has been doing and her answer is, "Oh, nothing much. I have to be so quiet during the day so Norman can sleep. When I come over here, at least I can speak above a whisper."

Johnny and I excuse ourselves because we still have things to do. As soon as we're out the door, we wink at each other and John says, "Toad, that was a real slick trick you had, having me call so you could get the phony deer poacher message to Snooks and then Nancy. Old Nail 'Em got the message just like you said and now we have him working nights and also have both Snooks and Nancy working for us!"

"Yeah, Johnny. We can pull that trick every once in a while, and I do believe we can keep him pretty well under control. Next time I'll make sure Snooks answers the phone so she'll know it's all legit." HA!

I tell Johnny "Maybe we should stop in at the Blue Danube and have a celebration drink or two. Our good fortunes are overwhelming! We're out-swaving 'em all!"

Johnny says, "I hate to burst your bubble, but you'll never out-swave Snooks, or at least not for long."

We enter the Blue Danube and we're the only ones there except the bartender. We order fuzzy navels for a change, and when our drinks arrive the bartender tells us a story about three astronauts; an American, a Russian and a Polock, sitting in a bar. The Russian says

158

"We Russians are the best astronauts in the world, because we were the first in orbit." The American says "We Americans are the best, because we were the first on the moon." Then the Polock says "Well, us Poles are the best, because we're going to be the first on the sun." With that the American and Russian say, "You'll burn up, you idiot!" The Polock says "Oh no, we won't! Do you think we're dumb? We're going at night."

About then Snarly Krautkramer and Rotgut O'Riley wander in so we go sit with them. Rotgut is already well on his way. He seldom adds anything sensible to a conversation, but then he doesn't seem to ever hurt anything or anybody either, he is sort of just accepted as a living test to see which will kill him first: Husky Musky or cigarettes. In fact, there are rumors that some Main Street businessmen have a pool as to which it will be. What they don't realize is, it will take an autopsy to tell and I'm afraid most of the pool money will go for the autopsy, so there won't be any money left for the winners. Sort of a catch twenty-two.

We don't find out a thing from Rotgut, but then we really didn't expect to. Sometimes I wonder who's smarter, Rotgut or the rest of us? In his semi-permanent pickled condition nothing ever bothers him, he's never upset, always happy, and it's a cinch he'll never have an ulcer. He doesn't even care who's President.

Now Snarly on the other hand, is almost always upset about something, and today it seems to be the way the toilet paper rolls are placed next to toilets. It seems like the roll is either just out of reach or around behind you where you can't stretch for it without throwing out your back. He says the Legislature should pass a law that toilet paper is always within easy reach; put it right in the building codes so the regulation has to be followed.

I ask Snarly why he's so all-fired up about toilet paper, and he says "A friend pulled a shoulder muscle while reaching for paper; had to go on medical disability but got no pay because it wasn't job related! He ended up on welfare, and who do you think pays the bill? Us taxpayers; all over a misplaced roll of toilet paper!"

159

I tell Snarly that I'm not so sure I want those idiots in Congress messing with our toilet paper after the way they legislated us into limited-water, non-flush toilets. I'll bet that flushing Legislator never thought once, while he sat there trying to figure out how to make a name for himself, that before he ruined every flush in the country, to just talk to a plumber.

It would have saved hundreds of man hours flushing a toilet that wouldn't ever flush right the first try, and seldom after several tries. There's just some things that should be left alone. No, I think we dasn't get the Legislature involved in any more bathroom, water and sanitation problems.

We finish our drinks and head on home; still happy over all our recent good fortune.

I tell Johnny that we should be ready to go to Bud's fishing derby picnic by noon. So if he wants to, he can drive by on the way and I'll be ready. In the meantime, when he gets home, call me right at 7 p.m., and I'll make sure Snooks answers and then I'll feed her a little more "news" to pass on to Nancy for Nugent. After all, we wouldn't want him to stagnate on his job for lack of work opportunity. HA!

When we pull up in front of the house Nancy's car is still there, so I tell Johnny he better come back in and maybe something will be said that will give us some more insight into Nugent's activities.

We see Yoko has gone home. Snooks offers us coffee but again Johnny says he'd rather have tea like they are. Both gals are all smiles. Something is going on, but they aren't giving out any information at all. We just ignore it. I know that sooner or later Snooks will tell all. Good or bad, it's hard for Snooks to keep a secret very long.

Snooks pours my coffee and Johnny's tea and then she says, "By the way, a Dr. Prickelhaupter called and would like you two to stop in Monday and see him." I'd like to ask a little more, but with Nancy sitting there, I just don't want to say or do anything that might alert Nail 'Em to the big secret knowledge we're dealing with.

Nancy tells us she must get on home as she has to make Norman's lunch to take with him this evening. Yep, boy, we really got him eating out of the palms of our hands. My brilliance for thinking up these diabolical tricks sometimes even scares me.

As Johnny leaves I walk out with him. He questions calling at 7 tonight. He wonders if maybe we should wait until Nugent wears this program out before we load any more on him? I tell John he's probably right; just keep Nail 'Em on an even steady pace, after all, there's no point in adding on more than he can handle. Just add it when we need it. That John is a good thinker; with us working together I know Nugent isn't gonna be any problem. We decide to skip tonight's call. After all, you can't improve on perfection. Boy, are we ever a swave combination.

Next morning I put aside a light spinning outfit and as soon as we have breakfast, and our morning tea-time visit from Yoko, I go down to the new Everything Homewise store, head back to the pet department and buy two nice bright little goldfish.

Just as I thought, the clerk puts them in plastic bags and asks how far I have to go? I tell him about two hours. So he pumps in some oxygen and says, "That should hold them all afternoon; no use taking any chances." He wants to know if I need a bowl, aquarium or fish food, and I assure him that none of his suggestions is necessary. I leave with a smile.

At home I place the plastic bags in a coat pocket and put it beside my fishing rod and small tackle box, just minutes ahead of Johnny's arrival. Johnny doesn't come in, just honks his horn. I kiss Snooks goodby and she says, "Now you two have a good day at Bud's."

I smile and tell her "I'm sure we will."

We arrive just as the big fishing contest begins. After several nice trout are caught, I wait until one is hooked a ways off from me, and while all the attention is directed to that area, I slip a hook just in the lip of one of the little goldfish and cast it out in the lake. Shortly after, Bud walks by and says "Hey Sport, you got a bite!"

"You're right Bud, I do." I set the hook and reel in.

Well I tell you, when that little goldfish ends up flopping around right in front of Bud's nose, his eyes get big as saucers and before he can say anything, I say "By golly, Bud, it looks like you owe me a million dollars, because that sure looks to me like a goldfish."

Bud scratches his head seeking an answer and finally stammers out, "Yeah, you win the million dollars all right; and I'm going to pay you off a dollar a year."

At which point I tell Bud, "That's fine, but in order to collect you're sure forcing me to live a lot longer than I ever intended."

As usual everybody has a good time as we always do at one of Bud's get-togethers. I give the two goldfish to Bud's grandson, who I'm sure will assure them a long and happy life.

# 14

# Espionage, Intrigue & Benz

Monday morning John picks me up and we head over to the Wonder What? Chemical Company to answer Dr. Prickelhaupter's request to see us. On the way, Johnny and I discuss what in the world could have gone wrong that he would need to see us again so soon. Johnny says, "You don't suppose they have it analyzed already, do you?"

I tell him that I very much doubt it. "I think it has something to do with costing us more money."

Again we have to go through old, permanent PMS at the reception desk. It would seem to me that an up-and-coming outfit would want a real sexy-looking, personality-plus, well-endowed blonde on that reception desk.

As we're waiting our turn I think about this and can come up with only one solution, and not wanting to ever pass up a chance to pick up a couple of quick, almost sure bets, I lean over and whisper to Johnny, "Betcha five she's a relative of the big boss and another five she's on the wife's side of the family."

Johnny whispers back, "I'll take both bets; now it's up to you to prove it." I'll go to work on this at the first and every opportunity.

She peaks over her glasses and whines out "Dr. Prickelhaupter will see you now."

We enter his office and this time at least he isn't busy with something else, but is frowning as though he has a problem. I say to him as we sit down, "You look sorta concerned Port, has that look got something to do with the gromafraw?"

Porter clears his throat and replies, "Gentlemen, yes, I'm afraid it does. Friday morning, noonish to be more precise, I had a visit from a government official inquiring into the nature of your business with us. Now I am concerned considerably by this visit."

Johnny pipes up and says, "Well Doctor, it would seem to me that you do not have a problem at all. We gave you a job to do, and gave you a deposit in all good faith, which, we were assured, included full confidentiality. Therefore, all you have to do, Doctor Prickelhaupter, is complete your work for us, and keep your mouth shut. Then we won't have to give any thought to a lawsuit against first, the company you work for, and second, you, yourself. Do I make myself clear?" I have never seen Johnny so blunt and straight-forward before.

Then Dr. P says he is very nervous about dealing with a government agent and asks if we are in some kind of inter-governmental espionage or maybe something sinister that could get us all in serious trouble? I ask Prickelhaupter which government agency came to him regarding our business with him? He says he was told not even to divulge anyone had been here at all, and he has already said more than he should.

After hearing what Johnny said, Dr. P decides that Tuesday morning when the agent returns, he will straight out tell him that by Federal law regarding customer confidentiality he cannot divulge any company business, therefore he can tell him nothing.

We tell him that we agree that it's his legal obligation to do so, and we expect him to honor it and not worry anymore about it. The Federal Government regulation protects him. Again we remind him to call us when he received the findings to our sample of gromafraw, at which time we will finish paying him.

We leave not finding out much to help us except the agent is due back in the morning. Johnny and I spend the better part of the next hour finding a suitable vantage point where we can use binoculars to watch who comes and goes to the Chemical Company office, without being detected ourselves. We are ready for an all-morning vigil if necessary. We'll find out who else is so interested in the makeup of the gromafraw juice.

164

We are really curious as to who else has so much interest in our little project. I'm really curious as to which agency it could be. I hope it's not that Tobacco and Firearms outfit; they cause more trouble than they fix. I wonder if the Tar Heels were followed too, or if it's just Johnny and me? Hopefully, we'll know in the morning. Johnny says he has a good pair of Navy surplus binoculars and he'll bring them along. I tell him I feel it best not to mention to Snooks what our morning activities are going to be, at least not until we know who we're dealing with.

When I get home Snooks is all excited about something she and Nancy are going to do tomorrow, and she couldn't care less about Johnny and me. There sure is an awful lot of secret activity going on, I wonder what she and Nancy have cooked up? I imagine it's something to do with their wheeling and dealing with all this antique hunting. The only clue Snooks gives me is that she and Nancy will be leaving early in the morning and likely will be gone for most of the day. They sure aren't going to a funeral or to visit a sick friend; they're far too excited and happy. I have to admit between what John and I are working on and whatever Snooks and Nancy are working on, the curiosity part of my brain is working overtime.

Snooks and Nancy have already gone by the time Johnny arrives Tuesday morning. We pack a couple of sandwiches and thermos of coffee; you just never know how long this stake-out may take, but we're prepared to stick it out till we learn something.

The one thing we hadn't planned on or given any thought to at all, happens. Somebody has parked his car in our well-chosen spot. This throws us into a wild-eyed frenzy trying to decide what's next? Johnny says, "Now what in hell are we going to do? The best laid plans are not always perfect. We gotta find another spot; that office opens in twenty minutes and we can't afford to miss a minute. This just makes the difference whether we're on a well organized stake out or just out.....period."

As we drive past the office I tell Johnny we have about fifteen minutes to try to find another spot. Two blocks down the street I look in my rear view mirror, and what do you know, a fellow is getting into the car in our spot. "Hey John, don't panic; the guy who's parked there just got in his car. We'll swing a right and circle around the block and by then, I think we'll have our parking place back."

Sure enough, the fellow must be leaving for work and we slide in, with five minutes to spare. We have averted what could have been a catastrophic, tragic twist of fate.

We prepare for a long, and if necessary, all-day vigil.

It's amazing the things you talk about when you're just sitting around killing time; and Johnny and I figure we're liable to be here killing quite a bit of it.

Johnny asks, "Have you ever wondered why they put the cotton in a bottle of pills? I spent a lot of time figuring that one out. They want you to think it's to protect the pills, but oh no, Toad, that's not it at all. It's really there so you can't pick up the bottle to shake it and find out it's really only half full; that's their way of legally cheating you. Nobody would buy a half-full bottle and pay full price if they knew it. Of course, after you open it and remove the cotton, you've broken the seal and can't get a refund, so by the time you know for sure you've been cheated, they Gotcha!"

"You know Johnny, I never gave it much thought, but I really didn't think an outfit that was out to make you healthy would do a thing like that."

To which Johnny responds, "Well then, why don't they put the pills in a bottle the size to hold what's in it without cotton? Another thing; you never ever see pills in a clear bottle unless it's full. That's also part of the scheme. You see a clear bottle that's clear full so you think all the bottles are full. They do that to lure you into a false sense of security. Now Toad, you just think about that, I know what I'm talking about. I call it the Pill Peddlers Pocket Picking or the PPPP."

Myself I have never had enough idle time on my hands to think of such trivia, but now that he mentions it, it sure does sound logical; I wonder if maybe that isn't the most expensive cotton in the country?

About now we spot a van drive up, a fellow get out and start up the steps. Johnny says "AH HA! This may be it; he's in uniform."

"John, you're all worked up. Take a look with your binoculars. He's got a sack of something, probably making a delivery of some kind."

Johnny says "Oh hell, you're right, Toad. It's that delivery guy from Dan's Donut Dunkin' Dive. I think he's just delivering some donuts for their morning coffee break. Well, I didn't think this was going to be easy."

We pour a spot of coffee and John remarks how he wishes he had tea instead. I ask if his stomach is still upset? "No," he answers, "But while I was trying to get my stomach settled I sorta got used to the taste of tea, and now I really have a craving for it."

Two more people enter the building but neither of them look like Government Agents according to Johnny, who is the one looking through the binoculars. I ask him, "Just exactly how do Government Agent people look different from people-people?" Johnny tells me that's real easy, because Government Agents always carry brief cases with locks on them and people-people don't carry anything; except women who always carry an emergency face paint repair kit. I say "Johnny, what are you talking about? I never heard of that." Johnny tells me the women call it a cosmetic bag.

"Toad, no woman is ever without one, except at bed time. I remember my sister Ingrid; at night she'd use something called cleansing cream and then wrinkle remover grease and then put those prickly hair rollers all over her head. When she finished, she sort of reminded me of a cross between a porcupine and a greased pig. A sure-fire killer of romantic ideas. I could never figure how she expected to catch a husband; it's no wonder she didn't marry until she was in her 40's." Boy, Johnny is really wound up today!

Eleven a.m. and still nothing, only three people have entered the building, plus the mailman, and we know even though he's a government agent, he sure as shootin' isn't our man. We decide to have a sandwich and more coffee. Johnny wonders if we heard

Prickelhaupter right? I tell him, "I imagine their company gets most of their business by mail. There sure isn't enough demand for their type business just in our little town; therefore, we shouldn't have a lot of foot traffic and that should make our job easier with fewer people to screen.

"We said we were going to wait, and I know Prickelhaupter said the fellow was coming back in the morning, and Johnny, the morning's not over yet. You just have to have more patience that's all. If you ever hunted ducks or geese you'd have learned a lot about patience."

We have our sandwiches and I sort of relax by just checkin' my eyelids for light leaks, when Johnny breaks the silence with, "HOLY COW! GUESS WHO? It's NUGENT! There he goes, big as all get out, walking right up the steps and into the building!"

I tell Johnny, "We should have guessed it would be him, but I didn't figure him high enough on the food chain to qualify as a government agent. He must have found out through some little leak from the gal's conversation, or he just accidentally happened to see us go into the building. I think it was probably something the women said, otherwise he might not have connected us going in there with anything that concerned him."

Johnny replies, "Anytime he sees you and me together, he knows it's got something to do with fishing, and if it's got something to do with fishing, it's sure to involve him! One thing for sure, he isn't dumb or lazy."

"That old saying 'fat, dumb and happy' doesn't apply to him; he's none of the three," I tell Johnny. "If he could ever catch us, it would change the happy part though."

"You know Toad, that Nugent, he doesn't miss a trick and he's really after us. We have to make sure we never give him a chance to ever catch us wrong. You know it makes sense he wouldn't show up early, not now that we have him working nights. I sure don't think we should force him into too tough a schedule. As much as we dislike him, it shouldn't be our intention to try to kill him.....just maybe drive him to drink."

"Well Johnny, after this victorious stroke of internal espionage, I think maybe we should relax and go fishing in the morning. There's a nice 9 a.m. tide, and we need to give that gromafraw another test. Let's head for home. We have our answer on this part of the puzzle."

When we arrive, Snooks and Nancy are each having a cocktail, and wearing big smiles and acting all happy happy. I ask, "How come home so early, what's the big occasion?"

Snooks tells me, "Secrets are never kept by telling them, so you'll just have to bide your time. Things are already beyond anything your fish-oriented minds could even begin to comprehend."

The gals offer us a drink too, but Johnny says he has some things he has to do and he'll pick me up in the morning in plenty of time to get our sand shrimp and still be there for low tide.

After Johnny leaves, the girls continue with their secret little party. Boy, there are so many things going on all at once, it's a real mind muddler. F'rinstance, why did Johnny have to leave in such a hurry? He acted like he was set for all day, but as soon as we were through early, he finds he has a bunch of stuff to do. Very strange. And what is so secret and making these two gals so happy? Snooks is even a little smart mouthed, and she's never like that unless it's something big and she's real sure she's on the winning side. Very strange.

The only thing we're sure of, is who the Government Agent turned out to be. But we still don't know why he is that interested, nor what chemical composition we're dealing with involving the gromafraw. Very strange. There's a lot of strange espionage and intrigue going on and I suppose the only real solution will come in time. Time should solve all these strange little problems eventually. Matter of fact, when you think about it, time almost always solves problems.

It's nearly 8:30 when Johnny picks me up. We head down to the bait shop, pick up our shrimp and head for the boat launch. This should be a nice relaxing day of fishing. We have some gromafraw and of course, it needs another test. It's a nice day and I guess the

Tar Heels haven't got their motor fixed yet, because there's no sign of them and they were our main competition.

We run up river to our favorite spot and anchor with our new quick-release anchor. We bait up and dip our shrimp in the gromafraw, make casts and we're fishin' again, the happiest part of life.

After about fifteen minutes, I tell Johnny that twice now I think I've seen the glint of something shiny off an object across the river in the bushes, up about two hundred yards, and if he will just stand hiding me a little so I can use the binoculars, I'll try to see who it is, and they won't know we're watching them.

Well, Johnny stands so I can see perfect, and am sure the other watchers can't tell I'm looking at them, as Johnny has me camouflaged behind him. I say, "John, I'll bet anything there's a guy over there with binoculars watching us. Yep, there is; and I'll give you one guess who."

Johnny says, "Don't tell me it's Nugent! I thought we had him working nights."

"Johnny, do you remember when you left yesterday, you said right in front of Nancy that you'd pick me up this morning in time to get our shrimp and make the tide?"

"By golly yes, I do remember. I just never gave it a thought." I tell him we just don't dare say a thing because after all, we can't blame Nancy for sticking up for Nugent. He's the love of her life and her husband, poor miserable girl. So it's up to us to be careful. However, now we know for sure she peddles everything, and it should be easy to keep him occupied and out of our hair, if we just use our heads.

"Johnny, I don't care if we catch any fish today or not. Let's just have some fun with Nugent.

"Why don't we pull up and anchor right off shore from him so he can hear every word we say, then we can feed him enough fresh 'information' and bull to keep him out of our hair for a long time." Johnny thinks that's a great idea. After all, Nugent has no idea we know he's there. I tell Johnny, "Let's not go directly there, but back and forth a few times like we're looking for something on the depth finder. We've really gotta be swave with Nugent, Johnny."

As we approach the shore where Nugent is hiding, we make a great to-do about running back and forth as though we're looking for a special spot. We know Nugent can hear every word as we holler to each other over the motor noise. Johnny calls out, "Those guys said it was in a deep spot out from that snag...sixty to sixty-five feet."

I call back, "Here it is! Run over it one more time. Yeah, this is it. Throw the anchor."

We settle back after baiting up and casting. Now it's time to start feeding Nugent little tidbits of false information with the hope of driving him stark raving. Start raving can go two ways: crazy, or mad, and we really don't care which form of lunacy we drive him into.

Johnny's first remark to turn Nugent stark raving, is: "What did those two guys say? I thought they said they got three over seven feet, or did I hear wrong?"

"Nope, that's the way I heard it; they kept them too, and that's really taking a chance, but then they said they fished at night, and if you're going to be real down-and-dirty illegal, night's sure the time to do it."

By now, I figure we have Nugent's ears glued to the same sound waves we're sending his way for sure. I say, "Johnny, I heard by the grape vine that old Nugent is going to have to ask for early retirement, or get canned and lose his pension, if he don't start cracking down on some of this rampant taking of oversized Sturgeon."

Johnny concedes "Well, that wouldn't be too far wrong. He hasn't done an honest day's work as long as he's been here. He's too dumb to ever make a good warden.

"There's a rumor going round that Nugent had to be transferred twice before they sent him here."

I ask "Why?"

Johnny says "I heard it was alcohol related, and he almost got canned then, but he only had one strike and they wanted to make it three before they let him out. Even a hardcore criminal gets three strikes, and as bad as Nugent is, they figure he deserves at least the same chance as a common criminal, which in my eyes he is only half-a-broken step above."

I tell Johnny, "Maybe we better start fishing nights and see if we can get a couple of those big ones. After all, that's the best time to break the law; under cover of darkness there sure won't be much danger of getting caught."

Johnny laughs and says, "Yeah, and there are good night tides all next week, maybe we better plan on fishing all the best night tides the rest of the season.

"I heard 'em talking down at the Plunkin Shack that Nugent wears panty hose and sleeps in silk jammies, too." John is not content to just drive him stark raving, he wants to go one step further and drive him PLUM stark raving, which is the all time bottom of the stark-raving barrel.

I help John along a little bit and answer, "Yeah John, I wouldn't doubt that a bit. I saw him drinking a dry martini with a straw. Now, nobody but a suckling new born would stoop to a thing like that. I have to agree he's gotta be a real wimp underneath that Smoky-bear hat and that little tin star."

Just then we hear a car door slam about a hundred yards away and a car leaving the premises just a snarlin' and growlin' as it wends it's way at high speed and low gear away from a festering source of irritation.

Mission accomplished. Our little trick seems to have worked to perfection. On the other hand, from our own point of view, we'll have to be doubly careful from now on. I would compare this with jabbing a bull in the butt with a sharp stick.

I tell Johnny maybe we should just pull anchor and mosey over there and see what kind of a stake-out he's got for himself. We do just that and find Nugent has a little lean-to with a canvas cover to keep out of the wind, rain and sun. Also, this is where he launches his boat. He has a muddy, makeshift launch, well camouflaged with brush; he's put a lot of time into concealing this spot.

No wonder he knows what we're doing almost before we do! Now we know another of his secrets, and another strike for our chance to win the battle of honesty against so called law-and-order. There is no honesty when one deals with the likes of Nugent. Anything goes, and that includes lying, which comes natural to a good fisherman anyway.

We still have an hour left of prime tide time so we decide to go back to our good fishing spot and see if maybe we can take at least one fish home. Sure enough, it isn't ten minutes until Johnny has a nice one on, and after following it around for another ten minutes, we notice some bubbles and soon after, a nice fish all legal and everything. By now it's time to pull up stakes (actually the anchor) and head home, another very successful day to say the least.

While cleaning the fish, Johnny again prepares one portion extra special. I ask him, "I suppose that piece of fish you took so much pain with has a specific destination, doesn't it?" Johnny acts just a little flustered that I've noticed his special efforts, but answers right back.

"Yes, it does. I'm taking that one to Tootie, she seems to really enjoy fresh Sturgeon and I enjoy giving her some whenever I can. Toad, you don't have a problem with that, do you?"

"Oh no Johnny, I think that very noble of you."

John must be tired, he sure bristled up over my teasing him a little about giving Tootie some fish. I switch the subject real quick and ask him if he punched his card for the fish he just brought home and he assures me he did. He says, "You don't need to worry Toad, I sure won't take a chance on letting Nugent get us; particularly after the treatment we gave him this afternoon. I'll bet you we'll be getting absolute priority treatment from now on."

I say, "Yes John, we're probably on the top of his Most Wanted list by now."

I invite him to come in and visit with Snooks before he leaves, but Johnny declines saying he's tired and thinks he'll just drop Tootie's fish off and head on home.

For a young man of mid-sixties I see no excuse for tiring so easily. Come to think about it, he's been acting tired a lot lately and I'm a little concerned. He may be anemic. Maybe he should take some iron, I hear iron is good for anemia. I think I'll suggest some iron to him.

After all, if he goes to the Doctor and says he seems tired all the time and wonders if he needs some iron, the Doctor will order a blood test and then say, "I found by your blood test you're anemic; you need some iron." And that'll cost $75 for a blood test and $150 for the Doctor to tell him what I'll already have told him.

That's one of the best things about Veterinanians; their patients can't talk so they don't get any hints as to what's wrong, they have to find out cold turkey. And the bill for the cold turkey diagnosis is usually less money because the dog or horse don't have any Medicare or supplemental insurance. However, I wouldn't be surprised to see some goofy politician pass a bill to give animals over a certain age some form of Medicare. That would of course, open the door for some insurance company to follow through with an Animal Medicare Supplement. I can see it now, Senate Bill #K-9 Medic introduced by Congressman Rhot Wiler.

Talking about insurance and stuff, when I enter the house Snooks says, "We just got a letter from that outfit where we bought our washer, dryer and microwave. They want to know if we want to extend our warranty insurance one year more. It's only an additional $125."

I say "Snooks, just write right across it in big bold letters, **"If your stuff was any damn good you wouldn't be so concerned about Warrantees running out."**

Snooks says, "Well, if you want to say a thing like that you just go right ahead, but I'm certainly not going to lower myself to a statement like that."

"All right Snooks, then just leave it on my desk and I'll do it; after all, I'm not bashful. I'll even mail it, I have some other things to get out. Do you want to ride down to the post office with me?" Snooks tells me she can't. She's right in the middle of making frosting for a cake.

When I return from the post office, Snooks wants to know exactly what I wrote about the extended insurance? I tell her "Snooks, I wrote exactly what I told you to write, and then I signed your name."

Talk about a short fuse! This one is about a tenth of one-half of a light second! Snooks explodes as if I had done her bodily harm of a criminal nature. "WHAT DO YOU MEAN YOU SIGNED MY NAME?!?"

"Snooks, Snooks, I don't think this is something to fling frosting all around the kitchen over. I just didn't see any harm in a little thing like that, and besides I doubt if you'll ever see any of those people. It's no big deal. I think you're having a PMS over-reaction."

"No Toad! You think you're so smart. You always have to bring up PMS. It's just that you can't be trusted alone to butter a piece of toast! I never know what in God's name to expect from you. This is a real low blow; how could you have the nerve, the audacity to sign my name to a piece of filth like that?"

There are times when a fellow semi-innocently gets in a mess, and he should learn that those are not the times to ever mention anything that will further agitate the female recipient. The one thing at a time like this NOT to mention is PMS, even though it might be true. Although I am aware of this, there are times I just don't follow the rules of the game. This will probably produce a week of silence.....that is, if I'm lucky. She has other ways of long-term punishment.

The next morning Nancy shows up and as soon as she arrives everybody is happy, giggling and smiling again. They pour themselves a little round of tea and I can see they are all excited. As I walk away into another room I can pick up bits and pieces of their conversation. One thing for sure, I hear Nancy tell Snooks that Norman is onto something really big. He wouldn't talk about it, but told Nancy he would be working a lot of nights for quite some time. AH HA!! Boy, have we got him in the palms of our hands. He swallowed the bait hook, line and sinker. I also hear them mentioning something about some dishes, then they giggle and Snooks hollers to me that she and Nancy have to be leaving as they have a 10 o'clock appointment downtown at the museum basement annex.

I don't know what they have up their sleeves, all I know is it's exciting to them. Probably some more dishes for Snooks, she has a mania for those fool things.

Never can understand about dishes, you don't need place settings for eight of everything when there's only two of you; two people can only eat off two plates. You might need enough for four people, but you sure don't need eight or more. The simple solution to that is.....never invite more than one couple at a time!

Also, all those fancy little cute designs around the edges of the dishes don't make the food taste any better. Matter of fact, the best meal I ever had was fresh, camp-prepared venison tenderloin and greasy, fried potatoes on an old beat-up tin plate, followed by exceptional camp coffee (including grounds) out of a sloshed-out, lable-removed, baked bean can. Now that's living! and flavors I'll never forget.

Women just don't understand it just ain't the dishes that makes the meal and adds the flavor; plain and simple, it's the cooking.

After the gals leave, I pour myself another cup of coffee and sit a spell to meditate all the strange goings on of the last several weeks, when John shows up. By the time he gets in the house I have his tea poured from Snooks' left-over pot, and can hardly wait to tell him the good news about Nugent putting in all those nights over a big deal. This really makes us feel good, real good. It just couldn't happen to a better person.

The phone rings. It's Doc Prickelhaupter and we can stop by and pick up the gromafraw analysis. We head down there, checkbook in hand, ready to get this important bit of information. When we arrive, Whiny Mouth sends us right in and Doc hands us an envelope and we pay him another $110 which is the balance due. Prickelhaupter says it's a complete chemical analysis and he's pleased they could get it so quickly for us.

We are so excited we just thank him and head home to take a look and find out just exactly what we have. At last the answer, the truth! My hands are shaking so bad I can't open the envelope and I hand it to Johnny. After some fumbling around he at last takes a peek and says, "WHAT IN HELL IS THIS STUFF? WE PAID HIM FOR THIS?" I take a look and it's just a whole bunch of words that don't mean nothing, nothing at all to us, words like: 5cc.amino acids, 3.8cc.tri tetra bromide, 6cc.sulfur dioxide, 10cc.hydrogen sulfide; not one word that tells us how to make it.

I tell Johnny that we got exactly what we ordered - a chemical analysis. We done did it to ourselves. Johnny gets on the phone and calls Prickelhaupter and explains that this is what we ordered not knowing any better, but is there anyway to say, break this down to show what common, garden-variety ingredients are in it so we can make the gromafraw juice up ourselves?

Doc says we should have been more specific. After all, we got what we ordered; but fortunately for a mere $50 more, they can break it down to plain down-on-the-farm type ingredients. He can have it ready in two days; he'll call us.

Boy, are we upset! All that money for something we can't read a word of, but at last we're going to get it right so we can make the juice ourselves, and that's really the bottom line. A bad set-back but not a total loss. It could have been worse, I guess. Johnny says, "Cheer up, Toad. After all, it's only money."

I say, "Yeah Johnny, but it's OUR money, that's what hurts."

We decide to spend another day on the river and get away from all these trials and tribulations. Johnny remarks, "It should be nice now that Nugent is so busy working nights. At least we won't have to worry about being spied on. I'll see you in the morning about 10; it's a late tide tomorrow."

Again the women head out by nine o'clock and just say they have eggs to lay, cookies to crumble, and mops to flop.....whatever that means.

Johnny picks me up on time as always. I'm glad because I detest

177

tardiness; I just don't see any reason for being late. Some people are always late. If a fellow dates a girl and she's always late for a date, that's the time to drop her, because you will never change her, it's just part of an inbred trait. I knew a gal once who figured if you had a dinner engagement 40 miles away, being on time meant leaving her house at the time she was supposed to arrive for dinner! She figured being late just didn't exist. It doesn't bother the person who's always late, but if they're with someone who prides himself on always being on time, they can have that person banging on the door to the loony bin.

Johnny and I arrive at the boat ramp and Shorty is there. We ask him if he's seen anything of Nugent lately and he says, "No, not for a couple weeks, normally he stops by every day or two." Yep, we've got him working nights for sure. AH HA!

We head up to our fishing spot and get everything ready; bait up, cast out and settle back for a nice day of Sturgeon fishin'. I think it's going to be hot today, the sun is already plenty warm. We land three fish in the first hour and they're all too small. Then I finally hook a nice one. We throw the anchor float and follow the fish. This one feels like it's going to be close, as to being a keeper, or a wee bit too big, like maybe over six feet.

Yeah, it's a warm day all right, that's one advantage the fish has. At least he's keeping cool down in the river water. I'm really working up a sweat. Sometimes a big fish is more like work than pleasure, particulatly under the blazing sun. I'm beginning to think I may have underestimated this one, it seems to be getting stronger with time or I'm getting weaker from dehydration under this hot sun.

Johnny says "Toad, you wouldn't be starting to weaken a little, would you? After all, you've only been at it an hour. Let's land this one and get back to normal fishing; or has it really got the best of you?"

"Well Johnny, I wouldn't say he's got the best of me, but at the moment I'm just not sure who's got who! I gain two inches and he runs off six feet. It's just a show of defiance but if he keeps showing me defiance like this, I doubt if I can out-defiance him, when my defiance comes in inches and his comes in feet."

Thirty minutes later, and I might add just about the time I think I might have to order a new back and pair of arms, I see the tell-tale bubbles and realize without any communication between us, that the fish is just as tired as I am, maybe even a little more. Ten more minutes and we finally get a look. This is an awesome sight! About ten feet of mean, stubborn, alligator temperament and looks. I have won! But secretly, I'm pleased to release it. Number one, it's not legal, and number two, we don't need the meat; yet we've sure had the fun.

Talking about fun, when the fish get that big, it's no longer fun.....it's work! I don't know how long it will take that fish to rest up and get back to normal, but I'm darn sure I'll be a while; like maybe next October. Right now I feel like I'm 95 and may not live long enough to ever recover. I ask Johnny if he would mind lifting the tab off a cold beer for me, I just don't have the strength right now.

"Boy," he says "you are in bad shape! What would you do if I wasn't here?"

"Johnny, I would just die of thirst, I guess.

"I can tell you one thing my friend, you better be in pretty good shape before you tackle these babies. Before next season I'm going to spend some time pumping iron. A guy needs every advantage he can get. One thing for sure, you can't tell the size of the fish by the size of the bite. That one bit like a marshmallow-mouthed, sick, sand dab! If I hadn't been watching real close, I could have missed that bite all together.

"I'm going to take the rest of the afternoon off, but let's go see if maybe we can get you connected up with a decent legal fish before we call it a day."

I don't understand why most big fish always seem to head up-river after they're hooked, unless it's to go with the current, which on an incoming tide is up-river. Johnny feels that is the reason. This fish took us about 400 yards up-river. Some day we'll have to fish an

179

outgoing tide and see what happens then.

After fishing another three hours, Johnny catches four more too small and one probably big enough but it just came unhooked after about twenty minutes. So today we go home empty-handed but a little wiser, and for me a few more sore muscles in the morning, I'm sure.

Johnny says, "You know Toad, we'd probably not be going home skunked if you hadn't been too scared to put a bait back in the water. I never saw a fish get the best of you before, or is your old age just ketchin' up with you?"

I listen to this line of ridicule all the way home, and I'm not going to say a thing until John gets one of those two- or three-hour battles on his hands. And I sure hope it's on a hot day like this, too! He's never battled one that big for that long, and he just doesn't know. He reminds me of politicians running for office. They're always telling us what great things they are going to do for us, but they really don't know, 'cause they haven't been there yet. John's time will come and I sure hope I'm there when it does.

Right now I feel like choking him, but I'm sure my hands are so weak and tired that I doubt if I could even make his eyes bug out.

As we drive into town Johnny realizes he has pushed me pretty far and says he thinks he won't come in, he'll just put the boat away and call it a day, but as we head down our street I see a car parked by our house that sure isn't one I recognize.

We pull up in front and John says, "Holy Cow! You must have some pretty rich friends or relatives. That's one of those little Mercedes Benz Roadsters. You don't find any of those as prizes in a Cracker Jack box."

"You're right, John. Hey, you better change your mind and come in and help me unravel this one."

As we enter the house, there sit Snooks and Nancy, each having a rum cola and obviously in the midst of some sort of celebration. "Snooks," I say "where's the people who own that little silver rig sitting out in front of the house? It doesn't belong to anybody I know,

180

because I don't fraternize with anybody in that monetary bracket.'

Nancy starts to giggle as Snooks replies, "Well Toad, for your information that 'rig,' as you call it, is a 1964 Mercedes-Benz 230 SL Roadster."

Here's Snooks with that smart-mouth attitude again. But I have a feeling she's in way over her head on this one.

I say "Snooks, I know pretty well what it is. The next thing I want to know is: where did it come from and who is the owner?"

Snooks puts her glass down with an authoritative thunk, reaches in her purse and pulls out a slip of paper, waves it around in front of her and says, "You want answers, Toad? Well, feast your peepers on this little O-ficial document." The smart mouth is getting smarter all the time, and before I even look at the paper, I have a sinking feeling what I'll find.

I take a look and it's a clear title with Snooks' full name in big bold letters. There ain't no doubt the car belongs to Snooks. "HOLY SMOKERUNY!" I say, and hand the paper to Johnny. I'm afraid to continue the conversation, because there is no way in God's world we can afford that car and I sure know it wasn't a gift! Snooks has bought herself a car! What would ever possess her to do such a thing? Maybe Nugent did put Nancy up to trying to break us like Johnny suggested some time ago. Yeah, that's got to be it. I knew this cosy little friendship would be our ruination.

I say, "Snooks, would you mind making me a double of whatever that is you have in your glass and th—,"

Johnny interrupts and says, "Please make that two, Snooks. I think I need one too. Holy Moley!"

I continue, "And then will you please sit a spell and tell us exactly how you managed a deal like this without money or brains?"

Snooks gets a silly little grin on her face, partly smart mouth and partly rum cola, somehow her appearance sort of reminds me of the look on the cat's face when it swallowed the mouse. She gets up, moseys over to the mixin's and ice bucket, makes two doubles, sweetens her own and Nancy's drinks, delivers them all and sits back down, ready to unravel a story that I hope will solve this mystery.

Snooks starts out with, "You remember that set of dishes, one hundred and ninety one pieces to be exact, that I bought at the antique store? You tried so hard to find out what I paid for them, and I might add, to no avail. Well, they had a little insignia on the bottom of each piece, and I got curious. So Nancy and I began to research everything on the Internet and any reference books on old china, etc.

"We finally found that they seemed to be part of a missing set of dishes ordered by President Rutherford B. Hayes! They were designed by Theodore Davis, a well-known artist of that time. For years the whereabouts of this set has been a mystery. A museum employee who knew about our search, called Mrs. Catie Crabtree Crocket, who's a noted authority on old china. She authenticated their origin and put us in touch with the Smithsonian who offered to buy them, and as they say, made me an offer I couldn't refuse!"

I have to admit, I'm surprised and a bit stunned. I say "All right Snooks, that's fine; but the car, what about the car?"

"You want to know about the car? I saw it down on Pat Phluckinger's used car lot. And for over a month, every time Nancy and I would drive by while checking on this big dishes deal, I'd tell Nancy I'd give a whole bunch to have that car for my very own, but I knew it was just a dream.

"When the sale of the dishes began to fall in place, we just stopped by the car lot one day out of curiosity, and Pat himself was there. So I said to him, just joking, 'Pat, that thing's been sitting there for over a month, and I doubt if it will ever move at that price. If you put a new set of tires on it, and knock five thousand off the sticker price, I just might be interested. I'd pay cash, of course.'

"He said 'What's wrong with you Snooks? You gotta be joking! Do you think I'd even consider a deal like that? That car is a real classic!'

"I just smiled and said, 'Pat, I didn't mean to insult you, but you just sharpen your pencil and think about it. My number's in the book.'

"Well, four days later Pat called and he was almost crying. He said I'd caught him at quarterly tax time and he was a little low on cash; and that he'd really be taking a terrible loss, but he'd have to accept my offer.

"In the meantime, the Smithsonian picked up the dishes and gave me a nice check which would cover everything. So I got my dream car sort of by accident."

"Snooks," I say, "that's all well and good, but what did the car actually cost?"

Snooks replies, "Three-hundred-seventy-five dollars."

"Snooks," I repeat, "what did the car cost?"

"I just told you, Toad. That's what I originally paid for those dishes; and that's really all I had in it. The rest was just luck and brains."

"Snooks, it is just impossible to get a Mercedes Benz Roadster f— o—,"

Snooks breaks in and says, "Yes, and with a pagoda roof no less, AND a new set of tires. Honey, that's not a 'MERCEDES Benz.' From now on, that's MY little Benz; my pride and joy."

Snooks reminds me I'd made a statement a few minutes earlier that I wondered how she managed this without money or brains and she thought she might admit to no money, but she really resented the crack about no brains, because any way you look at it, it took a lot of brains.

I have to apologize for the brain part of that statement. What she did was a pretty shrewd bit of wheeling and dealing all right.

I'm glad this is all out in the open and explained. I couldn't handle all that secrecy much longer. I also know I'm never, ever going to know the actual price of that car. I'm even more glad Nancy doesn't know what I've been thinking.

Nancy tells us it's time for her to leave and get Norman's lunch ready for night patrol and Johnny says he must leave also. After they're gone, I look at Snooks, get up and give her a big hug and tell her, "Snooks, I'm proud of you, you done good."

# 15

## Our Itchy Dilemma

While Snooks and I are having our morning coffee and a butterhorn, she tells me, "Honey, every day Yoko asks when you two guys are going to take Itchy fishing. It gets a little embarrassing to keep making excuses. I know you really don't want to take him, but I'm sick and tired of alibing for you any longer, and I refuse to continue side-stepping an issue that really is going to have to be settled sooner or later."

"Snooks, we'll have to wait now until the next string of good tides, unless we go at night, and I can't think of anything worse than a total non-fisherman, out for montstrous fish on his first trip, in the total blackness of night.....with a fish cop hiding in the bushes just waiting for a chance to make our lives miserable."

Johnny shows up and Snooks pours him his tea, and then she starts on poor John about us taking Itchy fishing.

The phone rings and when I answer it some gal calls me by name and says first thing, "How are you today?"

I tell her "I'm fine; but anybody who starts the conversation concerned about my health really wants to sell me something. Just what is it you're selling?"

She tells me, "Bottled water."

I tell her, "Thanks, but we have a faucet." She hangs up.

I say to Johnny, "Have you ever noticed when they start right off asking about your health, they're always going to try to sell you something?" Johnny says he's never given it a thought before, but he thinks I'm probably right.

Phone rings again and this time it's the Chemical outfit and they have broken down our gromafraw into what they call a simple, non-chemical evaluation. I tell Johnny and he's ready to go and I'm sure glad, because I need some time to think about how to handle this Itchy fishing trip that keeps rearing it's ugly head every few days.

First thing at the Wonder What? Chemical Company we pay our additional fifty bucks to Whiny Mouth, pick up our evaluation without ever seeing Doc Prickelhaupter at all. But this time, we take a peek before we leave just to make sure we can understand it, and we can. It's amazing what's in it! There is no doubt the original recipe came from the Tar Heels themselves. It reads like this:

5 Tbs.————Anise oil
1 Cup————Puree of raw shrimp
1 Tsp.————Concentrated skunk scent
8 Tbs.————Powdered green bread mold
1 Cup————Puree of sockeye salmon eggs
1 Tsp.————Snuff
1 Cup————Stale beer.

Seems like a lot to have to pay for a bunch of leftovers, but on the other hand it shore do work! We run downtown and get two copies made, one for each of us and the original will go in the safety deposit box.

On the way back home I tell Johnny, "We have a real serious dilemma that just can't be side stepped any longer. We are going to have to take Itchy fishing some day and soon."

Johnny asks, "Has he ever fished at all?"

"I don't think so, Johnny. I feel the only thing he knows about fishing is what his father taught him and that was all from old-country Japan. All Itchy really knows about it gardening."

Johnny says, "Well, if he's as neat in our boat as he is with his garden, he shouldn't be much trouble. I just can't stand to see the way some of these people mess up their boats. Some of them even throw the fish right on the deck! don't use a fish box, sometimes don't even have one! Can you imagine that? They make their boat stink and smell just like a hog pen! I'm sorry, but for me to enjoy fishing, I have to have a clean, organized boat. If you notice the people who get in serious troubles, like cuts and imbedded hooks, are people who always have sloppy, messy boats."

"John, I doubt if that will be our problem. It'll be more trying to keep him out of trouble because he won't listen. He's so eager to want to be a part of everything. You know how people who want to help, but don't know anything, can get in the way. I think that will be more our trouble. Sort of like trying to babysit a wild, four-year old with a box of matches in a firecracker factory."

I tell Johnny I'll get in touch with Itchy and make a date for him to go with us. In the meantime, and since Johnny is talking about it, we've only cleaned the boat out real good once since we bought it. Not that it's real dirty, but if you don't keep at them they can get pretty bad, pretty quick. It's either clean the boat or go night fishing. Personally, I'd rather just leave the whole night time program up to Nugent.....alone.....by himself.

When we get back to the house Nancy and Snooks have taken off for a spin in her little Benz, as she calls it. I'm still curious as to just how much moola she had to put out for that little beauty. Johnny says to wait until she licenses it next time and I can get a pretty good idea from the amount of excise tax she has to pay; it's based on car value.

Sometimes Johnny surprises me with his novel yet practical ideas. He must read a lot to always know so much. I notice readers and cross-word puzzle workers always know more trivia or just junk than other people.

We pick up the boat and set it in the back yard where it's near to water and handy to everything, and we tie into a first-class afternoon of spit and polish. Even then it looks like another half day's work, at least.

The women drive up and ask if we can help them remove the top. They would like to be real sporty and drive around in the sunshine and warm breeze for awhile. Breezes and sunshine? All they really want is to show off the new car.

I guess I can't blame them, we feel the same way about our boat. It's what you call pride of ownership. It shows up every time somebody's got something better than the first guy, and it can vary from owning a football team to possessing the gromafraw.

We decide to call it a day and finish our clean-up tomorrow. Johnny comes in for a short gin and tonic before he goes home. While we're relaxing and enjoying a little bull session, who pops in but Itchy?

We offer him a drink but he tells us "Onee one dwink good for Japanese; that is sake. I no have dwink, but maybe some tea?" Well, there's some left-over tea from morning so we give him that, and he has the gall to tell us "You not so good at make tea, not like Snookah." What he doesn't know is that 'Snookah' made it early this morning; he just has no taste for tea that has aged. He's just too fussy about his tea that's for sure. It's too bad when a person becomes so specialized in his taste, that he no longer can enjoy the good old run-of-the-mill stuff.

While Itchy is tea sippin' I can see he really wants to say something to us, but hasn't quite figured out how to come out with it. He's probably afraid he might botch it up and miss his chance. I say, "Itchy, you sorty look like you got something on your mind, do you want to tell us about it?"

This is the chance Itchy has hoped for, and waited for, and he blurts out, "You guys fish wots now. Maybe one time you have woom take Itchy and ketch b-i-g one! I be no twouboe."

"Itchy, as a matter of fact we were just talking about how pleased we would be to have you go fishing with us; but you probably can only go once because you have to get a temporary license, and that's not good for very long. The real license for a whole season is way too expensive, when you probably only go once."

"What I need? Bwing wunch? Need wod? When we go? How soon? Oh boy, oh boy, Itchy happy, you betcha!"

I say, "Now Itchy, just put your eye balls back in your skull, and we'll cover these things one at a time.

187

"It'll be a week before the tides are good again and wh—e—"

Itchy breaks in and asks "What you mean 'tide?' What ah tide stuff?"

I tell him, "The river water goes up and down twice a day because the moon is after it."

Itchy nods and says, "Ahwedy Itchy undahstan. Moon chase watah. Evah catch watah? How can moon chase watah when Itchy no see moon; it hide in sky sometime, what about when hide in cwowds?"

"Johnny, I have to go pee. Will you please go ahead and answer this last question for him?"

I don't have to pee, I just go out in the kitchen and pour another shot of gin in my glass; I need time to think. I hope John is not in as much trouble as I was, but I'm sure he is. I think we've already bit off more than we can chew.

Itchy is just like a four-year old, and anybody knows no matter how intelligent you are, a four-year old can tie you up in five minutes with a question that's impossible to answer. I don't know why it is or what it is, but four-year olds have a knack of making anyone feel pretty stupid. Normally, it doesn't take them long either. A little older or a little younger is never a problem. "Four" seems to be the magic number.

When I go back, Johnny is all red-faced and flustered, and Itchy has a very quizzical look on his face. Johnny says, "We'll talk more about that some other time, Itchy."

We tell him all he need worry about is a temporary Sturgeon license and his lunch, everything else we will bring, that's all he'll need.....period. As far as clothes, just dress like anybody would on a boat depending on what kind of weather we have. That's all, he doesn't need to worry about another thing. We'll let him know far enough ahead, but it will be sometime next week.

Itchy heads for home, happy as a kid on the last day of school.

The phone rings and it's Weasel. He tells me he found out that Cora Cogger, or Whiny Mouth the receptionist, at the Wonder What?

Chemical Company, is the sister of Clutia Cladwaller who is married to Chick Cladwaller, the owner of the Chemical Company. I ask Weasel to repeat that to Johnny. After all, I've got ten bucks riding on this little deal. After Johnny talks to Weasel he grins, pulls out his wallet and pays me ten bucks and says, "Boy, you sure had that one figured right. I guess when you think about it though, it had to be a forced issue rather than a choice issue, with a non-plus person in a plus-person job."

Snooks comes home about ten minutes after Johnny leaves. She has dropped Nancy off at her place. I ask Snooks if she doesn't think things have quieted down enough maybe she could take me for a spin in her little Benz. I offer to buy dinner at the El Toro.

I have to shower and change clothes after cleaning the boat, which takes about thirty minutes and we're on our way. This is one smooth-riding auto. I wonder to myself if I'll ever get to drive it?

At the restaurant, we start out with a big Margarita apiece and a quesadillas. By the time we finish that, we decide we're already full and don't need dinner. Back home we go and call it a day.

As I turn out the light I say to Snooks, "Honey, do you know what excise tax is? What is an 'excise' anyway? You have 'gas' tax, 'liquor' tax and all sorts of taxes, but just what is an 'excise?' Myself, I don't recall ever seeing one."

Snooks groans and replies, "Toad, I wish you'd say these things during the day instead of giving me something to ponder all night long. Why do you think this stuff up always at bed time?"

Johnny shows up while Snooks and I are on our morning coffee and about the same time Yoko drops in. Snooks and I have coffee and John and Yoko have tea. Johnny asks Yoko, "Where's Itchy this morning?"

Yoko says, "Oh, he one happy man to go fish foah big fish on boat. He go down to woah su'plus stoah to pick up sometings he need foah fish twip."

We tell her, "Yoko, he won't need anything but a temporary Sturgeon license and his lunch."

189

Smiling, Yoko says "I fix Itchy nice wunch; put in some tweats foah you fewoes awso."

"That sure isn't necessary, Yoko, but it would be nice. We thank you ahead of time for the nice thought."

Johnny and I leave the two women and head back outside to finish our job cleaning the boat. We thought we were pretty clean, but even so things get misplaced and soiled just with normal everyday use. The boat needed more attention than we thought and it takes the better part of another day.

Itchy comes over about the time we're through and wants to help clean up the boat, but we tell him we're nearly through and we only have room for two people working in the boat at one time. We ask him what he had to pick up at the war surplus store that he'll need for the fishing trip? He just gives us a smile so big that his eyes squint right up to where he can't see, and says, "I got big fishing twip su'pwise. No tell anybody; big su'pwise."

We finish up and head in for a glass of nice cold lemonade with Snooks. The boat is all spick and span and ready to go. Johnny says, "I wonder what Itchy's got up his sleeve and what his big surprise will be?"

"Johnny, I have no idea; but when Itchy does these things, I get about as nervous as a bee caught away from the hive in a hail storm."

We finally decide that tide, weather and everything look about right for Tuesday morning and we'll take Itchy for his day afloat then. I tell Johnny I'll let him know.

I ask John, "What rod should we fix up for him? After all we don't want to take a chance on one of our new expensive ones."

Johnny says he has an old black Harnell that he's had for years, a beauty, should be just right for a person of small stature who has no experience. It's one tough rod and it can really take punishment.

Snooks says Yoko told her that Itchy is so excited he isn't even sleeping well at night, just tells her he is catching big fish all night long. I sure hope we can get him into a nice fish. It would be the highlight of his whole year, I think.

When Johnny goes home, I call Itchy and tell him to be over at our house Tuesday morning by 8:30 and ready to go, because we're going fishing for sure. When I hang up Snooks asks me what the big smile is for, and I tell her "I just can't help it. When I talked to Itchy, he got so all-fired excited, you'd think he just won the lottery."

Everything coasts along pretty much normal until Tuesday morning. Johnny shows up with the boat in tow and right on time here comes Itchy. Johnny takes one look and says, "My God, Toad! Do you see what I see coming out of Itchy's house? What is it?"

I say "Johnny, I'm not sure, but by the look of things, I think Itchy has joined the Japanese Imperial Navy!" Johnny asks if we'll really have to take him out in public in front of everybody looking like that? I tell him I'm afraid we will.

As I watch Itchy approach - dressed in full Navy dress whites, with a chest full of medals - I remember hearing that his uncle was an Admiral in the Japanese Imperial Navy. Of course Itchy would want to wear that special uniform; and come to think of it, he's done exactly what I told him to do, "just dress like anybody would on a boat." And last, but not least, he has a Japanese officer's sword and one of those funny looking sideways Admiral hats. He looks like he's ready to board the Missouri to surrender; only difference is he looks far too happy.

Yoko comes with him. They act like he's going on a battle cruiser for an extended six-month stay. She's as excited as he is; is carrying a sea-type duffel bag, and has his lunch in a little round wicker Japanese basket sort of thing. We can't begin to imagine what will be in the duffel bag.

I could sort of expect a woman to bring a duffel bag; after all, the most important thing to a woman is not if she's going to catch fish but will she get sunburned? Or how many mosquitoes and bugs will there be? Will she have to touch worms and bait her own hook? And of course, how does she look? Is her hair all right? Is the eye make up going to run in the rain? In the heat? Does she look cute in her hat?

I'm always amazed at women's attitudes. You'd think they were trying to seduce the fish! But I never saw a fish that cared or knew the difference anyway.

As Yoko and Itchy finally near the boat, Yoko is beaming all over and says, "My Itchy wook handsome in uncle fishing cwoes, and he buy sword at woah su'pwus wast week! I fix nice wunch for Itchy and put extwa tweats foah evahbody."

I say "Yoko, he looks real swave, but tell me, what is he going to need that sword for just to go fishing?"

Itchy answers back, "Membah I say to you, Itchy have big su'pwise? I buy soad to cwean big fish when we ketch 'em." Johnny looks at me and rolls his eyes. Yep, this is really going to be a day to remember all right.

The kisses and hugs that go between Itchy and Yoko! You'd think he was going on six months sea duty without sight of land! At last we load up everything, and hope in all the confusion we haven't left anything behind, confusion can screw up the best-laid plans.

Itchy crawls in the back seat and immediately runs into a problem, he's shut the car door on his sword which didn't seem to follow him all the way into the car. After several minutes of door slamming, and I presume Japanese profanity, we finally get everything in and settled, and take off.

We don't go two miles when Itchy hollers, "Man in nex cah want's visit us. He fwendwy and waving and pointing." We tell Itchy it's nothing at all; it's the cup on top of the motor, someone wants to warn us that it might fall off and we'll lose it. Itchy is very curious as to why the cup is there and we spend considerable time explaining, but can tell we really never get the message across to Itchy's satisfaction. Sorta like the tide business.

My greatest fear is that we'll have to expose him to public view in that outlandish get-up he's wearing. If we're real lucky, we can get by everybody but the boat-launch fishermen; that's one place we just have to be, and of course, the one we'd most like to avoid.

As we drive along, I see Itchy's funny Japanese admiral hat is brushing the roof of the car and so ask him if he wouldn't be more comfortable if he took it off? Itchy answers "Oh no, it paht of my fishing cwoes and I feah bettah since I go fish to weave it on. Compweet outfit wook bettah."

Just to carry on a conversation with Itchy and try to make him feel comfortable and relaxed I say, "Now Itchy is ready to go fishing. He has his fishing uniform and his temporary license and his lunch. Itchy is really ready to fish."

Itchy gets a funny look on his face about the same as a kid who's just tasted castor oil for the first time. He shouts out, "HOWEE HIWOSHIMA! In ah da excitement I get wapped up in fishing cwoes and fohget about dat tempowawy wicense."

I tell Itchy not to worry, then ask John if he knows of any little out-of-the-way place we can stop and get Itchy's license for him? I'd do almost anything to keep him out of the bait shop and public eye, particularly where those public eyes know Johnny and me.

Johnny thinks maybe Blinky's Hardware on the Mall in the next little town will do. I ask him "Can't you find some place a little more out of the way than a Mall?"

"Actually, there is no Mall," Johnny says. "They just call two or three old buildings the Mall, and two of the buildings aren't even rented. The whole town only has two hundred people. I've never seen over three people in the hardware at any one time, and most often two of them are clerks. Ten people in there at once and you'd think they were having a summer give-away special! I'm quite sure they sell fishing licenses, at least they did four years ago."

It's only a mile off the beaten path to Blinky's Hardware on the Mall, which, after Johnny describes it, sounds just perfect. When we get there Itchy says, "Boy, we wucky to find wicense pwace so quick. Now I get tempowawy wicense and be okey-dokey to fish."

Johnny says, "Itchy, you just stay in the car till I go in and make sure they do sell fishing licenses." Johnny checks and comes out with a big smile and says they do sell them, and there are no other customers right now, so Itchy can get waited on right away. I'm sure

John said that more for my benefit than Itchy's. We decide we better go in with him just in case he needs any help.

After staring at Itchy in stunned amazement, the first thing the clerk wants to know is what kind of fishing license Itchy wants? We tell the clerk he wants a Sturgeon license. Itchy pipes up and says, "You betcha Itchy need tempowawy wicense." The clerk asks Itchy why he doesn't get a full-year license, it's only three dollars more and would be a lot cheaper in the long fun! I can see Itchy is pondering this.

Just thinking about a repeat performance of this morning, ties my stomach up in collywobble cramps. This is a terrible spot to be in. I hesitate long enough to see if Johnny can come up with a quick answer.....but he doesn't. However, he does ask Itchy a question about his birthplace and while he has diverted Itchy's attention, I grab the opportunity. I've got to be real swave and in a hurry too. I tell the clerk "Just visiting."

The clerk then gets out the temporary license book and prepares to fill it out saying to Itchy, "Yes, in your case a temporary license would be best." Itchy doesn't question this and we are saved from, I feel, a near brush with future fishing catastrophes unparalleled in the history of Sturgeon fishing.

The first two or three questions go along pretty well; name and place of birth. Then he asks Itchy his age. Well, Itchy has side-stepped this question as long as I've known him. He says, "Age not impo'tant. I heah now, dat what impo'tant." He will not tell the clerk how old he is; he just keeps saying "In Japan nobody ask, nobody keep twack."

I step in and tell the clerk, "Don't make an international situation out of this. Just take a guess and put it down." The clerk is upset by now and says he can't do that as all Orientals look the same to him, and they don't show their age. The clerk says he could be anywhere from thirty to seventy, and he can't even guess. I tell him to put down fifty-five and we'll take a chance that's sort of in the middle. If we can't guess any closer, nobody else can either. The clerk accepts this logic and continues.

This whole process should have taken ten minutes, but in Itchy's case we're close to half an hour, but it's finally finished to everybody's satisfaction, and we're on our way again. Next stop - bait shop.

On the way out of the hardware store I get signals across for Johnny to go in and get the bait and I'll stay in the car and keep the little admiral out of sight and possibly trouble. When we get to the bait shop Johnny says, "I'll go get the bait. It'll only take a minute."

Itchy says, "I wike go see bait shop, too." But I tell him we never both go in, it's just too crowded and they don't like too many people in there at one time; it just leads to thefts. So again he listens and we save another exposure of Japanese Admiral Itchy.

Everything goes fine until we arrive at the boat launch and of course Itchy is out and watching every move. He just doesn't seem to want to miss a thing. Shorty hollers over and asks, "Where did you pick that up, Toad?"

I just laugh and holler back "Hitch hiking!"

Itchy right away thinks he should go over and get acquainted, but Johnny says, "No Itchy, we don't have time now. We have to get everything loaded and be on our way." We get by without much more than stares and grins, and those not nearly as bad as we had feared.

We hurry faster than normal to cut down on the length of time we have Itchy exposed in his fishing uniform. At last we put Itchy in the boat and back our rig down the ramp to launch; Johnny backing down the ramp, Itchy in the boat out of harm's way and me holding the rope tied to the boat to control it once it is off the trailer and in the water.

Everything goes smooth, the boat is afloat and all looks well. I have the rope to pull the boat back to shore so Johnny and I can board and get under way. I watch as Johnny drives the car and trailer over to the parking area. I'm in no hurry to pull the boat to shore until Johnny parks the car and is ready to board.

All at once Itchy, who is afloat in the boat, goes absolutely stark-raving crazy, but in Japanese! And I can't understand a word he's saying. But man! He is upset! He keeps looking down at his feet as he hollers. If we lived down in the south I'd swear there was an eight-foot water moccasin loose in there with him. Needless to say, I pull him to shore as fast as possible, which is nowhere near fast enough to suit Itchy. He's hollering and screaming all the way. When the boat is still six feet from shore Itchy jumps over the side into water clear over his knees and staggers and sloshes around headed for dry land. I finally get him by the jacket collar and holler at the top of my lungs, "TALK ENGLISH! TALK ENGLISH! WHAT IN HELL IS WRONG?"

Still obviously upset, Itchy finally says "You guys not my fwiends! You twy push Itchy out in deep watah and dwown him! I say to Yoko and Snookah you two vewy bad!" I look in the boat and Holy Mackerel! It's filling with water! When we cleaned it up we forgot to put the drain plug back in, and now we have about six-inch deep water all over the floor of the boat and gaining gallons buy the second. No wonder Itchy figures Buddha was ready to take him to the promised land.

While I'm trying to get Itchy calmed down, Johnny arrives on the double, jumps in the boat, puts the plug in it's proper place and turns on the bilge pump; thus diverting a possible overdose of moisture.

After about ten minutes we get both the boat drained and Itchy calmed down and we're ready to travel. Itchy is still watching us over his shoulder, as he's just not sure yet we hadn't intended to do him in. He says, "I not know why you shove Itchy out in deep watah in weaky sinky boat, 'wess you want to wiquidate him in wiquid suwwoundings. I need talk Snookah and Yoko."

Johnny says, "You know, I don't know why he got so all-fired excited over a thing like that. He was never more than fifteen feet from shore, you'd think he couldn't swim."

Very quietly I say, "John, he can't."

Johnny then says, "Well for heaven's sake, get a life jacket on him quick because the catastrophe odds are not in our favor today!"

196

We head on down to the fishing hole with Itchy standing up, facing into the breeze. Somehow very reminiscent of the pictures of Washington crossing the Delaware, only I doubt if Washington had on a fluffy, orange life jacket.

As we ease our way into our favorite spot Johnny hollers, "O.K.! Dump the anchor and float!" I look where the float and anchor are always stored and I'm just looking at bare planking——no anchor or float in sight.

I yell back to Johnny over the motor noise, "We don't have any anchor or float!"

Johnny yells back, "What did you say?"

"John," I shout, "we don't have the float and anchor! It just isn't here; it's not in the boat, it's gone! Gone, I say!"

Johnny says, "Yeah, I was afraid I heard that right the first time."

"Well, I'll dig the other one out and hook it to the regular steel airplane cable; only problem will be every time we hook a fish, we'll have to pull anchor to give chase, which is a nuisance after we've got used to the quick-release method.

"Here's the other one. It could be worse John, we could be without an anchor at all."

At last we anchor and are busy rigging all our tackle and getting everything ready to do some real serious fishing.

The next thing we hear is another blast of excited Japanese. While we've been getting everything ready, Itchy has become fascinated with the live sand shrimp and has put his fingers in the bait bucket, and of course, one of the shrimp has pinched Itchy's finger. He's more startled than hurt, but is wildly waving his arm over his head and loudly uttering numerous Japanese profanities, while the sand shrimp dangles firmly from his finger, hanging on with the tenacity of a baby bulldog. Johnny utters a mumbling phrase, something not quite audible about Itchy's hollering, but sounding like, "My God, give me a four-year old any day!" At least that's what it sounds like to me.

Before we get Itchy settled down he has jerked the sand shrimp

197

off, and his finger is bleeding about a half drop through a quarter-inch long scratch. Itchy insists on some iodine and a Band Aid out of our first aid kit. He tells us, "You could get bad disease fwom t'ing wike dat. You gotta be ca'efoe." So we dig out everything in or near the first aid kit, and get him protected with all kinds of salves, ointments and of course, a Band Aid. Another twenty minutes wasted.

We cast Itchy's bait out for him and hand him the rod to tend, then proceed to cast the other two baits, Johnny's and mine. Itchy asks, "What you call dat when you thwow bait out in watah?"

"Itchy," I answer, "that's called casting and we will do tha—t—fo—"

Itchy interrupts and says, "Dat casting wook wike weah fun, next time Itchy do dat."

Johnny says, "If you've never done it, it just isn't as easy as it looks, Itchy. Besides, we're more than glad to help you, we'll tend to most of the casting. It'll save time in the long run I'm sure." I'm just not sure all this sinks in with Itchy, but I hope so.

At last we settle down to fishing. Everything is go.

Johnny has a bottle of beer and Itchy decides he'd like one too, and reaches in his duffel bag and drags out a bottle of Japanese beer and of all things, a bag of potato chips to have with his beer.

If there is anything to mess a boat up quick, it seems to be potato chips. I don't know why, I guess it's because they're just fragile and break and crumble easy. Itchy is eating his potato chips and, I might add, breaking and dropping pieces all over. You'd think he could hear and feel them crunching under his feet, but no. He seems more engrossed in bragging about how much better Japanese beer is than weak, watery American beer.

Pretty soon Itchy says, "Ho boy, Yoko send awong tweat to go wit wunch and beah; I get us some now. I ahmos fo'get." Well, he brings out this quart jar of something that closely resembles raw fish in some kind of brine. Itchy takes off the lid and sets some out on a piece of foil and says "You guys twy Yoko's tweat, you wike much."

Johnny and I each reluctantly take a big piece; we would gladly have taken a small piece but there are no small pieces. Johnny says, "You know itchy, if I didn't know better, I'd swear it looks like raw fish and by golly, it tastes like raw f-i—s-."

Itchy says, "Johnny, you one smaht fedda! Is waw fish! Japanese sushi vewy good tweat fwom Yoko just fo' you guys." I swear this bite is suddenly enlarging with every chew and after a great deal of effort and one gagging gulp I manage to swallow it. But keeping it down may be a bigger problem.

Johnny is having trouble too, but not near as much as me. After all, the Swedes do eat pickled fish which actually is raw too, but not raw-raw like this raw, I'm sure. Worst of all, the jar is still almost full! God have mercy.

Johnny asks, "Itchy, what kind of fish is it made from?"

"It mostwy cahp, maybe some eoh."

Johnny says "I'm sure sorry Itchy, but you know I'm real allergic to carp. I break out in a bad rash and get double bi-lateral vision in both eyes."

"Ho boy," Itchy says, "dat too bad, but weave moah fo' Itchy."

I have to give old John credit, he does think fast in a tight situation.

I say "Itchy, did you say maybe eel? If there's even a chance there is any eel, why I'm going to have to pass, too. I get terrible cramps and bad diarrhea from eating eel. What a terrible shame, because this is very good and absolutely tasty, and was really a thoughtful treat from Yoko."

Itchy says "Yoko going to be weah unhappy. She fix tweat and you guys awergic, but it give Itchy ah he can eat!" At which point he dives right into the jar and downs three more pieces in about three minutes flat. I don't know how he can enjoy it, although I'm sure some of our problem has to be in our minds. Actually, it didn't start to become hard to chew until I found out it was raw fish. Johnny was lucky, he spit his over the side while Itchy wasn't looking. I had to swallow mine. I guess you can't win 'em all. Itchy is happy though and consumes half the jar of this rare Japanese treat by the time he finishes his beer.

Nobody's had a bite in twenty minutes and we all reel in and most of our bait is gone, but when it comes to re-baiting Itchy is glad to let us bait up for him. He says, "I not touch dose. No, no, dey bad for Itchy." Johnny has just started in on a sandwich and sets it aside to help bait up.

We put Itchy's bait on first, but make the mistake of baiting all outfits before we cast any of them, and while we're busy baiting Johnny's and mine, Itchy decides to try his luck casting. We look up from our task after hearing the sound of garbled Japanese mixed with the sound of a rapidly whirling reel spool.

Too late we find Itchy has not taken heed of our message about casting, and has just had to try his hand at this seemingly easy task; finding to his amazement and our chagrin that he is now the proud possessor of a monumental back-lash of line on his reel.

Itchy looks at it very puzzled and says, "Ho boy! Wat Itchy got now? How dis happen so fast? Wat you caw dis?"

Johnny answers, "A hellava mess."

I can see Johnny's outlook is beginning to wear a little thin around the edges. I say, "Itchy, that's called a back lash and that's why we told you not to try to cast."

Itchy answers, "It wook easy. Itchy on'y twy be big he'p."

Johnny doesn't say a word, but slowly shakes his head and I can see his jaw muscles tense every few seconds. Yep, Johnny is close to blowing a cork but he's doing his level best to ride out the storm. After a minute or two he says, "Toad, you cast those other two baits out, and I'll work on this snarl and see if there's any chance. If not, we'll just have to put on all new line. I'll give it a try and see; I usually have pretty good luck with these, but this is a real bad one."

After about ten minutes Johnny is interrupted by the screech and clatter of half a dozen sea gulls all fluttering around one that is sitting on a nearby piling. John looks up from the snarl of line and with a warm smile says, "I always like to listen to the racket of a bunch of sea gulls. They always sound so happy and seem to be calling others to come and share with them. I wonder what they've found to eat that's so interesting?"

Itchy pipes up and says, "One come and take Johnny's sandwich. Johnny wight, dey aw happy to sha'e it togeddah wit uddah happy bi'ds."

John looks where he had set his sandwich down and sure enough it's gone. One has snuck in and stolen it while John was busy. This further irritates Johnny and he just goes back to work on the snarled line, muttering, "Damned worthless, obnoxious, scavenger, nuisance birds! God should never have created them!"

Johnny continues, "That sandwich had a special imported hard Italian salami with a nice slice of Walla Walla sweet onion, some extra sharp cheddar, laced with a liberal amount of imported German limburger cheese on rye: a rare treat to waste on those miserable birds."

After half-an-hour John decides this snarl is one even too much for him and he begins to remove and replace the entire line; which takes an additional twenty minutes to cut the old line off and rewind new on the reel, but at last it's ready. Johnny baits it up, casts it out and hands it to Itchy with the comment, "Don't forget, we'll do the casting."

At last we're finally all fishing at the same time. Itchy then decides to have another beer and eat some fried rice from a carton, with chopsticks no less. Now a Japanese is about as clever with chopsticks as a hummingbird is with his flying, but an excited Japanese has a certain amount of dexterity error and Itchy's seems to be showing. He's dribbling little pieces of rice between the carton and his mouth. I'd say maybe a twenty-percent loss. Of course the loss is watched closely by Johnny and me as it dribbles, unnoticed by Itchy, to the floor among the crushed, ground-in pieces of potato chips.

Johnny says "Itchy, you ought to be pretty good with those chopsticks when you learn how to use them and what to use them on. I would think noodles, but never rice."

Itchy replies, "Itchy usuwy do weal good, but excitement and fishing make Itchy ne'vous and unsteady and he weal sowy." Itchy finishes his beer and rice and settles back to concentrate on serious fishing, but that only lasts probably ten minutes and he begins fidgeting around and gets worse by the minute. It seems even as excited as he is about fishing, his attention span is equal to that of about a three-year old.

Finally I ask him, "Itchy, what's the trouble?"

He says, "Itchy dwank two big bottoe of beah and now got to wee."

Johnny asks, "Toad, what did he say his trouble is, doesn't he like Japanese beer?"

"John, he has no trouble with the beer except now it has gone through him and he has to 'wee', he says."

Johnny says, "Oh pee. Well, tell him to 'wee' over the side, there's nobody around."

I tell Itchy to just wee over the side but he tells me he would just much rather have a bucket so he can turn his back because he is too bashful to wee in front of anybody. I get the pee bucket for Itchy, and Johnny and I turn our backs and we wait—and—wait—and—wait—some—more. After about five minutes I ask Itchy "Are you about through?"

Itchy is muttering something in Japanese, then says, "No, Itchy got bad pwobwem. Dis mo'ning I so excited about fishing twip I accidentwy put sho'ts on backwa'rds. Got no opening; can't find it. Got to go to shoah and take off cwoes and tu'n sho'ts awound so it wo'k."

Johnny asks, "Itchy, can't you do that right here in the boat?"

Itchy answers, "I go to shoah to wee anyhow 'cause can't make wo'k in fwont of peopoe even wit you tu'n awound. Itchy weo bashfo about wee, got to go to shoah and be awone and hide. Den Itchy be fine, tu'n sho'ts awound and can wee in pwivate okey-dokey."

Johnny never says a word, just shakes his head and starts vigorously reeling in his line. Itchy and I do the same; then Johnny hauls in the anchor just as vigorously. I can see he is about at the end of his rope; jaw muscles really working overtime.

I interrupt the silence and tell John that Nugent's hide-out will be the closest place to shore and should work fine for Itchy.

Johnny heads that way and as we let itchy go ashore, Johnny says, "Itchy, when you change your clothes why don't you leave the sword off? After all, we won't be cleaning fish until we catch some and even then we'll clean them at home. The sword is a little awkward getting around in a small boat, particularly when it isn't needed yet." I'm sure Johnny could have used a much less diplomatic way of approaching the sword situation, but I'll have to give him credit, he really controls himself well.

Itchy's answer to the sword suggestion is "Okey-dokey, but Itchy want to be weady when time come to cween fish, you know."

While Itchy is changing his clothes around and weeing, Johnny and I each open another beer and Johnny remarks that he has one more sandwich but he wants to make sure before he even thinks of starting it, that he's going to have a chance to finish it. I tell him this is probably the best chance he'll have. Johnny agrees and takes two or three bites; then we hear great thrashing and wallowing around in the brush, followed by a very excited Japanese battle cry "AHH HEEE!" then more loud Japanese phrases.

Johnny says, "My God! What can it be now? Sounds like he's killin' snakes!" I never knew that old John was a mind reader, but he shore as shootin' is, because out of the bushes comes Itchy, sword in one hand and a four-foot long, decapitated, black water snake held high overhead in the other hand.

With a big smile Itchy says, "Boy, wook what Itchy got! Swo'd weawy wo'k good; take home and have Yoko make nice batch of snake soup. Have you ovah fo' dinnah fo' weal wa'e Japanese tweat."

Well, I don't know about Johnny, but snakes are the one thing in the whole world that turn me instantly into a quivering, helpless, terrified moron. I holler at Itchy as I work my way to the farthest point in the bow of our small boat, wishing we had a battleship deck instead of a dinky sixteen-foot overall dinghy. I don't need to guess about Johnny, as he is crawling all over me, trying to eke out an extra foot of safe distance between us and the snake, using me as a sort of ladder.

I finally stutter and stammer out in a hoarse screeching croak to Itchy, to get rid of that slinky, crawly reptile critter as quick as he can or he will have to find his way home overland through the mire and muck of the muddy tide flats!

Itchy stops in his tracks, loses his smile and exuberance and asks, "You want Itchy thwow away wa'e tweat for Japanese soup?"

I yell "Yes, Itchy! If you're going to get back in this boat, GET RID OF IT NOW AND FOREVER!"

Johnny shouts "YES, Itchy. GET RID OF IT! Why don't you take it back and put it on that chair by the little table? Just sort of coil it up so it looks natural."

Boy, like I've said before, Johnny can think better and quicker under stress than anybody I ever knew. This is a real swave idea to say the least. I remark to Johnny, "This will be a rare treat for Nugent when he comes out on night patrol and sits down in the dark on the remains of that reptile. I'd give almost anything to see his reaction to that. HA!"

Johnny says, "Yeah, and Nugent would probably have enjoyed watching us spill our beer and scramble around on the now squished remains of my sandwich, while trying to flee in terror from Itchy's choice morsel. I guess I just wasn't destined to eat at all today."

Once Itchy gets rid of the snake we let him back in the boat and head back to our fishing spot. All together we have lost another forty minutes of fishing time before we're back to serious fishing.

Itchy is still muttering about the loss of a choice item for Yoko to make into soup.

Johnny says, "You know Toad, I don't think after that little episode that I would ever be able to have dinner out," and he points a hidden finger toward Itchy, "because you would never in God's name know what the bill-of-fare might be."

"Johnny, you have no idea how many times that very thought has gone through my mind at a dinner invitation. There were times I was glad I didn't know, but on the other hand a person's imagination can many times be worse than fact. But we seem to stay healthy so it can't be all bad, and the intentions are really wonderful. Most of the time so is the food, taste-wise, that is."

Johnny and I are just in the middle of a discussion as to why the fish aren't biting even with the gromafraw, when we're interrupted by Itchy whispering, "Oh, oh, wooky. Someding tug on my wine, wee witto bit, pwobabwy guppy. Not vewy big."

Johnny and I can tell by the bite that it's a Sturgeon. You can almost always tell a Sturgeon bite. The only thing you can't tell is the size of the fish by the size of the bite. Sometimes a wee little bite can be six feet or more of muscle and meanness; you just never know.

I tell Itchy, "The next time the 'guppy' bites, you rare back on the rod just as hard as you can and quick, too." Well Itchy does exactly that and ends up flat on his back but still holding the rod. We get him on his feet and tell him to reel the fish in now.

Itchy reels until the line is tight and he cannot move a thing. He says "Itchy caught on bottom of wivah. No moah fish."

Johnny and I have seen this many times, sometimes it even fools the experts. All at once Itchy's line moves over about ten feet and stops again. Itchy's eyes get as big as saucers and he shouts. "HOE-WEE YOKOHAMA! SOMEDING BIG DOWN DEAH AND IT GOT ITCHY!"

I start to reel in our lines. Johnny is already pulling the anchor and we drift off with the fish. We know it's large and will take a lot of time and patience with Itchy, our total-neophyte fisherman. I hope we can all weather the storm.

I tell Itchy "Keep the rod tip up!"

Itchy asks "Up where?"

I tell him, "Up toward the sky." I've got a feeling this is going to be like a three-ring circus full of clowns. Johnny reaches over and checks the drag on Itchy's reel. After all, if it's too tight it will take less time but produce more hazards and could even tire out our new fisherman.

It's a give-and-take battle for about twenty-five minutes when Itchy says, "How many moah owahs maybe dis going to be? Itchy stahting get soah ahms and ti'ed back."

Landing this fish will take much longer than it usually does, because Itchy has no idea how to pump or play a fish. He just stands there and cranks away constantly on the reel handle, whether the line is coming in or going out. I doubt if Itchy has any idea if he is gaining or losing the battle. I'm almost sure he's losing the battle though, because he's having more trouble all the time keeping the tip of his rod up.

There's nothing we can do now but try to maneuver the boat so we stay close to the fish. Normally, I would say as much trouble and time as this is taking, the fish is probably too big to keep, but with Itchy not having any idea how to play the fish we just can't tell. We'll just have to stay with it till we can see it. In the meantime, we'll watch and try to advise our over-excited Itchy.

I open another beer and just stand back and watch. Up till now, even though I have been watching, I haven't been really seeing. Here we are with a guy playing a fish in a Japanese Admiral's dress uniform, hat and all, (we did get the sword away from him) and over the top of this ridiculous regalia is a bright orange, fluffy life jacket. I now visualize what an idiotic scene this would produce to anyone going by in another boat. We've been lucky and have seen nobody else. But now I hear another craft approaching from down river, and I think our luck is about to change.

The other boat spots us with a fish on and draws up close to see just what we have. All at once one of them pulls out a fancy camera with a big telephoto lens and begins snapping pictures from all angles. We can hear them laugh, then they wave and holler, "Good luck!" and whiz away on up river.

206

Itchy says, "Boy, nice people take Itchy's pichah. Itchy wish could get pichah fwom dem some day. You know who dey ah?"

"No Itchy, I don't. I never saw them before, but if your fish is legal and we can keep it, we'll get a camera and take your picture when we get home. But first Itchy, you have to catch it."

"Oh boy! Itchy shuah wike dat. I get busy and catch fish if ahms don't faw off oah back bweak fi'st."

At last the tell-tale bubbles show and we know the fish is finally conceding the battle. About five minutes later we get our first look. Itchy yells "Hooeeee Yokohama! Itchy no got fish! He got big cwockadile!"

"No Itchy, you have a nice big Sturgeon. But hold on now, we'll have to do some checking to see if it's legal. It looks real close."

After considerable maneuvering, measuring and guessing, Johnny and I feel it is about an inch too long and we'll have to re-lease it. We explain to Itchy that we can't keep it, we just can't take a chance on Nugent getting his claws on us. Itchy thinks about this, then says "Toad, you hoed wod foah Itchy one minute."

I take the rod and Itchy grabs his sword and waves it wildly over his head. Johnny yells, "Itchy! Put that thing down before you hurt somebody!"

Itchy's reply is "YAaaaaaa HEeeeeeee! Itchy hu't somebody if he don't keep biggest fish Itchy evah see to catch! Got to show Yoko and Snookah. You betcha we keep!"

After several minutes of deliberation, Johnny and I say we'll tie the fish up and get a more accurate measurement before we decide whether it's best for us to die sliced to ribbons, or to spend our lives in prison after Nugent gets through with us.

We find the fish to be one quarter inch too long! Itchy wouldn't care if it was ten feet too long! He is determined to keep it regardless of anything. Johnny says "Let's tie it up along side and maybe Itchy'll weaken after while and we can turn it loose."

"John, it's only a quarter inch too long, if we kill it and put it in the boat, the sun will dry it a little and it'll lose at least a half inch, and we'll all live to see another day. Otherwise, I think we're goners, because Itchy just isn't about to back down."

We finally kill it and wrestle it into the boat. But in dragging it over the side we scrape it's gills and the first thing you know we have blood all over the floor and spreading everywhere with little splatters flying around with each dying, thrashing movement.

I look at Johnny and his jaw muscles are really working now. If there is anything he likes, it's a neat and tidy boat at all times, I mean eat-on-the-floor type clean! and this is probably the worst mess either of us have ever seen. Our hours of cleaning the boat last week were wasted.

Johnny looks around in disgust and says, "This looks worse than the time I had to decapitate a dozen chickens for Uncle Hank's family picnic and barbecue. Never will forget those chickens...beheaded and floppin', flutterin' and bleedin' all over everything in sight! What a mess. We'll be a few days cleaning this up. I wish we had turned it loose like we first said."

"Johnny, if you remember it wasn't that easy a choice. It was more a choice between a samurai carving session or keeping the fish. Frankly, I'd be glad to take a week off and clean up the boat, and I'll bet Itchy would be glad to help us." John's reply is just an upward rolling of his eyes.

After five-to-ten minutes the fish finally quits thrashing around, but now the floor is so slick we have trouble walking around, so we get a couple towels and sponges and using river water, at least clean it up to the point we can stand without feeling we're ice skating.

Itchy says, "Boy, fish shuah do bweed a wot. Nevah know dey ho'd dat many gawons."

Well, I can see that Johnny has really had it and he says, "It's getting late. I shouldn't have put the anchor out again. We're going to have to go."

"Yeah John, we've had quite a day and we still have a fish to clean when we get home."

Johnny says, "Quite a day is the understatement of the year, to say the least. Never saw anything quite like it before, but thank God it's over.....almost."

"John, if you'll reel up and put things away and get Itchy squared around on that punch card before we get a visit from old Nugent, I'll pull the anchor."

He agrees and I get busy on the anchor. Johnny gets everything about picked up in the mess when he asks me, "Toad, haven't you got that anchor pulled yet?"

I say, "No, John. It's hung up tighter than all git out on something down there. I can't budge it." Johnny takes a try at it and after fifteen frustrating minutes we realize it just ain't gonna break loose.

Johnny says, "Give me the cutters out of the tool box. We'll have to cut this steel cable."

I look around and then tell him, "John, the tool kit isn't here. We forgot to put it back in the boat after we cleaned it the other day. I can see it now in the shed with the quick-release anchor and float."

"Then how in hell" asks John "are we going to get loose and out of here?"

"Johnny, don't panic. I'll get the hook file out of the tackle box. Should have us loose in about ten minutes at most."

Forty minutes later John asks, "Would you like me to spell you a while on the filing you're doing?"

"Yeah, Johnny. I'm makin' headway, must be nigh on half-way through, but this steel cable is tough!" John takes over and after probably thirty minutes more frees us from our hung-up anchor.

We finish off the trip without further incident, God knows we've had more troubles than any man deserves in a month of Sundays, and ours were all in one day! When we arrive home, we make sure to take several pictures of Itchy and his big Sturgeon; then Johnny and I proceed to clean and filet the fish while Itchy expounds at great length to Yoko and Snooks. He does not help to clean the fish and the big sword was never needed at all, a lucky break for sure.

Itchy tells the girls all about his unusual day of fishing and even tells Yoko that we would not let him bring home "nice snake big

enough foah soup and even few snake steaks." The very thought just turns my stomach and makes me feel like my complexion has become a pale green. Snake steaks, what a repulsive, gut wrenching, gagging thought. I hope I don't dream about it.

When we're finished, we divide up the cleaned fish and Itchy and Yoko head off for home, all smiles and excitement.

I say to John, "Why don't you come on in and we'll have a cool drink and talk over a few future resolutions and agreements." Johnny agrees and we chat about what a screwed-up day we've had and vow that never, ever, again, nohow, no way! will we ever take a total non-fishing type person fishing with us again.

Before Johnny leaves, we agree to meet in the morning and start the big boat cleaning project. Then I head for bed totally exhausted, even too tired to give Snooks any little thoughts to keep her thinking half the night. Whenever that happens, I know I really am tired. All I can do is just say "Night, Snooks."

# 16

# Smoke, Fire & Headlines

Johnny shows up just after breakfast and just in time for morning coffee and tea. He still looks tired and I ask, "How did you sleep last night, John?" He replies that he didn't sleep well at all, he had nightmares all night.

Then he turns to Snooks and says, "Snooks, in your wildest imagination you could not begin to guess how our day went yesterday. If somebody told me I had to live it all over again, I think I would consider suicide as the lesser of two evils."

Putting down his cup he asks "Can you imagine a day controlled by Murphy's Law and a Japanese Admiral with everything wrong, from his shorts on backwards to swinging a samurai sword and killing snakes to bring home to eat? That's just for starters. I could go on all day but I'm trying to forget it, not relive it, God forbid."

After our coffee we gather up the things we need to clean the boat. By the time we get around to the actual chore, the sun has had time to work on that dried blood and the odor is horrendous. We decide to pull the drain plug and get in with a scrub brush and high pressure nozzle and just go after it tooth and toenail.

About half way through we hear the distant wail of a fire siren. We ignore it until it's close proximity demands our total attention. Two trucks pull up in front of the house on the other side of Itchy and Yoko. It's a rental house that belongs to our mutual neighbor Vic, who lives just across the street.

Vic is one of those do-it-yourself fixer-upper people. Now I've got nothing against do-it-yourselfers, but a do-it-yourselfer has to be thinking all the time to keep ahead of the inspectors and the building permit people. Sometimes those people can turn a good do-it-yourselfer into a call-for-helper type person. Up until now, Vic has been a dyed-in-the-wool fixer-upper type person and understandably so.

If you have rental property you just about have to fix things yourself to come out financially. You can't pay a plumber or an electrician forty or fifty dollars an hour or, God forbid, sometimes even more!

This is one time when poor old Vic was gonna do a little home improvement but his mind must have wandered just a bit and he made one fatal error and exposure is now eminent.

Johnny and I stand off to one side as the firemen talk to Vic who is trying to get them to hold up a minute before they demolish most of the building with their fire axes trying to locate the blaze. Vic tells them that there is no blaze! He threw in a couple of bug fumigation bombs to clean the place before re-renting it, but he forgot to shut off the system for his automatic smoke alarm and fire detector first. He tells the firemen that he tried to make his wife go in and retrieve the bug bombs as soon as he realized his mistake but she said, "I'm no bug and you're not gonna fumigate me, big boy!"

The firemen then ask Vic why he didn't go in and retrieve the bombs himself? Vic says he's allergic to smoke, even had to give up cigarettes because of it.

This is finally straightened out to the satisfaction of the firemen, and our amusement, but they continue for twenty minutes to have Vic fill out papers and documents to clear the department from making a seemingly ridiculous false alarm run. Furthermore, it throws the blame squarely on Vic who right now hasn't thought of any follow up. That thought will sink in after the initial shock and all the attention fades away.....like during the middle of his sleepless night tonight.

I hope this little incident doesn't turn an expert do-it-yourselfer into a call-for-helper. Vic is one of the best do-it-yourselfers I've ever seen. I just can't imagine what his mind must have been on to screw up so bad this time.

212

After all the excitement, we return to the clean-up job and are still amazed the boat could get so messed up in one trip, but if you ever took Itchy along you would understand it. After three hours I tell Johnny we better break for lunch, and I understand our favorite restaurant has a little Olympia oyster pan-fry special today and if he'd like, we'll try it and lunch is on me. After all, I feel that's the least I can do after getting Johnny involved in yesterday's fishing fiasco. It really wasn't my fault though, it was one of those things a person just can't avoid and still save face. I hope it never happens again but I can see how it could happen all right.

We knock off for lunch and enjoy the break, and get to see a lot of our friends who we normally wouldn't see. Weasel is there with Doc Crandle, and he comes over and gives us a little choice gossip: it seems that our local used-car dealer got caught and fined for running the odometers back on a bunch of used cars. I always figure you have to watch used-car dealers almost as much as insurance adjusters.

Lunch arrives and our oyster fry is even better than we expected. You just can't beat these little Olympias for flavor. An oyster lover just ain't lived till he's had a pan fry of these little guys.

We leave very satisfied and head back to work. On the way we see a big billowy cloud of smoke in the sky and Johnny says, "You know Toad, that smoke looks like it's over by the Wonder What? Chemical Company."

"Well hey, Johnny, let's go check it out. After all, I've always enjoyed a good fire ever since I was a kid."

As we round the corner, Johnny says "HOLY SMUT! IT IS THE CHEMICAL COMPANY! Boy, that fire's already out of control. There's two big fire companies there already."

We park a ways away and walk up close and see Cora Cogger, old Whiney Mouth, wringing her hands, and Chick Cladwaller talking excitedly to a couple of the firemen. Out of curiosity we get close enough to hear the conversation and it seems Cladwaller is telling them that the safe with all the company's secret formulas is in that roaring blaze, and he must have it! He offers fifty thousand dollars to the firemen who can get the safe out. They dive in with renewed vigor but cannot calm the roaring, out-of-control blaze. In desperation he boosts the ante to one hundred thousand, but even this incentive is not enough to create any hope of retrieving the safe.

Through all the noise we hear another siren, and we see a little old fire truck with half-a-dozen volunteer firemen coming to the fire full bore wide open! They roar right into the center of the blaze with no hesitation. After about twenty minutes they calm the blaze. Chick yells "Get the safe out!" and they go back and return with the safe intact. Chick says, "Fellows, I applaud your bravery and dedication, and thank you one and all. Here's your check for one hundred thousand dollars for saving my safe and it's vauable contents. Now, what do you fellows intend to do with your money?"

The captain accepts the check and says to Chick, "Well sir, the first thing we're going to do is get the brakes fixed on this damn truck!"

We leave because by now quite a crowd has gathered and we have seen the best of it anyway. When we get home Snooks and Nancy drive up in Snooks' little Benz; seems they've been antiquing, looking for another bonanza but with no luck.

I tell Snooks and Nancy it was more exciting around home than traipsing off to the city antiquing because we got in on two fires to watch. Actually only one, as Vic only had smoke problems, intentional sort of, and when I told them what happened to Vic they agree it sounds like the sort of thing that could only happen to Vic; that's about the third time the firemen have been there on a false alarm.

The girls had wondered about the chemical plant and seen the smoke, but figured it was safer to stay away and read about it in the paper. Personally, I like to see all the activity and smell the smoke and feel the heat. I guess it's all in how your interest runs.

Nancy leaves saying she has to get "his" lunch ready for his night-time vigil on the river. Glad she mentioned that, now we know we still have him working nights.

Snooks goes over to Grandma Two Dogs. Grandma has bought herself a computer and knows nothing about them at all, and asked Snooks to come and show her how to turn the bloomin' thing on! This should be a frustrating experience for Snooks; teaching someone how to run a computer when that someone cannot balance a check book!

Johnny and I return to our clean-up chores, it's beginning to look like we should be able to finish by the end of the day.....IF we don't have any more interruptions. One thing almost for certain it won't be another fire, two in one day is already unheard of.

Sure as shootin' we do get an interruption. Itchy and Yoko coming running out of their house, frantically waving the just delivered afternoon daily paper. We finally make out that Itchy has his picture on the front page. There he is big as life, in full color, with his entire Japanese Admiral's uniform blazing back at us with big headlines JAPANESE DIGNITARY ENJOYS LOCAL FISHING. It seems the people in the small boat we saw on the river who were frantically taking Itchy's picture, were newspaper reporters on an outing, and being always on the lookout for news, grabbed onto Itchy in uniform. Then without any thought of facts proceeded to cook up a big phony story at Itchy's expense; but to Itchy and Yoko, it's one of life's greatest moments! Personally, I wouldn't be caught dead in a situation like that and I'm thankful neither Johnny nor I are in the picture.

The camera crew only wanted the little Admiral. After sharing this tribute with us, Itchy and Yoko head for home. Itchy all smiles and Yoko saying how proud she is of him and the picture showing the big fish he's catching.

We finish with the boat clean up just about the same time Snooks comes home from Grandma Two Dogs' place. As I start to pour a little relaxation drink for two over-worked boat cleaner uppers, Snooks walks in saying, "I don't care what you're drinking, pour me a double just like it. If you two think Itchy is frustrating on a fishing trip, I'll trade you Grandma Two Dogs any day!"

It seems some smart computer salesman caught Grandma Two

Dogs in a weak moment and sold her the latest, fastest pentium all-out computer with printer, scanner, C.D. Rom. You name it, she's got it. He told her now she could talk to her grandkids on the E-mail anytime she wanted and for almost free. "I told her the first thing we had to do was boot up. And right off she said she couldn't because he didn't sell her any computer boots and I should take her to town to get a pair! Fifteen minutes later, she learned how to boot up without boot-up boots, and that was just the beginning. She had a guy stop in and get her on the Internet but she's afraid to send a letter, because she can't figure out where to paste the stamp!" Snooks says.

"Grandma renamed her mouse 'Mickey' because she hates mice and that's the only mouse she ever liked. She doesn't know what a browser is, she says it sounds too much like you're being nosy. She sees no reason for a file, she already has one of those for her finger-nails and doesn't need another. Things like C.D. Rom, DOS, Icons, Floppy Discs, Recycle Bin, Log On, Screen Savers, Paint Brush, and many, many more are just totally out of her realm of thought, let alone imagination.

"I did think about having her take some lessons from our friend Mike Painter. He has the patience of Job and knowledge to help, but Mike's our friend and he's far too young to let go crazy."

Sipping her drink Snooks continues, "Finally, I told Grandma to contact the people who sold her the computer; they're the ones who told her how easy it was to be able to E-mail her kids and grandkids messages. Those people deserve the headache. For Grandma Two Dogs it will never be easy, and may be an impossibility."

Itchy and Yoko again run in with their newspaper and show Snooks the big color picture on the front page of Itchy fishing. Itchy acts about as pleased as if he had just been elected President. Yoko is so pleased and proud of Itchy that she's about to explode. We don't say anything to throw cold water on this show of exuberance. But if he hadn't been wearing the goofy Admiral's outfit, nobody would have given him a second look! It just isn't at all what the reporters have made it look like. I guess we can't knock it too much though, because it sure has made Itchy and Yoko happy. Some good comes from almost everything.

# 17

# One More Time

As I walk in the kitchen Snooks is drinking her morning coffee, a big smile on her face. I pour myself a cup and sit down beside her and ask, "Snooks, what is so confounded amusing at 8 a.m., before breakfast or the morning paper?"

Snooks laughs and says, "Well, I just thought of something Grandma Two Dogs said last night. She said she knew she could handle the computer all right because she has been taking two Ginkgo Biloba pills every day. They're supposed to improve your memory and brain power. When I asked her if they're working, she replied 'Yep, I think so, at least when I remember to take them.' That should give you some idea of her chances for computer success, don't you think?"

About this time Johnny pops in and hollers "Pot hot?" Snooks gets up and pours John a cup of hot water and puts in a tea bag. A real all-out, devout coffee-drinking Swede has done a Japanese about face and switched totally to tea.....for reasons still a mystery to me.

I tell John how pleased I am the boat is all cleaned up and how glad I am that we learned our lesson on taking other people fishing with us; particularly any non-fishing persons. "Just to be safe," I tell him, "we should eliminate everybody. After all, we bought it for our own pleasure, and not every other Tom, Dick and Harry."

Johnny clears his throat and looks down in his cup but does not give me a positive answer, in fact gives no answer at all.....in fact, a total silence. I suddenly have a sick feeling that for some ungodly reason he doesn't agree with me. You would think after our recent experience with Itchy, still so fresh on his mind, he would be only too glad and quick to totally agree; but no, something sinister is afoot!

Under the table Snooks is hammering on my leg with her soccer ball swing and I suddenly realize that Snooks has picked up on something that's oblivious to me. It's that sixth sense that females have. Just another small thing that makes them think they are superior beings.

"Johnny," I ask, "is there some reason you don't agree?"

Johnny says, "I gotta go to the bathroom."

During his quick trip down the hall I say to Snooks, "Something is bothering him. He acts like he stopped to think and forgot to start again. I don't believe he had to go to the bathroom in a quick flash like that; if he did, he better always stay ten feet from a rest area or he could have an accident."

Snooks replies, "I think Johnny has a problem and he just needed time to think."

When he returns, John clears his throat and begins, "Toad, I don't know how to say this, but before we took Itchy fishing, one time when I took Tootie some fish, she asked if we could take her fishing one of these days and, well, in view of the bargain she gave us on the boat and all, I just couldn't say no. I had no idea the troubles a non-fishing type person could cause and now I'm committed. I'd take her myself, but the way the last trip went, I think it will take both of us. I'm really sorry. She says Sturgeon fishing was always her favorite but her husband wouldn't fish for them, he only went after salmon and steelhead."

"Johnny, you're on your own. I wouldn't get in another mess like the last one without either committing a murder or having a stroke!"

Snooks pipes up and says, "Now Honey, that's no attitude to have. Johnny went along and suffered through Itchy and he made Tootie a promise before he knew how it would be. I think it's up to you now, to go along and back Johnny up. Then if you two want to never take anybody else it will be O.K., but you really have to help Johnny on this."

I don't know why Snooks either can't keep her mouth shut on matters that don't concern her or just act dumb and leave the room. It seems like no matter what, I'm always the one wrong. But this time, (and I'll never ever let Snooks know,) this time she does make sense.

Johnny doesn't answer; he doesn't want to step in over his head, but the smile on his face indicates that Snooks has tossed him a life preserver and to save face I'll have to go along. Life can be cruel at times.

I say, "Johnny, you did put up with Itchy and his odd antics and I can't see where Tootie can be any worse. We can take her and baby her along I suppose for one trip, but then after that we draw the line.....no more, just you and me."

Again Snooks pipes up and blabbers out something that sounds remotely like "But what if she's a good fisherperson?"

"Snooks, if I heard you right, you think there might be some chance Tootie could be a good fisherperson? Well, let me tell you something, I have fished with several so-called 'good fisherpersons' and all they care about is how they look, and little goodies to nibble on, plus a great big bag of non-essentials like suntan cream, mosquito dope, lipstick, extra clothing, and always a bag of potato chips just like Itchy did, and oh yes! A big, broad-brimmed straw hat.....mustn't get our noses burned, you know. But yes, I'll go along and help you Johnny, this one time. And when, pray tell, is it going to be convenient for Tootie to grace us with her presence?"

Once more Snooks sticks her nose in and says, "Toad, (I wish she had never heard about that Toad stuff) if you're going to go, then do it gracefully. You didn't hear any comments like that from Johnny when you took Itchy fishing, did you? Try to be a man about it and quit whining like a two-year old. Get a smile on your face and go along for her sake and Johnny's too; act as if you're really enjoying her company, not like a grumpy old bear with a belly ache."

I do wish Snooks would learn to mind her own affairs and leave mine alone. Even the few times she might be right, she doesn't have to say anything in front of other people. Some of them might even believe what she says and I'd rather it wasn't at my expense. Besides, I already said I'd go, there's no reason to just keep draggin' this through the mud.

Another thing, I just don't know why Snooks pushes me into these awkward situations. She never hesitates. It seems like she just looks for openings to put me in the middle of unwanted dilemmas. Getting tangled up with Nancy was one of those ugly situations that unbeknownst to Snooks, worked out to Johnny's and my benefit. We now have a pipeline to keep tabs on Nugent's every movement and make things happen to our advantage. Which of course, is what you must have to cope with a rat like Nugent. This could be called a positive situation. Needless to say, Snooks provides me with very few positive situations.

I decide to take Snooks' advice though, hopefully without her being aware that she had any influence on the outcome of my decision. I never want to let her know that she has any positive influence on my actions or I'd be in for an attempt for her to try to totally dominate all my thinking.

I say, "Well Johnny, when do you think Tootie would like to have us take her fishing?"

Johnny replies, "Oh, I don't think she needs much notice. We have a good tide on this coming Thursday, and I'll ask her if that would be all right. Does that sound all right too, Toad?"

"Gee Johnny, I'm not sure. I think I have an appointment with the dentist on Thursday."

Snooks, the little darling, pipes up and says, "Toad, your dental appointment is the next Thursday, you have nothing in the way this coming Thursday."

I was hoping I could stall for a little more time to get used to the idea, but again Snooks doesn't seem to know when to keep out of other people's business.

On a serious matter like this, one always needs some getting-used-to-the-idea time. I say, "Yeah, Johnny, you check with Tootie and get back to me. Thursday sounds just fine." I feel like a kid who hesitates jumping into cold water and finally decides to just jump in and get it over with. I go ahead and take the plunge. I accept Thursday and leave the rest up to Johnny.

Johnny leaves, all smiles, to go tell Tootie and I tell Snooks that he seemed in an awful hurry, "Ya know Snooks, Johnny almost acted like he was going to enjoy taking Tootie fishing with us. I doubt if he really has any idea how it's going to be. Bathroom privileges are going to be a big problem right off the bat. I wonder if Johnny has given any thought at all to the anatomical plumbing differences and the complications to be involved shortly after she consumes about two bottles of beer.....that is, if she drinks beer."

Snooks says "It won't matter what type of beverage Tootie drinks, the end result will be the same. Just don't worry about things that haven't happened and may not happen at all. You know Toad, you just might have a good time despite your negative attitude."

"Not a chance Snooks! It can't be better than Itchy, and that was a total disaster for all concerned but Itchy!

"We'll have to be casting for her and baiting her hook and I can think of untold problems. Itchy was probably a picnic compared to this deal John has got us into."

Snooks answers, "Toad, you've stewed around all day about this! Why don't you get it out of your mind because it's almost bed-time and if you don't forget it, you'll not sleep all night. I guarantee you, I'll go sleep in the spare bedroom if you roll and toss and thrash around all night."

Just then the phone rings. Snooks answers it, talks for a several minutes and says, "Oh my yes, I think that's delightful, and I know Toad will be pleased."

After she hangs up I ask, "Who was that? And what may I ask, am I going to be so all-fired pleased about?"

"That was Johnny, and he says Tootie is looking forward eagerly to her fishing trip and will fix a lunch for all three of you. Isn't that nice of her to be so thoughtful?"

"Sure, sure," I say. "I can just imagine what lunch will be: little home-made goodies and of course, potato chips. It sure won't be good stuff that will stick to your ribs. I think I'll just throw in a big sandwich with lots of good fisherman type staples to keep us going."

Snooks replies, "Oh no, you won't! That would be a terrible insult to that poor kind lady. Boy, are you negative! Please do your best to give this poor girl the benefit of a fair chance before you condemn her. Try to be more like Johnny just for once. Remember now, you owe Johnny a nice trip. He wasn't this way at all when you took Itchy. Try to be decent."

Too soon Thursday arrives, and Johnny is here to pick me up. At least now I won't have to listen to Snooks' constant verbal harangue; she is still giving me wifely advice as I leave.

As we drive along to Tootie's, my only thought is: it's only one day out of my life and no matter how bad, I'll suffer through it with a smile for Johnny's sake. At least I'll be the only one who knows how miserable I really feel.

We pull up in front of Tootie's house and there she sits on the front porch waiting for us with a fishing rod and a medium-sized lunch bucket. I notice she's wearing a plain, half-worn out, faded, red-checkered mackinaw, that even has a hole in one elbow. Little old worn baseball cap and looks like no make-up at all. I must say I sure didn't expect this for starters.

She puts the rod in the boat and the lunch bucket in the car trunk just like she's been doing it for nigh on as long as we have, and then tells us that she got her punch card and license yesterday so we wouldn't have to waste time doing that today. She also says she bought and put 100 yards of new 40-pound test line on her reel because she was afraid the old line was not heavy enough and she wanted to be prepared.

I know how it is taking women fishing. So far, she just doesn't seem to fit the female fisherperson pattern, but then I know when we get to baiting hooks with pinching sand shrimp, we'll separate the men from the non-men in a mighty big hurry and her true colors will show real sudden like.

Tootie proceeds to tell us how much she enjoys the opportunity to go Sturgeon fishing with us and that her dear departed husband never really liked Sturgeon because he had grown up with the mistaken idea that they were next to the bottom rung of the fish ladder. Yugo was almost a fly-fishing purist until one time he found out by accident that non-fly fishermen catch more fish with half the pain and effort. The 'pain' part being the doctor removing a deeply imbedded fly from behind his right ear, which seemed to have found it's way home, so to speak, on a back cast just after starting forward momentum. The 'effort' part being when he tried not to cry, blubber and scream as the doctor dug the hook out of his ear cartilage. Tootie laughingly continues "It was at this point that Yugo suddenly became a non-fly fishing purist. He became more of a catch 'em any way you can purist, but he was still too pure to stoop to Sturgeon."

It turns out that Tootie's love for Sturgeon came from a few successful trips with her father who thought Sturgeon were the epitome of all forms of fish life and at the very top rung of the fish ladder. Tootie said her husband and her dad never spoke to each other after they found out where the other stood on piscatorial pleasure.

We arrive at the bait shop and to my absolute utter amazement Tootie says, "Fellas, I'll go in and get the shrimp; after all, I want to pay my way here. How many dozen do we need?" I just sort of look at Johnny and he stammers out something about six dozen and asks if she minds if we go in with her? We figure after all, she surely will need our expert advice. I doubt if she knows a sand shrimp from a can of worms! We go in and she proceeds to open all the cartons in the refrigerator, to smell each one and put it back, then goes to Lou the owner and asks if this is his total supply of sand shrimp and Lou tells her no, he has more in the back room storage refrigerator. She goes with Lou and comes out with six cartons, informing Lou as she walks to the cash register that the others out front are almost dead and he should throw them out as they are no longer prime bait. She says, "Sir, they smell; fresh ones don't." Then she smiles, pays the bill and turns to us saying, "You boys can take these to the ice chest in the boat, I'm headed for the little girls' room."

We head out to the car and boat. Johnny says, "Kee-ripes, Toad! I can't believe I saw what I saw."

"Johnny, I saw what you saw, but there just ain't no way we saw what we think we saw! It had to be some sort of a tackle shop in-house miracle mirage.....I think. Tootie knows more about pickin'good bait than we do! I never would have known to check for freshness by smelling, would you?"

"No Toad, me neither."

"Yeah, John, it's sort of spoo-o.....look out, here she comes."

We get back in the car and head for the boat launch and John says, "Tootie, we went in to help you pick out the bait but we see you're wise to the old smell-the-carton-for-freshness trick, too."

Tootie answers, "Yes, my father, bless him, taught me that trick years ago, but I could never convince Yugo of it's value. He wasn't one to accept any ideas from Father even though Yugo knew they were to his advantage."

We arrive at the boat launch and as I'm backing down the ramp to launch, Tootie asks, "Toad, are you sure the drain plug is secure?"

Before I can answer that very logical question, Johnny answers, "Yeah, Tootie, I checked it last night."

Then Tootie asks "Johnny, are you sure the bitter end is tight to the boat?" Man-oh-man! am I glad she asked Johnny that question, because that's one that went right over the top of my broad knowledge of nautical terms. Johnny hesitates just long enough for me to take a quick glance at his big round, bewildered lookin', baby-blue eyes and I know he's no better off than I am; better him than me. Boy! That was close.

Johnny finally stammers out, "Yeah, Tootie, I checked that last night, too." Sounds to me like Johnny done a lot of checkin' stuff last night and I'd bet a nickel to a pinch of goose do-do that he hasn't any more idea of the "bitter end" of what the hell ever, than I do! But like I say, he can think quicker in a tight spot than almost anybody I know. Snooks being the one exception.

Then Tootie says, "Johnny, hand me the working end and I'll make sure it doesn't drift out once it's afloat."

Johnny thinks quick and says, "Help yourself, Tootie. I've got to make a run to the little boys' room." Again Johnny is thinking fast and has side-stepped another mysterious bit of nautical (I think) terminology. Just out of curiosity, I look in the rearview mirror and see Tootie pick up the loose end of the rope and walk along as we back into the water. The boat floats free and as I pull up, she holds the rope and guides the boat back to shore.

I guess I can put two-and-two together and come up with four! The "working end" has to be the loose end of the rope from the boat, and if that's correct, then the "bitter end" will have to be the end of the rope tied to the boat. Ha! S-w-a-v-e, that's me. Have no idea why they would call it the "bitter end," but it just has to be. I sure hope I'm right; what else could it be?

Tootie holds the boat as I drive the car and trailer up into the parking area and Johnny meets me as I'm locking the car. He says, "What in the world is that woman talking about? What's the bitter end? It's gonna be the bitter end for her if she doesn't start talking sense."

"Johnny, Johnny, my boy, you should know what she's talking about. The 'bitter end' is the end of the rope tied to the boat, and the 'working end' is the end you hold in your hand. I thought you knew that. I learned that twenty years ago; I just don't feel the need to be so precise."

John says, "Yeah, in a pig's eye! I'll bet you never heard that kind of talk before either. If you're so smart, then what is the rest of the rope called? Now tell me that right quick, Toad."

I say, "Johnny, everybody knows that's just plain rope. That's sure no big mystery, I'm sure even you knew that. You know John, a rope has to have two ends, show me a one-ended rope and I'll show you how to eat chicken broth with a fork. If a rope has two ends then they have to be called something to keep them apart. Right or left, or even this end and t'uther end would be simple, but somebody just wanted to be smart and called them the 'bitter end' and the 'working end'."

In complete confusion Johnny says, "I never heard of some of this stuff she seems to know so much about."

As we crawl in the boat and fire up the outboard, Tootie asks, "How far do we have to go?"

I say, "Not far Tootie, only about twenty minutes."

Tootie answers, "I'll help rig up the outfits, or I can run the boat while you rig up; but if you do the rigging up, I want to put a shrimp harness on my outfit. It keeps the shrimp alive longer. I tied up some last night if you fellows want to try it."

Oh boy, here we go again. I have to see this shrimp harness; that's a new one on me. I don't know if Johnny heard her, he's sitting real close to the noise of the big motor and I don't see any look of surprise or bewilderment.

Johnny runs the boat and Tootie and I rig up the rods with terminal tackle sinkers and all, but when she gets to hers, she puts on a long shank hook with two little, teenie-weenie rubber bands wrapped right to the farthest ends of the hook shank.

I can't wait for two things: I want to see how in tarnation she rigs the shrimp on that contraption and, I hope I'm looking at Johnny when he discovers this latest little development.

As we approach our designated fishing spot, Johnny idles into position preparing to drop the anchor and break-away float. Tootie watches intently as I lower the anchor and lay the float on the water and slip the remaining rope to the clamp cleat on the deck, ready to pull loose on an instant's notice. Tootie is quite taken up with this arrangement, but wonders really why we need it? Johnny is more than glad to inform her that when you have a large fish take off fast, you don't always have time to pull the anchor, and the float will hold it in place.

Her remark is, "Too bad my daddy couldn't have known about that, he lost a lot of big Sturgeon just for that reason." Johnny has a smug smile on his face. So far this is the first thing we've been able to teach, up to now it's been all learn.

Out of politeness, Johnny decides to bait up Tootie first and as he grabs a sand shrimp in one hand and hook in the other he stops, gets a puzzled look on his face and asks, "Tootie, just how do you go about properly baiting this rigamajig?"

Tootie replies, "Here Johnny, let me show you.

"You slide head in the loop of the front band and tail through the back band and the head of another shrimp through the egg loop and put the hook through the tail. That way at least one shrimp stays alive and on the hook longer." Then Johnny and I watch as she reaches in the bucket without even looking and grabs two wiggly shrimp and proceeds to show us how to bait our hook with her new-fangled hook harness.

We have just been put back in the learning cycle which we had momentarily escaped. Tootie finishes her baiting demonstration and Johnny says, "Tootie, if you'd like I'll caa-aa...." but by this time Tootie is already standing and makes a cast back of the boat that is an absolute thing of beauty. One other time I saw a cast like this; it won the casting championship at the State Fair in '75. Tootie never even stopped talking during, before or after she made that cast. I don't think it was out of the ordinary for her at all. I look over to John and he's wearing a mixture of expressions. If you know what an expression of bewilderment and disbelief looks like, well then, you have an idea of the basic look I would imagine to be on both our faces.

Three things we have found out real quick to add to our already vast world of wonderment: Tootie ain't afraid of sand shrimp, she knows how to bait her hook, and she sure as hell knows how to cast!

I can see where in the future Johnny and I are going to have many hours of discussion over this strange turn of events.

We all get baited up and begin real serious-type fishing and just settle back and wait. Tootie remarks "You guys didn't offer me any of whatever that was you dunked your sand shrimp in before you cast, what gives here anyway?"

I myself didn't know she noticed, but then this gal don't miss much of nuthin'. Again quick thinking Johnny says, "Tootie, that's what we call gromafraw juice and we think it improves our chance for bites by at least 65%, and we would have done the same for your shrimp, but you cast before we could give you the final pre-cast dunk job."

John is s-w-a-ve!

Tootie says O.K., but for her next cast she wants some of that stuff because she doesn't want anybody to have any advantage over anybody else and it looks right now like maybe we were trying to do something like that.

As we sit waiting for a bite Tootie asks if we noticed the fellow fishing with three rods as we made our run up river? Boy, I tell you, this gal don't miss nothin' at all!

"Oh him," Johnny says. "We call him 'Three Rod Bob.' He always fishes with too many rods. He's got a pair of scissors handy so if things look a mite dangerous, such as a visit from Warden Nugent, he can quickly snip two lines and he's home free. No law against extra rods in rod holders."

"Yeah." I say, "Bob's idea is this: he has one outfit fishing regular proven fish-catching methods, and the other two he calls experimental; meaning things he thinks might catch fish. You know, things he wants to try but doesn't want to waste good fishing time to experiment with. He says the extra two rods are Experimental Piscatorial Puzzles or EPP. One nice thing is, if one of his experiments proves to be a sure fish catching winner, he's always glad to pass his findings on to the rest of us."

"Three Rod Bob doesn't worry us at all," adds Johnny. "Except that maybe sooner or later old Nugent will outsmart him. So you see Tootie, in a way he takes all the risks and we get all the benefits. Yeah, Three Rod is really all right."

Johnny and I have our rods in rod holders but Tootie won't put hers down, holds it all the time. I ask, "Tootie, how's come you ain't puttin' that rod in a rod holder and relaxin' a mite, like for a cup of coffee or a sandwich?"

Tootie replies, "More fish are lost between seeing a bite and feeling a bite. With fish that bite as light as Sturgeon, you can't fish lazy. You have to hold your rod and be ever alert for the slightest indication of anything around your bait. Many times when you see the bite and pick up your rod and wait to feel the bite, it's probably already too late."

Johnny and I look at each other and neither says a word because what Tootie has said sure makes sense. We think she is right again but with our rods in rod holders, it sort of makes us both feel like a couple of kids caught with their pinkies in the cookie jar.

All at once Tootie rares back on that rod and if there hadn't been a back in her seat she would have ended up flat on the deck. She says, "Clear the decks for action fellas! I got a beauty!" By this time we're not surprised at anything Tootie does and she plays this fish like a veteran. After getting our outfits in and out of the way, we slip loose from the anchor and drift with the tide and fish. Twenty minutes later Tootie says, "Well, it won't be long now, I see bubbles and that's my sign it's beginning to tire." She even knows about the bubbles and tired fish! I really have to change my original ideas about taking her fishing; she knows her fishing for sure! Somebody taught this gal a lot; we had no idea she knew anything at all.

We soon see the fish and find it to be a nice keeper without any question. Johnny nets it and Tootie says, "Johnny, just string that fella on a rope and keep him alive till we finish the day and then we can tend to him."

Johnny informs Tootie that as much as we'd like to see her keep fishing we can't take a chance on party fishing with Nugent so hot to toss us in the bucket for any minor infraction of the law. Tootie punches her card and says that's fine with her; she will tend to baiting and lunch detail, sort of a glorified deck hand so to speak.

She says, "Fellas, if you'll hand me that 'wee' bucket and turn you backs I'll tend to a small matter here so I can give all my concentration to more important duties at hand." There's no running for shore and hiding in the brush; so far this little gal has done no wrong.

Johnny thinks maybe he'd like a beer and a sandwich and Tootie says, "Fine, coming right up. I also have some hard-boiled eggs, sharp cheddar slices and for sandwiches, peanut butter and jelly or ham on rye topped with a nice slice of Walla Walla sweet onion. Take your choice; I also fried some chicken."

However, before Johnny gets his lunch we have to land another fish, this time it's Johnny's and it also turns out to be a nice legal fish. After running a rope through it's gills, it joins the other one on our tether. Now this leaves me the only one fishing, hopefully, after a quick shrimp dip in the gromafraw juice, I won't be too long. It would end a perfect day if each of us catches a nice one and we don't have to spend a half day with only one of us fishing.

Johnny and Tootie go back to the beer and lunch. We just manage to finish before I tie into what hopefully, will be our last fish of the day. It proves to be another nice fish, and after fifteen minutes it surfaces and Johnny nets it, places it on the stringer with the other two and says, "Well, what a great day! We all got our fish in record time.

"Let's have another beer and toast our success before we clean things up and head for home, but first I'll kill these fish."

As Johnny grabs a club to dispatch the fish, Tootie pipes up and says, "Johnny, wait a sec, just give me that sharp long-bladed knife and I'll split their gills and bleed them. The meat is always so much nicer if you do. You know how it is, you guys wouldn't think of not bleeding an animal after killing it and this is the same." Seems like Johnny and I have heard this before. I figured I knew just about everything about fishing these things, but it seems like there's a few stones still unturned. We're not too old to learn, but I never figured any of it would be from the likes of Tootie.

She reaches over the side and operates on each fish, saying as she does, "Now, let's have that beer and in about ten minutes we can lay those fish in here on this tarp and there will be no muss, no fuss, and no blood." We relax and have our beer and just sit and discuss what a nice day we've had; weather, company, and fish, all the way around.

All at once down the river roars this big jet sled with an inboard engine and it's on us before you can say 'Jack Robinson.'

Guess who? None other than good ole Nugent with a couple deputies out to make life miserable for as many fishermen as they can cover with a fast boat and ticket book. As they pull up tight to our boat Nugent says, "All right, let's see each of your licenses and punch cards, and be quick about it. We don't have all day, ya know."

It looks to me like Nugent is trying to show off a bit in front of the two young deputies, and maybe we should just push him as far as we can without getting ourselves in over our heads.

"You know Nugent," I say, "you checked our licenses not over three weeks ago. Have you forgotten or is this the first sign of senility and mental retardation of one who is definitely on the down-hill slide of life expectancy?"

Nugent tries to ignore this but the sudden facial flush gives his true feelings away as he answers, "Just your punch cards. Let's just make sure they're up to date as of right now, with all these fresh caught fish."

Oh, how he'd like to find us wrong. He checks mine and then Johnny's and last asks for Tootie's license and punch card. Tootie says, "I don't think I have all that but I'll sure give you what I have." Right away Nugent perks up, he thinks at last he's going to get us.

I don't know what's the matter with Tootie, but before I can correct her, she winks at Johnny and me and we keep quiet just to see what will develop. Nugent says, as he smiles from ear-to-ear with anticipation, "Well little lady, let's see just what you do have." Tootie digs around in her wallet and hands something to Nugent. He looks and says "This is your driver's license. If this is it, then you can't catch fish legally with one of these, and I'm so sorry, but I'll just have to give you a citation.

"Now, let's see. No fishing license, no Sturgeon license and no punch card. My, my, and one illegal fish which, if I wasn't a nice guy, I would hold you all collectively responsible for."

Tootie says, "I met your wife a while back. She seemed like such a nice lady; I'm surprised she can still be so pleasant in view of whom she has to put up with." Nugent flushes again but makes no reply. He can hardly contain himself, he's too excited about finally getting to write a ticket to someone in our party.

Nugent has his book out and is asking the usual questions when Tootie interrupts and says, "I knew some game wardens once back in the 60's, and they were a fine group of honest, hard-working dedicated men.....gentlemen, all. It seems since then there has been a steady decline in quality personnel. It's too bad you couldn't have found other means of employment before you fell into this category, sir. I hope these young men with you rise above the standards you're setting for them."

Nugent is now shaking so bad he cannot continue to write and turns to one of the deputies and says, "You finish fillin' out this citation while I measure these fish."

Johnny says, "Nugent, unless your eyes have deteriorated along with your brain, there's really no need to measure those fish. One quick glance will show you they're all well inside the legal limit."

Nugent doesn't seem to hear; he measures each one anyway. I say, "Nugent, you're shakin' so bad I doubt if you can get an honest measure; maybe you better turn that over to the other deputy and then you can just concentrate more on being your usual obnoxious self and lower your blood pressure and stall your funeral a little longer."

The ticket is finally filled out and handed back to Nugent to validate and present to Tootie for signature. Nugent, now all smiles, hands it to her and says, "I'm so sorry, but I'll have to confiscate all three fish because it's obvious one is illegal but not knowing which one, I'll have to take them all."

Nugent grabs the tether and with help from the two deputies,

233

drags all three fish aboard their boat and just before they get ready to take off with our catch he says, "I'll see you all in court on Tuesday."

Johnny says, "Hold on just a darn minute, Nugent! Tootie, I thought you said you had a fishing license and a Sturgeon license."

"Oh my, yes!" Tootie says. "You gentlemen got me so flustered I forgot all about that. If you'll just wait one minute I'll see if I can't locate them for you."

She then digs around in her wallet again, and comes up with the valid fishing license, Sturgeon license and punch card. Nugent's little plan is starting to unravel right before his eyes, but he has one ace left. He says, "Yes, your licenses seem to be in order." He doesn't even look at the punch card because if she forgot she had it, then she sure didn't remember to punch it.

"I'll have to just re-write your citation for not punching today's catch on your punch card." So Nugent tears up the other tickets and proceeds to write a new one for failure to have a valid punch card.

We know she punched her card because we watched her do it! We're wondering just what Tootie has up her sleeve now. He writes out the new citation and then Johnny says, "Nugent, you're assuming her punch card isn't punched. Before you make a complete fool of yourself, you should check her card."

Through gritted teeth Nugent says, "I'll check it, but there's no way it can be punched!"

He checks.....it is.....Nugent is absolutely purple with rage. He bellows "Just how in hell can this be punched when she forgot she even had it? It's an impossibility! How could this happen?"

Tootie smiles and says, "Well, when I knew for sure I was going fishing today I was so sure I would catch a fish that I just went ahead and punched my card. If I hadn't caught one, I wouldn't be out anything; but I was so sure I would, I just went ahead and did it. I guess it all worked out for the best, didn't it, sir?"

Nugent is tearing the second ticket into little tiny pieces and casting them on the water, absolutely speechless and beaten.

But Tootie is not through, she says, "Mr. Nugent sir, I'm very sorry, but I must make a citizen's arrest for littering. However, we'll make an exception in your case if you'll just pick up all those little pieces of paper that are drifting aimlessly away on the water. I do hope you'll be more considerate of the environment in the future."

Nugent gets out a little trout net and scoops up all the little torn ticket pieces. I think he is probably churning up a fresh batch of buttermilk on the inside but in the presence of the two deputies he knows he's wrong and must honor Tootie's request. He's caught with his pants down, so to speak. He stops momentarily and Tootie says, "Reach way out there to your left. You missed one wee bit. Now, if you will be so kind as to transfer our catch to our boat, we'll forget this entire ugly incident. I hope you young men have learned a valuable lesson from Officer Nugent's inability to satisfactorily carry out his law-enforcement duties."

Now, I have never in my life seen anyone needle anybody better than Tootie did Nugent. I've always considered myself to be a first class needler, but I swear I can't hold a candle to this gal. I just got a post-graduate course from an expert.

Nugent returns our fish and pushes off from our boat, soon roaring away without another word. Tootie says "I hope that mean man doesn't get to Three Rod Bob before he gets his lines snipped. After all, like you said, he's doing the fishing research for the rest of us at the expense of Nugent possibly nailing him."

We head on back to the boat launch and home after what I would consider an almost perfect day. In fact, it was perfect! Even Nugent's intrusion turned out to be a plus.

The fellows at the boat launch gather round and admire our catch. It seems no one else has had much luck. These guys think it's the boat, but we know the gromafraw is a big help that they'll probably never know about.....at least not from us.

We load up and head home. On the way Tootie asks, "Have either of you tried slip-bobber fishing for Jack salmon?" Johnny and I look at each other and think here we go again; we're about to learn

235

another lesson. We admit we haven't, and Tootie says, "Next fall when the Jacks are running, I'll show you something almost as much fun as Sturgeon fishing." It's amazing all Tootie seems to know.

As we near home I ask Tootie if she wants us to drop her off at home or does she want to get in on the fish cleaning detail? Her answer is: "Fellas, it's not all fun; let's all join in on this little chore and we'll get it done in no time at all."

We all work together and have the fish cleaned in no time, just like Tootie said. Then we divide up the fish in vacuum-packed packages.

Johnny says, "I'll give Tootie a lift home and see you in the morning."

Tootie says, "Toad, if you'll bring Snooks and Johnny over tomorrow evening for a dinner of fresh, batter-dipped, deep-fried Sturgeon pieces, I'll be the cook. Come early for a drink, around 5:30, say."

I reply with a smile, "Tootie, that will be a real treat and I'll see that we're all there on time." I must say this has been a perfect day, yes-siree, absolutely perfect.

# 18

# Strange Revelations

As I walk in the house Snooks is waiting, all ears, to find out how our day went. Her first remark is, "Well Toad, you look like it might not have been too bad a day. At least that scowl you left with this morning seems to be gone. In fact, if I didn't know better, I'd say you look almost like you could smile real easy. Can that be true? Could it be that for once in your life, your sixth sense let you down? Could it be that you might even have enjoyed your day of fishing?"

Rose is in one of her needly moods I can see, but it's no problem today. I can cope with anything she throws at me, which would have been difficult if it had not been such a good day.

"Yes Snooks, we had a real fantastic day, and you're right, my ninety-nine-percent-perfect-sixth-sense was one-hundred percent wrong! In fact, not only was it a nice day, it was a fantastic day! Tootie is a born fisherperson. She knows fishin' stuff that most fishermen are not even aware of. Not only that, but she can cast, bait her hook, and also she puts up a lunch beyond belief. She not only holds up her end, but does more than her share of everything."

Snooks says, "You see, I told you Tootie was a nice lady, but you wouldn't take my word, you had to worry yourself to death for a whole week. Next time you might listen to me and save yourself a lot of frustration."

There's one thing about Snooks, she's always eager to hand out free information. Too bad she can't charge for it, we'd be wealthy.

When I tell Snooks that we are invited with Johnny to Tootie's place tomorrow about five for drinks and dinner with fresh, batter-dipped Sturgeon, Snooks says, "How nice of Tootie. I'll call and see if there's anything I can bring." I tell her to go ahead and ask, but from what I've seen Tootie won't want us to bring a thing, she'll have everything under control.

Snooks calls and those two are talking and laughing on the phone for twenty minutes. When she finally hangs up she says, "My gracious, that little lady is really wound up! She thinks you and Johnny are just like little gods. She said she hasn't enjoyed a day so much in many a moon, and sure hopes you two will ask her again; and you're right, she said her plans are all made; we just need to bring ourselves and our appetites. My, but she seems nice. I'm really looking forward to our evening out."

Johnny swings by for a cup of tea the next morning and right away Snooks is quizzing him as to how he enjoyed our day's fishing with Tootie. Johnny remarks that Tootie sure does know a lot about fishing. Snooks says she talked with her and Tootie would sure enjoy another invitation, and I can see Johnny is sort of waiting to see what I have to say, so I tell him that as far as I'm concerned, yesterday was a pleasure and Tootie can go along anytime she wants to go. Johnny says, "Yeah, she sure wasn't any trouble. We'll take her once in a while as long as she'll fix a nice lunch for us. Boy, she really can fix a first-class lunch."

Johnny leaves but says he'll meet us at Tootie's about five. Right away Snooks is trying to think of something we can take as a gift and finally decides on a couple pint jars of our own smoked and canned Sturgeon. I don't know why you always have to take something every time you go visit somebody, but it seems to be something somebody started and now you have to do it to keep up with the Jones' I guess.

The phone rings and it's Peggy Parkinfarker. She wants us to come over and play cards with her and Pete next Thursday evening. We check; we're free, so it's a date. Snooks says, "Boy, are we getting popular; invited out two nights in the same week. Don't Pete and Peggy live pretty close to Tootie?"

"Yeah," I say. "I think they live on the same street but about a block apart on opposite sides of the street; about four doors down from Angus and Mamie O'leary, the newlyweds."

Snooks gets a funny little grin on her face. I have to ask, "All right Snooks, what prompts that sly little grin just now? If I had to hazard a guess I'd say you know something I'd probably like to know. Are you going to tell me or leave me in suspense all day?"

Snooks says, "Well, I'll tell you, but you have to promise not to tell a soul."

I reply quickly, "O.K. Snooks, I promise. Now what's the big secret?"

"Well, when you mentioned Angus and Mamie it reminded me of a conversation Mamie and I had in the supermarket just yesterday."

"Yes, yes, Snooks, go on."

"Well, I ran into Mamie and asked how she and Angus were going and she said, 'Not speaking at the moment.' I asked what the trouble was and she said, 'Let's go sit down and have a cup of coffee and I'll tell you what Angus did.

"'Monday he came home with a gift for me, all wrapped up in a pretty box with a beautiful ribbon. He said, 'Bought you something, honey. Take a look.' Well, I unwrapped it and guess what? It was a flimsy little negligee, but so skimpy there was absolutely nothing to it at all! I told him, 'Angus, I'm not wearing a thing like that! There's nothing to it.....it's almost vulgar!' He kept after me and pestering and all, so I finally told him, 'O.K., I'll let you have just one look.' As I headed into the bedroom to change I thought to myself, I'm going to fool him. I'll just come out with nothing on, totally naked except for my earrings and high heels. So I came out and turned around like I was modeling it and asked Angus how he liked it? He said, 'Holy cow! For what I paid for that, you'd have thought they'd at least have ironed out the wrinkles, wouldn't you?'"

I really have to laugh; I can just picture it all, and Snooks says, "We might think it's funny, but Mamie sure didn't and I'd say things will be pretty cool in the O'Leary household for quite a spell. Remember now, you promised not to tell a soul, not even Johnny, or I'll see that you get the same treatment as Angus. After all, Mamie told me in strict confidence."

I remind Snooks that a promise is a promise and no matter what, I won't breathe a word to anybody. Snooks looks at me with a look of distrust. I never can figure why she doesn't ever totally trust or believe me.

We arrive at Tootie's right on time and Johnny is already there, drink in hand. Tootie takes our wraps and the jars of smoked Sturgeon. Right away she says, "I've heard about your smoked fish. Let's open this right now and try some with a little blue cheese and crackers. I made up a pitcher of margaritas from a recipe I picked up in Guadalajara. Shall we have a little drink before dinner?"

As soon as we're all settled, Tootie tells us how much she enjoyed her fishing trip, and we assure her that we will be glad to have her with us on some trips in the future, as long as she'll fix the lunch. She says the lunch is a pleasure to fix for two guys who enjoy eating like we do.

Tootie wonders if we heard about the trick Truman Halftrack pulled on his friend Artie Farkler when Artie had his big garage sale last week? It seems that Artie is a born worrier and Truman waited until the garage sale was in full swing then he had a friend who was visiting from out of town go over to Artie's, walk around looking at things and finally pick out an item he wanted and ask "Who's putting on this sale?" Artie was standing close by and said he was, and asked why the man wanted to know?

The fellow then tells Artie to show his City and also County Garage Sale Permits, which, he says, should be exposed in plain sight. He shows Artie a little dimestore badge, but by this time Artie doesn't even give it a second look because he's never heard of a Garage Sale Permit and he's instantly a bundle of nerves. While he is stammering around trying to prove his ignorance, the "Inspector" is paying no attention but asking for name, address and phone number to write in an official looking little notebook.

Now this is when Truman steps in and really gets abusive with his out-of-town friend who is posing as the "Inspector." Artie of course, doesn't want to ruffle any feathers because he's convinced he's wrong, and for Truman to step in now can do nothing but make things a lot worse for himself. Artie says, "Truman, just leave it alone."

But Truman says, "Artie, you don't have to take this from some dim-wit county moron. Check on your rights! I never heard of a Garage Sale Permit."

At last the "Inspector" tells Artie that he was just going to issue a warning ticket but with this loud-mouth, trouble maker's added insults he's going to throw the book at Artie and will expect to see him in court on Thursday. In the meantime, Artie is free on his personal recognizance, unless his mouthy friend continues to insult a county official.

The "Inspector" leaves and now Artie is mad at Truman and the whole glorious garage sale day is ruined. Artie is a nervous wreck and mad besides. Now Truman is wondering when Artie finds out the truth, is he going to forgive Truman or are things going to be worse? In the end, it looks like Truman bit off more than he could chew and now the shoe is on the other foot.

This gives all of us a conversation piece for about half an hour. During that time Tootie pours us all another margarita and says she must start dinner. Snooks starts to ask Tootie if she can help when Johnny says, "Tootie, I'll batter the fish while you tend the deep fryer." We all end up going to the kitchen and helping, and it's just a real nice friendly atmosphere. Tootie has a knack of making everyone feel right at home.

The dinner is fantastic; the batter-dipped Sturgeon is a rare treat and Tootie is a good hostess and cook on top of it all. As we get ready to leave, Johnny holds back and decides to stay and help Tootie clean things up.

On the way home Snooks starts in with an assumption that there is a little something going on between Tootie and Johnny. I say, "Snooks, why do you always have to try to read something into something that has no earthly foundation at all?"

Snooks replies, "I'm just more observant than you are. I'll bet Johnny is more acquainted with that household than meets the eye." I ask her to just give me one reason to feel that situation could exist. "O.K." Snooks says, "I'll even give you two: Number one, John was ready to go in a strange kitchen and help with the dinner preparations. That really was my place but he interrupted my offer to help and placed himself in that position, which showed me a familiarity beyond what we had thought. Number two, Johnny's desire to stay and help clean up the kitchen, just another indication.

"I'm so sure of myself Toad, that I'll just bet you a weekend at the beach against a night at the opera that I'm right, and we'll let the bet ride until it's proven one way or the other. Besides, I saw a couple little looks go between those two that also triggered my suspicions. You want to take my bet?"

"Sure," I say "but I know you're wrong Snooks, because if there was anything like you're suggesting, Johnny would have mentioned something to me, and he's never even indicated he knows how to spell her name! I'm a sure winner for a weekend at the beach. You just enjoy trying to make something out of nothing."

This just proves to me that women are always looking for any way to dig up something to gossip about. They all really love to gossip, and it seems my Snooks is no exception. I'll have to admit some gals are more addicted to the gossip bug than others, but there's no doubt it's a born-in natural trait. Men simply do not have it. Snooks has tried to make something out of nothing at Johnny's expense. All Johnny was trying to do was be a gentleman. It will be a pleasure to see her lose this bet.

"Snooks, my dear, I promised you I'd not mention the O'Leary's and the negligee event. Now I'd like you to not start asking Johnny any little hidden questions about his activities. Because if there is anything, such as you seem to think there is, we should let John tell us on his own without trying to trick him. Can you promise me you won't start asking questions?"

Snooks' evasive answer is, "Well, it sounds from that remark that maybe you too have some questions as to his association with Tootie."

I say "No, Snooks. I just want an answer to my question, and all you're doing is side-stepping it. Since I had to make a promise, I think you should, too."

Snooks decides that she will promise as long as I'll keep my promise; if I say anything about O'Leary's then she might get inquisitive with Johnny. Funny, but she seems to always hold the ace in the hole.

As we crawl into bed I say, "Snooks, have you ever noticed when you see a flock of sheep that there always seems to be one black sheep in the flock? Did you ever stop to wonder why just one black sheep?"

Snooks replies, "Frankly, I don't care why, but frequently you seem to find a reason to give me some no-good, unearthly question to mull around and ruin my night's sleep."

"Snooks, it's just something to keep you from thinking all night about some off-hand, no basis, intuition you think you have about poor Johnny. Now good night, Snooks. It's way past your bed time.....particularly when you probably won't sleep too well anyway."

Over morning coffee I ask Snooks where Nancy is? Haven't seen her much lately, and Snooks informs me that Nugent is retiring soon and Nancy is getting things ready for his retirement party and making plans for things to do together after they retire. I ask Snooks why in the world she hasn't informed me of this choice piece of news and her answer is, "I'm just not one to gossip you know."

This means at last we'll be rid of a real adverse factor in our fishing pleasure. But on the other hand, Nugent was always an easy challenge as long as we were right. I won't miss his underhanded trickery though. I tell Snooks not to plan on my attendance at a retirement party for someone I dislike as much as Nugent. Snooks replies "I think he'll be just as glad you're not there as you will be."

I'm reminded that this is the evening we go to Pete and Peggy Parkinfarker's for cards and I'd better get a trim. After breakfast I go right down to Jerry's and get in line for my haircut. It seems that there are very few good barbers left like Jerry, everybody else has turned into a hair stylist, which seems about the same except the stylists don't know as much as the good old barber, and they get paid more. A good plain barber seems to be going the way of the Dodo bird.

It seems like a barber shop is always a prime place for men to pick up any loose news going around. I guess this is about as close as men get to gossiping. Billy Booze, Hank Edwards and Arty Farkler are there already ahead of me and Jerry has Snarly Krautkramer in the chair, just finishing up on the razor trim.

I say "Hi" all the way around, and then ask Billy what he and Hank have been up to since that frog accident last fall? Billy says "Not much" and wants to know if we've heard about the service station north of town that advertises free sex with a fill-up? It seems that the contest rule is simple: free sex with every fill up.....all you have to do is pick the correct number from one to ten. Well, Billy filled his car and guessed seven and the service station guy said he was sorry but he was thinking of four, but told Billy and Hank to come back next week and try again, which they did. This time Billy picked six and the guy said he was sorry but he was thinking of eight. They were telling us all about it and Billy says, "You know, I think that contest is crooked."

Then Artie Farkler pipes up and says, "No, it ain't! My wife won twice last week."

So Billy decides they better give it one more try. "After all," he says, "it ain't every day you can get a chance at free sex."

I can't wait to get home and tell Snooks about this conversation over the free sex with a fill-up. Her response is, "Is that all you fellows talk about when you get together? I'm just telling you Sport, don't get any bright ideas about filling your tank and trying your luck or you may end up without a car to put gas in!"

During lunch Snooks again mentions how much she was impressed by Tootie and what a nice lady she is. Snooks must be really impressed to bring it up again. During this conversation who stops by for a chat but none other than Tootie herself. She says she just happened to be going by and thought she'd stop in and tell us how much she enjoyed our get-together and she hopes we can do it often. Snooks tells Tootie she's glad to hear that and we sure will and real soon, too. So it sort of looks like the feelings are mutual.

After dinner we go over to Pete and Peggy's for a wicked game of Hearts. Hearts is a game you never want to play with anyone but good friends, because it can get real vicious, frustrating, and nasty. During the course of the evening, mixed in with all the usual harmless social conversation, Snooks mentions having met Tootie and what a fine lady she is. She adds, "It's a shame such a pleasant, attractive lady lost her husband and now lives alone. I hope someday she'll find some nice man and again have companionship."

I'm sitting here just wondering if Snooks hasn't just broken her promise of silence about Johnny. Snooks is slippery as an eel when she wants to be and I think this is one of those times; but the frustrating thing is, there's no way to prove it and Snooks will probably sidestep any question I might throw in that direction later in the confines of our own home.

Snooks has just thrown out the baited hook and Peg jumps in and swallows hook, line and sinker without any hesitation. Peg has fallen prey to Snooks' trickery, I'm sure, because Peg is not one to gossip or cause anyone's business to become meat for inquisitive nosy busybodies.

"Snooks," Peg says, "don't feel too sorry for poor Tootie, because frequently she has an overnight gentleman visitor. It's been going on quite regular for the last three months or so now. It seems he shows up just after dark, with shaving kit no less, and leaves just before daylight." Snooks flips me a knowing triumphant look; had she been sitting next to me she'd have been kicking violently at my leg; but I'm safe, she's too far away this time. The "overnighter" could be somebody else. This is all circumstantial; it could be anybody. Snooks just knows now that Tootie has a friend, not necessarily by any means Johnny.

We go on playing and after a couple games we have coffee and apple pie. We say our good-byes and as soon as we're in the car Snooks asks, "Would you mind driving down by Tootie's on the way home?"

I say, "Snooks, that was a real underhanded bit of trickery that you pulled on poor Peg to gain information about Tootie."

"It was just normal conversation, and besides Peggy told it willingly. I didn't ask."

"No, but you put forth the suggestion you knew would lead into the answer you received. I think it's a dirty, low-down trick and I'm ashamed of you."

Rose's answer, "Just cut the idle chatter and drive by Tootie's on the way home. Let's just see for ourselves, shall we?"

Tootie's is only about a block-and-a-half up the same street as Parkinfarker's, only on the other side of the street, so it's sure not out of the way. So instead of an argument I drive by and there's no car in front of Tootie's which should set the detective back on her heels for a spell.

Next morning at breakfast I mention to Snooks that she has forfeited her bet by bringing Tootie up at Parkinfarker's last night and Snooks immediately informs me the bet was to say nothing to Johnny; any other avenue of information was not included.

Snooks thinks like a lawyer. It is often said a fool acts as his own lawyer and when I argue with Snooks I usually end up like that fool and always on the short end of whatever is in question.

I hate to say it, but I'm beginning to think way back in one corner of my mind that there's a possibility I may have to attend the opera. If Johnny is the "overnighter" why hasn't he confided in me? If nothing else, it would have saved me from making such a bet as I did. I've put myself in a position to possibly have to live out one of my most horrible nightmares in reality. An opera! A necktie! Screeching singers and music in Italian or something else I can't understand. God forbid! I would never have made such a bet had I felt there was the faintest chance of losing.

Snooks had suspicions or she would never have bet and now that Peg has verified part of those suspicions you can be assured Snooks will not rest until she has the answer.

Next morning just in the middle of our coffee Johnny drives up and I say to Snooks, "Johnny's here. Better fix him a cup of tea, but keep in mind one word to lead him into a conversation like you did Peg and you'll never see the curtain rise on your opera bet, even if your suspicions turn out to be true."

Johnny has his cup of tea but says he has many things to do and just wanted to stop by and tell us how he enjoyed his evening at Tootie's with us. Snooks replies that we also enjoyed Tootie and the evening and what a fine lady she is. Then Snooks adds, "She would make quite a catch for some lucky man."

Boy, she is pushin' her opera luck right to the limit on that one! Johnny replies, "Yeah, maybe." It was not said in any way that would give Snoop a chance to gain any clues, and as much as she'd like to pursue it further she also realizes that she has pushed things right to the limit.

Johnny leaves and right away I voice my thoughts about her pushing her luck on the comments but her answer is, "You might just as well give up grasping at straws, because if it proves to be Johnny, and only time will tell, then Buster, you're on your way to buy opera tickets."

Nothing more is said until about two hours after dark and Snooks pipes up and says, "It's such a nice evening, let's go out for an ice cream cone."

"Snooks, that sounds like a great idea."

As soon as we're in the car Snooks says, "Why don't we drive by Tootie's? It's almost right on the way." I instantly realize that I have been totally hornswaggled into checking out Tootie's residence. It really wasn't an ice cream cone that was on Snooks' conniving, evil mind.

I have very little choice but to drive by. I'm sure it will save another long, drawn-out argument which I'm bound to lose anyway. Two blocks away Old Eagle Eye says, "Well, what do you know? It looks like a car in front of Tootie's." As we get closer she adds, "Well, for goodness sake! It's the same make, year and color as Johnny's, and now that we're real close, it seems to have the same license plate numbers as Johnny's. I would almost say that even you would have to admit that car has to be Johnny's."

I say "Snooks, this don't prove anything. He may just have stopped by for a few minutes to chat."

Snooks says, "Let's check by again before we go home and see if it's a short chat or maybe an all night chat.....shall we? In fact, why don't we take in the late movie after our ice cream cone and just check again on our way home from the show?"

"Snooks," I say, "the movie don't let out till almost one o'clock; that's pretty late for us, don't you think?"

Snooks replies, "We don't have to get up early. Let's just do it." So we do, knowing full well that it isn't a profound interest in the movie, but an excuse to be able to check on Johnny with what Snooks hopes will be proof positive.

After the movie we drive by Tootie's and all the lights are out.....but Johnny's car is still parked out in front. I must admit this looks like proof positive. Much to my surprise, Snooks does not gloat, in fact she does not say a word; which in itself is very upsetting.

Just as we're turning out the light on the bedside stand Snooks says, "Better pick up some opera tickets tomorrow.....just wanted to give you a little thought to sleep on, Dear. Good night." Rose can be cruel at times.

I really don't sleep much, not entirely because of the good night thought Snooks put in my head, but mostly in disbelief at Johnny not letting me know what was going on. He should have known he could trust me to keep a secret. Now just because he didn't, I'm stuck having to suffer through a fate worse than death.....an opera! I'm just a little upset with John.

After breakfast I tell Snooks I've got to run down to Peak's Plunkin Shack and pick up some swivels. Matter of fact, I just have to go get those opera tickets and also see if I can find Johnny and have a heart-to-heart talk with him. I've just got to hear it right from the horse's mouth before I'll believe it. Not that I blame him a bit; all I'm upset about is that he didn't tell me.

It's a funny thing but when you want to find somebody you never have any luck, and that's sure the case today. I drive around to every place that I ever heard of John going to, and that started with his house and then working my way around to any place I've heard him mention, but no luck.

I pick up the opera tickets last. I guess it was a matter of putting off the worst till last. Would you believe I had to stand in line twenty minutes to get those fool tickets? And the opera is a week away at that! I guess there are more crazy people in the world than a fellow ever figured.

The one place I didn't think to look for Johnny was at our house and would you know as I round the corner after a two-hour search there sits his car in our driveway. It looks like this just isn't my day.

As I walk in the house I can tell instantly something is different for sure. There sits Snooks, Tootie, and Johnny with an opened bottle of champagne and clinking glasses at 11:30 a.m.! Now this would strike even the most non-observant as mighty peculiar.

I ask, "What pray tell, is this big mid-morning celebration all about?"

Snooks says, "My dear, Johnny and Tootie have a wonderful announcement to make."

Johnny flushes just a bit and Tootie says, "Go ahead and tell them, Hon." Johnny clears his throat and proceeds to tell us that he and Tootie are going to sneak away next week to Reno for a long week-end and get married.

Snooks says, "Well, I'm just thrilled as can be! I don't think I could

249

have received any more thrilling and wonderful news."

I say that it's sure wonderful and we wish them all the best. Tootie wants to know if we would take her on another nice fishing trip after they get back and I assure her it will be a pleasure any time. We kill the champagne, and the happy couple head out hand-in-hand.

Snooks doesn't wait until the latch clicks on the door before she says, "What night are our tickets for the opera?" I tell her a week from Saturday and she says, "How coincidental, that's the night Johnny and Tootie plan to be married."

I say, "Yeah, I don't know how they can be so happy, and I so miserable at the same time, and it all came about over the same situation."

# 19

# Operantics

Snooks informs me that next Saturday night is a busy night for many. Johnny and Tootie will be getting married, and it's also the night of Nugent's retirement party. "And that's nice," Snooks says. "A retirement party, a wedding and an opera; and you lucked out with the opera. What do you intend to wear?" I tell her I figure I'll wear my pin-stripe, navy-blue suit, the one I always wear to sad affairs like funerals. Snooks reminds me that at the get-together after B.B. Brain Bennet's funeral I spilled mustard on the left lapel of that suit and she doesn't think it's been to the cleaners since.

"Not to worry Snooks, I wiped that mustard off slick and clean with a paper napkin. There's no reason to worry about that."

But Snooks persists and says, "That suit has to go to the cleaners pronto to be sure and get it back in time. So I'll drop it off on my way to the city when I look for a new outfit for the occasion."

"Snooks, you have plenty of things to wear. Why do you need something new?"

She tells me she might see someone at the opera who would re-member seeing her in an outfit she'd worn somewhere before. An absolute female no-no, not understood by males at all.

I think it stems from the clothing people brain washing women over a long period of time until now it's a known fact. The women have fallen for the old "got-to-have-something-new-for-every-occasion trick.'

The week passes all too soon, and is pretty uneventful. We don't see Johnny or Tootie or hardly anybody; they're all busy on some big project or other, and before I know it, it's Saturday morning. It's funny how fast things come along that you don't want to come along at all. The suit isn't back from the cleaners yet; maybe I'll luck out and not have to go to the opera at all. I must be using mental telepathy because about the same time I think of the suit Snooks says, "I better call the cleaners about your suit, it isn't back yet and they promised it yesterday." Snooks makes the call and says, "WHAT! You mean to tell me it's not ready yet? Why? OH MY! Well, we'll just have to do something else; but this isn't the last you'll hear of this matter, let me tell you that, Buster!"

Snooks slams the phone down and says, "Those idiots sent your suit to the wrong address with a new delivery boy on the van; and now, those people are gone for a week!"

Quickly I put in, "Well Snooks, it's no big deal. It's not like it's the end of the world. We really can put it off for a year or two, you know."

Snooks is in no mood for any kind of humor particularly from me, and certainly not right now. She replies, "You're not getting off that easy! You made a bet, you have tickets; we go come hell or high water!

"You just trot right down to that tuxedo rental place and get decked out in a style that will look well with the new gown I bought. And since you don't have much time, I'd suggest you tend to it like yesterday!" This just adds insult to injury; I didn't even wear one of those git-ups to my own wedding and now I'm stuck for sure, and Snooks is in no mood for me to go against her iron will.

I trot down to see about a rental and all the time I'm praying they won't have my size or some freak thing will still save me, but luck is not to be on my side today. The tux shop has just what I need; they almost act like they were just waiting for me. It's just uncanny and it's my lucky day, they tell me. The suit is half price if I get it back by noon Monday. Just another of life's tragic lucky breaks, I guess.

When I return, Snooks is overjoyed to see I found just what she sent me after. She tells me she'd thought about going with me to make sure I got the right thing but she called the shop while I was on the way and they told her not to worry, they would fix me up just fine. Which explains why they had things all laid out and waiting and knew what I needed even before I did. Rose just isn't going to let anything spoil her night at the opera. Well, I'll tell you something; this will be the first and last time, so she better make the most of it!

Snooks is all bubbly smiles, and says, "This is going to be special, I have read about Luigi Mancinelli, and been interested in his operas, and this is his best, 'Ero e Leandro.' Also, this is the first time it's been presented in the States and we'll be there! My gracious, but this will be special and a time to remember."

Personally I'd find watching paint dry, or a piano recital for four-year olds to be much more entertaining.

The dreaded words are finally announced. Snooks hollers and says, "Honey, it's time to dress. After all, we don't want to be late now, do we?"

"No Snooks," I mumble, "we wouldn't want to be late, because once they turn out the lights it'd be difficult to find our seats, wouldn't it?" Just because she won the bet is no reason to have this attitude of triumphant superiority. Johnny really could have saved me if he just had let me know what was going on between him and Tootie. I doubt if he will ever know how his little bit of inconsideration could cause me so much misery.

I figure I better go along; too late to retreat now. I start to dress and spend nearly an hour getting everything to look just right. A look in the mirror and I must admit I cut a pretty dashing figure. We'll turn a few heads to be sure when we enter the halls of misery.

Snooks asks, "Are you about ready?"

I holler back and say, "Yeah, just finishing moussing and combing my hair."

Snooks says, "When you're ready, step out here and let me see how nice my darling looks in his first ever tuxedo! I'll just bet you're a sight to behold."

Well, when I step out to the close scrutiny of Snooks I'm sure not prepared for her reaction. She says, "WHERE IN GOD'S NAME DID

YOU COME UP WITH THAT?"

"That what?" I ask.

"That hideous looking, bright, overdone polkadot green-and-orange long necktie! That thing wouldn't even fit in at a class reunion picnic! Don't you know you need a bow tie with that outfit? Surely you must know that. Didn't they put one in the box with the tux when you got it?"

"Yes Snooks, there's one in the box, but you know how I hate any necktie and I thought this one would at least give things a little dash and color. Those dinky little bow ties are for the birds; they went out twenty years ago. I think they threw one in just in case I didn't have a tie at all."

"Oh no, my dear husband. They threw that in because it's the proper thing to wear with a tuxedo and to first-class, dress-up social occasions like Presidential inaugurations, Governers' balls and the opera. Now you go put on that dinky little tie before the one you're wearing makes me nauseated. And hurry, we've no time to waste."

Already I've had a serious crisis even before any crisis at all could possibly be expected. I just hope this is not a look at things to come. In the car I tell Snooks that she looks stunning in her new gown, but I think she might be a little over-dressed, more like she's going to the President's Inauguration or the Governor's Ball, not just a little old opera. Snooks doesn't act as though she heard me but she did, I can tell by the sound of her teeth grinding.

We arrive, and the first thing, some guy comes up and wants to park our car. I tell him, "I've got a driver's license and I got this far so I'll just tend to parkin' it myself."

Snooks breaks right in like she hasn't even heard me and tells this total stranger that it would be a pleasure to let him park our car. Now, she won't even let me drive after two or three beers, but she turns it over to a complete stranger without even a breathalizer. Sometimes I do declare, this woman is hard to understand.

As we walk in I tell Snooks, "I think that was a bum thing to do and I hope he don't sell our car. He looked like he needed money."

254

Snooks informs me that this is called 'valet parking' and it's done at most first-class social functions. I don't know how Snooks got so smart and I missed to much. She must have been soaking up knowledge while I was hunting and fishin' and enjoying nature. I'll have to disagree a little bit though, because Sid Snodgrass told me about something like this at a prize fight at the Indian casino, and you sure wouldn't classify that as a top-notch social function, I don't think.

We're finally ushered to our seats wading through a mass of humanity, each person trying to impress somebody else. It looks like hardly anybody is here to enjoy the evening's attraction. Mostly just showing off furs and diamonds. Funny thing though about furs, there aren't so many around any more now that it's become unpopular to let an animal run naked while you bask in his skin. Looks also to a casual observer that there's only a handful of men attending who look as though they have any intention of enjoying this affair. Probably pushed, tricked, or threatened into attendance. It's amazing what can be accomplished by cutting off a guy's sex life, poor devils.

We were given programs at the door when we entered and after being seated I take a quick look and it tells all about what we're going to see and hear. I ask Snooks, "What's the matter with these theater people? Don't they think we can watch and tell what's going on? Do they think we're too dumb to figure out a simple little play concocted years before computers, telephones and electricity? This thing goes clear back to 1892 before life ever became so trying. Looks to me like someone wants to make a simple thing look complicated. If they want to give us helpful directions they could tell us how to talk to a real person at the telephone company. Now that would be a real help! This program is just to impress us and make us think the show is worth what our tickets cost, which I'm sure it isn't."

A couple comes in and is seated right next to me. The man isn't saying much, sort of like me, but boy! she is thrilled and carrying on about her vast knowledge of other operas and how she thinks this one will compare to *Pagliacci*, which she "simply adored," and how she always enjoys *La Traviata*. Then she starts in on some composers. I have the misfortune of having her sit right next to me. It could have been her husband, the silent one, but no, I luck out with gabby. This is all just a disgusting show of knowledge to impress. Well, I don't need to be impressed. She turns to me and asks, "Don't you just love the works of Rimski Korsakov?"

I say, "Yeah, ol' Ripped Hiscorsetoff, he's one of the best all right." I get instant reaction from two sides simultaneously. A breath-taking left elbow in my rib cage from Snooks, and eyebrows raised over a nose so high in the air on my left that she's apt to run out of oxygen pretty quick.

I turn to Snooks because I'm in no mood to look up this gal's nostrils all night. Snooks whispers with a scowl, "If you don't know what you're talking about.....don't talk!"

I answer in a low whisper, "Well, I didn't start the conversation; gabby did, and it would have been impolite to just ignore her."

The lights go out and the stage is the only thing lit. The music starts, all kinds of instruments playing at random, a little here, a little there, but no tune or rhythm I can follow. None of it makes much sense. After fifteen minutes, I lean over and ask Snooks, "Why didn't they tune their instruments before the show started instead of taking up our time?"

Snooks replies through clenched teeth, "It's not a 'show.' It's an opera, you idiot. The musicians are half way through the opening number."

They sure as hell fooled me.

I look over at Nose Holes on my left and she has her hands clasped to her breast, eyes rolled back in her head like she's in some kind of an exotic trance. I knew right off she was short a few cards in her deck, and now I'm sure of it. Anybody who can get this carried away over a bunch of guys who can't even carry a tune should listen to the Hoosier Hot Shots and find out what real music is all about. Yeah, and old Spike could teach her a thing or two about good enjoyable music, too.

Next thing on the menu is some guy, who weighs about four hundred pounds, comes out and starts in babbling in what I figure is Greek, but Snooks says is Italian. Whichever. You can't understand a word of it and I don't think anyone wants you to either. I ask Snooks if opera singers are all fat but she don't give me an answer, just glares. I could ask Nose Holes but she's so far gone she wouldn't hear me and besides I have a distinct feeling she doesn't care to talk to me. I don't know why she thinks she's so superior, I'll bet she drank beer in high school right along with the rest of us. Time just seems to change some people.

Next on the stage comes some gal screechin' and bellerin' like she's really having an Italian attack of some kind. I say "Snooks, why don't somebody call 911 for that gal before it's too late?" Snooks just glares at me and Nose Holes comes out of her trance long enough to hear me and stick her nose up in the air again. I bet if she knew she needed to blow her nose she wouldn't be so all-fired anxious to show off her nose holes at every opportunity.

At last the program says it's Intermission. I ask Snooks if this is a pee break? Boy, do I get another dirty look! My question solves one thing though, Nose Holes heard me ask Snooks and now she has turned her back on me completely, and I must say it's a better view than I had before.

I have no idea what all is involved with Intermission, but let me tell you, it's much more like a Society Who's Who, show-of-wealth pee break than just an ordinary break like at Tony's Tavern after three pitchers of beer.

For any who is interested, they serve a nice mild white wine, probably the best part of the evening, and after I have three quick glasses Snooks drags me away and remarks rather emphatically, "That will be enough wine for you. Let's mingle."

Mingling means walk around and listen to everybody rave about what a wonderful voice the fat guy has and then try to compare it with some other fat guy at an opera they attended in Rome, Paris,

Budapest, Minske, Vladivostock.....or you name it! Anywhere to impress and outdo anyone else. It reminds me of the old saying: "The first liar don't have a chance."

Snooks says, "Don't try to outdo anybody because you may be good, but you don't have a chance with this bunch." Which is the first indication that Snooks and I might agree on something about this fiasco.

One fellow strikes up a conversation with me while Snooks is in the powder room. He inquires, "Quite a production, isn't it? I'm really looking forward to the second act."

I reply, "Yeah, but for my money it won't stack up to Blazing Saddles. Now there was a production!"

He looks at me sort of funny, then slowly begins to lose his stability, and turns a pasty white. Just as Snooks comes out of the restroom she sees him stagger over to a small table to gain some necessary support. Snooks remarks, "My, that fellow looks sick. I wonder what's wrong?"

I reply, "Snooks, I have no idea."

Heading back to our seats for the second act, I'm thinking what a pleasant time Johnny is having while I'm stuck to suffer through this mess for another hour or more. Johnny really let me down on this one.

I notice right off there's been a change in the seating arrangement. Nose Holes has made her husband sit next to me. Well, that's just fine with me. I wasn't enjoying her company any more than she was mine. I can tell she's said something to him because he also turns his back on me and spends all his time conversing with her.

The second act starts out entirely different than the first. A gal playing the haunting strains of a flute begins and it's quite soothing and meloooooo——I set the hook! It's on probably the prize biggest Sturgeon of my life! On and on the battle rages, gain a little line, lose a lot of line. Back is killing me. Sun is blazing hot. There he is! Big as big! Just one look and gone again. Can't last much longer. It seems like hours; my arms are like lead weights. Should have been pumpin' iron. Lose twenty yards of hard-earned line, everything points to a real tussle. More line out, can't hold him; burned, blistered thumb, all line going.....down to the last five yards, two yards, two feet; tighten the drag to the breaking point! Gained back a foot, my back is definitely broken, it'll never be the same. With a loud snap! the line breaks and I suddenly fall clear back into my opera seat, wringing wet with perspiration. All eyes for twenty feet in every direction are looking right at me.

My God, what did I do to deserve all this attention? There sits Snooks, bent over in her seat with her head in her hands, just shaking her head. The flute is long gone and now the music is just a lot of loud, loud clanging and banging. Enough to wake the dead for sure. I ask Snooks "What's all the fuss about? Why is everybody looking at us?" She still don't answer, just sits there holding her head.

She finally looks my way and her face is beet red and she says in a raspy whisper, "Shut up! I'll tell you when we get out of here. In the meantime, don't act like you even know me."

Well, I'm now oblivious to the opera because all I can think about is what might have created all the horrified stares aimed right at us; a few little titters and snickers going on, too.

I must have played that beautiful, big fish longer than I thought because the second act is over, and in my mind much faster than the first. At last I can get out of here. I think I'd rather rob a bee tree naked, than suffer through the likes of this ever again.

As we leave, Snooks walks briskly ahead of me and pays no attention as to whether I'm keeping up with her or not. The valet brings our car around and Snooks takes over and drives us home. It's a silent, long drive. I'm afraid to ask but I have the feeling that Snooks is silently trying to stifle a desire to commit premeditated murder.

The silence continues as we get ready for bed. Just before we turn out the lights I try to strike up a conversation by asking Snooks, "Why do they use sterilized needles for lethal injections?"

Snooks only reply is: "Shut up and go to sleep."

Next morning over wake-up coffee I finally get up nerve enough to take the bull by the horns and find out just what kind of trouble I'm really in. It's not fair to be in this much trouble and not even have any idea why, who or what.

"Snooks," I say, " as painful as it might be for you, I think you should have the decency to tell me what in the world caused all the snickers and wild-eyed stares aimed in our direction at the opera last night."

Snooks looks into her coffee cup, stirs slowly and finally speaks. "I have never in my life been so mortified and embarrassed as last night. After thinking it over, however, I was partly to blame. I should have known better than to serve you navy bean soup and a weiner and sauerkraut sandwich the same evening when we were going to a function like that.

"I didn't mind your little light, almost like a kitten purring, snore. The flute was restful, and made a relaxing, beautiful sound. After the flute there was one loud clang of large cymbals, then silence. I'll admit the loud percussion after the haunting flute was enough to startle anybody, but you timed things just right to interrupt the total silence immediately after the percussion of those cymbals. Yes, you filled the silence.....with the unmistakable sound of passing gas. Part of my mortification involved wondering if per chance they all might have thought it was me."

"You know Snooks, the way you were holding your head and all, I'll bet there's a good chance some of them could have thought that all right."

"I can say one thing, my friend," Snooks continues "after that display of crepitation you need not ever worry about being asked, forced, or for that matter, even allowed to another function of that nature!

"When Tootie and Johnny get home, I'll see if Tootie would care to accompany me in the future. I really like her and want to get to know her better. I can't ask dear Nancy because she's indicated that she and Norman will probably move to California. He just doesn't feel comfortable living in an area where he feels he has no friends."

I tell her, "Yeah, he's got that right! If I was him, I'd fear for my life, the way he treated us."

I'm glad I'll never have to go to another opera, but I'll have to admit I would never purposely have gone to such extremes to get out of it. But then, it wasn't on purpose or knowingly. HA!

# 20

# The Screamin' Battery

Life is suddenly becoming more beautifuller than it's been in a long time. One giant step for all sportsmen and particularly fishermen and particularly me.....in getting rid of Nugent. Next big step is never, ever having to think about suffering through another opera. I even had a slight headache from that cheap wine they served at half time. Also, Johnny and Tootie make a happy couple, and it looks like it will be a beautiful foursome now with Snooks and Tootie liking one another as they do. We should all have a lot in common and enjoy doing things together.

Come Tuesday morning Johnny and Tootie stop by. They just got back from Reno late last night and they're all excited and just bubbling over with love, enthusiasm and good cheer. Ain't love grand? I can remember when Snooks used to call me her "something special" now it's her "idiot child." It's funny how time turns those little pet names around, even "idiot child" is said with still a certain sense of fondness and mischief.

After telling us about their wedding trip, Tootie pipes up and says, "Toad, now I'm really serious, when can we go fishing again? I just love that Sturgeon fishing. I guess I can't get enough of it."

I tell her, "Tide's right Thursday. How about that?"

Tootie asks Johnny and his answer is, "When it comes to Sturgeon, I'm ready any time, day or night, summer or winter, sick or well."

I think that statement sounds remotely like something left over from a wedding ceremony.

Then Tootie asks, "Snooks, you'll come with us, won't you?"

Snooks replies, "When you get a boat big enough where I can walk around a few steps. Then I'll be there with bells on, but three's plenty in that little boat."

Wednesday morning I wake with a terrible pain in my right big toe and ankle and cannot even put my foot on the floor without getting the screaming collywobbles. I ask Snooks to call Johnny and Tootie and tell them there's no way I can go fishing tomorrow, that I have such a terrible pain in my foot and ankle that I can hardly walk. Snooks makes the call for me, then says that Johnny wants to talk with me for a minute.

John asks if I happened to drink quite a bit of wine while they were gone, and I say, "Yeah, how did you know? I drank wine at the opera."

Johnny says "I'd bet a nickel to a pinch of goose crap that you have an acute attack of gout; I had it once and it's terrible."

"You got that right, John. I can hardly stand to even look at my foot; and any pressure, like walking, is just out of the question."

Johnny says, "You get ready and I'll be right over and run you over to Doc Crandle's. They have pills to clear that up in no time at all."

I tell him, "I'll be ready all right, but hurry!"

We're lucky when we get to Doc's office, he's had a cancellation and I only have to wait about ten minutes. Doc looks at me hobbling in and says, "Looks like gout clear from here."

"O.K." I say "then just give me some of those magic little pills you have to get rid of this misery."

Doc says, "Not so fast now. It's not quite that simple, first we need a blood test. Otherwise I don't know what strength medication you need."

Well, I'm in no mood to argue and it sounds sensible at that. The nurse comes in and draws off a vial of blood and I ask if it takes that much just to check on gout? She replies, "No, but we always take enough to check on a number of things. This test is called a Screen and Battery, and will tell us about everything from kidney function to liver condition. It's really marvelous what this will tell us."

"Well," I say, "all I'm here for is just to get this gout cured as quick as possible. My kidneys work real well; I'm up almost every two hours at night."

The nurse says, "Sounds like you're right about kidneys, but it also sounds to me like you could have some prostate enlargement."

I've just learned a valuable lesson: don't volunteer any information at a doctor's office, because nurses and doctors will figure out some way to make you unhealthy, even when you feel good.

Pretty quick Doc comes in with a little sample bottle of pills and says, "Take one twice a day and if you're not fine by Monday, come back in. Incidentally, have Helen give you an appointment to come in as soon as we get your blood test results back from the lab, probably the middle of next week."

I make my appointment and Helen hands me another little sample bottle. I say, "Doc already gave me some gout pills."

Helen says, "Those may upset your stomach. Take these, one at the same time, to keep from possibly devloping an ulcer." One pill to save you from the other pill, now that's a strange arrangement.

I limp out with Johnny's help and as we head home in the car Johnny says, "Well Toad, Old Doc Crandle really pulled a fast one on you, didn't he?"

"No John, I don't think so. He gave me sample pills to get rid of the gout. I don't even have to pay to get a prescription filled. I thought that was pretty nice of him."

Johnny continues, "Didn't he tell you that he'd have to have a blood test before he could treat you?"

"Yeah he did, but he still treated me; he gave me the medication."

Johnny laughs and says, "You still don't figure it out, do you? He said he had to have a blood test before he treated you, but instead he treated you before he got the results from the blood test; in fact, before that blood hardly left your arm."

"By gosh, I see what you're saying. That old son-of-a-gun really slickered me on that one."

Johnny says, "Yes he did, and by this time next week, chances are you'll be on more pills for stuff you never heard of than you can imagine. You may think you're healthy just 'cause you don't smoke, but that's only part of it. You are now the newest member of Doc Crandle's pill parade." Johnny continues, "I know all about this because I joined his parade a couple years ago under very similar circumstances. You're sunk now. You should never have given him any blood."

"But Johnny," I say, "I couldn't help it. He said he couldn't tell how much medication to give me without the blood test, and I would have done anything to stop the pain."

"Doc knew that," Johnny laughs, "and that's why you fell in line so easy. It was purely a matter of pain and timing; Doc's a master at that trick. That's how he got half the people in town on his pill parade. Join the crowd, Sucker."

Johnny helps me in the house and then remarks that he thinks he and Tootie will take the boat and go fishing tomorrow anyway, and I'm glad they're going. I wouldn't want to feel I'm holding them up. I tell Johnny by all means go. I'll catch up as soon as I get rid of this gout.

Snooks wants to know what Doc Crandle did for me and I tell her he tricked me into a screamin' battery. Snooks asks, "In the name of heaven, what is a 'screamin' battery'?"

"Snooks, it's a trick blood test that tells everything you don't want anybody to know. All about your kidneys, liver, diabetes, gout, even cholesteral. I didn't want all that, but Doc Crandle tricked me into it and now when he gets the results back from the lab he wants me back to give me more pills to make everything come out even. Johnny told me all about how Doc tricks you into getting this fool blood test.

"Snooks, bring me a glass of water so I can take another pill."

Snooks says, "You'll get service around here a lot quicker if you put a 'please' in front of your demands, even if you do feel like you're about to die." Rose can be cruel and thoughtless at times.

I give Snooks my appointment card for my next visit with Doc, and down the pills. In the meantime, I'm looking forward to the pain relief from the magic pills that Doc gave me.

Two days of hell and at last the pills are doing their job. Now maybe I can get a decent night's sleep tonight. I feel almost human again today. "Snooks, answer the phone——Please."

Snooks says, "Now you're learning.

"It's Doc Crandle's office and they want you in first thing in the morning; something showed up on your blood test that they need to see you about right away."

"Snooks, did you find out what the problem is and why such an all-fired big hurry?"

Her answer of "No, with serious things they only talk direct to the one involved," does little to give me confidence.

"I wish I knew how long I have left, I wonder it it's fatal? If so, I hope I don't linger."

Snooks says, "Well, I can see that's the end of a good night's sleep tonight. Personally, I wouldn't worry till I had something to worry about. But Toad, you just go ahead and do it your way." Rose is even more cruel than I ever suspected.

Snooks was right; not one wink of sleep all night. Maybe if I'd had regular checkups and that blood test earlier, I might have saved my life, but it's too late for that now. I hope I have time to get my will in order. I'll just go in the morning and get the sad, sad news straight from the horse's mouth.

Morning at last, I don't know why worrying nights are always longer than normal nights. I'd study that, but I don't want to spend my last days on worthless trivia only suitable for government grants.

Snooks asks, "What would you like for breakfast, Hon?"

I tell her, "Snooks, there's no way I could eat breakfast with the grim shadow of death hanging over my head. A person can't eat when faced with a monumental crisis of this nature. I'll try however, to get a cup of coffee down. I'd even smoke a cigarette again this morning if I had one. After all, there's no point in trying to take care

266

of oneself if one's days are numbered anyway.

"Snooks, I know I'm an hour-and-a half early, but I think I'll just mosey on down to Doc's office now. Maybe they'll have a cancellation or something."

Snooks tells me I might as well, I can worry better closer to the tragic news than by sitting home. Rose even shows a mean streak now and then.

I might as well have stayed home. Doc is in surgery until time for my appointment. So it's just worry and try to read his year-and-a-half old magazines. Why would you have a *News Week* magazine on the table that dates back six months? That's not my idea of current news.

At last they call me in and right off I tell Doc, "If I don't have long left, don't beat around the bush, come right out with it now."

Doc says, "Oh my, no. Your triglycerides are totally off the chart and we have to get things in line before it becomes a serious problem. Your uric acid is high and that caused your goat. Your cholesterol is 320; we'll need some medication for that, and your blood sugar is a little high but we can control that with medication, too. Also, we'll need to get your blood pressure down a bit. However, liver, kidney, iron and potassium are fine.

"I'll write prescriptions for pills for blood pressure, triglycerides, cholesterol and blood sugar, plus three other prescriptions for side effects that follow along for almost everybody on this type of medication. One of those is to control constipation, and another for depression. Fill these prescriptions and check back in three months for another blood test. In the meantime, call if you have any dizziness, swollen ankles or ringing in your ears."

"Geez, Doc, how long do you think I'll be on all this medication?"

"Probably the rest of your life."

"Don't you cure things anymore?"

"Once in a while, but mostly by surgery, not pills."

Seven prescriptions and $158.45 later and I'm back home and Snooks asks, "Well, how long do you have? Should I call Bob down at the mortuary?"

I tell her "Snooks, I'll be here as long as the rest of you unless I run out of money to stay on Doc Crandle's pill parade. Seven prescriptions! Four for stuff they found on that fool blood test and three more to keep me from getting sick off the four supposedly to keep me well! I'm definitely on Doc Crandal's pill parade."

# 21

# Tootie's Tar Heel Triumph

Tootie calls and says she and Johnny are on their way over for morning tea, coffee or whatever, and are bringing some fresh-baked cookies. I tell Snooks, "Let's take them out some night this week for a nice wedding dinner celebration." Snooks thinks that's a great idea and we'll set up a date when they arrive.

During our morning get-together across the kitchen table, Tootie has to tell us all about their day's fishing. "I know I've said it before, but I just love that Sturgeon fishing! I doubt I could ever get enough of it. It's so much more of a challenge than any other local fishing, and tastes so good at the table.

"Snooks, I remember what you said about fishing with us and just give me time and I'll think of some way we can all go and enjoy it together."

Then our conversation switches to taking them to dinner and they are really pleased with the idea. Tootie says, "Great! I picked up a new outfit in Reno and I've been hoping for a chance to wear it. This dinner will be just a perfect opportunity."

Snooks says, "I have a new one bought on my last visit to the city so it's a nice opportunity for both of us."

Johnny says, "That ought to be quite a show, both of you with new duds."

The women make dinner plans and Johnny and I discuss other more trivial things, like my gout. I tell him all about my outcome with the blood test and that his prediction was absolutely right. Old Doc Crandle has me hooked on his pill parade forever. "Johnny, you were right. I should never have given in to the blood test, but as I said before, I didn't have much choice with Doc's little medical tricks and maneuvers."

We settle on the special dinner for next Tuesday and Tootie wants to go fishing on Thursday. Johnny says she read the tide book and it's another good day. We agree on both dinner and fishing and promise to pick them up Tuesday about six and take them out for the evening.

After they leave Snooks says, "I'm really looking forward to the dinner. I'm very fond of both of them."

"Yes Snooks, I can see many happy times together with those two."

The next day Tootie and Snooks are so happy about the up-coming dinner that they make calls back and forth for what seems like most of the day. Snooks tells me some of the calls are Tootie telling her about something her darling Johnny did or said that really delighted her. Snooks tells me all about it and I say, "Yeah, ain't love grand? But remember Snooks, the candle of love grows dimmer with age."

Snooks says, "You men just don't understand matters of the heart. HA!"

The evening arrives and Snooks steps out ready to leave in a terrific new outfit and I have to admit it's a knockout on her. I compliment her and she tells me it's a one-of-a-kind and she was lucky it fit so well without much alteration. I know better than to ask the price because Snooks will go into her turtle-in-a-shell, evasive tactics and I'll find out nothing.

She slips on a wrap as it's a little chilly out. I tell her it's a shame to have to cover her dress but she smiles and says "Take the camera and I'll let you take a picture or two at dinner."

"Snooks, that's an excellent idea anyway. I'm sure John and Tootie would like to remember the happy occasion, too."

It's just dark when we pick them up. I'd have liked to have been early enough to get to the Governor House in daylight because the entrance garden is really spectacular this time of year, but I guess you can't have everything.

Tootie squeals with glee as we turn in at the Governor House and remarks, "What a nice choice! You can't beat their seafood anywhere."

We park and walk through to the restaurant. The gals check their wraps. Snooks looks at Tootie and Tootie looks at Snooks. The silence is similar to that of a small child who has fallen, and is really, really quiet while sucking in enough air to tell the world all about it's troubles. It seems both gals are wearing a "One-of-a-kind" outfit. The exact SAME "One-of-a-kind!"

I've heard about these things happening, but never figured I'd observe such a catastrophic calamity first hand. I say, "Hey John, look! The gold dust twins."

By this time the intake of air is accomplished and the sputtering begins. Snooks says, "Aldridge's Exclusive told me this is a 'One-of-a-kind'."

Tootie says, "The shop in Reno assured me of the same thing."

Then, much to my surprise, Snooks and Tootie start to laugh at the same time and Tootie says, "Well Snooks, it just goes to show; we both have good taste."

Snooks replies, "Yes, but in this small town we don't dare go out without checking to see whose turn it is! Tootie, let's both dress up tomorrow and go down to Aldridge's and see what excuse they come up with. Their explanation should be worth the price of admission." The gals decide it's an excellent idea and both ask me to take their picture as further proof, and just for posterity, too.

I can see the way they handled this situation that these two will never have any big disagreements. A beautiful friendship in the making.

Laughter over the matching, "One-of-a-kind" outfits, and a couple of margaritas before dinner, furthers our enjoyment of Dungeness crab cocktails followed by a main course of New Zealand lobster tails with melted butter.

Truly an evening thoroughly enjoyed and, I'm sure, long to be remembered. I'm glad I brought along the camera. Pictures always enhance pleasant memories.

The next big event, at least for Tootie, is the upcoming promised fishing trip Thursday. However, the next big event for Snooks is to go with Tootie into Aldridge's in the morning as soon as the store opens. I'm glad I'm not the managers of Aldridge's, I have a feeling they will have met their match with these two.

Bright and early Snooks puts on her look-alike outfit and takes off in her little Benz to pick up Tootie in her look-alike outfit to do battle with Aldridge's, giant of the industry. About half-an hour later Johnny comes over and we both wait with great anticipation to learn the outcome of this battle between the two Davids and Goliath. Personally, my money is with our wives. I think they're perfectly capable of the challenge.

The gals are back in about three hours eager to give us a blow-by-blow description of their morning at Aldridge's. At first, they had trouble seeing the manager; they were told an appointment would be needed. But when Snooks explained the problem would be on the evening TV news, because they had been tricked into this One-of-a-kind sham, the clerks suddenly found the manager was free.... "he just had a cancellation in his busy schedule."

When informed if there wasn't a drastic settlement right now to correct this con-job, the next move would be to see our attorney. Tootie laughs and says, "The wind went out of his sails in a hurry when he found we were serious. He decided we should both immediately be outfitted in new and non-matching outfits in exchange for those we were wearing. We were escorted around the store to pick out anything we wanted, price being of no consideration. We could choose the most elegant non-matching items available. Red carpet treatment all the way, even alterations on the house."

"Then," says Snooks, "the manager hoped these new garments would make up for our terrible embarrassment, and that we would not speak ill of their store and it's fine reputation. He was at a total loss to understand how such a thing could possibly happen. Needless to say, Tootie and I were living proof it did happen and he was really backed up against the wall."

"Plus," adds Tootie, "luncheon tickets for the two of us at Reynoldo's any time in the future we want to go!"

I say, "Snooks, why didn't you make him include Johnny and me on those lunch tickets?"

Snooks replies, "I thought we were doing pretty well. We didn't want to push him over the edge. Besides, you weren't the ones caught in matching outfits, nor were you the ones to do battle with Aldridge's."

I never should have said anything; Snooks seems to always have an answer to outdo my questions.

"Well, now that we have that settled, are we still on for fishing Thursday?" I can see right quick that Tootie is truly a person who enjoys her fishing, and I can't help but feel real admiration for such an all-fired, dedicated fishin' female as this. I thought Johnny and I were about as far gone as one could get, but Tootie makes us look like fishin' Sturgeon is sort of a lackadaisical hobby. Tootie is what you might call a truly totally dedicated Sturgeon Fishin' Fanatic.

I assure Tootie "Thursday's trip is definitely as high on the priority list as we can put it, and come morning we'll be on the way for sure."

Tootie says, "I get so excited now, that I know I won't sleep all night. I just hook and fight Sturgeon in my half sleep for most of the night."

Next morning Johnny and Tootie arrive half an hour early. Johnny says, "I know we're early but Tootie couldn't sleep; up at five, had the lunch and everything ready by six, said she just had to keep busy, so here we are."

Tootie bought a new reel and she loaded it with 40-pound test line. She says, "I just can't wait to try it. It has a fast 6:1 gear ratio, 200 yard 40 pound. line capacity, and a light-weight graphite frame with ball bearings throughout; the lastest thing." This gal knows more about equipment than most pros.

We finally launch and Tootie runs the boat while Johnny and I rig up. She pulls slowly into our favorite spot, and drops the break-away anchor. By then we're rigged and baited; no lost time. This gal is just a real joy to have along. Johnny made the catch of the century when he landed this one, make no mistake about that.

We dip the shrimp in the gromafraw juice, cast and relax, just waiting for our first bite. The conversation covers topics from our President's antics to the upcoming Super Bowl, when we hear off in the distance, the sound of an outboard that put-put-puts, and every now and then there's a stutter, like it's gasping it's last.

The sound seems to ring a bell of recognition. It soon becomes loud enough to occupy our immediate attention and Tootie says, "That motor sounds like it's got a stuck valve. I hope they have a paddle."

Johnny looks at me and says, "You know Toad, that sure sounds like the tar heels. I wonder how they got that old outboard back in running order." John tells Tootie that it sounds like the guys we got the gromafraw from.

I say, "John, hand me the binoculars. They'll be coming around the far bend pretty quick." As they come in sight I say, "HOLY CRIMINIES! Johnny, it is them! And they got the same little boat and motor; but they're towing a monstrosity, the likes of which only they could come up with. I just can't describe it. Here Johnny, take a look for yourself."

Johnny looks and continues to look. He's just like me; he can't believe his eyes. He just shakes his bead and then hands the glasses to Tootie who is the first to attempt a description. Her remark is, "My, how ingeniously quaint."

They put-put-put right along the far bank and never give us a wave or a look. "Johnny," I say, "see where they go, because if you remember, they told us somebody was in their favorite spot and that's why they moved in here next to us. This spot was their second choice."

Johnny says, "I'll watch. I just can't take my eyes off that mess. It

looks like about a 15x25 foot raft with a little 10x12 foot shack on it, and an awning to sit under out of the sun in their lawn chairs. They've probably been working on that ever since we saw them last. There's a stovepipe coming out the side of that shack, so they must have a stove in there.....yeah, that's right. There's even some chopped wood piled up on one side of the shack. Incidentally, the shack is covered with black tar paper which should keep the rain out and an old, rusty, corrugated tin roof. What an outfit! They probably figure it's like dying and going to heaven compared with that leaky little boat, otherwise there's no way it would float without them bailing all the time like before. Personally, I wouldn't be caught dead on a crazy rig like that."

Tootie says, "I'll bet they're happy as two bear cubs robbing a bee tree." Tootie grabs her camera and with a little grin on her face, takes several pictures as it slowly put-put-puts by.

From that moment on, Tootie seems to have lost her fishing concentration, in fact if I didn't know better, I'd say she almost acts like she'd like to get out of here because she has other things on her mind. She continues to fish, but her heart just isn't in it. For the life of me I can't figure this sudden change. She spends more time eating and less time checking her bait and other important chores connected with good, heads-up fishing practices.

Fishing turns out to be poor even with the gromafraw; and it just isn't anywhere good enough to hold our interest. When Tootie finally asks how long before high tide both Johnny and I decide it's probably better to throw in the towel and try again another day under more suitable conditions. However, we do take time to run up river to see excactly where the Tar Heels decided to go as the prime fishing spot. As soon as we locate the spot and check some good landmarks, we about-face and head for home.

Even the ride home is different, everyone's quiet. Tootie's mind is preoccupired on something a long way from where we are, I can see that. I'll sic Snooks on her and see if she can find out what we did to cause such a drastic change in her interest.

Over breakfast coffee I tell Snooks that Tootie has got something on her mind and Snooks answers, "Yes, I know, she called last night to tell me that I wouldn't see her today. She had to make a trip to the city and would be gone most of the day. I agree with you, there's something strange going on. I just hope she isn't coming down with the flu or something."

I say, "Call Johnny——please, and have him run over for toast and tea and we'll see if he knows anything."

Johnny arrives shortly and he is just as mystified as we are at Tootie's strange behaviour. He says, "I don't think she's sick, or anything. That little gal has some big deal on her mind, but she sure doesn't want to let any of us in on it."

More to keep Johnny from worrying about Tootie than anything else, I say, "Well, Johnny, let's run over to Sam Sackrider's place and see how he's doing. I heard he fell and broke three or four ribs." Johnny agrees and we drive over to Sam's.

Sadie, Sam's wife, informs us that Sam just went down to the library to pick up some books to read, and should be back shortly. She invites us in to have coffee and wait. We ask how Sam is feeling and Sadie says much better since he got involved in that speed-reading course he's taking. Sadie says, "You know Sam is tight as the bark on a tree, but he shelled out $350 for this fancy course on speed reading and it seems at least to be taking his mind off his sore ribs."

While we're sitting there drinking coffee I see the morning paper on the table and pick it up and read two fairly short articles real thoroughly, almost memorizing them. Sam shows up and he's all smiles, just so glad to have friends come to visit. I ask, "Sam, what's this I hear about you taking a speed-reading course?"

Sam says, "Yeah boy, and what a difference it makes! I've only had five lessons and already I can see a world of improvement."

"You know Sam," I say "I was always the poorest reader in class at school, reading was always tough as can be for me, and I wonder if it would help me any?"

Sam says, "Yeah, I'm sure it would."

"Well Sam, before I put out that kind of money, I'd like to make sure.

"Let's take an article out of the paper and both read it; then Sadie or Johnny can ask us some questions and see who seems to have retained and learned the most from the article."

I thumb through the paper and of course pick out an article I've already digested. I say, "Now Sam, here's one not too long. Let's both read it and then see who gets the most out of it. You with your course, or me with my poor reading disability."

Sam thinks that's an excellent idea and he starts out first. He waves his hand back and forth across the page like he's trying to put out a fire or bat away pesky mosquitoes; really a sight to behold. He finishes and I take my turn. I try to take just a wee mite longer than Sam but without all the puttin-out-fire antics. With a deal like this, you really got to be s-w-a-v-e.

I finish and Johnny reads the article and asks us a number of questions pertaining to it's contents. Well you know, poor old Sam missed so much of that article, that I just plum beat him all to smithereens.

I can see that Sam is more than a little upset and I say, "Sam, you probably just got grabbed by the fickle finger of fate on that one. Let's take another article and try it again." Sam is visibly upset, his rosy-red face and stutter give him away; but still game, he agrees.

Again I thumb through the paper acting real nonchalant, I pick another article and say, "Sam, here's another article, let's try this one." Sam snatches the paper out of my hand and goes through his fanning exercises, only this time with much more vigor. At last he finishes and flips the paper over to me. I proceed to read the article, again not taking a great deal more time than Sam and again Johnny quizzes us on the article content and again Sam is a sad distance behind me on article knowledge retention.

Sam by now is livid, the red face has turned to almost purple. I say, "You know Sam, three hundred and fifty dollars is a lot a of moola to put out on something that you don't gain anything out of. I'm sure glad we ran that little test. I gotta thank you for keeping me from throwing my money away on the likes of that speedy course they took you on."

Sam jumps up from the table and we hear him in the bathroom going through the agony of wretching and throwing up. Sadie says, "That must just about be tearing poor old Sam apart with those sore ribs and all."

As we're leaving and head down the walk, Johnny says, "That was a real dirty trick Toad; and I hope nobody else saw how you set that up."

"Yeah Johnny, but I had no idea he was taking that speed reading so serious."

Johnny replies, "For Sam to spend $350 on anything! you should have known he was serious."

John is right. It was a dirty trick to pull on poor old Sam, sore ribs and all. But then you just don't get a golden opportunity like that often and the devil got me, I just couldn't pass it up. Hopefully Sam may even have learned something of value himself.

Johnny, my dear friend, just can't wait to tell Snooks about the trick I pulled on Sam Sackrider, and now Snooks is upset with me, too.

The only thing that saves me is Tootie showing up, all smiles and excited, and with a stack of brochures and information you can't believe.

Tootie says, "You know yesterday when the Tar Heels came along with that strange contraption, my mind instantly saw possibilities that Toad and Johnny totally missed. I could think of nothing else! so I went out this morning to get all the information I could, and here's what I came up with."

With that, Tootie lays out brochures about small- to medium-size houseboats for us to look at. My first comment is, "Tootie, these all look great, but where do you think we're going to come up with money for anything is this class?"

Tootie replies, "My dear, departed Yugo left me with more money that I will ever need and I intend to enjoy it.

"Fishing season is really over and I'd like us all to become involved in my plan. Can't you just see it? A houseboat with all the conveniences of home: washer, dryer, refrigerator......oh, just all those things; two bedrooms and a covered deck to walk around on. A home on the water! We can stay out and fish as long as we want. We have our little jet to chase unmanageable fish and also to use as a taxi to run to the boat launch and car to get groceries and any supplies we need. Just think! We could even do some night fishing! All with the comforts of home. We have till next season to find what we want and outfit it."

Snooks says, "Now I'm beginning to get really interested in fishing again. This sounds absolutely wonderful!"

"Really something for all of us to look forward to" I say. "I would never have thought the Tar Heels would furnish the idea to have four people this excited about next season."

Tootie didn't miss what was right before our eyes. We pop the cork on a bottle of champagne to toast Tootie's idea. As we clink our glasses together I say, "A salute to Tootie and Tootie's Tar Heels."

Johnny says, "I can hardly wait for the Tar Heel Dream to come true. Next season should be a Sturgeon season to end all seasons, and the beginning of many years of fantastic fun and Sturgeon fishin' 'ala exceptionale'."